LIGHT
OF THE LAST

CONTENTS

A NOTE FROM CHUCK BLACK

This is a speculative work of fiction not intended to confuse or diminish the truth of God's holy and inspired Word. Where the Bible is silent, I have taken literary freedom to construct a fictional account of the angels of heaven and their association and interaction with each other and with humanity. The intent of this book is, through fiction, to open our eyes to the reality of spiritual warfare as described in Scripture. I have made every attempt not to contradict the Bible in any way but rather to use it as a foundation upon which to inspire serious contemplation about our eternity and ultimately to give honor and glory to God. The Readers Guide that follows will carefully delineate the truth of God's Word from the fiction of this story. Please take the time to read and understand it so that there is no confusion regarding solid biblical doctrine.

CAST OF CHARACTERS

Drew Carter   main human character
Validus   main angel character, last angel created

HUMANS

Sydney Carlyle   main female character
Kathryn Carter   Drew's mother
Jake Blanchard   Drew's mentor & stepfather
Benjamin Berg   friend of Drew Carter; technical genius
Piper   member of Ben's tech team
Ridge   member of Ben's tech team
Crypt   member of Ben's tech team
Jester   member of Ben's tech team
Thomas Reed   FBI agent
Mr. Ross   mysterious observer
Aashif Hakeem Jabbar leader of the Islamic Global Alliance (IGA)

VALIDUS'S WARRIORS

Persimus   gifted at human translation
Sason   gifted at mass translation
Jayt   gifted at weapons
Brumak   gifted at strength
Crenshaw   gifted at prophecy
Rake   gifted at speed

GUARDIAN

Tren   assigned with Validus to protect Drew Carter

ARCHANGELS

Michael   leader of the Warrior Order
Gabriel   leader of the Messenger Order
Raphael   second to Gabriel in the Messenger Order

ANGEL COMMANDERS

| Danick | general of the second-generation of warrior angels |
| Brandt | great leader of first- and second-generation warriors |

FALLEN COMMANDERS

Niturni	former close friend of Validus
Zurock	a regional commander on the West Coast
Tinsalik Barob	rebel Fallen

1

INTERROGATION

Drew Carter sat in a white room on a white chair in front of a white table. His hands were handcuffed to a bar in the middle of the table.

A hundred images and emotions flashed through his mind. He had saved Sydney, Shana, and Micah, but he was worried for Reverend Ray Branson. No one would tell him anything about the reverend's condition. He cringed at the thought that the kindest man he had ever known might be dead . . . dead because of him.

Drew tried to clear his mind. It took a few moments, but slowly he pushed his emotions down. He closed his eyes and welcomed the serenity of the room. His entire body sighed at the reprieve from a constantly overloaded sensory system. It was the first time since that fateful accident in the lab at Drayle University that he didn't have to concentrate on filtering out all the stimuli of a chaotic world. Though still too bright, the white room with its absence of movement soothed his eyes. The cool surface of the table relaxed his muscles. The clean, filtered air lulled his olfactory nerves to minimal activity. But the sweetest sensation of all was the *near* silence of the interrogation room. For a normal person, the silence would have been absolute. For Drew, it was close enough. He didn't have to concentrate at all to ignore the extremely dampened sounds outside the room.

For now, there were no invaders, neither light nor dark. In this sterile room he could almost convince himself that it was all a bad dream, that the invaders weren't real and that if he could just clear himself and Sydney, life would be normal. Oh, how he dreamed of normal!

Drew was tempted to shut down completely, but he knew he had to mentally prepare for the interrogation to come. How much did they know? How much should he tell? Was prison his destination regardless of what he said? After

all, he had assaulted two FBI agents. No matter what the outcome or his motivation, they would never let that slide. Severe repercussions were inevitable.

His thoughts turned to Ben. He hoped his quirky genius friend would stay
levelheaded enough to implement the alternate plan. Ben was on his own now,
once again lost in the sea of humanity. He had learned a lot and now his ability
to disappear would determine if he lived or died. Drew shuddered to think of
Ben up against an invisible enemy by himself.

And finally there was Sydney Carlyle. What would her role be in all of
this? Drew had determined that the FBI was clueless in regard to the invader
war, but Sydney was not. Was she a secret agent of the light invaders? Her actions in the warehouse had directly affected the outcome, giving the light invaders the upper hand right when they needed it. He would have to conceal her
abilities from the FBI too.

After two hours of analyzing and preparing himself, he grew tired. He laid
his head on the table between his outstretched arms and tried to relax again.
How long would they leave him there?

With his ear against the table surface, some of the sounds in the building
were amplified enough for him to pick up, especially with the calm of the room
soothing his other senses. He filtered out the whir of the air-conditioning system, footsteps, and a low rumble of background noise that must be voices.
There was one set of voices much stronger than the rest. If he concentrated, he
could just make out the words.

"What have we learned from the girl?"

Drew lifted his head and put his other ear to the table to see if the voices
were any clearer, but it was the same. He turned his head so his face was away
from the one-way mirror to his left and concentrated.

". . . don't think she's trying to hide anything. No record. Looks like she
just got mixed up with the wrong guy."

"That's irrelevant. She's an accomplice to a man suspected of plotting the
massacre at Drayle University, and she aided and abetted him when she knew
he was running from the FBI. She's not innocent, and she's got a cell with her
name on it too."

Drew's heart sank. He had ruined Sydney's life by asking for her help and
bringing her into this mess. His stomach knotted as he thought of his beautiful, innocent Sydney sitting in a prison cell. He had to do everything in his

power to negotiate on her behalf, no matter what it might cost him. Humility and honesty were his best play, as long as he didn't mention the invaders. If the FBI believed he was schizophrenic, there would be nothing he could do on Sydney's behalf. He wondered how much she had told them. If he knew, he might have an advantage.

"Do you buy her bit regarding the industrial espionage? Seems far-fetched."

"Don't know. We need to find Berg. He's the biggest piece we're missing. Let's go find out what this criminal knows."

"Hey, Lewis, this guy can't be all bad. Even the police think he's some sort of hero. And if he did what those kids said he did . . . I don't know."

"Come on, Reed, he assaulted both of us, and he knew we were federal agents. That alone puts him behind bars for a long time. This jerk is going down before there are any more shootings and innocent lives lost. Don't get soft on me. Got it?"

"Yeah, I got it, but . . ."

"But what?"

"The warehouse . . . I was there, Lewis. Do you know what he did in that building to save those people?"

"Yeah, he went on another shooting rampage."

"He shot eleven gang members. None of them died."

"Maybe he's just a lousy shot."

"Or maybe he's an expert shot."

"Are you soft on this guy, Reed? Do I need to look for another investigator?"

"No. I'm just saying that this guy may actually be one of the good guys. That's all. Let's let the evidence speak for itself."

"Absolutely, Reed, and it's screaming for a conviction!"

Drew heard a door open.

"Agents Lewis, Reed, this is Mr. Ross. He's with the Department of Justice." This voice was one of authority, probably Lewis's and Reed's supervisor.

"Department of Justice? With all due respect, we're with the Department of Justice—oh . . . I see. Why are you here, Mr. Ross? This is still my investigation, isn't it?"

"I'm just here to observe. Are you well prepared for this interrogation?"

"Of course."

Silence.

"Is there something we should know?" That was Reed's voice.

"Do you know who you've got in there?"

Drew's heart began to quicken. This Mr. Ross scared him. He seemed too smart.

"Yeah, a sadistic jerk who gets his kicks murdering students and assaulting federal agents." That was Lewis.

More silence.

"I've been watching Carter for the last year. I can promise you, he is anything but that."

"How's that possible, sir? Lewis and I have been looking for Carter since Drayle and just yesterday discovered his location. How could you have been watching him?"

"Just go do your job, gentlemen," Mr. Ross said quietly.

"Don't screw this up, Lewis. We need this information, and you need this to go well," the supervisor said flatly.

Drew heard some unintelligible sounds and a door open and close again. He took a deep breath, then sat up as the door to the interrogation room opened. He thought of Sydney and Reverend Ray and was able to give the agents a genuine look of apprehension.

One of the agents sat across the table from Drew while the other leaned against the wall to his right, opposite the one-way mirror. Drew recognized him as the younger of the two agents he had overpowered earlier, which meant he must be Reed. He was lean with dark hair, twenty-five to thirty years old. He didn't look happy. The aggressive agent would be the interrogator, Lewis. He was shorter, five-nineish with a stocky build, ten years older than Reed and nearly bald. A Band-Aid covered a small cut and a nasty bruise just above his left eye. This was the agent Drew had slammed into the car and knocked out.

This was not going to go well.

Lewis opened a folder in front of him, then reached into his pocket and set a digital recorder on the table between them. "I am Federal Agent Lewis, this is Agent Reed. Will you approve of our recording this questioning?" Lewis asked.

Drew nodded. He appreciated the cold, professional demeanor Lewis was displaying, knowing the agent probably wanted to cold-cock him to get even.

Lewis pushed the Record button.

"Before we ask you any questions, you must understand your rights. You have the right to remain silent. Anything you say can be used against you in court. You have the right to talk to a lawyer for advice before we ask you any questions. You have the right to have a lawyer with you during the questioning. If you cannot afford a lawyer, one will be appointed for you before any questioning, if you wish. If you decide to answer questions now without a lawyer, you have the right to stop answering at any time. If you understand your rights and you are willing to answer questions without a lawyer present, sign here."

Lewis placed a sheet of paper and a pen within Drew's reach. Drew looked over his rights once more, thinking through whether he should have a lawyer present.

"I also have the right to a phone call," Drew said. "I'd like to talk to Jake Blanchard."

"You do have the right to make a phone call. However, a phone call to Jake Blanchard may jeopardize our continuing investigation. Is there someone else you would like to talk to?"

Drew frowned. That meant Jake was being investigated too. Probably because of the money and fake IDs he'd given Drew before Drew left to search for Ben. It felt like everyone good was under investigation while everyone bad was walking free. He didn't like it.

"No." Drew grabbed the pen and signed the paper.

"You are being charged with eleven counts of aggravated assault, two counts of aggravated assault against federal agents, and illegal possession of a deadly weapon in a school safety zone. Other charges may or may not be counted against you as the investigation continues. Do you understand the charges against you?"

"Yes, but I will only answer your questions on one condition."

Lewis looked at him with a countenance of stone. "We are not in a position to make concessions or deals in exchange for information."

"This one's easy. I want to know the medical condition of Reverend Ray Branson."

Lewis just stared at him for a moment, looking as though he didn't want to give Drew anything.

"I just want to know if he's going to make it," Drew said. "He's my friend. Please."

Lewis finally nodded. Agent Reed disappeared through the door and returned two minutes later. Drew studied his eyes for some hint of his message.

"Reverend Branson is in serious condition but stable. They will know if he will make a full recovery within the next twenty-four hours." Reed gave Drew a subtle nod.

Drew lowered his head. "Thank you." Ray had a wife and two beautiful children to fight for. Drew convinced himself that his friend would make it.

He looked back up at Agent Lewis. "Why don't you tell me about your involvement in the shooting at Drayle University on Thursday, May 8, 2014?" Lewis asked.

Drew shook his head. "It began eight months before that. I have to start there for you to understand."

Lewis crossed his arms and leaned back in his chair. "Start wherever you like. We have plenty of time."

Drew took a deep breath. "It all began with the death of Dr. Waseem, a physics professor at Drayle. My friend Benjamin Berg was his lab assistant. Dr. Waseem had received a grant for his groundbreaking work on the acceleration of light. Ben came to me one day, concerned because Dr. Waseem had disappeared. Later we discovered that he had died in a car accident, which seemed fishy to us. Ben and I attempted to re-create the lab experiment Dr. Waseem was working on, but the equipment exploded."

Lewis held up his hand to stop Drew. "Why did you try to repeat the lab experiment?"

"Because Ben believed that Dr. Waseem had successfully accelerated light and that his death was not accidental. We were trying to confirm his findings as proof."

"Proof of what?" Lewis asked.

Drew hesitated. "Proof that Dr. Waseem and his research were the victims of industrial espionage and possibly sabotage."

Lewis glanced toward Reed. Reed just raised an eyebrow.

"If you were convinced, why didn't you take this to the police?" Reed asked.

"Because we needed proof. No one was going to listen to a couple of college students about something this big. Besides, we were nervous that whoever was behind this may have been watching us. We were afraid for ourselves and our families."

"That's quite the conspiracy theory, Carter. How does this have anything to do with the shooting at Drayle University?" Lewis sneered.

"The accident burned Ben, and I went blind for a few months. During that time, Ben became paranoid. You see, Ben had helped Dr. Waseem conduct the research and was the only one who could re-create the experiment. He began to fear for his life, so he disappeared. When I recovered from my injuries, I knew I had to find him. That took me to Drayle, because I knew I had to disappear too, but I needed to say good-bye to someone first."

"Who?" Lewis prompted.

"Sydney Carlyle. And for the record, I want you to know that whatever you think I've done and whatever charges you have against me, Sydney had nothing to do with any of it. The only thing she is guilty of is trying to help me find Benjamin Berg. She is innocent on all counts," Drew pleaded.

Lewis smirked. "We know better, Carter. Ms. Carlyle was an accomplice of yours from the day she set foot in Chicago. She was supposed to report any contact with you to us, and she didn't. She's given us her statement. I wouldn't worry about trying to protect Carlyle, because she doesn't appear to be worried about protecting you. Now what happened at Drayle? Why did you have weapons in your car on a college campus?" Lewis's voice was strained.

Drew shook his head. "I wasn't thinking. I should have parked off campus. I had the gun and knives because I didn't know who I might come across in my search for Ben. If these people had truly killed Dr. Waseem, I wanted to be prepared."

Lewis huffed. "Supposing your story to be true and Dr. Waseem had been killed by some questionable people, you think you would be able to defend yourself and Berg?" He smirked. "Against professionals?"

Drew wasn't sure how much he wanted the FBI to know about how skilled he was. "Well, I knew I'd have a better chance with weapons than without them."

Lewis glared at Drew. "What is your association with Duncan Terance McGruger?"

Drew shook his head. "Who is he?"

Lewis smirked again. "Don't play dumb, Carter."

"I'm sorry. I don't know that name."

"He's the guy who killed nine students at Drayle. How can you not know his name?" Reed asked, leaning against the wall again.

"I . . . I disappeared off the grid for months. No television, no computers, no technology for weeks. I guess I never heard his name."

Both agents just stared at Drew, expressionless. Reed pushed off from the wall and walked behind Drew. Lewis glanced up at his partner. Some message was exchanged.

"How stupid do you think we are, Carter? You were there, you coordinated the attack with him, and now you want us to believe that you don't even know his name?" Anger flushed Lewis's cheeks as he struggled to keep control.

Drew was getting angry too. This guy had had it in for him even before Drew had knocked him out. Now there was no hope.

Lewis continued. "How was it that you were in the same building as McGruger when he started shooting students?"

"Sydney had a class in that building. I walked her to her class, and as I was leaving—" Drew stopped as he remembered the shots ringing out, the students screaming and crying. People had been dying all around him and all he could think about was trying to save Sydney. He recovered himself. "As I was leaving, the shooting started."

Lewis's eyes narrowed. "What did McGruger tell you to do then?"

Drew clenched his teeth and reminded himself that this was a tactic to get him to trip up. "Nothing! I'd never seen the guy until that day."

Reed walked from behind Drew to his left side and gave Lewis a stern look. "What did you do next?" Reed asked.

"I was on the stairs. I tried to pull some of the students to safety. One girl was shot in the leg, so I carried her back to Sydney's class and got two guys to take her out the back way. We got some of the students out, but the gunman cut off our exit. That's when he came into our room. The professor and I tried to keep the door shut, but he got shot and the gunman got in."

"The professor stated that you agreed to bar the door but then let the gunman into the room," Lewis said flatly. "Was that part of your plan with McGruger?"

"What? No! I told you I never knew that guy. Why would I let him in and then try to stop him?"

Lewis leaned forward. "You tell me."

"I don't know. I guess I was stunned for a moment. I remember thinking, what if this guy was connected with the people who killed Dr. Waseem? What if he was coming after me?"

For a moment, no one said anything.

"Is that what you believe?" Reed finally asked. "That they were coming after you?"

Drew realized that he was starting to sound like a conspiracy nut. He shook his head. "No. I realized that I was just in the wrong place at the wrong time. This McGruger guy was just some nut job on a rampage. All I wanted to do was to keep Sydney safe and stop the killing."

Lewis scoffed. "Sure."

Drew tried to ignore Lewis's sarcasm. "Once the gunman made the room, I charged him. He slammed into the wall and was knocked out." He shrugged. "That's it. I had nothing to do with the shooting except trying to stop it. Look, there was an entire classroom of witnesses you must have questioned. What about the professor? Surely he told you."

Lewis just frowned. "Why did you run? Why did you leave your car there, a car with weapons inside it? Were those backup weapons for McGruger? If you were innocent, why run?" The agent leaned forward again. "Sure looks bad from where we're sitting."

"Because I knew the campus would immediately go on lockdown. I would be detained and questioned for hours."

"So what?" Reed asked. "You waited eight months. What's a few more hours?"

Drew sighed. He felt manipulated, and Lewis was intent on making him look guilty. "My face would have been all over television for days, especially since I had stopped the gunman. I couldn't take a chance on those responsible making the connection between me and the incident at the lab."

"Oh, I see; you were afraid of the secret assassin that killed Waseem."

Drew stared at Lewis, trying to control his anger. The agent had no clue what was happening. Drew was the only person on the planet who could see the global invasion of mankind, and he was stuck in an FBI interrogation chamber, trying to convince two skeptical dimwits that he was a good guy.

"I don't think you have any idea how significant Dr. Waseem's discovery is. His work on light acceleration has the potential to revolutionize the technology industry. Telecommunications, data storage, weaponization. It would be the single most significant discovery in the last one hundred years, and it would be worth billions." Drew leaned forward and stared right into Lewis's eyes. "That's why I ran. And that's why Ben ran."

Lewis stared right back at him, anger seething in his eyes. "Carter, regardless of the evidence for or against you at Drayle University, you were in possession of illegal weapons in a school safety zone, you purposely evaded the FBI and impeded our investigation, and then subsequently assaulted two federal agents with deadly weapons." Lewis leaned in close to Drew and lowered his voice. "Assault with a deadly weapon against a federal agent carries up to twenty years in prison . . . for each offense! Do you understand how serious these charges are against you?"

Drew's heart sank. He glared at Lewis. Honesty and humility weren't going to gain him a thing. "Yeah, I get it," he snapped, regretting his tone before he finished the comeback.

Lewis stood up and leaned over the table. "I suggest you reconsider your story and start telling the truth!" He slammed the table with his fist.

The room fell silent.

Drew was frustrated, angry, and discouraged. It seemed so hopeless. He hung his head, resigned to finish out his life behind the bars of a prison cell.

2

A LIFE FOR A LIFE

The door to the interrogation room opened and an older gentleman leaned in. Drew guessed him to be Lewis's supervisor.

"Agents Lewis, Reed. A word."

Lewis grabbed the recorder. "You'd better think this over, Carter."

The two agents left the room, and Drew put his head facedown on the table. How had he come to this? All he ever wanted to do was play football, find a pretty wife, and be a normal guy. Now the world was crashing down on him like a boot snuffing out the life of an insignificant ant.

Even if he could by some miracle convince them he was telling the truth, it wouldn't change the fact that both he and Sydney had serious charges against them. If only they really knew what was at stake. If only he could tell someone the *whole* truth!

Drew waited until he was sure the agents were back in the observation room and then slowly turned his head away, placing his ear on the surface of the table.

"—jerk is lying. And he coordinated the story with Carlyle. I'm going to keep at these two until one of them cracks and starts telling the truth."

"No, you're not, Agent Lewis. Your line of questioning is coercive and has already jeopardized our ability to use this information in a court of law. As of now, consider yourself removed as the lead investigator on this case."

"Come on, Graham—"

"Furthermore," the supervisor continued, his voice firm and unyielding, "because of your inability to contain the suspect last night, coupled with your breach in FBI interrogation policy, I have no choice but to place you under review. Report to my office at 0800 tomorrow. Dismissed!"

There was a long pause; then a door slowly opened and closed.

"Agent Reed. You've been on this case with Lewis from the beginning. I'm bringing Mathews in as senior investigator, and you'll stay on as his assistant, but until then, this is your investigation. Finish up the interrogation, and get us something we can use."

"Yes sir."

"What's your opinion of Mr. Carter, Agent Reed?" This was the soft voice of the mysterious Mr. Ross again.

"Well, sir, I'm not sure what to think, but I know this—he could have killed us both last night if he'd wanted to. And . . ." There was a long pause. "I don't know too many guys who could take on an entire gang and come out alive."

"I want you to find out where Berg is," the supervisor said, "and I want you to bargain Sydney Carlyle's freedom for his confession to the shooting at Drayle."

"What if he really wasn't involved?"

"Just do it."

"Yes sir."

The door closed and Drew pretended to continue to rest. When the door to the interrogation room opened, he slowly lifted his head. As Reed entered the room, Drew looked behind him as if he were expecting Agent Lewis to follow.

Reed sat across the table from Drew. He placed the recorder on the table again and pressed Record. He looked at Drew, pursed his lips, and took a deep breath. "How are you doing, Carter? Can I get you anything?"

Drew squinted. He looked over at the one-way mirror. "Is this the good-cop–bad-cop play now?"

Reed forced a quick smile. "Listen, Carter. You may have fooled the students in that classroom and even the professor. But no one brings weapons like you had in your vehicle onto a college campus without serious ill intentions. We know you were plotting something. Your presence with those weapons on the same day as the shooting at Drayle is too coincidental. You're in deep, Carter, and your assault against federal agents has already bought you a one-way ticket to the pen."

Drew knew what was coming, but that didn't make it any easier. The shame for his mother would be the worst to bear. She and Jake would have to believe he had gone insane. The thick black cloud of an unfair life strangled him once more. His head hung low.

"I'm prepared to make you a deal," Reed said. Drew detected the slightest hint of regret in his tone. "Give me your confession to the shooting at Drayle, and we'll drop all the charges against Sydney Carlyle."

Drew slowly lifted his head and glared at Reed. His whole body felt twice as heavy as it had just a few moments ago.

"I'll give you my confession, but you have to drop the charges against Sydney Carlyle, Jake Blanchard, and Benjamin Berg, and you stop all investigation on each of them."

Reed glared back, brows furrowed. He closed the file in front of him. "Carter, you're in no position to bargain."

"And I want five minutes alone with Sydney, no one listening. Those are my terms. Without my confession, you've got nothing to tie me to that shooting, and I have a room full of witnesses against it."

Reed frowned, then stood and left the room. Before Drew had a chance to listen in again, Reed returned.

"Okay, Carter. You've got a deal. But I will be present when you talk with Carlyle, and we still want to talk to Berg. No exceptions." Reed put his index finger on the table between them. "You'd better take it, Carter. It's as good as it's going to get for you." He actually looked sympathetic.

Drew slowly nodded.

Reed left the file closed but turned on the recorder and looked at Drew, waiting.

Drew took a deep breath. "McGruger and I planned the whole thing out the week before. When I got to campus, I realized I couldn't do it, so I tried to stop him, but I was too late. I ran 'cause I figured the FBI would know I was in on it. The students thought I was a hero, but actually I was part of the whole thing."

Reed crossed his arms and glared at Drew. "If that's true, then why do we have surveillance footage of you every day in Rivercrest for two weeks prior to the shooting? Grocery store, fitness center, bank."

"We planned it out online in a chat room," Drew replied.

"We pulled all your phone and Internet records—no McGruger. You're not a very good liar."

Drew shook his head in confused frustration. "What do you want from me, Agent Reed? I'm giving you a confession. That was the deal. Now I have to prove that I did it?"

Reed just stared at him, and Drew knew he was struggling. The agent ran his hand through his hair. "We're going to go over that part of the story in detail. Right now I want you to tell me what happened after the shooting at Drayle. Where did you go?"

"After Drayle?" Drew asked.

Reed nodded.

"Do you want the story based on me being involved in the shooting at Drayle or the story based on me not being involved in the shooting?"

Reed fidgeted and quickly glanced toward the mirror. "Don't get smart, Carter. Just tell me the truth."

Drew backed off. He didn't want to turn Reed into a real enemy. "I'm sorry. I'm not trying to be disrespectful. I'm just a little tense here." He shrugged. "I'm going to give you the truth, and you can do with it as you please." Drew thought back to his decision to divert north to the Boundary Waters in Minnesota. "I was nervous that I might be tracked by whoever was responsible for Dr. Waseem's death, so I decided to go off-grid and disappear in the Superior National Forest in Minnesota until I could verify that no one was following me. I stayed there for six weeks and then made my way to Chicago."

"Did you hide out in a cabin?"

Drew shook his head. "No, I just camped."

"But we found most of your supplies still in your car," Reed said.

"I've had some training in survival. Besides, it was only six weeks."

Reed grunted. "Go on."

"Once I hit Chicago I started looking for Ben. He had given me a clue that he would be there, so I methodically started searching all the computer tech companies until I found him. That's when Sydney came into the picture."

"Did you ask her to come help you?"

Drew hesitated, wishing she had listened to him when he asked her to stay away. He would have to choose his words carefully so as not to incriminate her. "We met accidentally at Reverend Branson's church. She was on a mission trip. When she found out I was in Chicago looking for Ben, I enlisted her help."

Agent Reed leaned forward. "She said she came to Chicago to help you—insisted on helping you—and you tried to stop her. Is that true, Carter?"

Drew was sick at heart. He sensed that Reed might actually be for him. How could he lie, but how could he not save Sydney?

"Sydney Carlyle truly is innocent . . . innocent of everything! I convinced her that Dr. Waseem's death was a murder, that Ben's life was in danger, and that these same people were after me. She just wanted to help find Ben and keep him safe."

Reed seemed to think about this for a moment. "So you found Berg, then what? Why did you stay in Chicago?"

"Ben and I realized we needed proof that Dr. Waseem's research was legitimate. We decided to attempt to rebuild the lab and conduct the experiment on our own."

Reed held up his hand. "How could you purchase multimillion-dollar lab equipment?" He shook his head. "It would take years to acquire that."

Drew nodded. "We knew that, but we had no choice. We decided we were going to see this through, even if it took ten years." Drew had to keep his trading on the exchange a secret. If the FBI knew he had been trading, they would find his account and then find Ben. "The equipment was incredibly expensive, even used. That's what kept us from being successful." Drew lowered his head. "I'm not sure it would have ever worked, but we had to try. Besides the equipment, Ben told me there were some calculations Dr. Waseem had derived that he didn't have access to. Evidently they were destroyed in the lab fire."

Reed made a few notes. "Why did the gang kidnap Carlyle and the Branson children?"

Drew looked up at Reed, not sure how to make this sound. "The gang wanted me, and they knew that Sydney was the best way to lure me in."

"Why were they after you? Were you encroaching on their territory?"

Drew offered a weak smile. "Yes, but not in the way that you think. I . . . I was trying to help people . . . people they were trying to hurt."

Reed just stared at Drew, waiting. "Why?" he finally asked.

Sadness overwhelmed Drew. Explaining why he helped people while facing prison was dealing face to face with the raw injustice of the world. *Good guys really never do win,* he thought.

"Because my dad fought and gave his life defending people who couldn't

defend themselves." Drew felt his eyes ache with rising tears and a lump forming in his throat. "And he taught me to do the same. He taught me that it's
wrong to do nothing when you have the power to do something."

Reed's eyes softened.

"That's why the gang was after me. Because I was interfering with their
attempt to control the area. They didn't like it. They wanted to kill me." Drew
looked straight into Reed's eyes. "Last night I told you I was one of the good
guys. It's the truth, whether you believe me or not. I don't care what you do to
me; I just want Sydney free from all of this."

Reed leaned forward. "Then help me help you. You tell us where we can
find Berg, and we'll wrap up this deal with Carlyle."

Drew shook his head. "I don't know where he is. We were supposed to
leave Chicago together, but when the Dragons kidnapped Sydney and the
Branson children and I was captured by you guys, that all changed."

"Where were you supposed to meet him?"

Drew hesitated. He doubted the FBI was buying the industrial espionage
story. If they found Ben, his life would be in danger because there would be
nothing the FBI could do to save him from the dark invaders.

"I'll tell you, but it doesn't matter. He won't be there."

"Why not?"

"Because we had a backup plan if things went sideways."

Reed looked perturbed. He began tapping his thumb on the table.

"I don't know where Ben is because we each devised our own alternate
plan if we were separated, captured, or killed. It was our firewall of security for
each other. As far as I know, he could be on his way to Singapore."

Reed didn't look happy, but he did look convinced. What made Drew
nervous was the fact that this Mr. Ross apparently had been watching them all
along. There was a good chance that Ross had men trailing Ben right now. He
hoped Ben's alternate plan had multiple decoys like they had talked about. Ben
had learned a lot in the last few months, and Drew hoped his brilliant mind
would take advantage of it.

"We're not done, but for now that's enough. Is there anything else you
want to say?" Reed asked.

Drew's mind made a sweep of every option and possible outcome he might
face. His situation was desperate. In the game of chess, there was a desperation

move that could be played to transport the king out of danger—the castle move. It was the only move in chess where a player was allowed to move two pieces in one turn. It often surprised the opponent if he wasn't paying close attention to your pieces.

"Yes, I do have one more thing to say." Drew looked to his left, directly at the one-way mirror where he knew the supervisor, Mr. Graham, and the mysterious Mr. Ross were standing. He looked back at Agent Reed. "I want to speak with Mr. Ross."

Reed's eyes opened wide before he could check his reaction. "Ah . . . who's Mr. Ross?"

Drew looked straight into his eyes. "I've been truthful with you, Reed, just as you've asked me to be. Please afford me the same honor."

Reed frowned, then glanced toward the glass. A few seconds later, the door opened. A man dressed in a dark gray Armani suit entered and walked to the table. Every step and movement of his body seemed preplanned, smooth, perfect. His white shirt, blue-and-white striped tie, and short gray hair that faded to white at his temples all conveyed exquisite style and intellect. He would command any room he entered.

Agent Reed rose to his feet as Mr. Ross approached. Ross looked down at Drew, then to Reed.

"I'm sorry, sir, I—"

Ross reached for the recorder and clicked it off. He handed it to Reed. "Remove Mr. Carter's handcuffs and leave us," he ordered.

Reed hesitated.

"It's all right, Agent Reed. Mr. Carter's not going to try anything, are you?" Ross looked at Drew. His eyes nearly pierced him through with discernment.

Drew shook his head. Reed removed Drew's handcuffs and walked toward the door.

"Agent Reed, make sure the observation room is clear too."

"Yes sir."

Drew rubbed his wrists, thankful for the space to move them again. Mr. Ross slid the other chair out and glided into a position facing Drew.

"Well, Mr. Carter." Ross held out his hands. "You wanted to see me and I'm here. What do you want?"

Drew cocked his head. "Who are you, and why are you here?"

Ross folded his hands and leaned forward on his elbows. "You are an unusual man, Mr. Carter, and you haven't been completely honest, have you?"

Drew swallowed hard, wondering what Ross was implying.

"I've been watching you for quite a while now. You know things you're not supposed to know. You see things you're not supposed to see. You can do things other men can't do. Isn't that so?"

Drew paused. How was he supposed to answer?

"I'm not sure what you mean," he said honestly, but inside he could feel his muscles begin to shiver.

And if Mr. Ross wasn't enough to unnerve him, a light invader stepped through the wall of the interrogation room and began walking around the two of them. Drew recognized him as the warrior who had talked to the large invader called Validus. Drew had to concentrate not to look at the menacing form circling them. The invader seemed fixated on Mr. Ross. He looked concerned, which concerned Drew.

Ross smiled with condescension. "I think you know exactly what I mean. You have skills very few others have. Skills that allow you to take out an entire gang without getting shot. Skills that allow you to locate a man in a city of millions and whisk him to safety in a taxi cab."

Drew's eyes widened.

"Skills that allow you to know my name, even though you've never met me."

Drew put his hand beneath the table to hide the slight tremble. Something strange was happening. The light invader stopped pacing and looked straight at Ross.

Ross leaned back in his chair, reached in his pocket, and pulled out a package of gum. He slowly and carefully removed the wrapper from one piece and slid it into his mouth. With a subtle smile, he offered the package to Drew. Drew shook his head and waited. Was this man a tool of the dark invaders? Perhaps tattooed, grungy gang members weren't their only avenues of influence.

"My job, Mr. Carter, is to find people just like you. People with skills. People with the potential to serve this great country like very few others can. I'm a talent seeker, Carter, and I must say that you have talent." Ross's smile widened.

The light invader fingered his sword and squinted at Ross.

"I don't understand," Drew said. "If you've been watching me, then why didn't you bring me in earlier?"

"Because I wasn't done evaluating your potential, and now I know what you are capable of. Jake Blanchard has trained you well, but you aren't as good as you can be . . . not yet, anyway."

Drew shook his head. "Who *are* you?"

Ross looked at Drew as if he were moving in for a checkmate. "I am the invisible brother of the intelligence community. Normally I don't make house calls like this; I leave that up to my recruiters. But when I began getting reports on you, I made an exception."

Drew lifted an eyebrow. *The NCS?* he wondered. Could it be possible that Ross was part of the National Clandestine Service, the most secretive organization in the US government?

Ross continued. "Years ago we discovered a problem. It's not a big secret that the FBI, the CIA, the NSA, Homeland Security, Military Intelligence, and a dozen other intelligence-gathering agencies don't communicate with each other very well. And because of that, there are resources and personnel that aren't utilized to their full potential. One of my jobs is to fix that problem. Because of my position, I have access to information that allows me to find—how shall I say it?—anomalies in the masses of humanity that we can utilize and position to our best advantage."

Ross's eyes narrowed and his pleasant gaze turned icy cold.

"At Drayle, you popped up on our radar, and we discovered an anomaly, Mr. Carter. The more I heard and observed, the more I realized what a shame it would be to have you waste away in a prison cell."

Drew was certain he came to the same conclusion that the light invader did, and at the same time. Mr. Ross didn't know about the invader war, at least not yet. The light invader glanced at Drew with a steely-eyed look, then bolted from the room. Drew took a deep breath, not sure whether to be discouraged or grateful.

"If you've been watching me, then you know I'm innocent," Drew stated.

Mr. Ross raised an eyebrow. "Innocent of assaulting two federal agents? Innocent of possessing illegal weapons on a college campus? Innocent of shooting eleven people in an abandoned warehouse?" Ross frowned. "Innocent intentions don't eliminate guilty actions. I can't obstruct the machine of justice in America, Carter."

Drew reclaimed some of his nerve. "Then why are you here, Mr. Ross?"

Ross leaned forward once again. "I can't obstruct justice, but I can divert it." He let a subtle smile cross his face again. "You come from a family of military honor, of patriotism. Why aren't you serving in the armed forces?"

Drew felt a knot form in his gut. Ross was talking about the life he wanted but would never have. "That was my intention before all of this happened. Before the physics lab accident."

"How would you like to serve your country after all, Carter?"

Before Drew could reply, Ross continued.

"I'm going to offer you an alternative to prison, but consider this carefully, for you will only have one chance to accept. And should you accept, it will be more dangerous, more grueling, and more lonely than prison ever could be."

Drew looked at Ross through narrowed eyes. "Which agency?"

"That would be up to me once you've completed the training . . . *if* you complete the training. A lot would depend on how well you do."

"I'm assuming this 'offer' requires me to give up all connections to my former life."

Ross nodded.

"What about my mother and Jake? What will you tell them . . . and Sydney?"

Ross puckered his lips. "How about the truth? Sometimes that actually works."

"The truth? I didn't think you guys did that very often."

"Only when it gives us a better advantage than lying," Ross replied. "We simply tell them that in your attempt to rescue Sydney, you assaulted two federal agents and are facing up to forty years in prison. The government offered you the option of serving in an agency. You will be highly supervised and restricted throughout your training and will have no connection with your former life until such time as the agency sees fit."

Drew thought how much better it sounded than some fabricated story, and certainly much better than prison, but also how painful it would be for his mother. He would also have to give up any hope of being with Sydney—the universe seemed intent on keeping them apart. But even more important, inside the intelligence community, Drew would have the opportunity to discover more about the invaders. He might be able to learn if there was some branch of the government that knew about them, or perhaps was even responsible for them.

"And you'll drop all charges against Jake, Sydney, and Ben?"

Ross nodded once. "If we make you disappear, then what's the point in charging them? Who would they have helped?"

Drew looked down at his hands and then back to Ross. "Okay, Mr. Ross, I'll do it. Can I see them before I . . . disappear?"

"It will be arranged," Ross said. "Reed will get you ready for the transition."

Ross got up to leave, then stared down at Drew. "Do you know where you're going?"

Drew stood up to face the mysterious man who seemed to know the answers to all the questions he asked. "The Farm."

Ross frowned. "To start with. And by the way, you only get one chance at this, Carter. Our washout rate is high. You screw this up and you're right back on the road to prison. You understand?"

Drew nodded. "I don't have a degree. I thought that was a prerequisite for CIA training."

"I can take care of that."

"Thank you, sir, for an opportunity to redeem all of this," Drew said.

Ross shook his head. "Don't thank me, Carter. I'm not doing you any favors. You'll find that out soon enough."

"Yes sir."

Ross strolled to the door, opened it, and then looked back for a brief moment as if to convince himself he had done the right thing. "Don't make me regret today."

Then Mr. Ross disappeared behind the white door.

THE HARD GOOD-BYE

Drew waited for Sydney. She would be the first one he said good-bye to since she was already in Chicago.

He raced through all the things he wanted to tell her. He hadn't prepared for this. There were so many things to say, and many of them couldn't be said. Drew couldn't deny it any longer—he loved Sydney, but she deserved a life full and free from him. He had bartered for her freedom, and now he had to let her go . . . completely. The ache in his heart was unbearable.

What a frustrating and bizarre turn of events. She seemed to know more than she let on, or was it that her innocence was a weapon against the dark invaders? Were purity and innocence weapons unto themselves? Drew thought he might go mad trying to figure it all out.

One thing he knew for sure, whether Sydney truly understood the invisible war of the invaders or not, they could not let the FBI know that they knew. Like Jake, his mother, and Dr. Fisher, they would consider him insane, and he would end up in an asylum instead of with the CIA or even in prison.

The door opened and Reed came in, followed by Sydney. For one brief moment, she looked so horribly sad, until she saw why Reed had brought her here.

Her face lit up like the sun. "Drew!"

She ran to him, and he embraced her. His heart flipped, which would make the next few minutes all the harder.

"Please don't touch the suspect," Reed said, his voice firm but not cold. He stood at the door just ten feet away with his hands behind his back.

Sydney turned and looked at him, then slipped away from Drew and sat across the table. Tears spilled from her eyes. It hurt to see her in such angst. He wanted to sweep her up and take her away to some faraway island, away from the mess he had brought into her life.

She wiped her eyes and opened her mouth, but Drew stopped her before she could say a word.

"Sydney, I need to tell you a few things. Please let me finish before you say anything."

She reached for his hands, and hers were trembling. He hated what he had done to her. Just before she touched him, she hesitated, glanced toward Reed, and retracted.

"Drew, I—" she began but Drew cut her off.

"I wish I could say these things without others listening, but they've only given us a few minutes." There it was, the hint not to talk about the invaders. "So here it goes . . . First, I need to tell you that I care more about you than you'll ever know, and I am sorry that I've brought this on you. I never wanted anything or anyone to hurt you." Drew lowered his gaze to the table and then back to her beautiful, sorrowful eyes. "Especially me."

Drew saw her straighten slightly, and a look of resolve filled her eyes. She was tough, and Drew loved her all the more for it. It made his next few words nearly impossible to say.

"Second, you need to move on with your life and forget about me."

Sydney shook her head, but Drew continued.

"I'm facing some serious charges. Truth is, Syd, it's going to be a long time before I . . . Well, you can't wait for me, and I don't want you to."

At that, Sydney looked lost. "But all you've ever done is help people." She seemed to recall something. "They said you assaulted two FBI agents, but I don't believe them." Her eyes pleaded with him. "I told them you would never do that."

"I'm sorry, Syd. It's true."

Sydney pulled back a few inches, shaking her head, eyes wide with bewilderment.

"I had to. They weren't going to let me come and save you. I knew it was wrong, but I couldn't risk losing you or Shana or Micah." Drew clenched his jaw. "I didn't care what the consequences were, I had to save you."

Sydney's eyes darted to the mirror, to Reed, then back to Drew. "But they must know it was to help—"

"That's not how it works. It doesn't change the fact that I assaulted two federal agents and stole their weapons. Those two offenses alone could get me forty years in prison. And then there's the eleven gang members I shot."

"In self-defense! We'll fight this together, Drew."

"No, Sydney. We'd lose. Even if I did it for the right reasons, law enforcement can't allow vigilantism."

"But you saved us from the gang. No one can do what you—"

Drew widened his eyes, and she immediately caught the hint. She froze; then her shoulders slumped. She looked defeated.

"You can't wait for me, Sydney. You must move on with your life, but you're going to be all right. I've agreed to cooperate with them. They agreed to drop all charges against you in exchange for my confession; then they offered me an alternative to prison. After today you won't see me again."

"What's going to happen to you, Drew?"

"I'm going to disappear again, but this time it's to serve our country."

A tear ran down her cheek. "I won't see you . . . ever?"

"It's either this or prison . . . either way—"

"One more minute, Carter," Reed called out.

Drew looked at Reed, then back at Sydney. She was shaking her head and tears streamed down her cheeks. She looked like she was going to blurt out something they would both regret. Deep down, he hoped it was her confession of love for him, but he also hoped it wasn't. He didn't think he could bear knowing and never living in the embrace of her love. He slowly shook his head, signaling her not to say it.

"I *have* to tell you something, Drew." Sydney reached for his hands, and Reed looked away.

"It will only hurt us both, Sydney." Drew's eyes reddened. "You deserve someone who can love you completely . . . who will be there for you every day." Drew pulled back his hands. "Good-bye, Sydney."

Reed walked toward Sydney and lifted a hand toward her. "Come along, Miss Carlyle."

Sydney stood and waited until Drew looked up at her; then she leaned over and grabbed his hand anyway. "I won't give up praying for you, Drew. You need to know that I'm praying that God and His mighty angels will keep you and protect you from the darkness! Ephesians 6:12 is your verse, Drew. It's real!"

Drew looked into her eyes and saw the same fire that he always did when she talked about her God. He had no response. Her gaze nearly haunted him. What did it mean? Was this a message about the invaders, or was she truly this deceived by her religious beliefs?

"Come," Reed said, gently laying a hand on her shoulder.

Drew didn't want her to go. He had protected her many times, but something felt reversed. Though he didn't see it now, the power that emanated from her during the battle with the Dragons was still there . . . still in her eyes . . . still in her soul.

Drew watched her walk to the door, and just before she left, she glanced over her shoulder at him. He locked that beautiful forlorn face in his memory. It might be the last time he ever saw her.

DARK SECRETS

On their journey back from Brazil, Persimus listened as Validus filled Tren in on what had happened, explaining how they had learned from Tinsalik Barob, a Fallen who had lost favor with Apollyon, that Drew Carter was foreseen to be the last salvation initiating the End of Days. It brought clarity to their mission and understanding as to why the Fallen were so intent on killing both Drew Carter and Sydney Carlyle. Sydney had the most influence on Carter, and her faith was their hope in bringing him to Christ. Until then, Validus and his team of guardian and warriors were tasked with keeping both of them alive and trying to keep them together.

Validus, Tren, and Persimus set down outside of Chicago and demorphed their wings. Minutes later they were entering the Chicago office of the Federal Bureau of Investigation.

Tren briefed Validus and Persimus as they made their way to Drew's interrogation room. "The observer who's been following Carter for months is a man named Ross. He's the director of the National Clandestine Service for the US government."

"The NCS director?" Validus asked.

Tren nodded.

"This can't be good. What happened?"

"Ross offered Carter the option of prison or to serve as an agent."

Validus huffed. He didn't even have to ask Tren what Carter chose. "And we thought protecting him was tough the last few months. With Carter's skills, Ross is going to put him right into the Special Operations Group when they're done training him. It doesn't get any more life-threatening than that. We're going to need help."

They entered the white interrogation room to see Carter at the table, resting his head on his arms. Validus couldn't help the twinge of sympathy he felt for Carter. There were so many things he wanted to fix in the man's life . . . a man whose heart was good. And yet without the Lord in his life, his options were extremely limited.

Tren motioned toward the one-way mirror, which did nothing to hinder their view through to the other side. One man was staring at Carter. His arms were crossed as he scrutinized his prisoner.

"That's Ross."

Validus looked at the man, then back at Tren. "What's the status of Carlyle? What is the FBI planning on doing with her?"

Tren shrugged. "Not sure. I'll find out." The guardian disappeared through the wall.

Validus looked back at Ross. He stepped through the wall into the observation room and circled Ross.

"What are you plotting, Mr. Ross?" Validus said. He looked back into the room at Carter and saw Persimus studying the man. Tren returned to the interrogation room a few minutes later, and Validus joined him and Persimus.

"Looks like Carter bargained for Carlyle's and Blanchard's freedom in exchange for a confession. She's being released. She looks pretty broken, though. I'm guessing he told her to move on."

Validus looked at Carter. "So he still doesn't know who we are."

"Probably not," Tren replied. "I'm sure neither one wanted to let the FBI know that Carter could see us."

Persimus finally broke his silence. "When am I going to get a clue as to what's going on?"

Validus looked at his friend of old. "I'm sorry, Persimus. I'll bring you up to speed. Tren, any idea when they're going to move Carter?"

"Not for a few days."

"Good, keep an eye on him. I'm going to take Persimus to Rivercrest and fill him in on what's happened."

Validus briefed Persimus as they traveled to Kansas, answering as many questions as he could before arriving at Carter's home.

"Carter's mother is Kathryn, and his mentor, now stepfather, is Jake Blanchard. I want you to know who they are because, in spite of Mr. Ross's intentions, I think their influence and involvement in Carter's life isn't over."

They entered the home to find Kathryn in her bedroom. Validus and Persimus watched as she slid a wooden box from the top shelf of the closet.

Validus looked at her, drawn to her much as he had been to a young girl of ancient Babylonian days. "She's not saved but has a good heart, just like her son."

"I can see that." Persimus looked at Validus. "There's something more here."

Validus was taken aback. Persimus sensed it too.

Kathryn opened the small cedar box and closed her eyes as the sweet fragrance of the aromatic wood sifted into her nostrils. Validus was soothed by the fragrance as well. When Kathryn opened her eyes, she put her hand to her mouth.

"Oh . . . oh my."

She lifted a sealed letter addressed to her. She held it to her heart.

"Jake," she called out.

Jake came quickly, seeming to sense the pain in her voice. "What is it, Kathryn?"

She looked up at him, tears brimming her eyes. She held the letter out for him to see. "I'm such a horrible daughter. This is a letter from my mother. She wrote it just before she died and made me promise not to read it until a year had passed. Then I lost my job, we moved to Kansas, and life became chaotic."

Kathryn stared at the letter as if she dared not open it. Jake sat on the couch beside her, and she handed him the letter. "Read it to me, please."

He took the letter. "Are you sure?"

She nodded.

Jake slipped a pocketknife under the upper fold of the envelope and slid the perfectly sharpened blade across the length of it. He pulled out the letter and opened it to reveal a page of exquisitely crafted cursive words. Validus and Persimus listened along with Kathryn.

My dearest sweet Kathryn,

I am so sorry that I must leave you at a time when you need me most. This world can be so harsh, and yet I will choose to bask in the joy I feel when I see the love you have for Drew.

It seems our family has endured more than our share of tragedy. I've asked you not to open this letter until one year after my passing so that the sadness in your heart may have ebbed before I share with you what has burdened our family for three generations. I apologize in advance, but I feel compelled to share it with you, lest by some other means you discover it for yourself and begrudge me for not being honest with you. I've never told you, and I never told your father because I did not want the dark of our past to obscure the brightness of our future.

My father and mother were indeed refugees who fled from Germany to Sweden in 1943 as you have been told, but there is more to the story. They fled to Sweden because my father was an SS German soldier trying to escape the atrocities that he was forced to be a part of during the war. Upon arriving in Sweden, he changed his name to Frederick Arnson. Three years later when he, my mother, and I made it to the US, he began working as a factory worker. Although his death when I was nine was considered a factory accident, my mother later told me that he took his own life, unable to bear the sorrow of such a horrid past. I can only imagine the torment he must have faced every day for the things that he saw and was a part of. I believe he was the victim of an evil regime, caught in the trap of fear, death, and conscience. I know you too felt the continual sorrow of Grandma Klara, especially when she spoke of Grandpa Frederick, but in spite of what he was forced to do, she loved him very much. Even now as an old woman, my eyes swell with tears as I remember his gentle hugs. He always called me his "sweet redemption." I believe that in the end, he was a brave man.

So now you know. My name was Liesl Kraus. I didn't want you to live in the shadow of our family history until I could share with you that you are free from it, as I have learned to be. I watched you and Ryan instill in Drew a love for people and the courage to stand up for the innocent. I am so proud of you. What a wonderful mother you are, and what a great young man he is becoming! You are my precious and sweet redemption.

With deepest love,
Mother

Jake wrapped his arms around Kathryn as she cried. "Oh, Jake, she would be so disappointed."

"No, Kathryn. You and I both know who Drew really is. Time will prove it out, I promise."

Validus hurt for Kathryn because she didn't know the truth. Drew was everything his grandmother had hoped he would be and so much more.

He knelt with wings spread and peered across the tear-soaked cheeks of Kathryn's sorrow. In spite of her great sadness, something deep stirred inside of him . . . something profound. Could it possibly be? The hair on the back of his neck stood straight. He looked up at Persimus and could tell that he felt it too.

Validus translated the letter from Kathryn's hands and stuffed it into his breast pocket just as her cell phone rang. She reached for the phone and handed it to Jake. The number was unlisted.

"Hello? This is Kathryn's husband, Jake Blanchard . . . I'll take the message . . . When and where? Is he . . . I want some authentication . . . We'll be there."

Jake terminated the phone call, and by now Kathryn was silent, searching Jake's eyes for some hint regarding the strange message. He didn't make her wait.

"It was the FBI. They have Drew and want us to come to Chicago."

"Come," Validus said to Persimus as he launched himself up through the roof of the house at breakneck speed.

He dared not fully consider it yet, but if what he suspected were true, then the Fallen's suspicions of Drew Carter fell far short of the truth. And if they knew, Apollyon would unleash the gates of hell on him. With each beat of his wings, his pulse quickened and the urgency of his mission amplified. Tren would have to protect Carter for a few days. Persimus and he had much to do in Europe.

Before long, Validus and Persimus set down on the western coast of the UK. Validus demorphed.

"Keep your wings." He handed Persimus the letter he had translated from

Kathryn. "I want you to trace their family line back as far as you can go. Meanwhile I have an appointment with General Brandt. Let's hope he is willing to hear me out."

"Very well. Where do we rejoin?"

"At the church in Hamburg in two days."

Persimus saluted and took flight. Validus kept to the ground and sprinted through the rural regions of the United Kingdom north toward Scotland, where Brandt's world headquarters was stationed. After a brief delay by the warriors on guard, Validus was able to gain an audience with General Brandt and petition his cause.

"General Brandt, warriors dissolved helping me get this information. Drew Carter is the last salvation, and I must keep him alive until he accepts Messiah. The Fallen will stop at nothing to kill him and stop the time line. I need at least five more warriors dedicated to Carter's protection."

Brandt squinted at Validus. "I know what my directives are, and I don't have enough warriors to accomplish them. I can't stop protecting the churches and their missions for one man, not to mention trying to keep Israel intact. Things are heating up there daily." Brandt shook his head. "You'll have to work with Malak to get your support."

"That's the problem, sir. Malak refuses to give me what I need. Every commander is tasked to the extreme and can't commit any of their warriors. I need a directive from you."

Validus hesitated to tell Brandt his suspicions, but evidently he was going to be denied his request anyway. Israel might be the key to making his point.

"There's more, General. I believe Carter is the one General Danick was looking for."

"What are you talking about?" Brandt seemed annoyed. He didn't like second petitions.

"When General Danick died, he told me to find the one we missed. I believe Carter's the one. Elohim hid him from the Fallen and now he's here."

Brandt eyed Validus suspiciously. Validus had helped General Danick trace the Messianic lineage for thousands of years. Then, when Jesus was born to complete the lineage, Danick had insisted that his tracing of Jewish lineages was still crucial to the fulfilling of End Times prophecy. He had chosen the lineage of the prophet Simeon because of the outpouring of the Holy Spirit on the man when Jesus was presented at the temple.

"Is that what all this is about?" Brandt stood up and walked away, shaking his head. He passed through the door of his office and into the command room.

Validus whisked through the door to stay with him. "But, General—"

Brandt stopped and turned on him. "Validus, Danick's tactics served us well for thousands of years, but since Messiah, there's been no point, and we wasted thousands of lives protecting lineages that got us nowhere. I will not, I repeat, will *not* spend lives and resources on some wild notion you have about Carter being part of some prophetic lineage. Is that clear?"

Two of Brandt's commanders were walking briskly toward them.

"Now, I have a war going on," Brandt said. "I don't have time for this. Dismissed, Commander Validus!"

Validus clenched his jaw and forced a salute, then backed away as Brandt engaged with his commanders. Validus took a few steps toward the door, wondering how he was going to keep Carter alive against impossible odds. Never before had he been so frustrated, so burdened with the responsibility of so great a mission without the authority to accomplish it. Only Persimus and Tren fully understood the significance.

"Messenger approaching, sir," Brandt's executive called out.

"It's about time. Send him directly to me as soon as he sets down."

"He's not setting down, sir. Should be here any—"

A brilliant white flash filled the room as the messenger transitioned from silver streak to a dead stop just inches before setting down on the stone floor of the castle. The urgency of his message was apparent by the rush of his arrival. The messenger's back was to Validus, but everyone in the room knew who it was—Raphael, second only to Gabriel in the Messenger Order. His pearl white wings were broad and strong, and he did not demorph them. His bronze hair and eyes were glowing as if he had just been in the presence of the Holy One.

"Archangel Raphael," Brandt began. "What news have you from Zion?"

Validus knew he should be on his way back to Carter, but he was compelled to stay just a moment longer and hear the news from heaven.

Raphael turned and looked about the room, his eyes resting momentarily on Validus. His presence made Validus feel small again, as if he were back six thousand years ago as the last and least of the heavenly host. His assignment to earth in the Middle Realm, Elohim's physical creation, had caused him to dispense with such ancient feelings, but here in the presence of one of the archangels, it was back, fresh and revived.

Raphael leaned close to Brandt and spoke in hushed tones. Validus could see Brandt's face over Raphael's winged shoulder. The general's brows furrowed as the news was whispered in his ear. He shook his head and made some attempt at protest, but Raphael would have none of it. Brandt's face turned red with anger, but he relented.

Validus decided that now would be a good time to leave. Whatever the news was, Brandt was clearly in no mood to grant anyone requests, especially him. He turned to quietly go but was halted by the deep voice of Raphael.

"Validus."

Validus froze and turned back to see the archangel walking toward him. "Sir?"

Raphael closed the gap and took a moment to scrutinize him. Was Validus to give a report on his mission?

The archangel's steel gaze eased slightly. "How is Tren?"

That was not the question Validus was expecting. "He . . . is well."

Raphael folded his wings slightly. "Before the second generation, we were friends."

Something inside Validus ached. He tried to deny that it was Niturni, but he could not. "He's a strong guardian. We work well together."

Raphael nodded. "Tell him . . . tell him to be careful. There are dangerous days ahead. Lead him well, Validus."

Validus nodded. Raphael stepped back, spread his wings, launched into the air, blurring into a silver streak before he had materialized through the timbered roof of the castle.

Validus glanced toward Brandt and saw the general staring at him, harsh and cold. He motioned for him to return.

Validus approached cautiously. "Sir?"

Brandt shook his head. "I should have known something like this was going to happen. The day you were reassigned, I should have known."

"What is it, General?" Validus dared ask.

Brandt put his hands on his hips and glared at him. His words came slowly. "I have been *authorized* to grant you the support you need."

Validus suppressed a smile. It wouldn't help. "Five warriors?" he asked a little too jubilantly.

"Yes." Brandt could hardly say the words. "And five hundred more when you need them," he added.

"What?" Validus exclaimed.

Brandt turned to his executive officer. "Sutton, see to the commanders. I need a few minutes with Commander Validus."

Sutton joined the waiting commanders, and Brandt pulled Validus back into his private room so they could talk. Brandt wanted background and details on Validus's mission with Carter. As the story unfolded, Validus felt justified by the response Brandt gave him. Finally someone other than Tren, Persimus, and he grasped the significance of Carter. Validus could see Brandt's strategic mind working.

"The Carter mission has escalated to global significance. You are now in command of the operation. Take your pick of the warriors you need, just don't take all of my continental commanders at once."

Validus smiled. "Don't worry, sir, I know exactly who I need, and none of them are your commanders. I don't need an army, not yet. What I need is stealth and skill. But when the time comes—"

"When the time comes, just say the word," Brandt finished.

Validus handed Brandt a folded paper. "Thank you, General. For now, I need the locations of these warriors and orders reassigning them to my command."

Brandt opened the paper and read the names. He looked up at Validus. "I can see why Danick chose you as his first and why this is your mission. Two of these won't like it."

Validus nodded. "They don't have to like it."

The corner of Brandt's mouth turned up. "Come."

They walked back into the war room, where Brandt handed the paper to Sutton. "Give Commander Validus the location of each of these warriors, and prepare orders for their transfer."

Sutton nodded. "Come with me, Commander."

"Godspeed, Validus," Brandt called out.

Validus saluted and followed Sutton. Thirty minutes later, Validus was deep in the heart of Russia, inwardly rejoicing that, at last, he would have the men he needed to fight Niturni.

5

KATHRYN AND JAKE

Late in the afternoon of the next day, Reed told Drew that his mother and Jake Blanchard had arrived and were waiting to see him.

"They'll be brought here as soon as they've been searched. I'll need to remain in the room with you."

"I understand."

An extra chair was brought in for Jake while Drew was waiting. He hadn't seen his mother for nearly a year. He wasn't sure how to even begin explaining himself or how to apologize for how he had left her. The minutes ticked by and Drew became more anxious with each passing one. Would she be happy, angry, sad? Twenty long minutes later, the door opened.

Reed entered, followed by Kathryn and then Jake. Drew's first glimpse of his mom hurt. She looked older, much older than she should have looked. There were many lines of worry etched in her face that he had never seen before.

"Drew!" Kathryn exclaimed. She ran to him, and Drew embraced her. He buried his face in her dark brown hair.

"Mom!" he whispered into her ear. "I'm so sorry . . . so very sorry." He swallowed the lump forming in his throat as he felt her trembling in his arms. She held on for a long while, and Reed didn't say a word. Jake stood silently by, a pillar of support for both of them, as he had been since Drew was twelve.

Kathryn finally stepped back and put her hands to his cheeks, tears streaming down her face.

Drew grabbed her hands. "It's okay, Mom. It's all going to be okay."

She dropped her hands and looked toward Jake. "Drew, Jake and I are married."

Drew couldn't contain the broad smile that spread across his face. He went to Jake and hugged him. He didn't say a word. He didn't need to.

Drew stepped back and grabbed his mother's hand. "I'm so glad! And if you don't mind my saying, it was way overdue!"

Kathryn leaned into Jake as he put an arm around her. They both looked a little embarrassed.

"I'm sorry I wasn't there." Drew's comment sobered the mood. "I have a lot of explaining to do, and I'm not sure how much they're going to let me." He nodded at Reed.

Kathryn and Jake sat down in the chairs designated for them as Drew pulled his chair from his side of the table so he could sit closer to his mom. Reed looked like he was going to say something but instead remained silent. Kathryn had a hard time not touching Drew, so he held her hands while he talked.

"Mom, Jake, there's no way I can justify disappearing. The story is long and bizarre, but ultimately it was so I could find Ben."

He took a few minutes to explain why he and Ben had disappeared and their efforts to establish proof of industrial espionage. Both Kathryn and Jake listened intently. Drew couldn't imagine what they both might be thinking. Did they believe him? Were they skeptical? Were they concerned for his mental health?

"What about all the questions about the school shooting, Drew?" Kathryn asked. "And now they are saying you assaulted two federal agents and were involved in more shootings here in Chicago. Tell me it's not true."

Drew looked toward Reed, who subtly shook his head.

Jake grabbed one of Kathryn's hands. "There are things the FBI doesn't want him to talk about."

Drew hung his head. When he looked back into her eyes, his heart broke. His mother had to know that he had not walked away from the man she raised him to be.

"Mom, what they've told you is true, but I also want you to know that everything I did was to save lives. I am the man you, Dad"—Drew looked at Jake with admiration and respect—"and Jake raised me to be. Please believe me."

Kathryn closed her eyes and more tears spilled out. "I do believe you, Drew. I just needed to hear it from you. Sydney told us what you did at Drayle. That's why I couldn't believe what they were saying."

Jake glanced at Reed. "But Drew, assaulting federal agents . . . there's no get-out-of-jail-free card for that, no matter what the reason."

"I know, but I had no choice."

Kathryn's face clouded with worry again.

"In exchange for my confession, they agreed to drop the charges against Sydney and anyone else who helped me." Drew glanced briefly toward Jake and squeezed his mother's hands. *Now for the really tough part.* "I'm looking at up to forty years in prison."

"Oh, Drew!" Kathryn said.

Drew shook his head. "But they offered me an alternative. I'm not sure how they found out about my skills, but I've been given a chance to train into an agency for the government in lieu of prison."

Kathryn's eyes illumined, and the creases in her face eased. "What does that mean, Drew?"

He bit his lip. He might as well say it as plainly as he could. "It means I won't be home for a very long time."

At that, Jake's eyes turned fierce. Drew knew that Jake understood exactly what it meant.

Jake clenched his teeth. "I'm as patriotic as it gets, but this isn't right, Drew. This is coercion. That's not how America operates!"

"I don't care what it is, Jake. It's my ticket out of prison, and I'm going to take it. You both know that I've always wanted to serve."

Jake looked at Drew, then glanced toward Kathryn, apparently unsure how to say what he wanted without bringing more distress to her. He lowered his voice. "Drew, we're talking CIA or even Special Operations Group . . . missions where your life is at stake."

"Like you and Dad," Drew interjected. "I've already been there, Jake, multiple times. I'd rather serve my country than rot in prison. Wouldn't you?"

Jake took a breath and his countenance softened. "Of course I would. I just don't like their method."

Drew looked at his mom, wondering how she would handle knowing what he might be doing. Her concern seemed tempered by an inner strength, and then he realized that Special Ops and living daily with a loved one serving in dangerous circumstances was part of her life. He respected her strength.

"Will we get to see you again before you leave?" Kathryn asked, stuffing some of her emotion away.

Drew shook his head. "This is it, Mom."

Kathryn looked to Jake, and he seemed to read her mind.

"Wherever they put him, he's going to be fine, Kathryn. I've seen what he can do."

Drew noticed that Reed took note of Jake's last comment.

"When do you go?" Kathryn asked.

"Soon." Drew shot a look toward Jake, and he nodded. If Drew were put on highly classified missions, there was no telling how long he would be away. He would let Jake explain that to Kathryn later . . . gently.

Reed allowed Drew to have a full hour with Kathryn and Jake. The good-bye was difficult, and Kathryn could hardly let go of him. When Jake hugged Drew, he held him a little longer too, but it was not for the sake of affection but rather for the message he whispered in his ear.

"Ryan Johnson, US Bank 325625775325."

Drew repeated the number in his mind three times. It was no coincidence that Jake had arranged an account number with multiple fives at perfect intervals, making memorization easy. The account was under the same name Jake had used for Drew's fake IDs long before.

Jake pulled back, put a hand on Drew's neck, and looked straight into his eyes. "You ever need anything, you know where to find me."

Drew nodded.

Jake put an arm around Kathryn to help her walk away.

THE GROUND
CRIES OUT

In all of history, never before had such a team of angelic skill been assembled. When Danick had asked Validus to handpick the Lineage Legion, he had learned the skills and abilities of the top five thousand angels on the planet, but for various reasons not all of them volunteered. Some felt they would serve Elohim best in their current command. Others were blunt in their opinions about the post-Messiah lineage cause. Validus would start with one such angel, Brumak.

The Fallen had droxans. The angels had Brumak. The few times Validus had seen him in action, he was astonished. Brumak was a tower of dark, muscled, angelic force, standing a full six inches taller than Validus and half again as thick. He had seen Brumak take sword slices and bullets that would have put two angels down, but the warrior kept coming. He had never seen him smile. Never.

Commander Porthan would be angry with Validus for taking Brumak, especially without a full explanation, but Validus didn't have that luxury. He set down in Tobolsk, Russia, and made his way to Commander Porthan's headquarters.

After a brief and heated exchange, Commander Porthan calmed and shook his head. "At least tell me who else you have."

"Persimus, Sason, Jayt, Crenshaw, and Rake," Validus replied.

Porthan tilted his head. "I can't begin to imagine what you have in mind, but that is going be the oddest detachment of warriors I have ever seen. Oh . . . and you get to tell Brumak." He smiled and handed the orders back to Validus.

"I figured so. Where is he?"

"On the front, of course. He stops only long enough for the Curing . . . when he needs it."

Validus found Brumak eating and recovering from multiple wounds. He sat on the ground, leaning against a large tree in the city square. His eyes were closed but his hand held tight to the sword at his side. Validus made sure to stay just out of its reach. He put his hands on his hips and spread his wings, hoping it might help some.

"Warrior Brumak."

The mountain of muscle stayed still. Beneath his sleek, shaved head, his eyes remained closed.

"This is the voice of Validus," the low voice of the angel rumbled. He slowly opened his eyes. "How goes the life of ease and comfort in America?"

Validus ignored the insult. "Are you able to fly?"

Brumak furrowed his brows. "I am."

Validus glared at him and waited just a moment, evaluating his decision to bring him into the team. "Then on your feet, warrior. You've been reassigned under my command, and we leave immediately."

Validus didn't wait for a reply. He turned and began walking away. He heard a growl and felt heavy footsteps in the ground beneath his feet. A few seconds later, a large shadow fell over Validus's right shoulder.

"Porthan must think I need a vacation," Brumak muttered.

Validus looked over and up at the massive warrior, his wings morphing to full spread. "I promise you more Fallen and droxan in one place than you have ever seen in your life, so keep your mouth in check or you'll be guarding sled dogs in Alaska."

Brumak snorted, then nodded. "Yes sir."

The odd duo launched into chilled air and turned east toward China.

In Beijing, Validus collected Jayt. In Australia, Sason; in Congo, Rake; and in Venezuela, Crenshaw.

When they arrived back in Chicago at the FBI complex, Tren was in the hall just outside the interrogation room. As the odd detachment of warriors set down around him, he lifted an eyebrow toward Validus. "Looks like you finally found some help."

Validus nodded. He pointed to the room Carter was in. "Warriors, our mission is the man inside this room. He can see you, so try not to be too conspicuous. Keep him alive."

Tren seemed to enjoy the varied responses from Brumak, Rake, Crenshaw, and Jayt.

"Tren's in charge while I'm away. I'll give you a full briefing when I return. Tren, a word, please."

Validus walked with Tren a few paces down the hallway. Until recently, Validus had been assigned as Tren's assistant, but recent developments surrounding Carter had changed everything. He needed to let the guardian know that the command of the operation had fully transferred to him. With other warriors involved and with the scope of the mission quickly broadening, it was the only way. He turned to address Tren, but the guardian held up his hand.

"You need not say anything. I know . . . and am relieved. I was told this morning when I was presented before Elohim."

Validus nodded. "You're a good angel, Tren, and I will be relying on you heavily in the days to come."

"Where are you off to now?"

"Persimus is following a lead on the ancestry of Carter. It may give us insight that the Fallen don't have. If I'm right, what we've seen in the last few months is just the beginning."

Tren looked surprised, at least as surprised as Validus had ever seen the cool, calculating guardian look. They turned to walk back to the waiting warriors.

"Don't take any guff from this crew," Validus warned.

"I can handle them," Tren said without cracking a smile, and Validus believed him.

Validus launched back into the air and flew east to meet Persimus in Hamburg. When he arrived, his friend was waiting.

"I've traced the family back to 367, but I'm not sure what you're looking for. There's nothing significant that I can see." Persimus swiped across his pages, revealing the thousands of lines. "Going one more generation means tracing 3,242 people."

"That should be far enough. Is there any infusion into the family line of Jewish blood?" Validus asked hopefully.

"I figured that's what you were looking for, but no, I'm sorry. It's Germanic all the way back."

Validus couldn't help the sinking feeling in his gut. Perhaps he had been wrong. He looked over Persimus's work, beginning with Carter and working backward. He pointed to Kathryn's grandfather.

"Frederick Kraus—the German soldier who changed his name, then killed himself."

Both angels became sober.

"Those were evil days," Persimus said as he looked on with Validus. "Especially for men like him. The death camps were Apollyon's vilest creations."

Validus grunted. "That's the intersection . . . it has to be. To which death camp was Frederick Kraus assigned, and when?"

Persimus swiped across his name. "Sobibór, April 1942 to October 1943."

"That's it, Persimus! It has to be. See if you can find any medical records for Klara Kraus, Frederick's wife. Look for Liesl's birth certificate. Then meet me at Sobibór."

The two angels parted, and Validus flew northeast toward eastern Poland, back in time to one of the most painful moments of his life.

He set down near what used to be the entrance to the death camp. A museum, statues, and memorials stood on the premises now. As Validus walked, the sights and sounds of the vicious battle replayed in his mind. He remembered the mighty Yortan sacrificing himself to save Eva and her daughter Anna Wiesenthal, the last of the lineage of Simeon that General Danick was convinced remained. They lost hundreds of warriors that fateful day, but evil was too great to overcome. Validus knelt down where he had last held General Danick in his arms, remembering the words as if the general had just spoken them.

You must find the one I missed.

Validus stayed still and silent for a long while, honoring his great commander. He had never dreamed that his search would bring him back to this camp of death and horror.

He looked up and saw where the gas chambers once stood. He walked to the place where Yortan had bled and dissolved away on the roof of one of the gas chambers. Although the prisoner revolt that occurred during Danick's attack on the death camp resulted in over half of the prisoners escaping, no prisoner had ever survived Lager III, the camp where the prisoners were gassed. Validus knelt down and touched the ground that cried out against the horror it was used for.

"Is it possible, little Anna? Is it possible?"

Persimus set down next to Validus, and he stood to greet him.

"Liesl's birth certificate," Persimus said, handing it to Validus.

Validus examined every detail. It seemed legitimate. "I guess I was wrong." He let the paper fall and dissolve away, back to the forgotten file in some German hospital.

"But here also is her death certificate," Persimus said.

"What?"

"Liesl Kraus died two days later. Whoever Kathryn's mother was, she wasn't Liesl Kraus."

Validus smiled, unable to contain the explosion of energy coursing through his veins. He grabbed Persimus's shoulders. "Her name was Anna Wiesenthal. Somehow, some way, Elohim saved her!" Validus looked up to heaven. "You didn't miss anyone, General Danick. You were right all along. Drew Carter is not only the last to be saved, he's the last of the lineage of Simeon, the prophet who proclaimed to the world the arrival of the Messiah!"

∽◦∾

Frederick Kraus thought he was serving his country as a patriot when he was swept up into the Schutzstaffel, or the SS, Adolf Hitler's elite and powerful protection squadron. Once in, there was no getting out, and over the course of time, Frederick found himself a prisoner of the Third Reich.

Now he was being punished and tormented by God for his crimes. Crimes too unthinkable to speak, and yet he lived them every day . . . and every night. His brief, fitful episodes of sleep were filled with the faces of men, women, and children from the Sobibór death camp. Worst of all was that he was a coward— too afraid of the other SS soldiers to try to stop the heinous treatment of prisoners, too afraid to run, and too afraid to take his own life. It was a miserable existence of fear, death, and nightmares. But what could one man do against an army of evil?

When his wife, Klara, became pregnant, he had hoped that their bringing life into the world would ease his torment, but their little Liesl was taken from them two days after she was born. Klara didn't know the horrors Frederick was a part of at the death camp, so the death of baby Liesl was all the more his punishment to bear as he watched the grief of his wife grow to utter despondency over the next two weeks.

When the young Jewish woman passed by him that day on the way to the gas chamber, she pleaded for him to save her child. It was more than he could bear, and the last thread of humanity inside him broke. She reached for him, and he turned away, once more too cowardly to do anything. But turning away did not save him. Her pleading eyes and voice were indelibly part of his memory now.

The diesel engines roared to life as thousands of Jews fell into death. He could take it no more. He went to the opposite end of the chamber, where there was a door to remove the bodies. Other prisoners and Ukrainian guards would be there to do the gruesome task of transporting and burning the bodies. When the engines were shut down, the doors of the chambers opened to exhaust the poisonous fumes.

And that's when every guard and prisoner froze and listened. The noise of the engines had drowned out the gunfire and screams from the other parts of the camp. It had to be a prison break. Sirens sounded, guns fired, and guards and prisoners were running everywhere. The other SS soldier, Scharführer Josef Vallaster, began yelling orders. First for the prisoners to return to their barracks, then for the Ukrainian soldiers to help put down the revolt. Any prisoners who didn't immediately return to their barracks were shot.

Frederick stood near the door of the gas chamber, his senses assaulted by the stench of carbon monoxide gas and urine and by the sounds of gunfire and screams. He was surrounded by hell, both inside his mind and outside of his body. He fell to his knees, crushed by the mountain of evil he could not escape, and set the muzzle of his pistol against his head. What could be worse than this existence? No matter what lay on the other side of eternity, his death would at least end his part in the execution of others.

His finger squeezed the trigger, but just a few ounces shy of releasing the firing pin, Frederick heard the muffled wail of a baby. He released the pressure on the trigger and leaned into the chamber. The cry was louder. Fredrick began pushing the twisted bodies aside until he saw the pale back of the young mother, sheltering her infant from the falling bodies around them. He gently lifted her body away so he could reach the infant. The babe lay on the cold floor surrounded by the stench of death.

How was it possible? He lifted the child from the tangled mass of corpses. Frederick cradled the babe just as he had done two weeks earlier with the lifeless form of his sweet Liesl. The child quit crying and peered into his eyes. For the first time in years, he felt a moment of peace in spite of the chaos and death that was swallowing the camp. In the powerfully innocent gaze of a Jewish child spared by God from the gas chamber, Frederick found courage. This child would not die! Frederick could not save thousands, but perhaps he could save one.

He drew his pistol and tucked it under his left arm beneath the cradled child, then stepped back out of the gas chamber and came face to face with Scharführer Vallaster. Lager III seemed empty except for the scattered bodies of dead prisoners.

"Scharführer Kraus, we are needed in Lager I! The revolt— What are you holding?"

"The infant survived the gas," Frederick replied.

Vallaster scowled. "The prisoners are all revolting. Kill it and come with me immediately!"

Frederick felt his fear rising up inside him as he faced the fury of Vallaster. "No!" he shouted over the continual bursts of gunfire in the other regions of the camp.

Vallaster's eyes bulged with fury. He reached for the child's legs to yank her from Frederick's embrace, but Frederick turned to his right, away from Vallaster, and knew his next action would be punishable by death. He pulled the trigger on his hidden pistol, which was now aimed at Vallaster. Two shots rang out, and the SS man fell to his knees, shock in his eyes and on his face. He then fell backward onto the ground.

Frederick didn't know what to do. He had saved a Jewish baby, shot a fellow SS leader, and was stuck in the middle of a death camp under revolt. He tried to keep from panicking as his mind searched for some way of escape. He would have to pass through Lager II and Lager I to get to the main gate and then to a motorbike or automobile. It seemed impossible, although he could use the mayhem of the revolt to help him. He quickly made his way to the building where the prisoners were made to remove their clothing and found a large bag with straps. He gently laid the baby in the bag and closed it.

He then went back to Vallaster's body and came upon an idea. Scharführer Vallaster was responsible for operating the rail-trolley that took the elderly and the sick from the railway to Lager III. He had been in the process of returning the rail-trolley to the main station when the revolt began, so it was running and ready to move. Frederick had learned how to operate the rail-trolley when Vallaster was on leave just a month earlier.

Frederick dragged Vallaster's body to the rail and lifted him onto the rail-trolley. He then placed the bag with the baby beside him at the controls. Within a few minutes he reached the main rail and the front gate. He grabbed the bag, hoping that by some miracle the child's cries would be muffled enough by the bag and drowned out by the continual machine-gun fire all around them. Near the gate, he ran to two Ukrainian guards.

"Scharführer Vallaster has been shot by the prisoners. He's badly wounded. Take him to the officer's quarters, and I will go for help!"

The two guards left their posts, which allowed Frederick to exit the compound on a motorbike. He turned onto the road to Wlodawa, which the Germans called Wolzek. That was where Klara would be, in the home that the Germans had appropriated to be quarters for SS officers at the camp.

Once home, Frederick opened the bag and lifted the wailing child out, gently placing her in Klara's arms.

"This is our Liesl, Klara. No one need know . . . No one must know."

Klara's eyes were wide with wonder and fear. Deep down, Frederick felt as though Klara knew of the horror of the camp, but she did not ask. This baby girl was the one small glimmer of hope in a place of horrid darkness.

Klara looked into the innocent eyes of the baby girl and nodded. Tears filled her eyes.

"Liesl," she whispered.

Frederick knelt in front of Klara. "What I have done to save her means that we must leave. We must flee to Sweden where many refugees are safe from the . . . the Nazis." Frederick found himself on the other side of the word now, and it felt right. "Do you understand what I'm saying?"

Klara nodded. "Yes, Frederick. Yes."

The next three weeks were treacherous for the young couple and their Liesl, but they eventually found safe haven in Sweden. When World War II ended, Frederick knew that America was the only place he had a chance to make a new life for himself and his family. In 1946, Frederick, Klara, and Liesl crossed the Atlantic to their new home. Frederick was ever hopeful that he had indeed left the evil of his past behind, but as Liesl grew, the little one he called his "sweet redemption" was also the face that haunted him each night in his dreams, for Liesl bore a striking resemblance to her mother.

VALIDUS AND THE VALIANTS

Validus and Persimus found Brumak, Sason, Jayt, Crenshaw, and Rake on the grounds outside the FBI building in Chicago.

Validus turned to Persimus. "Unless Carter is in danger, bring Tren down here. We need to brief up."

Persimus disappeared and was back a minute later with Tren.

The seven warriors and Tren stood in a circle on the east grounds of the FBI complex. Validus took a moment to read the face of each of these valiant angels. The apparent disinterest on the faces of Brumak and Jayt discouraged him. Validus didn't consider himself a great orator, but he needed the right words today to set the hearts and minds of his men straight for the mission ahead.

"Holy angels of the Most High God, some of you may be wondering why you have been reassigned under my command to be the watch guard of one man sitting in an FBI holding cell. When we are finished with this briefing, I want no misgivings, no misunderstandings, no lack of commitment, and no uncertainty as to the significance of this mission. If any of you are still struggling, I don't want you on this team. Is that clear?"

Validus briefly glanced at each angel and received an affirmation from all. He continued.

"First, the directive for this mission came from Archangel Michael. My reassignment from continental commander to mission commander came from Archangel Gabriel, and the authority for me to recruit each of you came from Archangel Raphael. When and if the day should come, I will bring five hundred warriors more to accomplish this mission.

"Second, every warrior and guardian still serving in the Middle Realm has survived over four thousand years of battle with the Fallen. We are all veterans of war, but I chose each of you for very specific reasons. Each of you has a unique skill set that will allow us to succeed in protecting Drew Carter." Validus stepped into the circle and pointed to the building fifty feet away. "Understand this: if he dies, we fail. And if we fail, Apollyon will revel in his pride as if he had thwarted the Great Purge."

Validus let his words marinate in their hearts and minds.

"Commander, why is Carter so important?" Crenshaw asked. "We've only heard rumors."

Validus crossed his arms. "Persimus and I just returned from a mission in South America. I went to seek out Tinsalik Barob."

The angels looked from one to another with surprise on their faces.

"The Fallen sent eight legions to stop me, but I found him. And what I learned from him brought clarity to this mission beyond anything I had expected. According to Barob, Apollyon devised a scheme to access the Hall of Ages. His purpose was to discover the trigger of the End of Days and thwart it, just as he did at the beginning of creation and just as he has tried to do ever since."

Validus scanned the faces of his men and could tell that all of them were hanging on each word he spoke.

"The Fallen discovered that Drew Carter is the trigger. The message from the infiltrators of the Hall of Ages was 'Drew Carter is the last.'"

"The last what?" Rake asked.

"The Book of Life is nearly full," Sason said, his eyes fixed on nothing but the air above them. "Carter is the last salvation."

"Carter is the trigger for the End of Days, and Apollyon is trying to thwart Elohim's plan once again," Validus added. "We must keep Carter alive until he is saved."

"Is Ruach Elohim drawing him?" Jayt asked.

"Yes, we believe so," Tren interjected. "Sydney Carlyle is a strong believer and has witnessed to him numerous times. She has great influence on him."

"But from what you've told us, the US government is separating them forever," Crenshaw added.

"That's true," Validus said. "And besides this, they are recruiting him to be a CIA operative. With his skills, he will most likely be assigned the most dangerous missions. Add to this the fact that the Fallen know he is the End Times trigger, and you can appreciate the challenges we face. Niturni is the North

American continental commander. He is resourceful and brilliant, and he will stop at nothing to destroy Carter."

Validus scanned the circle of warriors again, searching for their hearts.

"There are a few things you need to know about Carter. As I've already told you, he can see us and the Fallen, though he can't hear us. Additionally he has speed and fighting abilities that rival that of an angel."

"Impossible!" Jayt said. "Humans are too slow, their senses too dull."

Tren shook his head. "Not Carter. You'll be impressed."

"Tren's right," Validus added. "Two days ago he single-handedly took on an entire gang in their hideout and defeated them. He is skilled in hand-to-hand and weapons. He even helped me destroy a droxan."

The last comment brought looks of disbelief from most of the angels.

"How—" Sason began, but Validus cut him off.

"It's a story for another time. Suffice it to say that Carter is well engaged in the battles of both realms."

"The CIA knows what they're doing in recruiting him," Tren added.

"Well, at least we're working with a human with skills," Rake said with a subtle smile.

"Yes, except that he has the spirit of a good Samaritan," Validus countered. "Couple that with the skills of an angel warrior, and you have an unsaved man who looks for trouble at every opportunity."

Validus watched Brumak cross his arms, his muscles bulging throughout his torso. There was no disinterest on his face anymore.

"There is something else you should know about Carter . . . something the Fallen don't know." Validus scanned beyond their circle to make sure his words would remain undiscovered by the Fallen. "We have recently discovered evidence that Drew Carter is of the lineage that General Danick was tracking before he was dissolved. Carter's grandmother survived the Sobibór death camp and is in fact the last of the lineage of Simeon. It makes sense why Elohim has His eye on this man."

Validus turned about to look each warrior in the eye. "It's up to us, warriors. I cannot promise you victory, only fierce battles against many legions of the Fallen. And I can promise you this—I am committed to the valiant calling of Elohim and to leading you, should you choose to remain as part of this team. What say you?"

"I am with you, Commander," Crenshaw said.

"And I," echoed Persimus, Sason, and Rake. A moment later, Jayt and Brumak followed.

Validus let the moment linger, then nodded. "Very well then. Some of you have fought together but most have not. It's going to be critical that we know each other's abilities." He turned toward Tren. Though the guardian didn't have the appearance of a warrior, his brown eyes and fair hair wore the look of experience. There was nothing soft about his handsome face.

"Tren was Carter's guardian and was reassigned to him when the Fallen began taking an interest. Until today I was assigned to assist him. Now he is my second in command." Validus gave the warriors all a stern look. They were not used to taking orders from a guardian, and he wanted to make sure they understood. "An order from Tren is an order from me. Tren knows Carter better than anyone, and he also has the gift of discerning the intentions of humans. I've never known him to be wrong in that regard."

Validus nodded toward Persimus. "Persimus has the ability to translate to human form with perfection and with longevity."

"Really?" Sason said with a hint of doubt. Warriors usually were not good at such a thing. "Let's see."

Persimus scanned to make sure no human eyes were on them. Then with just a wisp of blue flame and faster than Validus had ever seen, Persimus translated to the perfect form of an FBI agent wearing an earpiece and sunglasses.

"That's easy. They're stiff black and whites," Sason said.

A second later, Persimus was a bag lady complete with ragged clothes, mangled hair, and tattered shawl.

Sason circled Persimus, evaluating every detail. He wrinkled his nose. "Whoa, that's impressive—even got the smell!"

Tren evaluated Persimus with a critical eye, then nodded his approval.

"How long can he maintain it?" Crenshaw asked Validus, knowing that Persimus could not hear or see them in translated form.

"As long as you need me to," Persimus replied in the hoarse voice of a ragged old woman.

Crenshaw's eyes opened wide, and the other warriors all looked confused. "How . . ." he began.

"Persimus has learned how to partially translate, thereby keeping one foot in both realms, if you will," Validus offered. "It's good enough to fool humans, demons, and angels alike, and he can maintain the translation indefinitely."

Sason shot Validus another skeptical look.

"How long were you the Brazilian boy in the favela?" Validus asked Persimus as he translated back to a warrior.

Persimus looked as though he didn't want to answer.

"Dispense with humility, warrior. We need to know the extent of everyone's abilities," Validus chided.

"Thirteen months," Persimus said.

This gained the respect of every one of the warriors, including Tren.

Validus looked at Sason. With dark brown eyes, black hair, olive skin, and a mouth framed by stubble, the warrior was always the first to speak his opinion, often without being asked.

"Since we're on the subject of translation, Sason has the ability to translate much larger objects than usual and maintain them for significant distances." Validus moved on. "I don't think I need to offer an explanation of Brumak's abilities. His strength and ability to carry a fight is legendary."

He nodded toward Jayt. This warrior was quiet, even compared to Tren. There was an air of confidence in everything he did. He had narrow eyes, straight black hair, and movements like a human ninja. "Jayt is our weapons specialist. He is an expert in every translatable weapon mankind has created, but his favorite . . ." Validus lifted a hand to the warrior.

Jayt opened his cream-colored knee-length trench coat to reveal an entire arsenal of handguns and grenades, but the majority of the space was filled with knives.

"Why knives?" Sason asked. "Seems archaic in the age of propulsion weapons."

Jayt stared at him as if he might throw one his way. "Because they're silent and deadly no matter the distance."

Sason raised an eyebrow and tilted his head. "If you're fast enough and accurate enough."

Jayt didn't respond.

"Can you actually do grenades?" Rake asked. "I've never heard of a warrior who was able to effectively translate explosives, let alone the resulting blast."

"I can translate the explosives and even the detonation, but I'm still working on the blast. The concussion is tricky and difficult to maintain. I have to get close to maintain it, and it gets dangerous," Jayt replied.

"I can imagine," Rake said.

Validus continued. "Rake is a warrior with speed, both with and without wings. He flies at near-messenger speed and runs nearly the same." He glanced at the red-headed warrior. Rake was the lighthearted one, but any brevity disappeared the instant a demon was near.

"And finally we have Crenshaw." Validus turned and looked into the mesmerizing pale-green eyes of the warrior. "Elohim has given Crenshaw the ability to sense and determine events moments before they happen. With what we will be facing from the Fallen, I'm looking to you to keep us alert. Over the last year, we've learned with Carter that the Fallen could attack at any time and at any place."

Crenshaw nodded.

"So you can see the future." Sason's questions were never really questions. They were statements of contest that demanded a response.

Crenshaw was unfazed. "Not far . . . usually only a few minutes and not usually with specificity. The more angels and demons involved, the easier it is to see."

Sason scrutinized Crenshaw but remained silent, much to Validus's surprise.

"I want demonstrations," Jayt said, eyes narrow with concern. "If this mission is going to be as dicey as you say, I want to see what they can do."

"Commander, we've got trouble," Crenshaw interjected. He looked west across the FBI complex lawn and pointed. "There."

"Numbers?"

"Unsure, but more than us," Crenshaw said drawing his sword.

"No time for exhibitions, Jayt." Validus drew his sword. "Tren, Rake, I can't imagine Carter is in danger inside the FBI holding cell but get there and make sure the Fallen aren't trying something with him. As soon as you are convinced he's safe, get back here."

The guardian and the warrior materialized through the southern wall of the building as the rest of the warriors prepared. A moment later, a line of more than fifty Fallen appeared. Some came from the west, some from the south.

They all carried swords and pistols but they stopped twenty yards away, as if they were waiting for something.

"Any droxans?" Validus asked Crenshaw.

"Not that I can tell."

Finally a demon stepped through the line. Validus recognized him as Zurock, one of the regional commanders on the West Coast. Validus had found it difficult to find a regional commander who could match the demon's tactics. Evidently Niturni had transferred Zurock to this region of the US to replace Durgank, and Validus suspected that it had everything to do with Carter.

Zurock walked up and down his line of demons, sneering at Validus and his men. Black, deep-set eyes glared with the hatred of six millennia. As an angel he would have been fair to look upon, with dark brown hair and a chiseled, handsome face, but now, after evil had done its work, his beauty had been transformed into a tool of fear and menace. Zurock clutched his sword, but he did not attack.

"What are they waiting for?" Sason said.

"For him," Crenshaw said, looking into the sky behind them.

Validus saw it too. A Fallen was descending, his dark wings spread wide, casting a shadow beneath him as he came. Validus's heart began to pound as his hand instinctively gripped his sword tighter. It was his ancient friend turned enemy, Niturni. He would land just a few yards from Validus, fearless and arrogant. Validus noticed that the other Fallen and even Zurock seemed intimidated by Niturni. *His power must be great indeed.*

Before Niturni's feet touched down, a wide, sickening smile spread across his dark face.

"Ah, Validus." Niturni's voice was thick with condescension. "So this is the pathetic and feeble band of warriors you've assembled." He slowly shook his head as he walked in front of Validus and his men as if inspecting them. "I expected so much more from you." He turned and looked at the FBI building where Carter was being held. "We will kill him, and there's nothing you can do to stop us. It's all falling perfectly into place, just as planned." He looked back at Validus. "You're such a predictable pawn, my old friend."

Even after six thousand years, Validus still fought his inclination to believe that he was the last and the least. How could he match the strength and brilliance of a fallen angel from the One Hundred—those first mighty angels created by Elohim to lead the angelic orders? The presence of the warriors beside him was a reminder, however, that he was not least, for Elohim had chosen him for this time and for this place.

"Niturni, your pride always precedes you, and it will be your undoing. Even if you could gain access to Carter, there is nothing in that building you could use to harm him."

Niturni laughed, then allowed his sadistic smile to fall from his face. His eyes turned icy cold as he glared at Validus. "I'm not here to destroy Carter . . . not today. I'm here to destroy you!"

Niturni turned his back on Validus and walked toward Zurock. "Kill them all!" he ordered as he flew up and behind Zurock and his demons.

"Keep our line tight," Validus ordered.

The Fallen unleashed a wall of bullets just ahead of their attack, but before a single round hit Validus's men, Sason stepped forward and swept his sword across the screaming pellets of lead, intercepting their translations and sending them back into the realm of humans. All that remained were miniature wisps of vapor where the bullets once were.

"Didn't know you could do that!" Validus said.

Validus, Crenshaw, and Persimus pulled and emptied their handguns into the horde of Fallen racing toward them while Jayt let eight knives silently follow. Brumak stepped forward and was the first to engage four demons at once. In one massive stroke, he cut through three of them and finished the fourth with a return slice, then turned, anxious for more.

A few seconds later, Validus saw Tren and Rake jump from the third story of the FBI building to join them. He watched as Rake morphed his wings midair and flew swiftly down toward the attacking Fallen. Two demons jumped upward to intercept him, and Validus worried for his man, but Rake twisted and dropped, swinging his blade in a perfect upward cut through one of the demons. The earth below swallowed the remnant green vapor. Rake then turned and demorphed his wings, smoothly transitioning to a perfect fighting stance beside Validus.

Validus looked for Zurock, but the coward hung back, watching his men attack while Niturni floated above him. Then it dawned on Validus that Niturni's real intention was to observe his opponent's team and discover their strengths and weaknesses. Whether Niturni was successful in defeating his team would be irrelevant, for Validus knew the demons would be replaced before the end of the day. This ruthless commander he had once called friend was sacrificing his warriors simply to explore Validus's team's capabilities.

Validus engaged two demons and put them down in short order. Now all eight of the angels stood side by side, skillfully eliminating each wave of Fallen that came at them. Brumak was a beast and by far dispensed with the most, but each of the others, including Tren, fought like the valiant angel warriors they were.

Another wave of fifteen Fallen was coming when Sason turned to Jayt. "Cast a grenade," he shouted.

Jayt shook his head. "Too close. It won't work."

"Let me worry about that. Just do it."

Jayt pulled the pin on a grenade and timed its explosion right as the fresh wave of Fallen would reach it, just twenty feet in front of their team.

Sason reached out his sword and focused, translating only the blast and resulting shockwave on the side facing the Fallen. Validus and his men felt nothing. Eight of the charging demons immediately dissolved to the Abyss and three others fell to the ground severely wounded. The remaining Fallen hesitated, unsure whether to attack or retreat. Neither angel nor demon had ever seen such a tactic before.

Brumak yelled with the fury of a lion and charged into the remaining Fallen. Jayt and Rake joined him. Within seconds the Fallen were gone.

Validus looked at Niturni, whose eyes were still cold and calculating. The demon hovered in silence, his wings slowly beating. He gave an order to Zurock, then turned and flew south.

The fight had only lasted a few minutes. The eight stood next to each other, looking in all directions for another assault. Brumak actually looked disappointed.

"What was that about?" Jayt asked.

"It was about finding out who we are," Validus said. "And I think they learned a lot."

Tren looked at Validus, pleased. "So did we."

The corner of Validus's mouth turned up. Tren was feeling what he felt. For the first time since being assigned to Carter, they had the angels they needed to protect him. And they were the best!

"That was remarkable!" Rake exclaimed with a broad grin. He was the first to sheath his sword. "And that grenade translation trick—where did that come from?" He looked at Sason and Jayt.

"I never could create the reaction to initiate an explosion," Sason said.

"And I could never expand the concussion," Jayt added.

Crenshaw kept studying the skies. "I see nothing, Commander," he said, sheathing his sword.

"We need a name," Rake said, still energized by the fight.

Jayt huffed and the other angels shook their heads.

"I'm serious. This team is unprecedented."

"It's not about us," Validus said. "It's about Carter and about keeping the will of Elohim. There will be no name."

Rake shook his head. "What a shame. Hey, how about the Valiants?"

"There will be no name," Validus repeated.

Validus stood so he could see each of his warriors. "This was just a taste of what's to come. Niturni was just probing. Those Fallen we faced were not their best, not by a long shot. There will be long periods of boredom punctuated by intense struggles for life and death. We can't afford to ever become complacent. By the time this is over, the odds are that not all of us will have survived, but I don't want to lose a single warrior or guardian. Is that clear?"

Validus's words sobered them. They were not words typical of a victory speech, but he had to keep his men focused. None of them had ever seen a mission like the Carter mission. And what lay ahead was as unpredictable as Apollyon's first sin.

"Very well. I want round-the-clock coverage on Carter. Tren, you'll manage shifts. Everyone cycles through except Brumak. No need to unnerve the man until it's necessary."

Tren nodded.

Validus turned his attention to the FBI building. "Let's see what the United States government has in store for Mr. Carter."

8

THE FARM

Five days after the FBI had taken Drew into custody, he was prepped for transportation. As a precaution, and perhaps for the benefit of the FBI's reputation, the handcuffs had been placed back on him. Two large FBI agents escorted him to the black Continental waiting to take him to the Farm, the CIA's training ground for agent candidates. Reed stood by the car, and behind him stood light invaders Drew had never seen before. As good as Drew had become at masking his knowledge of their presence, these two made it difficult because they were staring at him as though they expected him to see them.

The FBI escorts placed him in the backseat of the car and shut the door, locking him in. Drew watched as one of the men turned to Reed with a smirk on his face.

"Hey, Reed, try to keep track of your gun this time."

"Real funny, Pruitt."

Reed slid into the driver's seat and shut the door. Drew could only imagine the harassment the agent had taken for letting him escape. It would probably take a long time before either Reed or Lewis would live that down. Drew wondered if he had permanently tarnished or even ruined their careers.

Reed drove the car off the FBI campus and onto the streets of Chicago toward the interstate. It seemed to Drew as though his two invisible companions were going to be with him for the duration. They rode in and on the vehicle as if they were guarding some precious cargo. Drew tried to ignore them.

Drew could see Agent Reed's eyes in the rearview mirror. He felt compelled to at least offer an apology.

"Agent Reed, I'm . . . ah . . . sorry about how this went down for you and Lewis. I really didn't have a choice."

He saw Reed look at him through the rearview mirror, but he said nothing. When Reed slowed the car and pulled over on a side street, Drew's heart quickened. Had he ruined the agent's career to the point of inciting revenge? How far would Reed go?

Reed stopped the car and put the gear lever in park. He stepped out of the car, and Drew's mind began to race through his options. The light invaders were watching Reed closely too. The agent opened the door and stepped back. He pulled back his jacket, and Drew knew he had only seconds to respond.

"Get out, Carter."

One of the invaders drew his sword and looked as though he were ready to take Reed out.

"I know you're upset, but don't make things worse," Drew appealed.

Reed squinted, then reached into his pocket and pulled out the keys to the handcuffs. He held them up. "What did you think I was going to do?"

Drew slowly stood up, still not convinced. He held out his hands. "Wasn't sure just how upset you were," he said with a weak grin.

Reed eyed Drew. "Before I take these off, let's get a few things straight. First, you've been injected with a micro GPS tracker, so no matter where you go, we can find you."

Drew remembered one morning feeling more tired than usual. He must have been drugged. He frowned. Earning the trust of the government would be a long time coming.

"Second, you embarrass me again or try something stupid, and I won't hesitate to shoot you. Are we clear?"

"Yeah, I'm clear."

Reed hesitated, evaluating Drew one last time.

"Okay." He unlocked the cuffs. "You can sit in the front with me. If Mr. Ross trusts you, then that's good enough for me. Besides"—Reed paused and looked straight into Drew's eyes—"I think you may be one of the good guys after all."

Drew nodded. "Thanks, and for what it's worth, I really am sorry."

Reed waved him to the passenger door. The invaders didn't relax but instead turned their attention from Reed to the surrounding streets, watching and evaluating.

"It's okay. Could be one the best things that's ever happened to me."

Drew opened the door and looked across the roof at Reed. "How's that?" he asked incredulously.

Reed slid into the vehicle and Drew followed. He looked over at Drew as he buckled his seat belt. "I put in for a transfer to the CIA months ago and was denied. Now Ross wants me to watchdog you, and I get my transfer." He put the car in gear. "Never saw that one coming."

Drew flashed a grin. "Back on the street in front of the church, I knew you were a solid guy."

Reed nodded. "I have to know one thing, though."

"Shoot."

"How did you get out of those handcuffs?"

Drew stared out the window, catching a glimpse of a dark invader pestering a woman as she walked down the street. He looked back at Reed. "Is this a requirement to fulfill my commitment?"

Reed tilted his head. "As far as I'm concerned, you're a fellow candidate for the CIA. You're not a prisoner, Carter. Heck, you weren't ever convicted, and the charges have been dropped, so no, I'm just asking."

Drew nodded. "Then I'm going to have to decline, because you would never believe me if I told you."

Reed changed lanes to make the on-ramp of the highway. "You're a bit of a mystery, Carter, but I'm going to figure you out one day."

"Mind if I ask you a question?" Drew asked.

"You can ask. Don't know if I can answer till I hear the question."

"So what's the story with Mr. Ross? Who is he . . . really?"

Reed took a moment to gather his thoughts. "Well, I can pretty much guarantee that Ross isn't his real name. All I can tell you is that his clearance and credentials are as high as I've ever seen. Beyond that, I can only speculate. It's pretty unusual for someone in his position to be concerned with an FBI case when there's no international threat."

Drew didn't know what to make of that. Something about Ross unnerved him. Something deep . . . something dark. He remembered that the light invader seemed to feel the same.

After a few minutes on the road, Drew asked Reed to check on Reverend Branson once more and was greatly relieved to hear that his friend was doing much better. The prognosis looked good.

Reed drove them to the airport, where they caught a flight to Hampton, Virginia. An agent was waiting for them, and they drove the last thirty-five miles in a black SUV. They arrived at Camp Peary in York County by five in the afternoon.

Drew couldn't help the excitement he felt as they drove up to the heavily guarded gate. Something about the military, guns, and special ops training resonated inside his being. He couldn't help it. He would have never picked this path to these gates, but he was here, and he loved it. Had Jake ever been here? There were parts of Jake's life that he never told, not even to Drew, and he often wondered what secrets lay in the gaps of Jake's life.

Reed offered identification at the gate. After confirming their arrival, the guard waved them through. Camp Peary's nine-thousand-acre military reservation was officially referred to as an Armed Forces Experimental Training Activity, but it was fairly well rumored that this was where the majority of the nation's clandestine training was accomplished. Now Drew knew it to be true.

Inside the compound they drove for a couple of miles before the SUV pulled up to a set of brown buildings. Through the window, Drew saw Validus staring at him. It was the first he'd seen the invader since his encounter in Chicago. The other familiar invader was with him. Drew didn't know his name and probably never would. Based on what he'd seen, this invader must be Validus's vice commander.

It was difficult for Drew to describe how he felt about seeing Validus. His presence indicated many things. That he was intent on helping Drew was clear, but to what end? And usually if Validus was near, so was trouble. How could there be any threat to Drew here, in the heart of a CIA training camp? Recalling the massive warrior's last words sent chills up and down Drew's spine. *They know who you are, and they are coming for you. They are all coming for you.* Drew didn't even know who "they" were or why were they coming for him.

"Carter!"

Reed's voice jolted him back to their reality. Drew turned and looked at him.

Reed shook his head. "Believe me, this is not the place to daydream. Let's go."

Drew and Reed were set up in living quarters next to each other. A new class for CIA training was to begin in ten days. Because of Drew's unusual route to the Farm, those days would be used to administer an IQ test, personality and psychological tests, a polygraph test, a medical examination, a physical fitness test, and a background check for a security clearance.

Drew had never taken an IQ test, so he didn't know what to expect. The questions relating to math, logic, spatial, and pattern recognition seemed extremely easy. Verbal and classification were a challenge, however. They never did tell him his score, but later Reed told him that something about his test had raised eyebrows. The personality test was just plain bizarre. Drew couldn't even begin to figure out what the right answers were or how such silly questions could give the CIA any useful information at all. He was nervous about the psychological evaluation and the polygraph test. If by some chance the test administrator stumbled on to the fact that he was seeing invaders, there would be nothing he could do to hide it. To his relief, he was able to skirt the invader issue and seemed to be given a green light to move on into the program.

The physical fitness test was a cinch for Drew. He had kept himself in superb physical condition. Mr. Lee, his tae kwon do instructor, had made sure of that. The medical exam went well too. For the hearing test, Drew had a good sense as to the frequency and amplitude range for normal people and shut down his responses just a little beyond that. Still, the examiner seemed surprised and had him repeat the test.

The last part of the medical exam was the eye examination. Drew couldn't help the knot in his stomach as he remembered the last eye exam his mother had taken him to back in Kansas.

"I see by your medical records that you had eye trauma in an accident nearly two years ago—that your vision was severely impaired. Says here that the ophthalmologist declared you legally blind." The doctor closed the file and looked at Drew. "I can't believe they've let you get this far."

"I can see fine, Doc," Drew said.

"I'll make that judgment, Mr. Carter. Let's start by looking at your retinas. That will tell me most everything I need to know."

The doctor examined Drew's eyes with the ophthalmoscope, seeming to take an extra long time to do so. When he was finished, he set the scope down and wrote a few notes.

"Well, I don't see any evidence of the trauma indicated in your record," the doctor said with a frown. He shook his head. "That kind of trauma doesn't just disappear."

Drew was relieved beyond measure but tried not to show it. He was just as surprised as the doctor.

"Perhaps the rest of the exam will reveal something," he said with a little too much enthusiasm.

The doctor set Drew up for the visual acuity test. Through the process, Drew took no small delight in watching the doctor become increasingly befuddled. He tried multiple tests with multiple charts to ensure Drew hadn't memorized them somehow. When it was over, he was left scratching his head.

Drew breezed through each of the remaining sections of the exam. The doctor finished writing in Drew's chart, then sat back and scrutinized him once more.

"Can't say as I have any reason to disqualify you, Mr. Carter." The doctor actually looked disappointed. "You're cleared for training." He closed the file and left the room without saying another word.

When training finally began, Drew was more than ready. He was enrolled in a class of thirty candidates—nine women and twenty-one men. Their primary instructor was a man by the name of Frank Hampton. He was unassuming in stature and appearance, but Drew could see decades of experience behind his probing eyes.

"You are the best and the brightest America has to offer, but that gets you nothing here except a seat in this room. How you use your skills and intellect will determine if you have the right stuff to become an agent we can use. As a career trainee, or CT, as we will refer to you, you will learn the tradecraft of a CIA operative. We will teach you how to jump out of planes and to escape and evade. We will instruct you on the use of weapons of every kind, including improvised weaponry, self-defense, demolition, agent acquisition, disguises, surveillance, secret writing, photography, sketching, technology and the improvised use thereof, and prisoner resistance and survival techniques. Everything is a test, so get ready to be pushed beyond your limits."

Drew looked around the room and wondered if anyone there was nearly as excited as he was. One thing he was certain about—he was the only one with a prison sentence riding on his success or failure.

Within the first couple of weeks, Drew began to stand out. His greatest struggle was determining just how much of his skill he should divulge. However, there were aspects of his training in which he didn't have to pretend a lack of skill, such as demolition, photography, and sketching—things Jake hadn't taught him—so he focused intently on that part of the tradecraft in particular.

Since Drew had arrived at the Farm, he had noticed that at least one light invader was with him at all times. Validus's vice commander seemed to be his usual guard, but several new faces had joined the rotation. He still wasn't sure what that meant.

Four weeks into the program, Drew, Reed, and three other CTs were playing cards one evening. Aaban Hadad looked like he was of Middle-Eastern descent. Nora Riggs was a dark-haired twenty-five-year-old from Boston, and Steven Connor was the son of a farmer in the Midwest.

"So, Carter," Connor said as he picked up his cards. "What's your secret? How are you already acing this program?"

"Yeah," Riggs piped in. "We've got months of training left, and you seem to already know this stuff. Where'd you come from?"

Reed looked over the top of his cards to see how Drew was going to answer.

"Are you kidding?" Drew said. "Did you see my sketch of the arms dealer? When I was done, he looked like a bad Charlie Brown."

Riggs smirked and glared at him. "You know that's not what we're talking about, Carter."

Drew finished arranging his cards. He shook his head. "My stepdad was a Ranger. He took me camping and started training me when I was twelve. I got nothin' over you guys except a little head start. In another month, you'll be running circles around me."

Reed snorted. "That's a bunch of baloney if I've ever heard it." He pointed at Drew. "I saw this guy—"

"Don't go there, Reed," Drew interrupted. "It's way too embarrassing for you." He glared at Reed, warning him.

"Wait . . . You guys knew each other before the Farm?" Hadad asked.

Drew raised an "I told you so" eyebrow at Reed.

"Only for a few days," Reed said. Drew relaxed, but then Reed smiled. "I used to be FBI, and I had to arrest Carter for his criminal activity."

"What!" Hadad, Riggs, and Connor were all on it.

"Get out! Is that true, Carter?" Connor asked with a big country grin.

Drew slowly set down his cards. "Thanks a lot, Reed. I can't wait for hand-to-hand tomorrow. I'm going to ask for you!"

"What happened?" Riggs asked, setting her cards on the table and leaning forward.

"Nothing!" Drew snapped. He was going to kill Reed. "Can we get on with this game?"

"Come on, Carter," Hadad pleaded. "Tell us. We'll all fess up to something afterward to make it fair."

Drew shot Reed a steely-eyed look and shook his head. He put his cards on the table. "You know, I'm getting tired, and tomorrow is supposed to be a rough day. I'm done."

Drew stood up and moved toward the door.

"Lighten up, Carter," Reed said.

"Shut up, Reed. I mean it."

Twenty minutes after Drew got back to his room, there was a knock on the door. It was Reed.

"Hey, I . . . I was out of line." Reed had a hard time looking Drew in the eye. "I didn't realize it was such a touchy subject. Won't happen again."

Drew couldn't even begin to explain his life to Reed and what the implications were of letting others know more than they needed to.

"It's all right," he said. "We're good."

Reed leaned up against the doorpost and crossed his arms. "They're right, though. I don't know you well, Carter, but I know you better than anyone else here. When you're ready, I'll be a friend, if I haven't screwed that up already."

Drew looked at Reed. It was a genuine offer, but he couldn't get past the notion that Ross was using Reed to keep an eye on him. How could there ever be any authentic friendship under those conditions?

"Thanks," Drew said. "Let's start by not highlighting me any more than necessary, okay?"

Reed smiled. He nodded, then turned to go to his own room.

The next day, Drew expected to be harassed relentlessly by Riggs, Connor, and Hadad and perhaps be tagged with some irritating nickname, but it didn't happen. Whatever Reed had told them, they offered Drew the space he was looking for.

Over the next few weeks, their little band of five grew tighter, and it was Drew who seemed to be the glue that brought them together. Hadad in particular seemed drawn to Drew. He took it upon himself to help them further their training at every opportunity, and because of it, they each maximized their potential in the program and became close friends. At the beginning of the program they were told that they would form relationships at the Farm that would last their entire careers, and Drew could certainly see how that was happening.

Although Drew loved the intensity of the training, there was an element of danger that none of the other CTs could see, one which Drew was aware of hourly. The security of the Farm did little to protect him and the other CTs from the attacks of the dark invaders.

From Drew's perspective, Validus and his men were in a continual state of war. Without the availability of the darkened minds and cultural situations outside the Farm, it appeared that the dark invaders were trying to capitalize on the potentially dangerous nature of the training conducted at the Farm. Whether they were being trained on tactical driving techniques, how to shoot rockets, or how to set and detonate explosives, there was opportunity every day for the dark invaders to take Drew out. With each week that passed, Drew found it more difficult to concentrate. He wondered if Validus and his men would ever grow weary in their protection of him.

At one point it looked as if the dark invaders were coming at him with a hundred warriors. That was when Drew saw him. He was the largest, fiercest warrior Drew had ever laid eyes on, and he didn't belong to the dark invaders—he was part of Validus's team. The "Hulk" took out two or three dark invaders at a time. The battle was as fierce as Drew had ever seen, and many of Validus's team were wounded.

What was this all about? It unnerved Drew enough to affect his training, and Reed and the rest of his friends began to notice. The warning that Validus had given him in the Chicago gang's warehouse certainly appeared warranted, but he didn't know what to do about it, let alone why he was the focus of such warfare between invaders.

Drew paced the floor in his room that night. How long could the light invaders maintain their protection? How long *would* they? And how would he die—a stray bullet, an unexplained pre-detonated bomb, electrocution? There were a hundred ways to die at the Farm if an unseen dark invader had access to him and enough time to pull it off. Drew was trapped. The Farm, prison, the city, the wilderness—it didn't matter where he went, they would be there.

A warrior with black hair and Asian eyes stepped through Drew's door to check on him. Drew looked at him, and the warrior stared back. He seemed annoyed, almost angry with Drew. A wound on his shoulder was still bleeding, but Drew had noticed that their wounds didn't last long. Either they healed or they died.

"I want to speak with Validus," Drew said quietly.

The warrior didn't seem to take kindly to his request and just continued to stare at him.

Drew squared off with him. "Why are you protecting me?"

The warrior lifted his chin slightly as he eyed Drew; then he turned and left. A few minutes later, Validus appeared. He too had multiple wounds from the battle. They looked painful. Drew didn't know how the warrior would respond, but he didn't waste time.

"You said they were after me. Why? Why me, and why are you protecting me?" Drew glanced at the warrior's arm, where a long gash was still dripping blood.

Validus hesitated. He clearly did not want to have this conversation.

Drew turned away in frustration. He walked a few steps, running his hand through his hair. "I don't know what's going on. I don't know what to do!"

The room began to glow blue, and Drew spun back around in time to see flames licking at the warrior's form as he finished materializing into the world of men. Drew looked at the warrior in awe. His arm was still bleeding, the blood dripping on the carpet at his feet.

Validus seemed to struggle with his words, restrained by something deep within him. "You are significant to the future of these people." He shook his head and grimaced either from the pain of his wounds or from the frustration of being limited in what he was allowed to say. He took a step toward Drew and pierced him with his penetrating eyes. "You must focus and learn and stay alive. Right now there is nothing you can do about our war." He turned his head slightly, as if he could hear something Drew could not. Then he looked at Drew one more time. "Stay alive!"

Validus grimaced, and the blue flames seeped from his body to enshroud him on his journey back to their realm. He then stepped through the wall and disappeared.

Drew knelt down to touch the blood-stained carpet. He lifted his hand and looked at the blood on his fingers.

"Hey, Carter," Reed said as he opened the door.

Drew looked up, then back to his fingers. The blood was gone and so was the stain on the carpet.

"What's up? You lose something?" Reed asked.

"Ah . . . no. Just getting ready to do a few push-ups."

Reed shook his head. "Yeah. This program is a little soft. We could all do with an extra workout." He smirked. "Card game in five minutes." He nodded, then closed the door.

Drew sat down on the floor and leaned up against the wall. It was a hard pill to swallow, that warriors were fighting, bleeding, and even dying for him, and he still didn't know why.

∽०∾

"I need permission to tell Carter, General!"

"I don't have the authority to give that to you, Validus." Brandt crossed his arms and leaned back in his chair.

"All it would take is for him to know who we are, and it would be done." Validus was frustrated. Carter seemed so ignorant of the obvious, and yet his salvation was the trigger point for the beginning of the End of Days. How could he not see it?

"You don't know that. Remember Elohim's people in the wilderness? They all saw greater miracles than Carter has seen, and Elohim caused the earth to swallow them because of their unbelief. What of the girl?"

Validus turned and walked away. "She's our best hope, but they are driven apart by the CIA now. He may never see her again." He turned back. "I understand that the gospel of the Messiah is reserved for men to preach, but messengers have given men revelations before. Request a messenger to reveal the truth of who we are to Carter."

Brandt seemed to consider Validus's request. "I'll put the request in. Meanwhile, get Carter and Carlyle together."

Validus nodded. "I'm working on it, but you can bet the Fallen will counter with everything they've got. They know the influence she has on him, and if we're successful in getting them together, the Fallen will unleash everything to keep him from salvation."

General Brandt stood up and walked toward Validus. "Then your team had better be ready."

Validus drew a deep breath. "Yes sir."

By the time Validus returned to his team at the Farm, all seven of them were outside Carter's quarters. They looked anxious. Persimus was pacing. When he saw Validus approach, he hurried to his friend.

"What is it, Persimus?"

"You have a visitor."

Brandt's request must have gone through, and the reply was fast.

"A messenger?" Validus asked, looking for the angel.

"Not a messenger," Persimus said. "It's Michael."

Validus froze. "Michael?"

Persimus nodded.

"Yeah," Jayt said with a grin. "Whatever you did over in Scotland must not have set well. He's not looking his usual pleasant self."

"Where is he?"

"He said he'd be at the church," Persimus replied.

Validus looked in the direction of the only church at Camp Peary, a remnant from the past. "Michael?" he asked again.

"We'll be right here if you need us," Crenshaw said.

"Thanks for the support," Validus said with a smirk. He straightened and made his way to the church.

When he entered, the mighty archangel stood at the front of the sanctuary, looking at the cross. Validus approached cautiously.

"That was a marvelously sad and victorious day." Michael's voice reverberated off the walls of the empty church. The archangel slowly turned and looked at Validus.

In spite of Validus's expectations, Michael's gaze was not full of judgment.

Though the fire still burned in his eyes, Validus was taken aback at the diminished fierceness that usually accompanied the first angel.

"Do you remember what Messiah told the disciple Thomas after He conquered death?"

Validus stood still below the mighty form of Michael.

"Thomas, because you have seen Me, you have believed," the archangel said as he stepped down to stand in front of Validus.

"Blessed are those who have not seen and yet have believed," Validus finished.

Michael looked at Validus, then seemed to look off into the distance beyond the walls of the church. "Walk with me."

He led Validus through the back wall of the church and into the thick woods of the camp.

"Validus, the burden of your mission with Carter is great, particularly because of his unbelief. Do you understand the significance of it? What will happen if you fail?"

"I believe so, sir. I am prepared to give my all."

Michael nodded. "Consider your actions carefully and remember, Elohim highly values the free will of men and women. Without faith, a man cannot please Him. Regardless of the outcome, Carter must come to faith *on his own.*" Michael's emphasis of those last three words was his message.

The archangel continued. "Drew Carter has already seen more than he needs to in order to believe. Do you know what's keeping him from faith in Messiah?"

Validus nodded. "The same thing that keeps most of mankind from Him. Pride."

Michael stopped near a brook that meandered through the camp, eventually spilling into the York River. The crisp sounds of the water babbling were filled with harmonics that reminded Validus of Zion.

"Yes. And the only way to penetrate a heart of pride is to break the man." Michael looked at Validus. "You have done well, but the future of Drew Carter is not cast. You must carry on, and you must prevail no matter the cost. And there will be cost."

"Yes sir. I understand."

Michael's wings morphed outward and upward, gleaming pearl-white in the midday sun. The archangel's gaze resumed the fierce fire of the First. Without another word, he launched upward toward heaven. Validus watched the silver streak arch toward the Puebloan Stairway until it faded away.

9

RISKY BUSINESS

Drew resolved to do his part. He couldn't afford to let the conflict between the light and dark invaders jeopardize his training. The distraction alone could cost him his life. He owed it to Validus and his team of warriors to remain focused and excel in his training, and that was exactly what he did. It helped that the encounters Validus and his team had with the dark invaders seemed to diminish. Evidently their message to the dark invaders was clear—we will stand our ground.

The rest of the training at the Farm went very well for Drew. There were moments when he didn't hold back, especially if he could get away without being seen or drawing undue attention to himself. At the end of eight months of training, Drew and Hadad were selected for an advanced course, whereas the rest of their crew were assigned to operational positions within the CIA.

"They're grooming you to be a NOC," Reed said.

A nonofficial cover agent, or NOC, pronounced "knock," carried the greatest risk of all. It was how the United States government disavowed involvement in shady operations outside not only the laws of nations but often outside the moral and ethical boundaries of society. Their missions were often the darkest of all, done in the name of national security without a nation to back them.

"I still don't think they trust me," Drew said. "Either way, you take care, Reed. I hope we can work together sometime."

Reed smiled. "Yeah, maybe we can be on the same team this time."

Drew laughed. "And I promise not to steal your gun."

Drew soaked up another four months of training before he was deemed a fully qualified CIA operative. The strange thing was that he wasn't given any particularly unusual assignment. In fact, he was honestly quite disappointed. Even though he would be a field operative, a lot of his job would be analyzing intelligence other agents had gathered. He wondered if it had to do with his history. Would he ever be trusted?

Drew felt strange leaving the Farm. The last four months of training were intense, and the nature of the training, along with the unusual skills that Drew had acquired as a result of the lab accident years earlier, completed him. He had to admit that he was anxious to be on an operation just to see what he could do. He told himself that such thinking was foolish and tried to temper his enthusiasm, but it didn't work.

Back in real life, Drew realized that the danger from invader attacks would be just as severe and probably worse, now that they had the minds of reprobate people to work with again. And because he was an agent with the CIA, his interaction with such people could be close and personal.

He processed in at CIA headquarters in Langley, Virginia, then caught a plane to Philadelphia, Pennsylvania, the next day, where he would be assigned for the foreseeable future.

Waiting for him at the airport was none other than Agent Reed. Drew was glad to see his friend, but also a little disappointed. Reed picked up on it.

"Just so you know, I haven't been given any directive regarding you," Reed said.

Drew threw his bags in the trunk and slammed it shut. "And the odds of us being assigned the same field office are . . . ?" he mocked.

Reed just shook his head.

"It's all right. I'm looking forward to working with you, Reed, regardless of what Ross, or whoever, really thinks of me. So much for being a NOC agent."

Once they were in the car and moving, Drew wanted to know more about what he would be doing. "So how's the job? Was the move from the FBI to the CIA a good plan?"

Reed shrugged. "It's about the same so far. The only difference is that now I read reports that come from *outside* instead of *inside* the US."

Drew grimaced. "Sounds wonderful. I guess it beats staring at prison bars."

It wasn't long before Drew realized that Reed hadn't underestimated the excitement of the job. Their primary mission at the Philadelphia office was to analyze intelligence gathered on foreign militant terrorist groups and ascertain threat levels for an attack on US ground. When 9/11 hit in 2001, the credibility and morale of the CIA took a nosedive for not having stopped it. As a result, budgets were increased, more people were hired, and they redoubled their efforts to stop terrorist attacks before the plans ever made it to America's shores. It was the primary focus of the Philadelphia office, although it was not its exclusive mission.

For the next few months, Drew settled into the mundane work of analyzing mountains of intelligence data. If there was any side-benefit, there didn't seem to be a lot that the dark invaders could use against him, so there was a bit of a reprieve not only for Drew but for Validus and his men.

During this time, Drew was finally able to spend some time thinking about Ben and about how he would go about searching for him. The problem was that he knew he was still being closely supervised and couldn't afford to draw attention to his friend. Instead, he turned his focus to trying to determine if the CIA or any other clandestine agency had any knowledge whatsoever of the invaders, either directly or indirectly.

After months of analysis work, Drew and Reed started being assigned field missions. Twice Drew was sent to Afghanistan to coordinate with an SOG team—a Special Operations Group—and participate in an intelligence-gathering mission regarding the Al-Qaeda terrorist organization. Validus and his team had no small amount of difficulty keeping the dark invaders at bay on the missions, but that couldn't be Drew's concern. He had to do his job and do it well.

Back in the States, Drew went over the files again, a mountain of intel that he and the rest of the agency had collected on the rising threat of retaliation efforts against the US by ISIS (the Islamic State of Iraq and Syria), Al-Qaeda, and Hamas—three Jihad terrorist organizations. Of significant note was a communiqué from the Mossad, Israel's intelligence organization, warning the United States of an impending threat by one or all three of the terrorist groups.

Something nagged at the back of Drew's mind as he reviewed the intel. He felt like he was looking at a collage of images that formed a larger image, but he was too close to see the big picture. There seemed to be a connection between recent terrorist attacks and threats from distinctly isolated and separate jihadist groups—groups with vastly different local goals. Drew kept coming back to the IGA, the Islamic Global Alliance. Though undirected to do so, he spent a significant amount of time trying to connect the IGA with ISIS, Hamas, the Muslim Brotherhood, and other Islamic militant groups, but each trail he followed was a dead end.

Until recently, Islamic groups were independent and disjointed, serving their own interests. Three years ago, a charismatic man named Aashif Hakeem Jabbar had offered a global vision and mission for the fastest growing religion in the world. Over one-fourth of the population of the world now claimed Islam as their faith. Jabbar created the IGA and brought unity to a splintered Islamic people while garnering support within world governments in Europe and in Russia. An ideologically unified group of such magnitude carried great political clout, and Jabbar was a brilliant politician. He maneuvered himself to the front stage of the political arena by denouncing all terrorist attacks, calling for cease-fires, and negotiating territory disputes between nations in conflict. He was an extremely intelligent and strategic leader with a degree in law from Oxford and a master's and a doctorate from Harvard.

At first, the CIA, like Drew, aggressively looked for a connection between Jabbar's IGA and other Islamic fundamentalist groups sponsoring terrorist attacks, but that was abandoned once the investigation dead-ended. Israel claimed there were ties between the IGA and the very terrorist attacks they denounced, but without definitive proof, they were gagged by mounting worldwide political pressure.

Once Drew's supervisor, Agent Sloan, discovered that he was investigating possible ties with the IGA, he gave Drew a clear directive that he was to discontinue such investigation and focus on the imminent threat of possible attacks within the US.

Drew complied and came to the conclusion that three US cities could be potential terrorist targets: New York, Houston, and Chicago. After his presentation, Sloan looked skeptical.

"This seems inconclusive, Carter, but I'll pass it on to Langley. If they validate it, they'll notify the FBI, Homeland Security, and the NSA." Sloan closed the report. "And now I'm putting you with Reed on the investigation of Andrés Zapata. We believe he is running an illegal arms and drug operation out of San Juan, Puerto Rico."

"But, sir, I've spent the last six months analyzing this, and I believe this threat to be imminent. Furthermore, specific targets haven't yet been determined. Shouldn't we continue on this investigation until the threat is confirmed or eliminated?"

Sloan handed Drew a new folder stamped Classified. "Our concern is outside the US. It's time to let the FBI and Homeland Security do their job on this. You and Reed need to review this file, and we'll brief the op Monday morning. Dismissed."

Drew left Sloan's office and headed to his cubicle. He was frustrated and surprised at Sloan's directive. He had spent months getting up to speed on international terrorist threats and in one stroke was derailed in an entirely new direction. Why?

"How'd it go?" Reed asked as he fell in step with Drew.

Drew shook his head. "It will be passed up the chain if they can validate the threat, and I've been reassigned to investigate Zapata."

"Hey, you're a junior agent. You shouldn't expect more than that. Besides, it sure beats Afghanistan. Puerto Rico has some nice beaches."

"Yeah, and a corrupt police force, a failing economy, and crime rates that rival Mexico." Drew handed Reed the file. "But I'm glad you're excited about the beaches, 'cause we're both on this one. You mind reviewing the file first? I need to do some wrap-up."

Reed grabbed the file. "Sure. Just don't poke your nose where it doesn't belong, Carter."

Reed peeled off to his cubicle, and Drew found his. He sat down and faced his computer. New York, Houston, Chicago—all three target rich for terrorists. The attacks on 9/11 were meant to cripple the US government, the economy, and the military. Drew considered the strategy of the terrorists and came to the conclusion that if another series of attacks happened, they would be to incite fear into the hearts of Americans, and the best way to do that was by hitting malls, restaurants, and coffee shops. Places where every American typically felt safe.

What Drew couldn't report to Sloan was that he knew why the terrorists were attacking—they were instigated by the dark invaders. It was maddening to be at the heart of protecting US interests and yet not be able to tell anyone who or what they were really fighting. There was no way that these third-world terrorist groups had the technology the invaders had, so whoever was behind it all, the terrorists were simply puppets in their hands.

Drew's mind ebbed away from dark invaders and their ISIS and Hamas pawns and turned to Sydney. It had been eighteen months since he'd last seen her, but there wasn't one day that went by when he didn't think of her, even in the midst of his most intense training. Drew had tried to methodically eliminate Sydney from his thoughts, but it seemed the harder he tried, the worse it got. In spite of his preoccupation with her, he truly hoped she had moved on, because he didn't want her going through what he was going through.

If he could determine that she had moved on in life without him, it would free him to move on without her. And even more important, he needed to settle in his mind once and for all if Sydney had any clandestine knowledge of the invaders.

Drew found himself staring at the CIA database screen, considering the possible consequences of investigating Sydney off the record. After ten minutes of mental deliberation, his need to know overwhelmed caution. His hands tapped the keys, initiating the search.

She was living in an apartment just two blocks off the University of Illinois campus. It didn't tell him much, other than she was probably close to finishing up her degree. There was only one way to get an accurate glimpse into her life from this distance. He tapped into her mobile-phone records and began perusing the last month of text messages she had sent and received. There it was—a guy. He went back further and discovered that texts from the guy started about three months ago.

As Drew read, emotions tore at his heart. She certainly had moved on. Logically he tried to convince himself he was free and relieved, but in his chest, he hurt. He fought his reaction to protect Sydney, but it was impossible.

He searched the corresponding mobile number and found a Dustin Willis as the owner. A quick search turned up nothing. The guy seemed clean, although his employment history was lackluster.

Drew shut down the search and tried to be at peace with what he had found, but it wasn't to be. Why did he feel so stunned? So unrelieved?

Monday afternoon, Drew and Reed met with Sloan and two analysts from Langley who were investigating Zapata's operation. A picture of Zapata and three other men flashed up on the large high-definition monitor on the front wall.

"This is Andrés Zapata and his three top hatchet men, Botello, Valarde, and Mancilla," Sloan said. "As far as we can tell, he is the leading drug trafficker in Puerto Rico. His rise in the drug arena has been fast and steady, aided by a corrupt police force and hard economic times for the island. Until now, we've just fed any intel we received on him to the DEA."

"What's changed?" Reed asked.

One of the analysts pointed to the next image that flashed on the monitor, a photo of Zapata talking with another man. "This is Kofi Sesay, an arms supplier to various rebel factions in central Africa. This was taken three weeks ago. And we have photos of other meetings as well."

Sloan resumed the briefing. "We believe that Zapata is expanding his operation to include weapons dealing. We suspect that he is trading drugs for weapons manufactured in the United States and then supplying the weapons to various terrorist organizations in the Middle East and in Africa. You two will pose as a US weapons supplier under the front company Armstrong Industries. Find out where his operation is, and get us his network of suppliers and dealers so we can make a bust.

"You'll be joining with a senior CIA operative in San Juan by the name of Carlos Hurtado. He has successfully gained the trust of Zapata's men by feeding them reliable contacts for their drugs. Once the drugs make stateside, we track them and make our busts far enough down the chain that Zapata doesn't suspect Hurtado. Hurtado's cover name is Soliz. He'll give you a situation report when you arrive," Sloan finished.

More details of the op were briefed and discussed, allowing Drew and Reed to ask questions until they were satisfied they had all the information they needed for the mission.

Two days later, they arrived in San Juan, Puerto Rico, where Agent Hurtado met and transported them to the La Concha Resort. In spite of being thirty-two, Agent Hurtado looked young and reckless. The sparse facial hair and colorful tattoo that stretched from his elbow to his shoulder added to the impression, but that was where the facade stopped. In the hotel room, Hurtado's brief was thorough and professional. Afterward he looked concerned. Drew figured he was analyzing their abilities and resolve.

"These guys don't mess around. If they think for a second you aren't the real deal, we're all dead. And they can get away with it."

"Then we'd better make sure they believe us," Drew said.

The following day, Agents Hurtado, Reed, and Carter arrived at Zapata's villa overlooking Costa Dorada Beach on the northwest shore of Puerto Rico. It was a scene right off a postcard, with white sandy beaches, teal-blue water, palm trees, and humid air thick enough to drink.

Drew scanned the area as they walked up the elaborate stone sidewalk. Validus and another light invader were waiting, swords drawn. Validus was shaking his head.

"Something's not right here," Drew said, slowing his gait.

Validus gave orders, and two more light invaders appeared. They entered the house ahead of Drew and his team.

"It's a little late for second thoughts now," Reed said.

Hurtado shot Drew a fierce gaze.

Drew readied himself as Botello, Zapata's main contact, greeted them at the entrance. "Ah, Soliz, come in, my friend."

"It's good to see you, Botello." Hurtado turned and looked at Reed and Drew. "This is Edward Davis and Kyle Moore."

Botello didn't greet them but instead led them into a broad marble foyer that opened to a two-story skylight ceiling twenty feet above. Drew followed with Hurtado on the right and Reed on his left.

Validus and his three warriors were each engaged with fierce dark invaders. Whatever happened now, Drew wouldn't be getting any help from them.

"These are the associates from Mr. Armstrong's organization I talked to you about on the phone," Hurtado said.

Botello turned and held up his hand at the same time that two men with handguns entered from the left and right, muzzles leveled on them. Botello smiled condescendingly. "And that, Soliz, was the biggest mistake of your life."

"Whoa," Hurtado said, lifting his hands in the air. "What are you doing, Botello?"

Botello's smiling face turned fierce as he pulled out his own .45 and stuck it in Hurtado's face. "You don't tell anyone about me or Zapata or our operation. That's not how we do business, you idiot!" He sneered at Reed and Drew. "These two could be cops or DEA agents for all I know."

Drew noted that the gunman to his right used a two-hand grip while the other gunman and Botello used the single-hand grip of inexperienced, cocky gang members. Drew stepped forward, next to Hurtado. "What is this, Soliz? I thought you said Zapata was looking to buy weapons."

Botello switched his target from Hurtado to Drew. "Shut up!"

Drew's senses ramped up. He watched Botello's trigger finger and listened for movement from the other two gunmen. He was too close to dodge the bullet, so he would have to anticipate if Botello made the shot. He needed to get one step closer to make a move.

Drew scowled back at Botello. "You insignificant pig! Threaten us and you threaten Mr. Armstrong."

He stepped toward Botello just as he heard the gunman to his right move in. He felt the cold tip of the man's barrel up against his right temple. Evidently this guy was just as dumb as the other.

Drew exploded into action. He simultaneously swept his right forearm up and back, pushing the gun off his head, while hook-kicking Botello's gun hand, which sent the .45 flying across the room. Drew wrapped his right arm around both of the gunman's arms while executing a powerful sidekick to Botello's chest. Both moves were done in less than a second. The gunman's barrel was now aimed at Reed and the other gunman, and a reactionary shot went off. Drew felt the concussion of the shot next to his chest just before he slammed the palm of his hand into the gunman's throat. In a fraction of a second, Drew torqued the gun from the gasping man's hand and turned his attention to the second gunman.

The wild shot had grazed Reed's arm but hit the other thug square in his right shoulder. Reed was moving to recover the weapon. Drew whipped his head back toward Botello, who was just getting up off the floor after stumbling backward. Drew snarled and walked toward him, but Botello pulled a knife and threw it at him. Drew froze the image of the spinning weapon in his mind, calculating the precise moment to react. When the blade was just inches from his chest, he twisted and caught the knife by its handle with his left hand without missing a single step in his approach toward Botello.

Drew stuck the gun in his belt to free his right hand. Botello looked frozen from panic as he realized that he was now facing a vengeful arms dealer. Drew grabbed Botello by the throat and slammed him up against the nearest wall. He put the knife to his throat and leaned to within two inches of his face.

"You want a war, Botello? You got one. Mr. Armstrong will decimate Zapata's operation within six months. I came here to make us both profitable, and you point a gun in my face? Bad move." Drew tightened his grip around Botello's throat. "We've got money, we've got ports, and we've got weapons. Now all you're going to have is a lot of pain."

"Wait . . . wait," Botello wheezed.

Drew wore a frown of contempt but hesitated. Botello's eyes widened with fear as Drew pressed the knife in close against his throat. Botello looked like he was struggling for air, so Drew lightened his grip just enough to let the man talk.

"I can set you up with a meeting with Mr. Zapata. We can still work this out!"

Hurtado stepped toward Drew. "He was just being cautious, Moore. We can all profit from this. You kill him now and we all lose."

Drew squinted, glaring into Botello's eyes. He let five long seconds elapse, then removed his hand and the knife from the man's throat.

"I won't do this with you again, Botello. Next time you threaten me or any of Mr. Armstrong's men, you die. I will personally see to it. Is that clear?"

Botello rubbed his neck as he nodded.

Drew pulled out a white business card with a single telephone number on it. He stuffed it in Botello's shirt pocket, then turned and walked toward the door. "Set up the meeting and call the number. We'll be there."

As Drew walked toward the door, Reed and Hurtado followed. He reached for the handle and then stuck the knife into the frame of the door. They left without saying another word.

They had driven off the compound before Hurtado looked at Reed, then at Drew. "You want to tell me what I just saw back there?"

"He's our up-and-coming superagent," Reed said, holding his arm tight.

Drew looked at Reed. "How bad is it?"

"I'm okay. Just hurts like—"

"Seriously," Hurtado interjected. "Where did you learn to move like that?"

Drew opened the glove compartment to see if there was something to put over Reed's wound until they stopped. "Chicago. I spent a lot of time dealing with thugs just like those."

He hoped that would suffice.

Back at the hotel, Drew found a first-aid kit and began cleaning and dressing Reed's arm.

"How do you do it, Carter?"

"Do what?" Drew asked.

Reed just shook his head. "I haven't been completely honest with you. Do you know why we're in Philadelphia together?" He winced as Drew finished cleaning the wound.

"Yeah . . . 'Cause I'm a rookie and you've got experience."

Reed snorted. "Seriously, do you?"

Drew stopped and looked at Reed's face. "Because Ross wants you to keep an eye on me."

Reed didn't say anything.

"How am I doing?" Drew asked with a slight grin.

"I cleared you three months after the Farm."

Drew was surprised by that. "Then why are you still with me?"

Reed gingerly felt the wound and nodded his appreciation. "Because there are no other agents like you, and Ross knows it. You see things no one else sees, Carter. It's uncanny. I've been with you long enough to know you're not normal. Hurtado saw that in one mission. So tell me how you do it. It will only make us better as a team."

Drew sobered. He looked at Reed, considering how his partner would handle the truth. He shook his head. "You would never believe me if I told you."

He started to get up from his chair, but Reed grabbed his arm.

"Carter, whatever it is you have is real and it works. I'll believe you. There's too much evidence not to believe you. Try me."

Drew once again faced the temptation to share the burden of this global battle for mankind with someone else. If only Ben had succeeded. If only he could find Ben now. If only he had physical proof for what he was seeing.

He looked Reed square in the eyes. "There is no secret, Reed. I've been training since I was twelve, and I have a knack for it."

"I don't believe you. Obviously you've had training, but nobody catches knives out of the air, and nobody can predict a situation going south before there are any indications." Reed reached for his shirt. "Just be straight with me."

"There's more going on here than just fighting drug lords, weapons dealers, and terrorism. A lot more," Drew said.

Reed squinted, anxious to hear more.

"All of these crimes are being orchestrated by an organization much bigger, much more evil than ISIS, Hamas, or people like Zapata."

Reed shook his head. "Like the IGA? Carter, that theory's been investigated."

"No. Bigger," Drew replied.

Reed cocked his head. "How do you mean? What proof do you have?"

Drew hesitated. Reed was a stand-up guy. Imagine what he and Ben could do with one more person on their side, trying to discover and reveal the truth about the invaders—especially another CIA agent. Drew opened his mouth to confess, then recanted. Reed would never buy into it.

"It's just a gut feeling I have. A sixth sense."

Reed looked disappointed. "Well, I can't argue with that. You have one heck of a sixth sense."

"Yeah, I guess so."

Reed waited for more, but Drew was done, and Reed seemed to sense it. Perhaps one day he might be ready to hear the truth, but it wouldn't be today.

Three days later, Hurtado, Reed, and Drew met with Zapata. This time, the meeting was in a public outdoor club, and much of the conversation was just social.

"I like to get to know my clients first," Zapata said with a wide smile as he sipped from his glass of Bacardi rum. "If I can't enjoy a drink and a meal with someone, I don't want to do business with him."

Drew looked at Zapata, disgusted by the filth he was pouring into the US. In his eyes, Drew saw the images of addicted teenagers, broken marriages, and abuse of every kind.

Drew smiled back. "Then let us drink and eat often, my friend, and the business will take care of itself."

At the end of the meal, Zapata lit a Cuban cigar and nodded at the pleasure the aroma brought him. "I think we may have a future together." White smoke pushed out from his nose and mouth with each word.

"On behalf of Mr. Armstrong and Armstrong Industries, we look forward to doing business with you."

Zapata eyed Drew and became very serious. He leaned forward. "Tell me, Mr. Moore, would Mr. Armstrong be averse to receiving additional cargo at your ports along with our payment for your goods? There would of course be significant compensation in exchange for receiving this cargo."

Drew leaned forward. "I can assure you that Mr. Armstrong is open to all forms of business." He leaned back slightly. "However, the risk versus gain ratio must be considered. What might the nature of this cargo be?"

Zapata took another long draw on his cigar as he eyed Drew and then Reed closely. "The kind that must be received at night and would disappear by morning without any effort on your part at all."

He was talking about human cargo. What kind, Drew wasn't sure, but this changed the entire scope of the mission. Was Zapata already doing this with other clients? Was this a possible terrorist route into the heart of America?

"Sounds promising. I'll have a discussion with Mr. Armstrong, and we can discuss details at our next meeting."

Zapata nodded and the meeting ended. They had not gained the intel they were hoping for, but it certainly would give the CIA a whole new avenue of investigation to pursue.

SYDNEY CARLYLE AND
THE WEAPONS DEALER

The debrief with Sloan went well, and his supervisor seemed pleased. Langley responded well too; they wanted Drew and Reed to continue establishing a connection with Zapata and his organization to see how much information they could gain before taking Zapata out. It was going to be a lengthy mission after all.

Over the next couple of weeks, Drew found it impossible not to check up on Sydney from time to time when there were breaks in the Zapata investigation. One late Friday afternoon, he read a few more texts and discovered that the last one sent just a few minutes ago read: *Can you meet Sat for lunch at Kally's . . . 12?* The reply from Sydney: *Love to. I work at 1:30. See you then!*

Drew shut down the search and sat back, a dangerous thought forming in his mind.

"Hey, Carter. Want to catch something to eat?" Reed said as he walked toward the elevators.

"Thanks, but no. I've got to take care of something tonight." *Where did that come from?*

"Okay. See you Monday."

Drew nodded and shut down his system. He left the building and entered the parking garage, trying to focus on the Zapata evidence they had gathered, but his thoughts always turned back to Sydney. He sat in his car with his keys in one hand and his cell phone in the other. He opened his airline app. Without consciously deciding to do so, he checked flights to Chicago. One was leaving in two hours, the last for the day. His report indicating Chicago as a possible target for ISIS flashed across his mind.

"What are you doing, Carter?" he said out loud. "Go home."

He clicked the phone off and started his car. At the garage exit he waited for a break in the traffic to turn left, toward home.

He rested his forehead on the steering wheel, took a deep breath, then flipped on the turn signal and took a right—to the airport. The carry-on with one set of clothes in his trunk was all he had, but it would get him through Sunday.

∽o∾

Validus could tell Tren had an important message by his hurried approach. It was unusual for the guardian.

"Carter is checking up on Carlyle," Tren said.

"We need an encounter, not just curiosity," Validus said.

"He's on his way to the airport as we speak," Tren replied. "To Chicago."

"Finally. How promising is an encounter?" Validus asked, hopeful.

"With a little help, I think we can make something happen. But that doesn't guarantee she'll witness or he'll listen if she does."

"Perhaps, but it's the best opportunity we'll have had since he left Chicago. If it doesn't happen, we're going to have to look at other options . . . options he's not going to like." Validus was encouraged. "Tell Crenshaw to gather the warriors and then get back to Carter. Keep him safe until we arrive."

Tren nodded. A few minutes later, the valiant warriors under Validus's command were ready for their briefing.

"Warriors, Tren believes Carter is about to attempt contact with Carlyle. If you thought the Fallen were doing everything to take him out in the last few weeks, you haven't seen anything yet. If Carter is indeed the last salvation that triggers the End of Days as prophesied by John, then Niturni will stop at nothing to prevent Carlyle from witnessing to Carter. Their lives will be at stake every minute of every day until he accepts Messiah. We must be alert and be prepared for anything. Car accidents, plane crashes, serial killers, diseases, natural disasters—there are no limits to what they might try."

"Why Carlyle? Couldn't another lead Carter to Messiah?" Crenshaw asked.

"Carlyle certainly has the strongest influence on him, but you're right.

There is another, and we just about lost him the last time Carter was in Chicago. We will need to provide cover for Reverend Branson and his family too."

Sason let out a low whistle. "You sure you got enough warriors, boss? Multiple assets to protect and only eight of us against who knows how many Fallen. If this is as high risk as you say, we could be outgunned in a heartbeat."

"Perhaps, but when two of our assets converge, so do we and our strength is double. If at any point I think this might escalate to century- or legion-level conflict, Commander Malak has two legions on standby for us. You all know as well as I do that the Carter mission is just one of thousands in this region. I can't jeopardize those missions unless I am absolutely sure it's necessary. If I make the call prematurely, the consequences could be just as dire."

Sason nodded.

"What we need during the next few days is intel, strategy, and precision." Validus looked at the circle of extraordinary warriors he had gathered. "I've selected each of you for a purpose. You do what you do best, and I'll make sure we have adequate force to accomplish the mission."

Each of them was on board.

"Rake and Jayt, I want you covering Reverend Branson. If something goes down at the church, the warrior there, Teriel, will offer support. He knows the score. Brumak, Sason, and Persimus, you're on Carlyle. Crenshaw, Tren is covering Carter. We'll join him as soon as we dismiss. Any questions?"

⚬⚬⚬

Six hours later, Drew was in a rental car heading for a hotel in downtown Chicago. He spent the next morning walking the streets of the Windy City, keeping an eye out for invaders.

Fifteen minutes before noon, Drew tucked the *Chicago Tribune* under his arm and walked into Kally's Bistro on Seventh and Fifteenth. He quickly scanned the restaurant. At the back he spotted the restroom sign and made his way there, capturing every detail and every face at the tables and in the booths as he went. Two girls taking a break from shopping, husband and wife meeting for lunch, man by himself expecting no one, divorced father with son and daughter for the weekend, young man waiting . . . waiting for his girlfriend.

Drew recognized Willis from his search. He was good-looking—wavy brown hair, dark eyes, clean-cut, religious—just Sydney's type. He even had a worn Bible on the table off to the side.

Drew made his way to the hall at the back of the bistro, passing a doorway that led to a set of tables under an awning outdoors. He went down the hallway, opened the door to the bathroom, and washed his hands in the sink. He ripped a paper towel from the dispenser a little harder than he had intended and looked in the mirror.

"This was a bad idea, Carter. You're just tormenting yourself."

Then he realized the torment was subconsciously what he wanted. Perhaps if the pain was deep enough, he would finally let her go. He clenched his teeth and resolved to see it out.

He had already mapped out the room and chosen his position. There were tables spaced throughout the center of the dining area and high-backed booths along the glass wall, which looked onto the outside tables under the awning. Willis was in one of the booths. Drew sat in the booth behind Willis, back to back with the man who was stealing his lovely Sydney.

"What can I get for you?" he heard the waitress ask Willis with a hint of sass.

"I'm waiting for someone, but I'll take a raspberry tea while I wait," Willis replied.

"Sure."

Drew heard the scratching of a pen on an order pad. A few seconds later, the waitress sidestepped and asked Drew the same question. He pointed to the smoked turkey sandwich about the same time he heard the door to the restaurant open.

"Want anything to drink besides water?"

Drew shook his head, hoping to be rid of her so he could focus on the table behind him. The waitress left.

Drew picked up a knife and polished it, then positioned it so he could see the reflection of the front of the bistro behind him. The slender form of a young woman was walking toward him. When she was nearly to the booth, Drew recognized Sydney, and his pulse quickened. It had been eighteen months since he last saw her. She was more beautiful than his memories, and he had to consciously remind himself to stay seated and out of her life.

"Hey, babe!" Willis called, and Drew had the urge to hit him.

"Hi, Dustin." Hearing her voice was almost harder than seeing her. Drew bit his lip as he watched Willis stand up and hug her.

Drew opened his newspaper, pretending to read one of the articles inside. The paper acted as a parabolic sound antenna, amplifying everything in the restaurant. He closed his eyes and focused on just the sounds coming from the booth behind him.

"Are we meeting for something special?" Sydney asked.

"No, sweetheart. I know you're busy tonight, and I couldn't wait until church tomorrow to see you, so I thought a lunch today might be nice."

"How thoughtful. I'm glad; this is nice."

Drew was trying to interpret Sydney's tone, but he wasn't sure. It had been so long since he'd seen her. He couldn't tell if she was completely taken with Willis.

Drew listened for fifty minutes as he ate and pretended to read. Their talk was trivial—work, friends, God, church. Willis seemed to have that one element that Drew never could quite swallow—belief in an all-knowing, all-powerful God.

Near the end of the meal, Sydney excused herself to go to the restroom, and Drew lifted the paper high around himself. As she walked by, her perfume teased him with memories of the past. He closed his eyes.

When she returned, she grabbed her jacket. "I'm sorry, Dustin, but I have to be at work in a few minutes. This was really nice, though. Thank you."

Willis stood up, and Drew could hear them embrace. "I'm glad you liked it, babe. Can I pick you up for church tomorrow?"

"Sure. I'll be ready at nine."

"Awesome. I have to stay to get the check, but you have a great rest of the day."

"Thanks. You too."

Drew heard the soft click of Sydney's shoes walking away. He hung his head and knew it was over. The pain was indeed great, but it was time for him to completely let her go. He folded the paper, took a deep breath, and grabbed the ticket the waitress had just placed on his table. He slid to the edge of the seat.

"Dude, how's it going?"

Drew stopped. He turned his head and got a glimpse through the vertical slats of the booth's high-back of another guy sliding into the seat opposite Willis, where Sydney had been sitting.

"Got her eating out of my hand. Another couple of months and she'll be ready," Willis replied.

Drew slid back into his seat.

"You are ice cold, man. Are you sure you can pull this off? You sure it's worth it?"

Willis stifled a laugh. He lowered his voice, but Drew had no problem hearing him. His senses were peaked. "Her dad is filthy rich. All I have to do is keep up this religious garbage a little longer, and I'm on easy street." Drew heard Willis thump the Bible on the table. "Listen, I was raised in this nonsense, and these fundamental freaks are taught to obey their husbands. Why wouldn't it be worth it? Money and a wife who does what I say. And when I'm tired of her, I'll get my thrills with some other lonely gorgeous babe."

Was this some joke Willis was playing on his friend? He considered the tone and reevaluated what he'd just heard. No, Sydney was definitely being conned.

"I'm telling you, I know a guy who pulled this off, and he is living the good life." Willis chuckled and his friend joined in the laughter.

Drew couldn't take it anymore. He left money on the table to cover the ticket, then slid out of the booth and made his way to the door that led to the outdoor tables so neither of the men would see him. He maneuvered through the tables under the awning and stepped over the waist-high black iron fence and onto the sidewalk. He circled back to the front of the bistro and reentered.

His mind was racing with all sorts of wild ideas, most of them ending with Willis in serious condition in the hospital. He considered telling Sydney outright but realized he couldn't do that and keep his cover. He had to think of another way.

He hesitated as he looked toward the booth where the two men sat. Drew wanted nothing more than to permanently wipe their silly Cheshire grins off their faces.

"You can seat yourself," the girl at the till said with a smile.

Drew gave her a quick smile, then walked toward the booth, nearly trembling in anger. He used the last few strides to get control of himself and play his role.

He stopped beside the booth and stared down at the two men. Willis was to his left and the other weasel was to his right. As the men looked up at Drew, he glared at them with a face of stone. No one said anything.

Just as Willis was opening his mouth to speak, Drew cut him off. "Dustin T. Willis?"

Willis squinted. "Maybe. Who are you?"

Drew pulled out his CIA Special Agent badge and flashed it so both men could see. "I'm Special Agent Grady, and I need to talk to you." He looked at the weasel friend. "Alone!"

"How do we know you're legit?" the weasel asked.

Drew slowly put the badge back into the inside breast pocket of his jacket. He held the jacket open far enough for the weasel to get a glimpse of his FN Five-Seven. Then he leaned toward the guy and smiled. "You'll know real quick unless you leave . . . now!"

The weasel glanced at Willis, then slid out of the booth and left. Drew took his place in the booth and crossed his hands in front of him as he stared Willis in the eye.

"I . . . I haven't done anything. What do you want with me?"

Drew pursed his lips and let the moment work for him. "We've been following you for some time, Mr. Willis, ever since you started seeing a Miss Sydney Carlyle three months ago." He waited, letting Willis react.

Willis's eyebrows lifted in surprise. "Why would the CIA care about that?"

"Keep your voice down," Drew scolded. "Do you know who Mr. Carlyle is, Mr. Willis?"

Willis squirmed in his seat. "He's the owner of a small aircraft manufacturing plant in Wichita, Kansas."

Drew nodded, even though he'd had no idea. Sydney never acted like a rich kid, and why was she in Rivercrest if her dad owned a plant in Wichita?

"Actually Mr. Carlyle is an international arms dealer, and his aircraft manufacturing company is a front. We've been trying to get close to him to get enough evidence to bring him down. So far we've been unsuccessful. That's why we're coming to you."

Willis swallowed hard and glanced nervously around the restaurant. "I . . . I don't understand. What can I do? I don't know anything."

Drew leaned forward on his forearms as if to tell even deeper secrets. "You're dating Mr. Carlyle's daughter. We want you to be our man on the inside, gathering evidence that we can use to bring his operation down. It would be a noble service to our country, Mr. Willis."

"But I—"

"Before you answer, I need to warn you about the risks. Mr. Carlyle is a very dangerous man. We have reason to believe that he has eliminated people he considered a threat, and his international ties are even more ruthless."

Drew let Willis absorb that. The man rubbed the back of his neck. Drew could see sweat forming on his forehead.

"But Sydney seems so innocent. And the whole church thing . . . I've met him."

Drew nodded. "We suspect that Miss Carlyle doesn't know about her father's illegal dealings. He's kept her isolated. And what more perfect cover for an arms dealer than a faithful church attendee?" He clenched his teeth. "People who fake their religious beliefs are some of the lowest scum of the earth."

He watched Willis cringe.

"We would protect you as much as possible, but in some situations you would be on your own. As soon as we have enough evidence, we will arrest him and seize all his assets. When we're done with him, he'll be spending the rest of his life in prison and won't have a dime to his name. It should only take a few months, if you're efficient."

Willis's eyes were getting wider with each piece of information Drew fed him. Drew could see the anxiety mounting.

"What's in it for me?" Willis asked.

Drew tilted his head. "What's in it for you?" he asked, his voice filled with surprise.

"Yeah. You know, what do I get if I do this?"

"Well, you would have the honor of knowing you served this great country and saved many—"

"What?" Willis's voice was incredulous. He tried to control the volume but his tone was intense. "You want me to risk my life for months and all I get is a 'good job'? You're nuts! No way! No way in heck would I do this!"

Drew had known all along exactly how an honorless guy like Willis would react. He held up his hand. "Calm down, Mr. Willis."

Willis started to get out of the booth, but Drew reached across and grabbed his arm.

"Sit down, Mr. Willis, or the meal you just ate may be your last." Drew glowered at him.

"What do you mean?" Willis asked, his voice quavering.

Drew released his grip, and Willis settled back into his seat.

"I'm sorry to hear that you won't do this for your country, but unfortunately by dating Mr. Carlyle's daughter, you've already placed yourself in a very precarious position."

"How so? I'll just dump her and move on."

Drew shook his head. "With the resources available to Mr. Carlyle, don't you think he already knows everything about you? Even though he's a ruthless weapons dealer, he's still a father who loves his daughter. You hurt her like that, believe me, her tears will not go unpunished."

Willis's eyes revealed his swelling panic, and Drew was enjoying it far too much. He drove it home.

"Her last boyfriend just disappeared. We still don't know what happened to him."

Willis's eyes nearly popped. He pointed a finger at Drew. "That's right. She said something about that guy. She wouldn't tell me what happened to him." Willis began rubbing his upper arm with his hand. "Oh man . . . What . . . what do I do?" He was on the verge of a complete meltdown.

Drew looked at Willis in disgust. "Are you sure you won't reconsider going in as an operative for us?"

Willis looked shocked. "No! No, of course not! I told you, that's nuts!"

Drew smirked. "Then I'm afraid there's nothing I can do for you."

He started to slide out of the booth. This time Willis reached across the table and grabbed Drew's arm.

"Please, Agent Grady, please help me! Surely there's something you can do."

Drew hesitated and tried to look sympathetic. He sighed and settled back into his seat. "There's only one way out of this for you. You're going to have to disappear and run, and I mean far away. Northern Canada or Greenland would be your safest bet."

"But I don't even have a passport. I can't leave the country!"

Drew shook his head again. "Then I suggest you get to the tip of northern Maine and hide out for the next two years. Maybe, just maybe, Mr. Carlyle will quit looking for you by then."

Willis put his head in his hands, but Drew kept working him.

"I hope you realize that everything I just told you is classified. You can't tell anyone anything about the Carlyle family. If word gets out and our investigation is jeopardized because you talked to someone, even your weasel friend, you'll have more than Mr. Carlyle after you."

"When should I go?"

Drew turned and scanned the restaurant. He looked skeptical. "You just had lunch with Miss Carlyle, right?"

Willis nodded.

Drew tilted his head. "Odds are that Mr. Carlyle had someone watching you. If he's still around and he's seen me talking to you, then you probably have less than twenty-four hours to make your move."

Willis looked at Drew, and he thought the guy was going to cry. "My life is ruined. What have I done?"

Drew looked at him sadly. "I guess you just messed with the wrong girl. Here." He handed Willis a napkin and a pen.

"What's this for?"

"I'm going to help you the best I can. You're going to write a note to Miss Carlyle, and it might buy you enough time to get out of town."

"Okay. What do I write?"

"Sydney, after much prayer I've come to the conclusion that God is telling me we are not right for each other."

"Yeah . . . yeah, this is good," Willis said with enthusiasm. Drew wanted to punch him. He continued for Sydney's sake.

"I wanted to tell you yesterday but couldn't bear to see you hurt. I'm leaving on a mission trip and may never see you again. I pray your life is filled with God's love and peace. Dustin."

Willis finished writing and looked at Drew with a glimmer of hope. "Do you think this will do it? How do I get this note to her?"

Drew took it from him. "Text her right now and say, 'Something came up, and I can't make it to church tomorrow. Please meet me at Kally's at two. Same table.'"

Willis typed with shaking hands. He hit Send and they waited. A few seconds later Sydney's reply came. Drew snatched the phone out of Willis's hands.

Okay. Everything all right?

Drew handed the phone back to Willis. "Type 'Everything's fine. See you tomorrow.'"

Willis typed and hit Send.

Drew stared at him. This scumbag had intended to destroy the most perfect girl Drew had ever met *and* her family. His punishment wasn't nearly enough, but it would have to do.

"That's it. If you leave tonight you should have a twenty-hour head start. You need to ditch the phone, change your identity, and never come anywhere within four states of the Carlyle family again. Got it?"

Willis nodded. "Okay, I got it." He looked nervously around the bistro, then stood up and started walking.

"Hey!" Drew called before Willis was more than a few steps away.

Willis turned around, and Drew held up his meal ticket and the forgotten Bible.

Willis reached back and grabbed the ticket. "You can keep the Bible. I won't need it anymore." He hurried to the till at the front of the bistro, paid, and left.

Drew stuffed the napkin note in his pocket, grabbed the Bible, and left the restaurant.

He went back to his hotel just a few blocks away. When he got to his room, he threw Willis's Bible onto the table in the corner and flipped on the TV. Tomorrow he would finish setting Sydney's life back in order and then catch his flight back to Philadelphia. Mission accomplished.

Drew flipped through all sixty-two channels twice and was reminded for the hundredth time that there was nothing worth watching. He clicked off the set and threw the remote to the other side of the bed.

The big black book stared at him from the corner of the room. Drew looked at it and shook his head. What did intelligent people like Sydney see in such malarkey?

He rolled over and tried to take an afternoon nap, but sleep eluded him. And every time he turned over, that book seemed to be waiting.

In frustration he got up from the bed and sat down at the table. He spun the book around until it was right side up. *The Holy Bible.*

Drew sighed. What a sham. He thumbed through the pages until one stuck and started reading out loud.

"The Gospel According to John. In the beginning was the Word, and the Word was with God, and the Word was God." He skipped a few verses. "And the Word became flesh and dwelt among us, and we beheld His glory, the glory as of the only begotten of the Father, full of grace and truth."

Drew stopped. Shivers went up and down his spine. "Dwelt among us," he said once more. *That is exactly what the invaders are doing . . . dwelling among us.*

He thumbed further through the Bible until he recognized a word, *Ephesians.* He stopped and remembered the message Sydney had given him over a year and a half ago in the FBI interrogation room. *"Ephesians 6:12 is your verse, Drew. It's real!"* she had said.

Drew turned pages until he found the reference.

"For we do not wrestle against flesh and blood, but against principalities, against powers, against the rulers of the darkness of this age, against spiritual hosts of wickedness in the heavenly places."

Drew froze, then read the verse again and again. It was eerily representative of what he was seeing.

He closed the book and stood up. He walked down to the lobby to buy a soda, and by the time he returned, his mind was in overdrive, racing with possibilities.

He walked over to the big black book and sat down. He turned to the first few pages.

"In the beginning God created . . ."

THE BURDEN
OF COMMAND

The next day, Drew arrived at Kally's Bistro at one thirty. He sat in the same booth Sydney and Willis had sat in the previous day. When the waitress came, he told her he had to leave and asked her to keep the booth open until his friend arrived. He slipped the waitress twenty bucks and asked her to give Willis's note to the girl who would come to the booth.

He then slipped through the door to the outdoor tables and positioned himself so he could see through the glass wall and into the booth he had just left. He ordered a piece of pie and a cup of coffee, then pretended to read his newspaper again, placing it at just the right position so he could see the booth but Sydney would not be able to see him.

Then he waited, dreading the hurt that his beloved Sydney was about to feel. He dreamed of a different life, of meeting Sydney without the chains of a CIA sentence or the knowledge of a worldwide invasion. Why couldn't he have normal? Why couldn't he have happiness?

A few minutes into his imaginings, Sydney came and sat down at the booth. Drew watched her every move, her charming smile, the brush of her hair over her ear, and the blink of her eyes.

"I'm sorry, Sydney," he whispered.

The waitress arrived, spoke a few words, and then handed Sydney the note. Drew watched as she read. When she was through, she slowly set the napkin on the table. At first she looked stunned, just staring at the empty seat across from her. Drew expected tears, but there were none. Perhaps she was tougher than he gave her credit for, or perhaps she would save the tears for later, in the privacy of her car or room.

He watched as she slowly turned and looked outside, setting her chin in her hand. She looked so sad. It took everything in him not to run in and take her in his arms, even though such selfish action would add years to her misery. It was done. She would never know it, but he had saved her once more.

He knew he should go, but he loved to watch her, and besides, there was no way to stand up without drawing her attention while she was looking out the window. At one point she changed her blank stare to a couple sitting at a distant table, and Drew considered making his escape.

Just then, a dark invader flashed through the restaurant behind Sydney. Drew had come to be able to identify the difference between a dark invader just watching and one about to engage in some ill-intentioned action. Drew turned to see if there might be more than one. He scanned the surrounding area and saw more activity from both the dark and light invaders. Something was up, but he couldn't tell just what it was yet.

When he turned back, Sydney had shifted and chosen his table to gaze at. The distraction of the invaders may have cost him his cover. He moved the newspaper so that not even the sliver of his eye could be seen, but of course he could not see her anymore either. Better to play it safe for a few minutes.

After three minutes he shifted the paper slightly to bring her back into view, but Sydney was gone. Before he could drop the paper and make his exit, he caught the teasing scent of her perfume, and he froze. Then came an enticing and soothing voice next to his right ear. He could feel her breath on his neck.

"Mister, did you just chase my boyfriend away?"

Drew slowly turned his head to see Sydney's sparkling blue eyes and a subtle smile that disarmed him like nothing else could.

"Hi, Syd," he said quietly.

Her eyes were impossible to read—surprise, anger, fear?

"Do you have any idea what's going through my mind right now?" She seemed to sense the secrecy he was supposedly shrouded in.

He wanted to jump up and hug her, but he couldn't bring any extra attention to them. He slowly pushed the chair on the opposite side of the table away with his foot. She took the cue, slipped around the table and sat down. Drew lowered the newspaper to see her eyes filled with wonder.

She leaned forward. "What . . . what are you doing here?" Her voice was trembling. "Are you in trouble?"

Drew cursed himself for having become distracted by the invaders. If Ross knew that he had made contact with Sydney, there was no telling what the repercussions would be. He took another scan. Activity in the invader realm seemed to have subsided. He checked for any potential real-world threats or observers. All seemed clear.

There was no lying his way out of this. She knew him too well.

He looked straight into her eyes. "I'm not in trouble. Not yet anyway. I'm sorry, Sydney. I can't tell you anything."

She raised an eyebrow, and her coy expression caused Drew's heart to skip a beat. "And you think I'm going to let you get away with that?"

He shrugged.

Sydney stared at him, then shook her head, closed her eyes, and said, "What do I do with that?" She opened her eyes, hopeful. "Are you telling me the truth?"

He reached across the table, and she gently laid her hand in his. The touch seemed to ease her mind, and the lines of worry on her face disappeared. She struggled with what to say.

"I can't believe you're here. I didn't know if I would ever see you again."

"You weren't supposed to, not for a long time, but—" He stopped short, not sure how much he should say.

"But you had to chase Dustin out of my life?" Sydney finished.

Drew grimaced. "Yeah, I guess you could put it that way." He focused on every detail of her face. "I guess I have some explaining to do."

Sydney pulled back her hand. She placed her elbows on the table, interlaced her hands, then rested her chin on the backs of her fingers and nodded. Drew just stared at her for a moment.

"What?" she asked.

"Well, first can you explain to me why you don't seem very devastated, or better yet, angry at me for messing up your love life?"

Sydney briefly dropped her gaze to the table, then looked back into Drew's eyes.

"The truth is, you saved me the trouble. Although Dustin seems like a nice guy, the Lord impressed upon me that he was definitely not the one. I never felt like I could trust him. You know what I mean?"

Drew laughed. "Yes, I know exactly what you mean."

"I don't know what you told him, but thanks for being used by God on my behalf."

Drew smiled and shook his head. There it was again, attributing the natural actions of circumstances to God.

Sydney's expression became quizzical. "What *did* you tell him, anyway?"

"Well . . ." Drew hesitated, then figured she might as well know. "I told him your father was a ruthless weapons dealer and that we needed him to gather information for us but that his life would be on the line the whole time."

Sydney laughed, but Drew didn't. Then horror filled her eyes. "You didn't!"

Drew nodded. "Yes . . . yes, actually I did."

Sydney's mouth dropped open, and she leaned back in her chair. "Drew, are you insane?"

He tilted his head. "I've wondered," he teased, but she was not amused. He leaned forward. "Sydney, your perceptions of Willis were right, except he was much more of a scumbag than you would have ever dreamed. He was scamming you, setting you up because he discovered your father was rich. Which, by the way, you never told me he owned an aircraft manufacturing plant in Wichita."

Sydney's mouth dropped open. "Are you sure about this, Drew?"

"I heard it from his own mouth. And all that religious stuff he was pretending to believe—total fake. I'm sorry, Syd, but I had to step in."

Sydney covered her mouth with her hand. Drew let her gasp a few times.

"Well, anyway, you won't be bothered by him again. He's so scared he's going to hide out in northern Maine for a couple of years." He shot her a wry smile.

She slowly lost her ghastly expression and began to laugh. Drew joined her until they both had tears coming down their cheeks. When they recovered, Sydney gazed into his eyes.

"How long have you been watching over me, Drew?"

He lowered his head and then looked into her penetrating eyes. "I guess about as long as you've been praying for me."

She reached across the table and touched his arm. A shockwave flooded his arm and body from her touch. "I started praying for you the day you said hi to me in the hall after speech."

Drew stared at her, remembering the day that she stole his heart playing hard to get. "Really?"

She nodded. "Really." Her eyes seemed so sad at that moment. "Have you figured it out yet?"

"Figured what out?"

"Those men you said you were seeing. Have you figured out who they are?"

He sobered. He looked around to make sure no one was close enough to hear and that there were no invaders nearby. Talk like this was institutional-worthy. He had to be careful even with Sydney.

"I think you should tell me who you think they are. You seem to have influence over them."

Sydney furrowed her eyebrows. "What do you mean?"

"Come on, Syd. I saw you nearly paralyze them. I need to know." Drew wasn't sure how far to take this. "Are you . . . Do you . . ." He watched her expression closely, but it was unchanged. "Who do you think they are?"

Sydney took a deep breath. "I think God is allowing you to see angels and demons."

Drew rolled his eyes. "Please don't play games with me, Syd. I saw what you did. There's nothing in your Bible that describes that. I think your devotion to this religious stuff is as fake as Willis's."

Sydney's eyes narrowed, then filled with fire. She pulled back. "Fake? What would you know about real faith, or better yet, the Bible?"

"I know because I read it," Drew shot back.

Sydney turned her head and looked at him out of the corner of her eye, trying to decide if he was teasing her. "When?"

"Last night."

"Ha! I don't believe you." She crossed her arms and glared at him.

"You don't believe me?" He lowered his voice to a whisper. "You believe that I'm seeing aliens from another dimension, but you don't believe I read the Bible last night?"

"It takes most people a year to read through the Bible, and you're telling me you read it in one night?"

"I'm a fast reader."

"Uh-huh. And if you read it that fast, how much do you remember?"

"Almost all of it."

Sydney eyed him skeptically. "Who were the sons of Noah?"

"Shem, Ham, and Japheth."

"Who's Hezekiah?"

"A king of Judah who turned out to be a pretty good dude. Man, the Bible's not much of a history book. The time line is all over the place. It's a pretty crazy book."

Sydney seemed stunned as she looked at Drew in amazement. "That's remarkable, Drew. I can't believe it. Then you know . . . you know what this is all about. You know who Jesus is and what He did on the cross for you."

Drew fidgeted. He couldn't deny that there were things he read that pricked his heart and made him uncomfortable. But in the end, he had to dismiss the spiritual mumbo jumbo because of science and because of what he was seeing. He looked at Sydney, trying hard to decide if she really did believe this religious stuff or if she was still playing him and was some secret agent of the invader realm. It was a moment when the burden of the world fell on him as he came to the conclusion that he and he alone was the only one who really knew what was happening. Or maybe he really was going insane, as Jake and his mother had thought.

"Here's what I got from reading that book, Syd. To an ancient, pretechnological civilization, alien invaders would look like gods. Everything in that book can be explained by it, especially if you could see what I've seen."

"It's more than a book, Drew, but until you have a heart to find God, His living Word will only be ink on paper to you. And consider this, to a modern technological civilization, angels and demons dwelling among us might look like alien invaders."

Drew opened his mouth for rebuttal, but no words came. He had never considered that, and it was so logical that he couldn't refute it.

"Sydney Carlyle, every time I'm with you, you surprise me."

He caught the blurred movement of a dark invader in the street behind Sydney. Sydney followed his gaze. Another invader came from the other direction.

"What is it, Drew?"

Drew did a quick 360 scan. Within seconds, dozens of light and dark invaders began converging around them. He spotted Validus commanding and engaging. Their focus seemed divided between someone on the street and Drew and Sydney.

The dark invaders were coming after them. But this trip was so random and spontaneous . . . how could they have known? He glanced at Sydney as his senses kicked into hyperdrive, evaluating the situation and possible threats.

"Do you come to this bistro often?" he asked as he continued to watch the invader realm escalate around them.

"Ah . . . yes. It's my favorite. What's going on, Drew?" Fear laced her words as she saw Drew begin to react.

❦

"Where are they?" Validus stood in front of Kally's Bistro. Persimus, Crenshaw, and Tren were next to him. Sason and Brumak were positioned at strategic locations around the restaurant, as were Rake and Jayt, who had rejoined them after determining that Reverend Branson was not a target. Crenshaw was looking, searching, feeling.

"Niturni's too smart to let this encounter happen without a fight. He's got too much at stake. I expected a legion of the Fallen."

Crenshaw turned and pointed. "There, Commander. Niturni didn't miss this—he planned it. He's going to try to kill them both at the same time!"

All at once, a dozen Fallen collapsed on them, jumping from second- and third-story buildings to pull them away from Carter and Carlyle. Validus instantly recognized them as some of Niturni's best.

❦

The invaders were now engaged in half a dozen fierce battles. Drew finally saw and understood the threat in an instant. A young man of Middle Eastern descent was walking toward the front entrance of the bistro. His jacket was too thick for the temperature and too thick for his build. He was a suicide bomber.

Drew wondered if his warning to Langley had been passed on to Homeland Security, the NSA, and the FBI. What were the odds that Drew just happened to be at the one place in the United States that had been targeted? It was beyond coincidental. Drew looked at Sydney and realized that this had to be about her.

He grabbed her hand and whipped her out of her seat. Though he couldn't abandon the eighty people at the restaurant, he could make sure she was safe first.

He was about to tell her to run out the back gate of the bistro's outdoor patio when he saw a second suicide bomber coming from that direction. The terrorist was just opening his coat to show his explosive-laden vest while chanting praises to Allah. This was a multiple bomber hit. There might even be a third. They were trapped.

It looked like Validus and another light invader were trying to get to Drew and Sydney, but it would be too late.

Drew flipped their solid metal table over on its side. "Get behind this and cover your ears!" he shouted to Sydney.

Then he charged the second man, who was just thirty feet away.

"Everybody hit the floor!" Drew shouted.

The suicide bombers were still too far away to cause the damage they wanted. Drew knew he had only seconds to save lives, but it would cost him his own. Screams of panic rose up, and some of the people in the outer courtyard of the bistro started to run into the restaurant, which was exactly what the terrorists wanted, right into the first suicide bomber's trap.

As Drew closed on the bomber coming into the courtyard, he looked for a dead man's switch, but the bomber's hands were holding open his coat and were free from any devices. It left only two other detonation options. The explosions were set to go off on a timer or they would be remotely triggered by an observer. Based on how the bomber tried to display his explosives to herd the people back into the restaurant, Drew guessed a remote detonator.

In less than a second, Drew pulled his FN and fired one shot aimed just above the bomber's vest, being careful not to hit the charges and set them off. The bullet penetrated the man's upper chest, but before he could fall, Drew lowered his shoulder and plowed into him, wrapping his left arm around him and lifting him into the air.

Just five feet behind the bomber was a line of parked cars on a side street. Drew took two steps and then hurled the man over the top of an SUV, hoping that the terrorist with the remote detonator was focused on the first bomber, who was just now approaching the entrance to the bistro. All Drew needed was three more seconds. The man's body flew across the hood of the SUV and slammed onto the pavement.

In the fraction of a second that it took for Drew to reverse his momentum, he saw Validus's massive warrior charge an attacking monster across the street. Drew dove back over the black iron fence toward Sydney, passing right through another light invader with his sword stretched out, ready to engage the multiple dark invaders surrounding the bomber.

Drew hit the ground beside Sydney. A waitress had joined her behind the table, shielding her. He careened into the brick wall of the bistro, unprotected by the table. He covered his ears as the pressure wave ripped through the air around them.

✎⊙✎

Once Validus understood the Fallen's plot, dread filled his soul. He had been outmaneuvered by his brilliant nemesis. The suicide bombers were protected by eight Fallen each. The closest threat to Carter was the bomber coming from the side street. Sason was closest, but he would soon be outmanned. Two demons engaged Validus as he tried to make his way toward Carter.

"Brumak, Rake, cover Carter! Persimus, you protect Carlyle. Jayt, Crenshaw, get to the primary bomber and take him out."

Validus cut through one of the warriors facing him and allowed Tren to take the second one, which freed him to move toward Carter and Carlyle again. He was almost to them when he heard Persimus cry out a warning just before translating into the form of a waitress.

Validus looked up to see Zurock jumping from the roof of the bistro to engage him. Validus had just enough time to raise his sword and deflect Zurock's powerful vertical cut. Precious seconds were lost as he saw Carter attack the bomber to save Carlyle. The Fallen had planned it well, and Validus knew he was about to lose both of them.

As if the Fallen weren't advantaged enough, a droxan materialized through the wall of the shop next door and charged Rake, Sason, and Brumak as they tried to give cover to Carter. Brumak didn't hesitate. He diverted to take on the droxan single-handedly as Sason and Rake took on the other Fallen guarding the bomber.

∽o∽

The explosion shook the earth and broke all the windows in a one-hundred-foot radius. The concussion hurt, but the SUV and the other parked cars had taken the majority of the blast, protecting the people in the courtyard. Smoke, fire, and shards of glass were everywhere.

But the worst of the threats was yet to come.

Drew crawled toward Sydney, wondering where the waitress had gone. He pulled Sydney from the ground and pushed her toward the side street.

"Run, Sydney. There's another bomb. Run!"

∽o∽

Sason translated two thirty-degree segments of the blast, which instantaneously dissolved six of the eight Fallen who were attacking. Rake's sword flew at the speed of lightning to deflect large pieces of metal and glass that would have impaled Carter and killed him instantly. Validus tried to disengage Zurock, but the regional commander would not give. Brumak's battle with the droxan was a sight to behold. Screeches of the demonic beast mingled with the war cries of one of Elohim's holy and mightiest of angels.

Every one of Validus's team was engaged in a life-and-death battle not only for themselves but for Carter and Carlyle. The heroic efforts of his men had helped his charges narrowly survive one suicide bomber, but how could they survive a second?

∽o∽

Sydney was dazed and bleeding, but it didn't look serious. She stumbled out of the courtyard across the twisted metal fence. Drew ran toward the front street. He looked through the broken windows of the bistro and saw the first bomber standing at the entrance of the restaurant fifty feet away, dazed and unsure as mayhem ensued. To Drew it looked as if the bomber was scared and losing his nerve.

Drew spotted Validus engaged with one of the most vicious dark invaders he had ever seen. Validus broke away momentarily and pointed toward a parked car just seventy-five yards up the street.

Drew crouched near a lamppost and took aim at the man sitting in the driver's seat. There was no way for Drew to determine if the man was just a spectator watching a disaster unfold or if he was a terrorist with his finger a microsecond away from pushing a button that would kill many innocent people. If Drew ran toward the car and the man did have the remote detonator, it would be over before he could get within fifty yards.

He scanned the area and saw that every light invader was engaged. Tactically it looked like the two dozen dark invaders were set in a perimeter to protect the suicide bomber and the man sitting in the car, and yet . . .

Drew considered the shot. It would have to be a perfect head shot, and it would have to be quick. If the observer thought the suicide bomber was losing nerve and might not enter the restaurant, he would detonate immediately.

Drew's mind raced through the calculations, estimating distance, bullet drop, and deflection from the glass of the windshield. The last was the most unpredictable. He figured the first round would shatter the glass and his second round would be the critical one. If he missed, he and thirty to forty more people would certainly die.

It was the moment of decision. Two pounds of pressure on the trigger was all that separated Drew from killing a terrorist or an innocent bystander.

Drew saw a dark invader racing toward him out of the corner of his eye.

∽o∾

Validus was desperate to free himself from Zurock and take out the bomber. The terrorist was hesitating because of the premature detonation of the first bomb. At fifty feet away, Carter was just on the edge of the lethal radius. If the bomber went inside the bistro to kill more people, Carter's survivability would go up, but a lot more people would die. A demon was trying to push the bomber toward Carter and not into the bistro, which confused the man. The observer sitting in the car down the street was the key.

Validus countered Zurock with a powerful cut and took a fraction of a second to point out the observer with the detonator to Carter. Validus then maneuvered toward the bomber. He saw a demon abandon his protection of the observer and attack Carter.

"Jayt!" Validus screamed.

Jayt deflected a slice from his opponent and then in one swift movement drew a knife, rolled, and let it fly silently toward the attacking demon. It struck at the same moment the sound of an FN Five-Seven shot rang out.

⚬⚬⚬

Drew squeezed the trigger and then followed immediately with four more shots. He didn't wait for the results but instead turned his aim on the bomber who was just entering the door. He had to get the bomber away from the people, no matter what had happened to the observer.

"Back away from the door!" he shouted. "Now!"

Drew nearly lost his nerve as a dark invader that looked part beast, part warrior screamed past him in the direction of the observer's car. He noticed that none of the light invaders even tried to stop it. Drew refocused on the terrorist.

The man turned, and Drew could see that he was just a teenage boy, a victim of radical extremist brainwashing. Sweat and fear covered his face.

"Your observer is dead. Back away from the door and lay down on the ground!" Drew shouted as he took a few slow steps toward the teen, his FN leveled at the terrorist's head. He shouted the command again, but this time in Arabic.

The boy let go of the door and slowly backed away. He began talking quickly in Arabic as tears streamed down his face.

"On the ground!" Drew shouted.

The teen complied.

"Don't move!"

Drew shouted orders to the people in the bistro to leave the restaurant through the back exit. He cleared the street and waited for the police and the FBI to arrive. When the SWAT team arrived, he briefed the captain and let their bomb squad take over.

Once the explosives were controlled and the terrorist was in custody, first-response teams arrived on the scene to treat dozens of wounded. Ambulances and fire trucks followed soon after, and of course, a half dozen news teams.

∽o∾

Once the bomb threat had been eliminated, Zurock disengaged, and he and his demons retreated.

One by one Validus's men came to him. Brumak looked to be in the worst shape. His left arm was bleeding badly where the droxan had torn chunks of flesh away. Persimus immediately began dressing the wound.

"This is bad, Validus," he said as he translated a bandage wrap from an EMT and quickly covered the wound, applying pressure to stop the bleeding.

Sason was the last to arrive, walking slowly. All of them were dealing with wounds, but when Validus saw Sason's cloak, he knew something much worse had happened.

"Commander," Sason winced. "I think you'll have to finish this without me."

Validus reached for him as he collapsed to his knees. He gently laid the wounded warrior on the ground and opened his cloak. Blood was everywhere.

"No, Sason," Validus pleaded. "Rake, get me water!"

"No, Commander. You and I both know this is over." Sason grimaced and lifted a hand. Validus grabbed it, his heart aching with remorse for not having been prepared for this day.

"It was an honor serving under your command, sir," Sason said.

Validus's hand slowly collapsed around the blue wisps of vapor that floated upward toward heaven. Sason had warned him about not having enough warriors to counter the threat, and he was the one who paid the price.

Validus's hand became a fist. This was what he hated most about command—the pain of loss because of his decisions. Every time it happened, he vowed it would never happen again. With deep sorrow, he lowered his head and remained still for a moment.

He fought the temptation to wallow in the agony of the moment, knowing his men needed him to rise above his selfish self-pity. He slowly stood, looking into the war-torn faces of his team. They all stood in the silence of respect for a fallen brother.

"This great loss will not be forgotten," Validus said. He looked at Brumak, his arm bright red with soaked gauze.

"I'll be fine, Commander. Tomorrow I will fight two droxans if need be."

Validus nodded. He turned and led them toward Carter and Carlyle.

"Men, as hard as this has been, this encounter is what we have been waiting for. As long as these two are together, there is great opportunity and great risk. Stay sharp. We may not be clear yet."

PROTECTING
THE ASSET

Before the news crews started filming, Drew found the lead FBI agent. "Agent Kalua, I need to get out of here before the news crews set up. I'll file my report and be available for any questions you have." Drew nodded toward the SUV taking off with the terrorist inside. "The CIA is going to want a turn with him once you're done."

"Sounds good, Agent Carter. And nice work," Kalua said. "A lot of people owe you their lives today. And that shot on the observer was one in a million. Gutsy."

Drew nodded his thanks, then turned and saw Sydney being treated for minor cuts on her legs from the glass shrapnel. He recovered most of her purse, which had been blown up against the wall near the table she'd hidden behind, then made his way toward her.

"She doing okay?" he asked the EMT.

She nodded. "She's in good shape. A lot better than most that were out here." The EMT picked up her bag and moved on.

Drew took a moment to look for Validus. The invader had gathered his men and was coming toward them. They looked bloody and battered. It had been a fierce battle for them, but Drew sensed a soberness that transcended the weariness of war. Someone was missing.

"Can you move, Syd? We need to get out of here." He offered her a hand.

Sydney took his hand and stood up. She looked determined, but as she rose, he felt her legs give out. He grabbed her around the waist and she held on.

"I'm okay . . . just a little dizzy."

"Take your time." Drew held her tight until he felt her strength return.

She looked up at him and nodded. "I'm good now."

When Drew turned to help Sydney to his car, a thin, dark-haired woman with penetrating brown eyes shoved a microphone in Drew's face. He had seen her before on one of Chicago's news programs. She was sharp, gutsy, and full of moxie. Her name was Sophia Bryant, and something about her caused people to believe her, no matter what their political affiliation. Drew remembered thinking that she would be working for FOX or CNN before long—she was that good. Her cameraman was filming just a few feet away.

"I understand you're the man who thwarted this terrorist bombing. Who are you, sir, and did you suspect a terrorist attack here today?"

Drew immediately turned his back to the camera.

"Please quit filming," he said with a side glance to Bryant. Of all the news crews, he wasn't surprised that she was not only first on the scene but had pinpointed exactly where to start the story.

"We just have a few questions for you. The people of Chicago need to know."

Drew held on to Sydney and tried to walk away, but Bryant and her cameraman would have none of it.

"Are you FBI?" Bryant asked. "Do you know of more attacks planned?"

Drew realized he had only one option. He turned and looked straight into her eyes, ignoring the camera.

"Miss Bryant, please don't film me or ask me questions." He pointed to the camera without breaking eye contact. "If you put my picture on your news station"—he paused, pouring as much honesty and warmth into his gaze as he could—"you will greatly jeopardize the security of this nation." He lowered his head slightly. "Please let me do what I've been trained to do—protect the people of Chicago. I respect you and your station. Please do the same for those of us who are putting our lives on the line for you."

Bryant's probing eyes softened, and she slowly dropped the mic. She made a cut motion to the cameraman, then looked at Sydney and Drew. "Okay, mystery man, I'm going to trust you."

Drew nodded. "Thank you. And I'm going to trust you."

Bryant flipped a business card out of her pocket and handed it to him. "You ever want to feed me a story that would, well, do the people good to hear, give me a call."

There was a gleam in her eye that caught Drew by surprise. He took the card and slipped it into his rear pocket. "Thanks."

Bryant nodded, then grabbed her cameraman and dove into getting coverage on the bombing.

Drew led Sydney to his car, which was parked a block and a half away. He was extremely aware of Validus and his force of warriors providing guard just a few feet away from them. Unlike their usual mode of operation, the invaders didn't even try to hide the fact that they were nearby.

Drew started driving, but he wasn't sure where to take Sydney. She was still stunned and in mild shock . . . silent.

"Where should I take you, Syd? Do you want to go back to your apartment?"

"No. I want to go wherever you're going."

Drew's plane back to Philadelphia left in two hours, but he wouldn't be on it. He drove back to his hotel and booked a room for one more night. He got a suite with a separate room so he could be near Sydney if she needed him.

Inside the room, Sydney sat on the couch. Four light invaders were nearby, two in the room and two outside. Drew guessed there were probably more on a perimeter watch. Their actions alone told him Sydney was key to whatever operation they were running. He had never seen such consistent attention before.

It was early evening, and the light coming through the window began to fade.

"I have to make a couple of phone calls, but I'll be right back," he said. "I promise you're going to be okay."

Sydney nodded.

Drew stepped out of the room and called headquarters. After quick elevation up the chain, it was determined that Reed would fly out to help Drew in the follow-up investigation. Drew cancelled his flight home and stepped back into the room. Sydney was still sitting on the couch, motionless.

Drew sat next to her, and she leaned into him. He wrapped an arm around her and held her for a long time, until she quit trembling. A few minutes later, her heavy breathing told him she was asleep.

He held her for half an hour more, then carried her to her bed. He eased her shoes off, covered her with a blanket, shut off the lights, and closed the door to her room most of the way so she wouldn't be disturbed by any noise he made.

When he turned around, Validus was still standing guard at the window, but the other invader was gone. Drew had never seen the mighty invader so concerned when there were no dark invaders in view.

Drew stared at the back of the hulking warrior. "Why did they attack today? Was this all because of Sydney?" he whispered. He knew the warrior's ears were more sensitive than his own.

Validus turned and stared at Drew. A long moment passed, but Drew didn't retreat. This invader had answers to his questions.

Finally, Validus walked over to Sydney's purse and reached inside. When he removed his hand, Drew saw that he had translated a tube of Sydney's lipstick. He removed the cap and let it fall, but it dissolved back into the purse before it hit the ground. Validus walked to the mirror in the room and began to write.

As the letters appeared, eerie chills flitted up and down Drew's spine. He knew that the message only existed in the invader realm, and that he was the only human who could read it.

They want to kill both of you.

Once Drew read the message, the letters dissolved to nothingness.

"A terrorist attack like that would take weeks to plan, and they knew she would be there. Why are they trying to kill her?" Drew whispered.

Validus hesitated, then wrote another message.

She has what you need.

"What do I need?" he whispered.

Validus didn't move. Evidently that question would go unanswered. *Why the mystery?* Drew wondered.

He turned away, disturbed and frustrated. Today was close. Sydney had almost died . . . again. Every time he was near her, tragedy struck. Whatever power she possessed that he needed, he couldn't take the chance that she would die first. He looked back at Validus.

"If I leave her forever, will they stop trying to kill her?"

The huge invader looked disgusted, almost angry. He dropped the lipstick tube, and it dissolved away.

Drew didn't need him to answer anyway. No matter what the light invaders wanted, Drew was not about to sacrifice Sydney for the sake of their mission or for his own life.

He glanced toward the bedroom where she was sleeping.

"Will you protect her?" he whispered, wondering if Validus was through with him.

The invader's fierce look softened slightly, and he offered one subtle nod; then he turned his back on Drew to stand guard at the window again.

In the morning, Drew ordered room service and brought breakfast to Sydney in bed—orange juice, scrambled eggs, sausage, fresh fruit, and yogurt.

Sydney yawned, sat up, and held her hand in front of her mouth. "Morning," she said shyly.

"Don't worry, my breath is just as bad. I'll keep my distance."

"Wow . . . I've never had this before," she said as Drew set the food across her lap.

"Come to think of it, neither have I."

Sydney smiled. "Some Saturday mornings I would serve my dad and mom breakfast in bed. I was so proud of my runny eggs and burnt toast." She laughed. "They raved about how delicious it was." She fixed her eyes on Drew. "Thank you."

"I only wish I'd cooked it myself, but you're probably glad I didn't."

He made two cups of coffee while Sydney ate. When she was done with her food, she came into the other room and sat on the couch next to Drew. He handed her a cup of steaming coffee, and she smiled her appreciation.

"I have a million questions to ask you," she said.

Drew looked down at the coffee cup in his hands, the steam swirling and disappearing into the air. Just like the essence of a dead invader.

"No doubt, but I won't be able to answer them, Syd. Being around me is dangerous." He looked into her eyes. "The less you know and the farther I am away from you, the safer you are."

Sydney seemed to know what was coming. "Drew, I've seen you do some amazing things . . . things normal people can't do. And if you really are seeing beings that no one else can see, then you are either seeing angels and demons or . . ." She paused.

Drew glared at her. "Or I'm crazy?"

She averted her gaze. "I didn't say that."

"But that's what you meant. Is that what you think I am, Sydney? Some nut job? Have you ever seriously considered the possibility that Ben and I might be right? That I've been telling the truth this whole time and that humanity is being manipulated?"

"By aliens?" Sydney snapped back. She made it sound as crazy as it seemed.

Drew started to stand up, but Sydney reached for his arm.

"Please don't go, Drew. It's just that this is all so bizarre. You're asking me to believe something that sounds crazy. You're asking a lot of me." Her voice trembled.

"Do you know how I knew where that detonator was?" Drew asked. "One of those invaders pointed to him, the same one who got me out of the FBI handcuffs so I could save you. It may be crazy, but it's true."

Drew felt his face flush with anger. He tried to calm down, but he was once again reminded that he was alone in this. If Sydney wouldn't believe him, no one would. He was alone, and he needed to operate alone. But as frustrated as he was with her, he still loved her. He looked at the mirror and was reminded of the message from Validus. The only way for her to be safe was for him to disappear out of her life.

Sydney slowly leaned over and rested her head on his shoulder. "Please don't leave me again, Drew."

He closed his eyes and calmed himself. Every time she was near him, he was amazed at the power she had over him. And this simple act of vulnerability didn't help. Her plea was almost more than he could bear.

"I'm not even supposed to be with you right now," he said quietly. "This impromptu trip to Chicago might be my undoing."

"But you saved hundreds of lives," Sydney said softly.

"Perhaps, but I broke protocol, and they'll be keeping a closer eye on me now than ever." He reached for her hand. "Syd, it's no coincidence that your life is in jeopardy whenever I'm near. You know that, don't you?"

She lifted her head and looked into his eyes.

"That's why I have to leave you . . . forever. I care too much about you to keep putting your life in danger."

Just then Validus materialized through the wall of the hotel room.

Sydney shook her head. "Drew, I *do* believe you. And I believe that God is drawing you to Him. These beings you call invaders . . . I wish you would open your eyes. There's a spiritual battle going on for your soul." She reached for his cheek. "Promise me one thing."

Drew shook his head, "I can't—"

She put her fingers over his lips. "If you care about me, you must promise me one thing."

How could he refuse her anything?

"Promise me that you will ask God to reveal Himself to you. Promise me that you will be willing to be convinced of the truth, no matter where it takes you. Promise me that you will read the Bible one more time with a heart to know the truth."

"Hey, hey, hey . . . that's three. You said one," he teased.

"It's only one really. A promise to get to know God."

Drew hesitated. It was contrary to everything he was feeling in his gut. He needed to find Benjamin again and blow this whole invader realm wide open.

"Isn't your job as an agent to discover the truth?" Her eyes began to fill. "Then why are you so resistant to discovering the truth about God? Are you that proud? You of all people, with the gifts and visions He has given you!"

Tears spilled down her cheeks, and her passionate plea rattled his heart.

"Hey," he said and lifted his hand to wipe her tears away. "Okay . . . I promise, Sydney. I promise."

She bit her lip and forced a smile through the tears. "And when you do, I don't care if it's thirty years from now, you find me and tell me. Okay?"

He nodded. "Okay. And now you have to promise me something."

Sydney wiped away the rest of her tears. Drew found the next few words the hardest he would ever speak in his life.

"You live your life, Syd. Where I'm going and what I have to do, no one in the world can follow. You deserve a life and a good one."

She turned away. "You hurt so much, Drew, I can hardly stand it."

He knew the hurt all too well. He was never so miserable and so happy as when he was with her.

She turned back. Drew lifted his hand to her cheek, and she leaned into it. "Promise?"

The tears spilled again, but she nodded.

Drew reached to grab a tissue for her and saw Validus staring at him. The warrior's grave expression was impossible to interpret. At least Drew had the word of the warrior that Sydney would be protected.

EXPOSING ALIENS

That was too close," Tren said.

Validus and his team were back in Philadelphia where they had a chance to debrief the last few days.

"Carter is too vulnerable as a CIA agent," Rake added.

"He's right, Commander," Crenshaw said. "The Fallen have too many opportunities and too much influence over the people the CIA is going after. One of these times we're going to be outmanned and too late. Then where will the world be?"

Jayt shook his head. "It's a shame, though. With time, Carter could make a significant impact on Apollyon's tactics to spread his destruction. Except for Messiah, since creation there's been no human with his capabilities in such a position to do good on the earth."

Validus considered the viewpoints of his warriors carefully.

"Rake and Crenshaw are right. Our primary mission is to keep Carter alive until he trusts in Messiah, regardless of the good he can do as an unsaved man. Carlyle is still our best option, since she has the most influence over him, but the momentum of their lives is moving apart, not toward each other." Validus looked around the table at his veteran warriors. "I'm open to suggestions. In spite of his vow to never see her again, we must get their lives to intersect."

There were a dozen ideas, and Validus considered them all, but none seemed viable. Tren and Persimus remained quiet, as they were always inclined. Validus would seek their council in private later.

When the debrief was over, Validus asked Persimus and Tren to stay behind. "Do either of you have anything to offer?"

Tren glanced toward Persimus, then back at Validus, his eyes seething with words unsaid.

"Speak freely, Tren," Validus said, crossing his arms.

"You have access to five hundred warriors, and you didn't call them in. We lost Sason because of it."

The guardian's words cut deep because they were true, and Validus had no rebuttal. His gaze went to the floor. "It was a mistake that I will live with for the rest of my life." He looked back up at Tren. "But don't think for a moment that the loss of Sason is the end of it. No matter how many warriors I call to the fight, we will lose men. Until Apollyon and his minions are cast into the lake of fire, we will fight and we will suffer loss. What happened in Chicago is something that will tear at me for a long time, but it won't stop me from ordering warriors into harm's way."

Tren glared back at Validus, but the edge of his anger was gone.

Validus turned to Persimus. "Do you have something to say to me?"

Persimus nodded. "It might take some time, but I think I have an idea. It's rather unorthodox, but it might get you what you want with Carter."

Validus tilted his head. "I'm all ears."

When Drew and Reed got back to Philadelphia, Drew was called into Sloan's office.

"What were you doing in Chicago, Carter?"

Drew hesitated. He had been working on an answer for days, but he couldn't come up with a good story, so he decided to tell the truth.

"I was checking up on an old girlfriend from college."

Sloan shook his head. "You expect me to believe that? And you just happened to be in the same place as a terrorist attack in one of the cities where you predicted it would happen?"

Drew stayed silent and looked guilty.

Sloan sighed. "Forget it, Carter. It's pretty hard for me to reprimand you because your actions saved a lot of lives. Besides, Langley wants you back on the investigation now. They want you to brief them on the investigation you presented."

Shortly after the attack in Chicago, Premier Jabbar of the IGA promised to work with the United States to eradicate terrorism, offering any support he could. Drew spent weeks following up the investigation of the suicide bombing. With the analysis of the intel he had conducted, coupled with additional information Premier Jabbar offered, the FBI was able to intercept and prevent two more attacks on US cities. Both the US intelligence community and Premier Jabbar were highly praised throughout the world for their successful partnership in stopping terrorism before it happened.

As was always the case after encountering Sydney, Drew was disquieted by her words, for they kept ringing in his mind. He didn't forget the promise he had made to her, but he did stuff it away for a while.

The whole encounter renewed his determination to find Ben. This time he would have to do it without her help.

He just hoped that his brainiac friend had finished the Light Accelerator by Stimulated Optical Kinetics project, or LASOK for short, and could prove to Sydney and the rest of the world that Drew was not crazy. Whatever missions he went on for the CIA paled in comparison to the one that would expose the aliens to the world. He needed Ben.

His search would be encumbered by the fact that he couldn't let anyone at the CIA know he was doing it. He would have to search on his own time and with his own resources, and it could take him months, even years to accomplish.

That was the plan, but what Drew didn't see coming was the attention he had won from his supervisors for his successful missions in Puerto Rico and Chicago. Within two months, Drew was being tagged for high-priority missions of every kind, and he excelled at them all. One of the consequences of such consuming responsibility was that his search for Ben did not transpire.

Drew and Reed worked well together, and occasionally they crossed paths with their previous Farm CTs, Riggs, Hadad, and Connor. On one mission, Drew teamed with Riggs and Hadad and came to highly respect their skills as CIA operatives in the field. Drew participated in two more missions with one of the Special Operations Group teams in Syria and in Iran. He could not deny the satisfaction he felt after a successful mission, knowing that he was serving his country well.

He noticed that Validus and most of his invaders did not seem to appreciate the added danger those missions brought. However, his team of seven performed like a squad of tactical superheroes, improving themselves with each mission, and two of the warriors, the large hulking warrior and the ninja-like warrior, seemed to thrive on it all.

Over the course of the next ten months, Drew and Reed became more than members of an operational team. Their friendship was forged in the fire of life-and-death situations. When lives were on the line, Drew didn't hold back on his abilities to eliminate threats, and Reed was astounded with each new skill that he witnessed.

"It's like you have radar that tells you what's going to happen before it happens," Reed said after one close call. "I swear you actually dodged that bullet." He looked Drew over for an entry wound. "When are you ever going to let me in on your secret?"

Drew looked at his friend and wondered once again: Could he?

"You just have to look for things that no one else sees."

Reed stared at Drew. "What kind of things? Are you saying you see things that no one else can see . . . things that aren't really there?"

Drew eyed Reed, not sure what he was implying but nervous that perhaps his actions might have given away what he was experiencing.

"Give it a rest, Reed. Everything's good, and we need to wrap up this mission."

Reed nodded, but he looked concerned.

A few days later, a car was waiting for Drew outside of his apartment building. As he approached, the driver rolled down his window and looked up at Drew.

It was Mr. Ross.

"Get in, Carter," Ross said, then rolled up his window and unlocked the doors.

Drew opened the passenger door and entered the vehicle. Ross began driving, and Drew wondered if there was a destination planned or if this was just a ride to talk.

"Well, you've certainly made a big splash your first two years in the agency," Ross said. "I thought I could pace you a little better by putting you out in Philadelphia, but I guess I was wrong."

"I don't follow, sir," Drew said, and he didn't.

"You've been doing a great job for us, Carter. Better than I'd hoped, actually."

"Thank you, sir. I'm glad you're not disappointed."

Ross looked over at him, and Drew knew there was something else coming.

"Tell me about your last Zapata mission."

"We successfully conducted our first exchange of weapons for drugs as directed. A micro GPS transmitter was placed in the butt of each weapon, and we are currently tracking them to the terrorist cells. From what I understand, our SOG teams are planning assault missions to take out the terrorists and recover the weapons before they are used against us, but you would know more about that than me. We're also following up on the lead that Zapata might be using his contacts in the US to smuggle terrorists in, but that's going to take some time to develop and investigate."

Was that what Ross was looking for?

"I'm interested more in what's not in the reports you submitted," Ross said.

Drew felt his pulse quicken. Wherever this was going, Drew didn't want to be there.

Ross waited.

"I'm not sure what you mean, sir."

Ross calmly pulled the car over to the curb in front of a three-story office complex. He put the car in park, then turned slightly in his seat so he could look Drew in the eye. Drew forced himself not to fidget. Ross was too smart, too discerning. Drew had learned that the first day he'd met him in the FBI interrogation room.

"When I put an agent in the field, regardless of how good he is, I have to know that he is psychologically and mentally able to handle the stress of life-and-death situations. We all deal with that stress differently, but I think you may be dealing with it in ways that are outside the scope of what our agency would deem as normal. Our reputation is on the line, Carter, especially in this day of terrorist attacks every time we turn around." Ross stopped and scrutinized Carter. "So tell me, Carter, are you seeing things that aren't there? Things that other agents can't see? Perhaps people that no one can see but you?"

Drew's world fell out from under him. This had to be from Reed. That scoundrel—that traitor! Why would he have reported such subjective opinions to his supervisors? But how did he know? Did Drew give away more than he realized as he was taking out enemies?

He didn't know how to respond.

"Is this from Reed, sir? He has no basis upon which to be concerned and certainly no basis upon which to make a report on me." Drew said, trying hard to keep his composure.

"You didn't answer my question, Carter. Are you seeing people that no one else can see?"

Drew considered lying, then justifying, but Ross would see through it all. He tried to form words to answer, but they would not come, and that in itself was an answer.

Ross just nodded. "Report to Dr. Whitton, suite 204." He looked at the office complex just a few steps to Drew's right. "I need a psychological evaluation performed, Agent Carter. I suggest you be forthright in answering any and all questions he asks of you."

Drew couldn't even look at Ross. There was no way he would understand, no way he would believe what was at stake. His story sounded so absurd that if he tried, Ross would instead drive him straight to an asylum.

He slowly opened the door and stepped out. Ross didn't wait to see if he would go in or not; the GPS tracker in Drew's body would tell him that.

Drew considered running, but that led to prison bars. He considered lying, but that led to prison bars. He considered telling the truth, but that led to an asylum.

He was trapped, and meanwhile, the dark invaders continued to wreak havoc on the ignorant species called man.

THE ILLUSION OF
THE SUBCONSCIOUS

When Drew opened the door to suite 204, the secretary looked up from her work. "You can go right in, Mr. Carter."

Drew saw the open door to his right. The placard read Dr. Whitton. Drew entered the room, sickened by the memories of Dr. Fisher, his sweeping voice thick with insinuation. Drew's senses ramped to full alert.

Why had he said anything to Reed? These people had no idea what was at stake. Any hope he'd had of using his position within the CIA to expose the invaders was now gone forever. What a fool he had been.

Drew scanned the room and stopped just a few feet inside the door. Something wasn't right.

"Welcome, Mr. Carter." A man dressed in slacks and a polo shirt stepped out from behind a large desk and came toward Drew. Silver hair, handsome face, fit body—the guy looked like he was meeting Drew for a tee time at the Links. And he acted like it too. A warm smile that wasn't overdone put Drew at ease.

"Dr. Whitton?" Drew asked, certain he was in the wrong place. This office looked too normal. No lounge chair, no framed credentials, and no bookshelves with psychoanalysis texts.

"Actually, Whitton will do. I've been in the CIA too long to use anything but last names." He held out his hand, and Drew automatically lifted his to meet it. His grip was firm. Whitton reached behind Drew and closed the door. "Can I get you something to drink?" he asked as he walked toward a small fridge in the corner. "I've got sodas and water."

"Ah, no thanks," Drew replied, even though he needed some water. He didn't want the doctor thinking he already had him at an advantage.

Whitton pulled out two chilled bottles of water and returned to his desk.

He set one on the side nearest a chair that was meant for Drew. "It's there if you want it." He circled back behind his desk and sat down. "Please sit down, Carter."

Drew sat down and glanced at the condensation forming on the transparent plastic bottle of water. Whitton cracked open his bottle and took a long draw until one third of the bottle was gone. He replaced the cap and took a deep breath.

"Okay, Carter, I know you think this is a bunch of baloney, and quite frankly, I might agree with you, but I have a job to do, and I'd appreciate it if we could make this as easy as possible for both of us. You've been sent to me, and I'm supposed to determine your level of mental and emotional stability for the sake of the CIA's interests." Whitton leaned back in his chair and put his hands across the back of his head. "Don't give me any lies, and I won't give you any either. Both of us serve our country, and we both have an obligation to figure out what's going on. The only way that's going to happen is for us to be completely honest with each other." He looked right into Drew's eyes. "You good with that?"

Drew was certainly caught off guard. Whitton's tone and mannerisms reminded Drew a little of Jake. He wondered if that was intentional and then dismissed the notion. The CIA was good but not that good. Drew wondered if he really could be completely honest with this guy, but then, what did he have to lose? Reed evidently already knew he was seeing things, and he'd told who knew how many others in his chain of command. It had obviously reached Mr. Ross.

Drew slowly nodded. "Sure."

Whitton looked a bit skeptical. "I'm going to tell you right now that one of the reasons I work for the CIA as a psychologist is because I don't need a lie detector to know if someone's telling the whole truth. It's a gift I have, just like you have the gift of analyzing a room and determining threats within seconds of entering. The CIA is very good at finding the best talent the nation has to offer. I'm not at Langley because I'm now a consultant Mr. Ross uses for 'special cases,' like yourself."

Drew believed Whitton. However, he decided he wasn't going to volunteer the truth. Whitton would have to ask for it.

Whitton stared at Drew in silence for a minute, and Drew took the

opportunity to reach for the water bottle. He downed half of it and then spun
the cap back on. He set the bottle back on the table and looked at Whitton.

Whitton was looking up at the ceiling. "I'm told you've been seeing things.
Are they people? Soldiers? Agents?"

Drew just stared at his water for a moment as he thought about Validus;
then he slowly nodded. "Soldiers of some kind, I guess." He hated hearing his
own voice say it to someone who would never believe him. He wanted to jump
up, run out of the office, and disappear, but Ross had made sure that was an
impossibility.

"Why are they here?"

That was a strange question. Drew looked up at Whitton. He thought about
it and realized that the most peaceful way through this was to tell the truth.

"I don't know."

"Do you think they're an invasion force, or are they simply some sort of
cloaked agents from the government?"

Drew shook his head. "I thought you said no baloney. You're talking like
you believe that what I'm seeing is real, and I know you don't."

Whitton slowly dropped his gaze from the ceiling to Drew's eyes. "Carter,
it doesn't matter whether I believe it or not. You believe it, and the only way to
find out what's really happening to you is for you to talk to me like I believe it.
So again, is this an invasion force or cloaked government agents?"

This was as hard as Drew thought it was going to be. He knew that the
moment he opened his mouth he would sound insane and further incriminate
himself. "I don't know."

"I don't believe you," Whitton said. "I think you do know, but if you're not
ready, fine. Tell me what they look like."

"Large and fast. The dark ones seem desperate to destroy us, and the light
ones seem . . . well, better than us."

Whitton thought for a moment. "So it's us and them. They aren't human?"

Drew fidgeted. "I don't know. I guess I would probably say no, although
it's possible. They are close to seven feet tall. One group seems intent on destroying us—mankind. The other seems intent on helping us survive. It's bizarre, I know. I—"

Whitton held up his hand. "Carter, let's not worry about trying to understand it. Just give me more details and help me see the whole puzzle."

Oddly, Whitton's attitude was refreshing. Drew took a breath and began to share more and more details. Never had he been able to share so completely with someone other than Ben, and that was a long time ago.

The more he talked, the better he felt, and Whitton gave no impression of analyzing or judging him. At times he seemed mesmerized by the stories Drew told. His questions were those of genuine curiosity. At one point Drew wondered if perhaps he had been so convincing that Whitton might actually believe him.

After two hours, Whitton stopped Drew, and he was quietly disappointed. It felt so good to get this out of his system. The burden had been great . . . much greater than he had even realized.

"Carter, your visions are truly fascinating. Tonight I don't want you to rehash anything or wonder if you should say more tomorrow. I know how good it feels to get a burden off your chest, and you've been carrying a lot. I want you to just enjoy the lifting of the weight. Got it?" He stuck out his hand.

Drew shook his hand and nodded.

"Good. For the time being, do not report to your office. Be back here at two tomorrow. I'm anxious to hear how you evaded one of them in the national park."

Drew didn't hear a hint of condescension in his tone. He really wanted to hear it.

Drew walked away fairly confused. Whatever technique Whitton had used on him had worked perfectly. He acknowledged that the man was extremely good, but it didn't diminish how good Drew felt just being able to talk about it.

The strangest part of all that he hadn't seen an invader, either light or dark, since Ross had shown up outside his apartment that morning and it was revealed that the CIA knew about his ability to see them. Were they worried they might be discovered? Were they plotting to take him out? Would the light invaders be upset and refuse to help him, or worse yet, have a hand in silencing him? These questions began to rob Drew of the "lifting of the burden" Whitton had talked about. He guessed that the doctor hadn't figured out how to handle those kind of thoughts.

The next day, Drew met with Whitton again, and the doctor was able to coax him into telling more of his story. As each chapter of Drew's life unfolded, Whitton's questions became more detailed and more intelligent. He asked about the invaders' weapons. What could and couldn't be translated? What motivated them? How were they able to influence people? When Drew shared about the three times the light invader named Validus had actually translated into the physical realm, Whitton was on the edge of his seat, soaking up every detail and asking a dozen questions about the incidents.

The sessions went on for over two weeks until at last Drew had shared it all in excruciating detail. Well, almost all. He had been able to avoid revealing how he'd raised money for the equipment that he and Ben purchased to re-create the LASOK, explaining that they only earned enough money to purchase substandard equipment. Drew knew that if he revealed the Chicago Mercantile Exchange venture, the CIA would be able to track the money and then find Ben. And if the CIA found Ben, so would the dark invaders. It was his last and only secret—a secret to keep Ben alive.

One day into the third week of his sessions, Drew sat down as Whitton opened a file on his desk. Drew took a deep breath. *Great,* he thought. *Here comes the psychoanalysis. Time to quit playing friend, Dr. Whitton.*

Whitton soberly turned the pages, and Drew waited in silence until Whitton finally looked up from the file.

"Your father was an American hero, Carter."

Drew felt like he'd been smacked. He hung his head as memories of his dad came rushing into his mind unsolicited and unwanted. Not now.

"Yeah, he was." It was all he could say or wanted to say.

"What was he like?"

Drew lifted his eyes and pushed the tears and the emotions down with fierce resolve. He didn't want to speak, knowing his voice would betray him. "Why are we doing this, Whitton?"

Whitton's countenance eased, expressing genuine sympathy and then sorrow. "My dad left home when I was eight. It took me thirty years before I could get to a place where I felt I could forgive him . . . if he ever asked for it. My mom"—Whitton shook his head—"My mom was my hero. I guess I always wondered what it would have been like with a dad as a hero too."

Whitton's eyes glazed over, and he stared at nothing for a few seconds, then snapped his gaze back to Drew. He took a breath. "And I need to know everything I can about you in order to make my report." He shot Drew a crooked smile.

Drew nodded. He had to admit it, Whitton was honest.

"I can't imagine any dad better than mine," Drew said. "He loved this country, he loved his wife, and he loved his son. And he died—" Drew's eyes immediately threatened tears, and his voice trembled. He swallowed hard and straightened his shoulders. "And he died fighting for our freedom and for the freedom of those whose names he didn't even know."

Whitton put a reverent hand on top of the file, which Drew realized must be his father's. "I'm sorry, Carter. Great men sacrifice greatly. What happened in the years after his death? How did your mom get on?"

Drew began to share his life story, beginning from the sorrowful day of his father's funeral. Over the course of the next few days, Drew unloaded his life story up to the day of the lab accident at Drayle University.

When it was over, Drew looked at Whitton, and his eyes were difficult to read. The CIA had indeed found a very talented man, because Drew felt exposed and unarmed. Deep down, though, he didn't regret it. At least he had finally gotten to say it, and not once did an invader, either light or dark, appear during Drew's sessions. It was quite peculiar, to say the least.

Whitton stood up and walked from behind his desk to stand next to Drew. He leaned against the desk, crossed his arms, and closed his eyes for a moment. When he opened them again, he looked at Drew.

"Carter, you are one unusual man, and I must say that I have *never* heard a story quite like yours. It's my job to analyze, report, and recommend. That's it. The CIA isn't in the business of therapy or rehabilitation."

Drew felt his chest caving inward. Something was crushing his soul.

Whitton's gaze turned serious. "Do you know who Mr. Ross is? Do you know how powerful a man he is?"

Drew shook his head. "I guess I don't."

Whitton smiled. It was the first subtly condescending action Drew had seen from him.

"Let's just say that these sessions we've had have been classified at the highest level. You and I are not to speak of them to anyone . . . ever. And furthermore, Mr. Ross has instructed me to help you, if possible."

Drew's brows furrowed. "Help me?"

"Yes, help you. But I'm not sure that's possible." Whitton stared at Drew as if trying to decide whether to take on the challenge.

Drew was getting uncomfortable. "I don't understand. What do you mean?"

"You're a smart man, Carter. I think you know what the probable outcome of all this is. If there were a way you could still serve your country and honor the service of your father, would you be open to considering it?"

"Of course, but I'm still not following."

Whitton walked over to the side of the room and grabbed a chair. He carried it back to Drew and sat down so he could face him eye to eye.

"Carter, you have one chance at getting this right, and it all depends on how you respond to what I'm about to say. All I'm asking is that you hear this out and give it careful consideration."

Drew was intimidated, excited, and apprehensive all at the same time. He had no idea what Whitton was about to say, but if it could keep him in the game, searching for the answer to the invaders, he would endure anything Whitton had to offer.

"I'm good. Let's go."

Whitton pursed his lips and nodded. "Carter, you have experienced one major tragedy after another. A father dying, a grandmother dying, football scholarships and hopes crushed, and perhaps worst of all, a friend dying in your lap due your lapse in judgment and focus. Add to that a lab accident that left you temporarily blind and a friend expelled from the university. Every human being, and I mean *every* one, has a limit to how much emotional pain they can handle."

Drew knew what was coming. He wanted to run, but his legs would not obey. He was breathing hard, huffing with each breath. His world was crumbling. He wanted to scream against the life he was condemned to live. *Why . . . why me?*

The moment froze, and he realized that Whitton had stopped talking. He looked at Drew in pity. As the realization of his fate drifted into Drew's mind, his body felt twice its weight. He didn't run because he couldn't run. He was as serious a liability to the CIA as a mole. They would never let him leave, let alone disappear. He would be watched forever.

It was all over. The invaders had won. Drew shook his head, anger slowly replacing his despondency. Protest rose within him, but Whitton preempted it.

"If you can't accept this, Carter, it's over. The first step in overcoming any serious problem is acknowledging that there is a problem. I don't expect you to get there in a day, but I do expect you to start the journey. Ross is bending every rule in the book for you. How far are you willing to bend for him?"

That was when he came. Validus stepped through the wall and into Whitton's office. The invader was fierce . . . angry.

Whitton followed Drew's gaze. "Do you see one? Right now?"

Validus looked at Whitton and then back at Drew. Drew didn't dare speak or move. Whitton stood up from his chair and walked toward the place Drew was looking, toward Validus, until he passed right through him. He put his hands on his hips as Validus frowned.

"Drew, your invader is angry, isn't he?"

Drew nearly fell out of his chair. Who was this guy? How did he know?

"He's angry, Drew, because your subconscious is being threatened by me. That's where he lives. It's where all of them live. This is how you've been able to cope with all the tragedy, the guilt, and the pain."

Drew's mouth opened, but he could form no words. Validus looked as if he were going to kill Whitton. Drew considered warning him, but . . . but what if Whitton was right?

Validus gave Whitton one last piercing gaze and vanished through the wall. Whitton came and sat in front of Drew again. He put a hand on Drew's knee.

"Think this through, Drew. Everyone has a limit. When Joey Houk died, you didn't know it, but your subconscious began looking for some way to help you deal with the pain, guilt, and remorse. It's a defense mechanism that all of us have. And when Berg came along with a fascination for alien life, your subconscious grabbed hold, waiting for the opportunity to give you an escape route from the reality of pain you'd been dealing with. That lab accident, your temporary blindness, Berg's expulsion from school—all of it was the catalyst to finally let your subconscious take over."

Drew listened and tried to reject it, but it made so much sense. He hated the loss in his life. He hated what it had cost him. Maybe it had affected him more than he realized.

"Think about it, Drew. Your subconscious has constructed the absolutely perfect escape for your conscious, and all it took was a willing, quirky friend and a blurry picture. Has anyone other than you ever seen one of these invaders?"

"Of course not; it would take a functioning LASOK or—"

Whitton cut him off. "A device that conveniently doesn't work and never will because Berg has convinced himself it's true too. Or it would take eyes like yours that no one else will ever be able to see through. Don't you see, Drew? It's a perfect setup."

Drew couldn't deny it. The LASOK seemed ever elusive. Everyone in school thought Berg was crazy, and so did Sydney, in the end.

"Even when your invader translated into our existence, did anyone see him? Don't you think it's more than coincidental that every time another person might see him, he would disappear?"

Drew sat stunned, trying to process Whitton's rational and logical words.

"Your subconscious will always orchestrate the scenario so that your invaders' existence is never revealed to anyone else. It must keep the charade going in order to protect you. Right now it's screaming against me and the words I'm speaking because this is the first time your subconscious has ever faced such exposure."

Whitton gave Drew a few seconds to process.

"There is a time when our subconscious reveals its alarming creativity and intelligence in a way that isn't damaging—in our dreams. Have you ever had a dream where other people in your dream say things or do things that surprise you? Perhaps do things that you would have never thought to do?"

Drew realized it was true. And honestly those dreams rather disturbed him.

"But your mind created those characters and their actions and their words, right? Those are created by our subconscious and can be so unique that our conscious mind is truly surprised. Are you following?"

Drew slowly nodded.

"Drew what if you were stuck in a dream and your subconscious was free to generate and create at will, surprising even your conscious mind?"

Drew began to shut down. His mind replayed all the encounters he had had with the invaders, looking for an exception to what Whitton was saying but finding none. Then he realized that everything Whitton was saying was true.

"You are stuck, not in a dream but in an altered state of mind that exists right on the fringe between your conscious and subconscious mind. And it is all in order to give you respite from dealing with the pain of severe loss."

Drew had no response. He was undone. Breached. Conquered. "I . . . I . . ."

Whitton seemed to know the depth of his distress. "Before I came to work for the CIA, I counseled hundreds of vets with posttraumatic stress disorder. Many men and women who served our country with courage and honor deal with it. You're not alone in this, Drew. The onset of PTSD can be delayed for months and even years after an event. Even before you became a CIA agent, your symptoms were classic. Always on guard for danger, overwhelming guilt, self-destructive behavior—in your case, canvassing the ghettos for action—trouble sleeping; the list goes on. Most of my patients experience distressing unwanted memories, flashbacks, or severe reactions to something that might remind them of the event. For you, it took a more advanced form." Whitton's face turned darkly sober. "You are suffering from schizophrenia."

Drew cringed. No. He would not accept it. There was too much evidence, too much to prove it was all real.

He shook his head. "How come I can react faster, see better, hear better?" he shot back at Whitton. "You can't explain that!"

Whitton straightened and lifted his chin. "The mind is still a mystery to us, Drew. We all know that most humans only use a small portion of their brain. We are all walking around with amazing untapped potential." He leaned forward and looked at Drew as if he were evaluating the results of an experiment. "Your schizophrenia has allowed you to tap into levels of your brain that most people will never use. It's put your subconscious into overdrive. Your extra abilities are unique, Drew, but not unprecedented. Remarkably, you have been able to harness the side effects of your schizophrenia to become a very efficient and productive agent for the United States government. It's why Mr. Ross hasn't given up on you. It's why I'm still talking to you and you're not on a one-way trip to a psychiatric hospital."

"But there are times when the invaders warn me of danger before there are any signs of it . . . before anyone else can see it," Drew protested.

"Your increased cognitive abilities are able to pick up clues, like a modern-day Sherlock Holmes, and predict dangerous situations developing. Then your subconscious fills in with invaders to add to the effect," Whitton explained.

Drew dropped his head into his hands. Was it possible? Had he gone insane?

Whitton put his hand on Drew's shoulder, but Drew didn't look up. "Drew, you have all the symptoms of schizophrenia. Thoughts of imminent danger, hearing voices, seeing people that no one else can hear or see. Surely you must have wondered along the way?"

Drew hated to admit it, but Whitton was right. He had often wondered if any of what he was seeing was real. But then something would happen, and he would be thrust right back into the dream, this blasted inescapable dream. Drew dropped his hands and stared at Whitton, grasping for some shred of hope that this wasn't all a wild fabrication of his broken mind.

"But what about the dark invader slashing through the tire on the church van? How do you explain that?"

Whitton nodded as if to agree with him. "Have you ever dreamed you were drowning only to wake and find that you were facedown in your pillow? Or that a police siren was sounding only to discover your alarm clock was going off? The subconscious is very powerful. It has the ability to shut down sensory input, craft a believable sequence of action, turn back the senses and chronologically rearrange events to make a seamless, believable story. The tire was a broken piece of glass or a popped valve stem. Your subconscious coincided the swipe of a dark invader's sword exactly when it needed to, possibly delaying your conscious mind's ability to hear the sound until it was time. Our subconscious can be a master time-line editor, and it does it all for your protection. For most people, this all happens while they sleep, but for you, it's happening while you're awake. But the results are the same: vivid, detailed visions and memories."

Drew was reeling. Whitton had a logical and plausible answer for everything Drew had experienced.

"There's a reason you didn't tell Sydney Carlyle about the invaders."

Drew looked at Whitton. He knew his own reasons, but he was afraid Whitton was about to dismantle those too, so he just waited.

"Revealing the invaders to Sydney would threaten everything your subconscious was trying to do. And that's exactly what happened, isn't it? She didn't believe you, and in order to keep the facade alive, you retreated from her. Your subconscious forced you to go away."

Whitton paused for a few seconds, then seemed to look right into Drew's heart with his sympathetic eyes. "You love Sydney, don't you?" He didn't wait for a response. "When you went to save her in the gang's hideout, your subconscious turned her into a hero. It's often what we do in our dreams with people we love. Rather than turn against her, which your subconscious knew was impossible because of your deep feelings for her, you turned her into an agent with great power. Your subconscious wove her into the story so you could still love her and not reject her. Although you love her, she's a threat to exposing the plots of your subconscious. It will never allow you to end up with her in spite of your love for her."

Drew turned his head away and stared at a painting on the far wall. He wanted to disappear, dissolve away just like his fabricated invaders. This was too embarrassing to deal with. His whole life he had imagined himself to be mentally strong. Now . . . now . . .

He turned back to Whitton and lowered his gaze to his trembling hands. "What do I do?" His voice was weak and muffled, but it was a sign that he was beginning to accept or at least consider Whitton's words.

"For now, nothing. You have a lot to process, and you've taken the first and most important step. You're acknowledging your condition. Many people with schizophrenia lead productive, normal lives."

Drew sat numb and dazed. The fabric of his life had been unraveled in an hour.

"Rest and think about all this, Drew. I can help you, now that you recognize it and want it."

The next day, Drew was afraid to go back, but he needed to know, no matter what it meant. He hated lies, especially those that people told themselves. It seemed as though he were guilty of the worst of it.

The first half of the session with Whitton was more logical and rational explanations of every situation that Drew could throw at him. The second half of the session, Drew was silent, slowly accepting the fact that he was schizophrenic. It was a hard pill to swallow.

"Why did this happen to me, Whitton?" Drew asked at the end of the session. "Why schizophrenia?"

"One percent of the population deals with some degree of schizophrenia. Often it follows family lines but not always, as in your case. I believe you experienced its onset because of repressed grief in your life. In all that you've told me, it doesn't sound like you ever let yourself properly grieve your losses. Your father's death, your grandmother's death, the loss of your dreams to play college football, Joey Houk's death—you never really grieved, and it may be because you needed to be strong for your mother." Whitton's gaze fell to the floor. "Believe me, Drew, I know what that's like."

Drew rubbed his eyes. All this time he thought he was some hero for the downtrodden, helping the weak, but in reality he was selfishly insane and trying to cope with his own mental weakness. It was too much.

"I'm going to help you, Carter. The most courageous thing you can do is face it and conquer it."

"Conquer it? What does that mean? I can make this go away?" Drew grasped this sliver of hope. All along he had wanted to go back to a normal life where invaders didn't exist—the life that most other people lived.

Whitton held up his hand. "Let me rephrase, Drew. Your schizophrenia is extremely defined and entwined with both your conscious and your subconscious. Most people with this condition learn how to rationally cope so they can live a somewhat normal life."

"How long does it last?" Drew asked.

"For most, their entire lives."

Drew's shoulders slumped. He shook his head.

"But now that you know it and are willing to deal with it, we can give you techniques so that it doesn't control you but rather you control it. That's what I meant by 'conquer.' In spite of how you are feeling right now, you're a tough, resilient agent. I've read your file. Are you willing?"

What choice did he have? He couldn't run, not from himself. Whitton seemed his only hope.

"Yeah." Drew nodded. "Help me, Whitton."

Over the next two months, Dr. Whitton treated Drew and began to reshape his thought processes, equipping him with coping techniques to deal with his schizophrenia.

There were times when invaders came or appeared to influence circumstances, but Drew recognized them for what they were and ignored them. Validus appeared twice. Drew found him the most difficult to deal with because he seemed so real and personal. Drew marveled at the power of his subconscious. Validus looked disappointed, almost ashamed that Drew had given in to Dr. Whitton's evaluation. Drew did his best to ignore Validus, but it was difficult. At least if he closed his eyes, everything went away, unlike many schizophrenics who dealt with constant voices.

At the end of eight weeks of therapy, Drew stood at the door, ready to leave Whitton's office.

Whitton's gentle smile was notably absent. "You've done well, Drew. I've submitted my final report to Mr. Ross. For the record, you are classified as severe posttraumatic stress disorder."

Drew lowered his head. In spite of the gift of not being labeled schizophrenic, he knew it was over. "Surely the CIA is done with me."

He looked at Whitton and read the answer in his eyes.

"I'm not sure, Carter. That's not for me to decide. I just know that you are going to do okay if you keep your wits about you. You're strong and you are able."

"So what now? Where do I go? What do I do?" Drew asked.

Whitton motioned for Drew to follow him to the window. He pulled back the curtain so they could see the street from his second-story office. A black car waited at the curb.

"I don't know, Carter, but I have a feeling you'll find some answers there."

Drew took a deep breath. He turned to Whitton and stuck out his hand. "Thanks for seeing me through this. I would have never made it without you."

Whitton gave him a firm grip. "You're a good man, Carter, and this world needs good men. Be careful out there."

Drew flashed a humble grin as Whitton reached up and squeezed Drew's shoulder. Then for a brief few seconds, his imaginative mighty warrior, Validus, appeared behind Whitton, eyes burning with anger.

Drew blinked hard, suppressing the flush of adrenalin that hit his veins.

When he opened his eyes, all was normal again, and Whitton's genuine smile reassured him that all was right with the world.

Drew exited the building and looked at the black car with darkened windows. The rear door opened, and he hesitated. How willing would the CIA be to allow a schizophrenic with secrets and tradecraft skill to walk free? Would prison be enough? Were the secrets and reputation of the CIA worth the life of one man?

Drew quelled rising thoughts of paranoia. Perhaps it was just his final debriefing out of the CIA and into civilian life. That was what he hoped for.

He pulled his leather gloves on a little tighter and then stepped into the car, sat down, and closed the door.

15

OUTCAST

A man sat beside Drew, staring out the opposite window. The car began moving, and the vibrant images of the world outside turned dark, gray, and cold.

"Carter, you are psychologically unfit for duty in the CIA or any other government agency."

Drew recognized the voice immediately. Ross turned and looked at Drew.

"Your dismissal as a CIA agent is effective immediately. Having recruited you, I felt it was only proper for me to personally tell you."

Although Drew knew it was coming, the impact on his gut was no less diminished. Hearing Ross state the sentence with such callousness crushed his soul. Drew looked out the window. He let the images wash by like an old silent movie. He felt numb, a spectator of some cinematic tragedy.

He frowned as one of his imaginary dark invaders looked up and straight into his eyes as he tormented a young teen girl walking down the street. Drew saw the emotional pain on the girl's face and knew that his subconscious had conjured up an invader to justify what he saw. Drew stared. The scene came and went like a dramatic moment in a slow motion sequence. Why him? Why crazy?

Drew turned and looked at Ross's stone face. "Are you taking me to prison, Mr. Ross?" he asked, emotionless.

Ross's glaring disappointment was hard to bear. "You've served our country well, even if only for a short time. That's worth something. No, I'm not taking you to prison. Your training, your missions, your identity are all classified. You are not to divulge any information in regard to your time in the CIA." His countenance eased slightly. "I recommend continued treatment. Your transition back to civilian life will be challenging without it."

Drew turned back to look out the window. What Ross was offering was a gift, but it still hurt. He was relieved and saddened at the same time.

They were passing a park filled with trees, benches, and walkways. The car pulled up to the curb and stopped.

Drew felt frozen, unable to leave the car. In the CIA he felt like he was making a difference, that his abilities were being utilized for something good. Now it was gone. Once he stepped back into the world as a civilian, that would be over forever. He looked back at Ross once more.

Then a sobering reality hit him. Ross was letting him go? It seemed unlikely. No, it seemed impossible. They would never let a crazy man with knowledge of the inner workings of the clandestine agencies free into the world. Fear began to well up inside him.

"Take a walk with me, Carter," Ross said and reached for his door handle.

In silence, Ross and Drew walked along an abandoned walkway into the trees. When they approached a bench, Ross motioned to it and Drew sat down. Was a gunman with a silencer waiting behind him? Drew wasn't sure of anything anymore.

"You're a bit of a dilemma for me, Agent Carter."

Agent? What?

"You made it through our psych evaluation at the Farm, and we turned you into a weapon. I can't let a weapon we've created walk around in society with the potential of going rogue on our citizens. No telling who you could pick as an enemy. You're an asset with the potential of becoming a serious liability. And your skills . . . well, they are second to none. So I find myself in a serious dilemma."

Now Ross was telling the truth. This was it. Drew fought the urgency to run, but how could he run from Ross, a man who had been tracking him for months before he even knew it?

Drew waited.

Ross shook his head. "You are the most normal crazy man I've ever come across. But the truth is, I don't care what kind of demons you have inside that head of yours, you're the best agent I've ever seen. That's why I'm going to make you a deal."

Drew lifted his gaze to meet Ross's. "What was all the baloney you said in the car? What's really going on, Ross?" He couldn't help but do a quick 360 scan.

"Relax, Carter. You're safe. Cars have ears. That was for show."

Drew didn't relax. "What kind of a deal?"

Ross hesitated, eyes narrow and serious. "There are certain missions that are too sensitive in nature even for the CIA to handle. Certain situations that require an extra measure of skill."

"You want me to operate under nonofficial cover. A NOC," Drew finished.

Ross's silence was answer enough.

"And if I refuse?"

Ross's brows furrowed. "Carter, don't force me to say things I don't want to say. I'm trying to help you here, and I'm bending every rule in the book to do so. If it weren't for me, you would be serving time in the pen for a school shooting and for assaulting two federal agents."

"What country?" Drew asked. He was imagining Afghanistan, Iraq, Iran, Venezuela. There were literally hundreds of hotspots throughout the world that the CIA could expend him on. As Drew thought about it, it made perfect sense. Ross would have him out of the country, and the CIA would find it easy to disavow any involvement should he get caught.

"You won't be overseas. You'll serve here in the US."

Drew looked sideways at Ross. "Isn't that rather . . . unconventional, even for the CIA?"

Ross didn't reply. Something felt fishy.

"I will not subvert my oath to defend my country, even if I'm not officially enlisted as an agent," Drew said firmly.

"Serving your country is what this is all about, you have my word. Any missions you are called to will come directly from me."

Drew didn't trust Ross, but what could he do? He felt like a pawn being manipulated by a chess master.

"Within the US, the CIA's mission is to collect foreign intelligence and to run technical operations against enemy threats."

"Why do you need a NOC within the US to accomplish that mission?"

Ross looked at Drew as if waiting for him to discover the answer . . . and he did.

"I see," Drew said. The brilliant sunshine, the smell of freshly cut grass, and a chilly fall breeze under other circumstances would have delighted Drew. Not now, not today. "And I'm the perfect cover, aren't I? A rogue spy with a history of schizophrenia. Tell me, Mr. Ross, is my role as a NOC CIA-sanctioned?" Drew looked straight into his eyes. "Or am I outside of even that nether bubble?"

Ross turned slightly so he could face Drew straight on. "I will be your only contact. No one in the CIA or any other government agency will know about you. As unorthodox as that may sound, even for the CIA, the missions I give will be part of an operation critical to the security of our nation. Trust is hard to come by in our business, but you're going to have to trust me. From this day forward, you will have no contact with any other agent in the CIA."

Validus appeared and came to stand right behind Ross. Drew didn't want to look at him, but he couldn't help it. The massive warrior was glaring at Ross, but Drew saw a nearly imperceptible nod. If he didn't trust Ross, could he trust his subconscious?

Drew leaned back against the park bench. "Okay. When I'm not on mission, what's my cover?"

"Anything you want it to be, as long as it looks normal to the populace."

"What about equipment, tech?" Drew asked.

Ross looked uneasy. "There can be no traces, not a single one. If you're caught with CIA tech, an investigation will point straight back to me."

"Mission funding?" Drew asked.

Ross reached into his pocket and gave him an envelope. Drew felt a wad of cash. If they were hundreds, he calculated it to be ten thousand dollars.

"This is it," Ross said. "Beyond this, you have to find your own funding. Just remember the prison cell you *won't* be living in."

The deal was getting worse by the moment. How could he fund any reasonable operation himself?

"What will my missions be?"

"The less you know now, the better. Just do the job we've trained you to do." A runner and her dog were approaching, so Ross conjured up some fake dialogue. "How's work, Josh? Are they keeping you busy at the firm?"

Drew responded, and after the woman disappeared, Ross reached into his pocket and withdrew a black box shaped a bit like a Taser. "Take off your coat."

Drew obliged. Ross set two exposed electrodes just behind his left shoulder, near his armpit, and pressed a button. The sensation stung and burned at the same time. Drew rubbed his shoulder to ease the pain.

"I've disabled your tracker. You're clean now."

"How will you contact me?"

Ross handed Carter a USB drive. "I've devised a code using hundreds of innocuous websites to transmit messages. Memorize the code and destroy the drive." He stood up and took a deep breath, then looked down at Drew. "Sometimes circumstances force our actions. I don't really have a choice, and neither do you. Show me you can be trusted, Carter, and perhaps the future can be different."

He turned to walk back to the waiting black car.

"Hey, Ross."

Ross turned and looked back at Drew.

"Since I'm unsupported, I'll need a job. Managing missions with a job is going to be difficult."

Ross shrugged. "Work it out, Carter. No one can know—no one! I'll be in touch."

Drew watched Ross return to the car and drive away. Guys like Ross with that kind of power were scary. Governments rose and fell on the shoulders of such men.

HOMEWARD BOUND

Validus, Tren, and Persimus watched Drew sitting on the park bench from a distance. Ross was gone, and Carter looked sad, alone, despondent. He was a broken man, and Validus hoped they had taken the right action.

"It was a risky move," Tren said. "He could have ended up in a mental institution. And now he doesn't even think we're real. What if he had been assigned overseas?"

Validus shook his head. "Not with how Ross intends to use him. We can use Ross to bring about our own purposes no matter what he has planned."

Persimus frowned. "I hope I haven't screwed this up. Now he's a CIA agent without the CIA to back him. He could be more vulnerable than before."

Validus shook his head. "Are you forgetting how risky his missions were getting those last few months? No, this is the right move. And we did accomplish exactly what we were hoping to. He is free to reengage as a civilian. Let's work on setting up an intersection with Sydney Carlyle." He turned to Persimus. "You did a great job orchestrating all of this."

Persimus nodded, but he looked worried. "We've ruined his reputation and his self-confidence. There's no telling what might be the consequences of that."

Validus considered Persimus's words. "Michael reminded me that when pride keeps a man from Messiah, he must be broken. His reputation and his self-confidence are the very things keeping him from the Truth. In two weeks, I want you to erase every record, both electronic and paper, in regard to his psychological evaluation and diagnosis. I don't want a single trace left anywhere."

The concern left Persimus's face. He would enjoy that mission.

Tren looked like he wanted to say something. Validus knew that the guardian was a deep thinker, and he had come to rely heavily on his intuition.

"What is it, Tren?"

"Is it possible that Carter may be here for more than . . ." The guardian stopped.

Validus nodded. "I've considered the same thing. Ross and his associates are trying to save America. Perhaps Elohim's plan for Carter is broader than we first thought."

Tren and Persimus looked at Validus, waiting for his next orders.

"Whatever happens, it doesn't change our mission. We need to keep him alive, and we need another Carlyle encounter."

∾o∾

It was a Wednesday evening just a few minutes before seven when Drew stepped out of the taxi and walked up to the door of his home in Rivercrest, Kansas. It had been years since he had been home. He lifted his hand to the door and realized he had never knocked on his own door before. It was a sign of just how far and how long he had been away from home. He hesitated as years of memories flashed across his mind. The wood felt strangely soft against his knuckles, almost as if he were in a dream.

When his mom opened the door, Drew wasn't sure what to expect, but all she did was gasp, then lunge at him, wrapping her arms around his neck. Drew hugged her back.

"Hello, Mom," he whispered.

Drew felt her warm tears on his neck and heard the soft sounds of her weeping. He hoped he could tell her everything one day so that her sorrow would at least be compensated with truth.

Drew looked over his mom's shoulder and saw Jake smiling as big as he had ever seen. Beside Jake stood Validus. Drew ignored the vision and nodded at Jake.

A few minutes later, Drew, Kathryn, and Jake were seated at the kitchen table, each with a glass of iced tea. For a few moments, Drew imagined that there were no visions and there was no CIA. It felt good to be home.

"What happened, Drew?" Jake asked. "How is it that they let you out?"

Drew took a deep breath and looked down at his glass of tea. Sadness overwhelmed him as he gathered the courage to tell them the truth.

"It turns out you guys were right from the beginning. They discovered I was seeing things, and I was diagnosed with severe PTSD. I was deemed unfit for service."

The room became awkwardly silent. Drew hoped that neither of them would ask about the elephant in the room—or in his case the imaginary alien in the room.

"I'm just thankful you're here," Kathryn said, unable to let go of his hand. Her smile faded as a thought crossed her mind. "You are going to stay, aren't you?"

Drew covered her hand with his free hand. "If you'll let me, at least for a while."

Kathryn laughed. "I'd have it no other way."

"What are your plans?" Jake asked.

Drew sat back in his chair, pulling his hands away from his mother so he could take a drink of his tea. "Well, I don't really have a lot of options. I was thinking about applying at the fitness center, but in the meantime I was wondering if you might have some grunt work I could do for you at the security company." He winced. "Considering my current state, I understand if that's not an option."

Kathryn's face lit up as she looked at Jake. "Jake's done really well with the company, Drew. I was even able to quit teaching so I could travel with him from time to time. Oh, Jake, can you work something out for Drew?"

Jake nodded. "I've got more than grunt work for you—"

Kathryn's eyes widened, and she gave him a stern look.

"Grunt work it is. Nice safe grunt work," he said sweeping his hand in a cutting motion across the table.

Drew laughed. "Thanks, Jake. It will be so good to have things back to normal."

Jake gave Drew the eye, but Drew just focused on his mother. He would deal with Jake later.

Drew smiled. He had missed his mother, and he'd missed Jake. Both of them filled such a gap in his life. The rest of the evening was spent eating, talking, laughing, and crying. For a few hours, Drew felt at peace.

Drew took the rest of the week acclimating to home and the new order of things with Jake as his stepfather. Though different, it was an easy transition. Jake had now been as much a part of Drew's life as his real father had been, and perhaps even more, especially when he was navigating through the tumultuous years of his youth.

Monday morning, Drew went with Jake to his security firm. Drew could tell Jake was full of questions by how little he was talking. As usual, however, he let Drew pick his own time to reveal things.

It had been nearly four years since Drew had last seen Jake's company, and even then Jake hadn't really shared much with Drew about what he did. He only knew that Jake provided security and that many of his employees were ex-military.

"I don't remember this being the way," Drew said as Jake drove west out of the city.

"I've relocated and expanded," Jake replied.

He turned onto a gated blacktop road. Near the gate a prominent stone sign read Fortress Security, Authorized Personnel Only. The fence ran north and south until it disappeared behind rows of trees. They drove a couple hundred yards up to a second entry, where a guard greeted them.

"Good morning, Greg," Jake said.

"Good morning, Jake," the guard replied with a smile. He reached inside the guard shack and the gate opened.

"Wow. Mom wasn't kidding. You really have done well," Drew said as he scanned the inner compound of the security firm. A stout but sharp-looking brick and steel building was centered on an acre lot.

"Don't get too carried away with assumptions, Drew. There's no excess in my firm. I keep it lean and simple. Your mother and I don't need much, so most of what I earn goes right back into the company."

"That I believe, but I bet you've got some great tech," Drew said with a wide grin. "And weapons."

Jake flashed a quick smile. "That I do. You're going to love the range out back."

"Range?"

Jake nodded. "I own twenty acres surrounding the firm. We have an entire range dedicated to training."

"What the heck, Jake?"

Jake raised an eyebrow. "Drew, I'm an ex-Ranger. My buds are ex–Special Forces from all branches. They're not wired to be mall cops." He winced.

"Although we have been known to handle that too. We offer security at every level, and I mean every level. We work closely with the authorities wherever our services are needed. We've even started to land a few government contracts."

Drew eyed Jake. "What about services that are needed by questionable people and companies?"

Jake nodded. "We get requests of every kind, but I only approve those that are legal and legitimate. I thoroughly investigate any potential client before accepting them."

Jake took the morning to show Drew the compound, and he was impressed. In a smaller way, it reminded him of the Farm. The men and women Jake had assembled were top flight, every one without exception. It was a testimony to the leadership skills Jake possessed. In just a few hours, Drew's respect for Jake elevated beyond the lofty place it already was.

Just before lunch, Jake took Drew to the range. In the weapons lodge, a man with a bushy mustache who looked to be about Jake's age met them.

"Drew this is Mick. He's my right-hand man around here."

Mick stuck out a large square hand. "I never knew your dad, but I heard a lot about him."

"Mick and I served together, in Afghanistan," Jake added.

Drew took Mick's hand. His shake was firm and nearly painful.

"Drew is looking to hire on with us," Jake said to Mick.

"You got prior service? Training?" Mick asked.

Drew pursed his lips. He wasn't sure how to answer. "No, not really."

Mick raised an eyebrow and looked at Jake.

"Just the eight years Jake trained me while I was growing up," Drew added.

Mick nodded. "Then let's see what you've got. Here are the weapons you asked for, Jake." Mick set a Springfield .40-caliber pistol and a Beretta 9mm on the counter before them.

Drew smiled. "Just like old times."

Jake turned to Drew. "I rely on Mick heavily, but I personally evaluate every employee—their skill set, their psychological condition, their mental prowess. When I vouch for man or woman to a client, my reputation and their life are on the line. No matter how big we get, I will not delegate that to anyone else." He looked at Drew. "There are no exceptions."

"I understand," Drew replied.

The first station for Drew was simple target practice at twenty-five, fifty, and seventy-five feet. When Mick pulled the targets in, he just silently nodded. Each of the three targets had a tight two-inch pattern in the center of the chest regardless of the distance.

Jake followed on the premise of staying current. "Too much time behind a desk will ruin a good shooter."

The next station required Drew to hit multiple targets behind various barriers. The sequence was timed. He actually held back so as not to reveal too much to Jake and Mick, but even still, his performance was superb. After the last sequence, Mick looked at the shot timer and eyed Jake. He flipped it around for Jake to see. Jake just nodded.

"And you taught him that?" Mick's voice was thick with skepticism.

"Yes, he did," Drew interjected. "Started when I was twelve."

Mick shook his head. "Well, kid, you've run circles around the old man."

Jake snarled at Mick, "Who you callin' old? How's it compare to your last run?"

"That's classified, and don't try to make this about me," Mick snapped back.

Jake offered a crooked smile. "Need to see anymore?"

Mick huffed. "I'm good, I'm good."

Drew cleared the weapon and handed it back to Mick. "Thanks."

After lunch Drew sat in a chair in Jake's office and looked at his mentor across the desk. Jake's hands were folded and his index fingers were resting against his lips.

"So what do you think?" Jake asked. "Do you want to work for Fortress Security?"

"What you've created here is incredible, Jake. I had no idea. Of course, I want to work for you."

Jake leaned back in his chair. "But . . ."

Drew had to give Jake something, otherwise his time at Fortress would be rife with lies and deception. He couldn't do that to Jake. Drew took a deep breath. "But you need to know that I may have extended periods of unexplained absences."

Jake's eyes narrowed. "I wondered. How often?"

"I have no idea."

"Well, at least your mother bought it."

Drew wanted to tell him everything, but Ross wouldn't allow it.

"And the psych eval . . . That was just a ruse to oust you from the agency?"

Drew wasn't sure how to answer. "Not exactly. Jake, you've always been able to read me like a book. You also know that there are things I can't tell you. I'm just asking for your help and your discretion. I'm serving our country—not the way I'd hoped, but I've been given a gift . . . and a curse for some reason." He looked down at his open hands. "It's complicated, and I'm asking you to trust me."

Jake leaned forward and looked at Drew the way he remembered his dad doing when he was just a boy. "Okay, but no matter how skilled you are—and by the way, I know you were holding back out there—a bullet still kills. You be careful. And if you need anything from me—*anything*—say the word."

Drew loved Jake. He was always a pillar, the lighthouse that told him where the solid ground was.

"I'm . . . I'm very grateful, Jake."

Jake nodded. "Mick will be the only one I'll have a challenge keeping this from, but I'll think of a way. If you can give me any warning, I can send him to check up on our other facilities."

Drew's eyes widened. "Other facilities?"

Jake smiled.

17

FINDING BEN AGAIN

Drew was a natural fit for Fortress Security, and Jake was grateful to have him. Drew learned that Jake had launched Fortress Security East Division just south of York, Pennsylvania, in an effort to be more conveniently located to gain government contracts. Before long they found it necessary to expand to a third facility located north of Los Angeles, which became their West Division. Rivercrest then became Fortress Central.

Jake's reputation among the Special Forces veterans afforded him the opportunity to build a security company that was both extremely skilled and efficient as well as reputable throughout the country. Six months after Drew joined Fortress, they began receiving international requests. It afforded Drew both the excuse and the opportunity to complete NOC missions for Ross with only minor diversions. Drew suspected that some of their international clients had been fed to them by Ross, for more than once did a NOC mission coincide with either a Fortress mission or a marketing and public relations call to a potential client.

Throughout his time with the CIA, Drew had been ever restless over the agonizing reality that Ben was still out there someplace. Now that he was settled in at Fortress, he decided it was time to put finding Ben at the top of his priority list.

They had come full circle. Ben was missing and probably paranoid again. Drew had been under the microscope while at the CIA and hadn't dared access his Chicago Mercantile trading account for fear of the CIA discovering Ben's whereabouts. In spite of being free from the prison of believing the alien invaders were real, Drew hadn't ruled out the possibility that the industrial espionage theory might still be a plausible one. If indeed the LASOK technology could be developed into telecommunication products or even weaponized, its worth would be incalculable. It was just that, if and when he found Ben, he wasn't sure how to tell his friend the truth. He decided he would deal with that when the time came.

The problem with searching for Ben was that this time his friend had left absolutely no clues as to where he might go. That pretty much left the entire United States to search. It seemed impossible, and thus far any leads Drew followed came up dead ends, including his attempt to access their Mercantile Exchange account. To Drew's dismay, he discovered that the account had been closed over a year and a half ago.

After days of thinking back over the months he had spent with Ben before their separation, Drew remembered that the last piece of equipment Ben needed to buy was an electron microscope. If he could find a reseller who had sold one not long after their separation, maybe he could trace the sale to Ben. And although it was three years ago and seemed like a long shot, at least it was something.

Drew sat down at his computer and opened a browser. He entered "electron microscope suppliers and resellers" into a search engine and waited. The wait icon spun and seemed to take longer than usual to respond. The screen filled with a long list of companies on the first page. Drew glanced at the number of results and felt his heart sink. About 8,260,000. He hung his head. Even if only one percent of the hits were valid, it still meant a search of over 82,000 links.

"Well, another dead end," Drew said. He moved the mouse to the red X in the corner of the screen just as a pop-up showing an ad for electron microscopes appeared.

Drew tried to exit the pop-up but it wouldn't go away. Then the ad disappeared and words appeared.

What took you so long?

Drew froze as he stared at the words. The cursor was on the line below, and it was blinking . . . waiting. Could it be? Goosebumps covered his body. He hit the W key on the keyboard, and the pop-up displayed the letter.

"Impossible," he whispered.

Who is this? he typed.

The cursor blinked and Drew waited.

I'm Alice. I was designed to find you.

The hairs on the back of Drew's neck stood straight. He should have realized that searching for electron microscopes from a Rivercrest IP address would raise flags.

Another message appeared: *Have you taken the blue pill?*

Drew typed: *Yes.*

What color is the night?

Drew typed: *Gray.*

What did you receive for graduation?

"Ben, you sly dog!" Drew smiled with excitement and typed: *A spoon.*

The cursor blinked. Then another message. *Please scan and verify security. Are we secure?*

Drew scanned for invaders and then realized that he didn't believe this stuff anymore. He fought the urge to get sucked into Ben's fantasy world again.

Yes.

Drew waited, hoping. He grabbed a pencil to write down any message Ben would send him, but it would not be needed.

Admiral David Glasgow Farragut, 9 p.m. Good-bye. The message displayed for a couple of seconds, and then the pop-up disappeared.

Drew sat back. All along Ben had been waiting for him. Drew searched for "Admiral David Glasgow Farragut," but the results were too broad. He added "monument" and found the result he was looking for.

"Madison Square Park? Seriously, Ben?"

For a man hiding from what he believed to be an alien invasion, it sure didn't seem like the center of New York City would be the place. Maybe Ben had gone off the deep end after all.

Drew immediately booked a flight to New York. He could leave early the next morning and be there by six o'clock in the evening, plenty of time for the 9:00 p.m. rendezvous.

By eight thirty the next evening, Drew was in Madison Square Park in New York, New York, the most densely populated city in the United States— precisely the place that Benjamin Berg shouldn't be. Drew began second-guessing himself. Was this a trap set by the industrial espionage group? Terrorists who had somehow discovered his connection to Ben?

Drew decided that even though his light invader friend wasn't real, there was no denying the fact that his subconscious had abilities his conscious didn't. This figment had helped him in the past, and perhaps he'd better at least pay attention to its warning signs. Validus and two of his companions seemed on the alert but not anticipating any serious threat. It eased Drew's nerves a little, but he still decided to play it safe.

Admiral David Glasgow Farragut's statue was on the north end of the park, so Drew found a park bench far enough away that he could see whomever might observe it. He watched every person far and near, waiting for his friend. Nine o'clock came and went, but there was no Ben. He waited until ten and then decided that Ben would have probably given him a day to get there. He would try again tomorrow night.

Drew stood up and left the park. At the curb, a cab waited. Drew opened the door to get in, but a man was already sitting on the far side of the seat. He was looking out the street-side window.

"Sorry," Drew said and stepped back.

Ben turned and looked up at him. "Do I have to stuff you in here like you did me?"

Drew smiled from ear to ear. He jumped into the cab and shut the door. "Ben!"

Ben smiled back. They locked hands and hugged. Drew sat back and looked at his friend. Ben looked good . . . almost too good.

Ben tapped the seat, and the driver took off. "I see you got Alice's message."

"Yeah, I—"

Ben leaned out of sight of the driver's rearview mirror and held his finger up to his lips.

"—did," Drew finished. "Thanks. Where are we going?"

Ben pulled a smartphone out of his pocket that showed a map and their location with a GPS pointer. Below the map, Drew saw a message flashing: "Observing."

"You'll see in a minute. How are you, Drew?"

"I'm good, Ben. Man, you look good. How's . . . life?" Drew wasn't sure how much Ben wanted him to say in the cab. Ben kept checking his phone and Drew sensed that he wanted to keep things surface-level.

"You hungry?" Ben asked as he swiped his screen and updated something.

"Yes, actually. I came directly over once I got the message. Haven't eaten anything since lunch," Drew replied, dying to get someplace to ask questions.

He glanced down at Ben's phone again, and this time the flashing message read: "Clear."

"Alice says we're clear." Ben leaned forward. "This will do," he called out to the cab driver.

"You sure?" the cabby asked.

"Yep." Ben handed him a twenty.

Drew looked out the window to see that they were back at Madison Square Park. What was going on?

Drew and Ben exited the cab and stood on the sidewalk. The cool night air held the sounds of New York life—cars, people, music.

Drew turned to Ben. "So—"

Ben grabbed Drew and gave him another hug. "It's so good to see you, Drew. Man, I missed you!"

"I missed you too, Ben. I'm sorry it took me so long." Drew sighed. "You wouldn't believe what's happened in the last three years."

"I can only imagine," Ben said. "Let's walk and you can fill me in."

Drew looked at Ben in awe as he led them down the street. At first Drew could hardly concentrate to tell him his story, because Ben seemed so solid, so together. It wasn't at all what he expected, nothing like the last time. Drew quietly considered two possibilities to explain Ben's state. Either Ben had given up on the whole notion of an alien invasion and was actually a normal, functioning person, or he had so lost it that his paranoia was being temporarily masked and would probably manifest itself before long. Either way, Drew was a little nervous about discovering what had really happened to Ben during the last three years.

They walked for five or six city blocks, passing up the delightful smells of Italian, Mexican, and Chinese restaurants along the way. Drew gave Ben the summarized version of his life, and his friend seemed to take it all in, asking questions to clarify some of the details. When he was done, Drew stopped and looked around, realizing they were nowhere near any restaurants. These blocks were exclusively office buildings, conference centers, and high-class hotels. It was now almost eleven, and the restaurants would all be closing.

"So . . . what about you, Ben? What's been going on with you?" This was where he would discover the true mental state of his friend.

Ben stuffed his hands in his coat pocket and motioned for them to keep walking . . . away from any food. "Well, my decoys to help me escape from Chicago must have worked, since I'm still alive," he said with a quirky laugh.

Of course you're alive, Drew thought. *There were never any real invaders to harm you in the first place.*

"You had some great ideas, by the way, using multiple vans and tunnels. But then I got to thinking about how I was going to carry on our work, not knowing if you would ever be back. So I decided to find a job first and disappear again as a nobody. And that led me here."

Ben stopped walking. Drew turned to face him. Ben shrugged.

"New York City?" Drew asked.

"Yes, but no . . . I mean *here*," Ben said, opening his hands and looking around them.

Drew looked all around, trying to figure out what his quirky friend was getting at. Ben finally pointed up. Drew followed and saw a big, blue high-tech sign that read NexTech.

"Here? NexTech? You found a job working here?"

Ben nodded. His grin was a little too big.

"Wow . . . that's great," Drew said, choosing to believe him for now. "How did you land this job without being discovered?"

"Not just any job. I'm the senior tech for the firm."

"Senior tech? Seriously? That's awesome. NexTech looks like an amazing company."

Ben laughed. "Yeah . . . NexTech is pretty amazing, huh?"

Drew looked up at the sign again and read the company slogan—Next Generation Technology Today. The glass doors and windows gave just a hint of what their capabilities were.

"What we could do with these resources and technology . . ." Drew whistled, contemplating how much faster they would be able to replicate Dr. Waseem's work. "If only we had something like this."

"We have something like this, my friend."

Drew didn't like his tease. "An abandoned warehouse and spare parts bought off the Internet are a far cry from the capabilities of NexTech."

Ben nodded. "Which is why I never used our money to rebuild the lab as we had planned."

Drew's heart sank. In spite of being convinced that the invaders actually didn't exist, there was a part of him that secretly wanted Ben to prove the world—and Dr. Whitton—wrong. By now he had expected Ben to be nearly done. Granted, the money would probably have run out, but there should have been enough to get them close.

"What are you saying, Ben? You never rebuilt the lab?" Anger laced his words.

"I didn't say that . . . exactly. The equipment we bought was junk. I realized it would never work, so instead I built NexTech."

Drew smirked. "You're an employee of NexTech, my friend. Have the invaders messed with your brain again?" he quipped, but deep down he wondered if perhaps there was truth to it. He had seen Ben nearly drop out of reality before.

"It's a front, Drew. I realized the best way to hide from the FBI, the invaders, everyone, was to hide in plain view, right under their noses. I needed a cover, and we needed better technology, so I took our money and designed a fake tech company with a fake board of directors and a fake CEO."

Drew shook his head. "I don't believe you. No one could pull that off."

Ben was as giddy as Drew had ever seen him. "Yeah, I know, right? Plus, who's going to take a computer geek like me seriously? So I hired an actor to play the corporate investor representing a board of directors, set up interviews, and brought in a real highflying tech manager to run the business. Hired myself, and voila . . . NexTech was born."

Drew was stunned. Did he dare believe him?

"The only problem was—" Ben stopped short, preoccupied with some secret problem.

"What problem, Ben? The money's all gone and there's still no lab? Is that it?" Drew pressed, trying to control himself.

"No. This fake company actually worked. It started making money. I had to hire real programmers, managers, accountants—all of it. It's really slowed down Dr. Waseem's work."

Drew looked sadly at Ben. The money was gone, Ben was clearly unstable again, Drew was schizophrenic, and there was no hope of ever turning Dr. Waseem's research into something profitable. *It's just as well,* Drew thought. His secret and foolish hope of Ben being able to throw him a lifeline to reality was finally over.

Drew put an arm around Ben. "It's okay, buddy. I'm here to help you out now."

"Yeah, and it's about time. It hasn't been easy on my own."

"I'm sure. I'm sorry it took me so long to get to you."

Ben waved him off and smiled. "It's all right." He looked up at the Nex-Tech building and glowing blue logo. "I've been plenty busy."

"Why don't we go get something to eat, and then you can show me where you're staying," Drew said, leading him back to where they might still be able to order a pizza at a pub.

"What? Don't you want to see it?" Ben asked.

"See what?" Drew asked.

"The LASOK, or at least how far I am." Ben started walking toward the darkened entrance of the NexTech building.

"Not now, Ben. I'm hungry." Drew was hoping this wouldn't get embarrassing and draw attention. "Come on."

Ben stopped and looked at Drew. "Your stomach is going to have to wait. I haven't worked my butt off so you can go eat a piece of pizza."

He turned and walked straight to the access pad. Drew ran to catch up to him.

"Ben . . . Ben, wait. Let's not—"

But before Drew could finish, Ben pulled out a white security card, swiped it near the pad, and then entered a ten-digit code. The red LED flashed green, and the solenoid lock on the door clicked open. Drew froze, but Ben opened the door and stepped halfway through it.

Ben glared at Drew. "I'm serious, you're going to have to wait 'cause I'm not going to."

Drew's mouth hung open as he stumbled across the low threshold of NexTech's gleaming entry. Inside, Drew gawked at the sterile glass-and-silver interior.

"You actually do work here?" Drew asked.

"What's wrong with you, man? I told you, we own the place."

Though still skeptical, Drew decided to let the next few minutes unfold without opening his mouth and potentially making a bigger fool of himself.

Ben took Drew up a wide staircase and through a couple of hallways lined with offices. One large room was filled with cubicles and open-area work centers. Off to the side was a large office with a beautiful view of the city.

"Are we still safe?" Ben asked.

Drew scanned and took a moment to scan outside too. He nodded. Ben swiped his card again, entered the key code, and the office door clicked open.

"It's impossible to have too much security," Ben whispered. Drew stayed silent.

Inside, the office was the largest and nicest he had seen in the building. Drew got nervous. It reminded him of the night they entered Dr. Waseem's lab.

Ben made sure to close the door and listen for the lock to engage. He walked over to his desk.

"This is your office . . . really?" Drew asked.

Ben looked disgusted. "This? You're impressed with *this*?"

Drew quit scanning the office and looked at his friend.

"Wait till you see this!"

Ben slid out a drawer, lifted a fake bottom, and placed his hand on a scanner. A white light rolled up and down the glass plate. Then Drew nearly fell over. Just to his left, a four-foot section of the wall slid away, revealing an entire room filled with the highest tech gadgetry money could buy.

"You have got to be kidding me!" Drew said. "You . . . you . . ." He didn't know how to respond. He was shocked and thrilled. "Ben, look what you've done! This is incredible!" He grabbed Ben and gave him a bear hug, lifting him up and setting him down. "You actually own NexTech? Really?"

"No, idiot. *We* own NexTech. You were the one who invested the money."

"Ha! This is amazing!"

Drew went into the lab, and there on the bench was the most beautiful sight he had seen in years. A gleaming new version of Dr. Waseem's LASOK. Drew ran to it and feasted his eyes on its beauty. He glanced up at Ben and saw his friend beaming.

"Does it work?"

Ben's smiled faded some. "Not yet. I'm still searching for Waseem's last equation, and I have a couple more pieces of equipment to install. But we're close, Drew. Really, really close."

18

NEXTECH CORPORATION

Drew and Ben spent most of the night catching up and exchanging stories, and Drew was delighted to find out that Ben had a fully stocked freezer of frozen pizzas. He learned that Ben and the team he assembled had created a new operating system for mobile devices that a major cell phone company picked up and leased from them, which skyrocketed them to the successful tech company they were. Ben dubbed his creation Leeloo.

Drew pulled out his cell. "Wait, you're the creator of Leeloo?"

Ben grabbed Drew's phone and accessed menus that Drew didn't know existed. He tapped in access codes and made updates, then handed it back. "There, now it's twice as fast and twice as powerful. They forced us to add limitations so they could program upgrades into their marketing plan. Yours are all unlocked."

Drew just smiled in wonder. Who knew that his genius friend also had a gift for business?

"Leeloo is a scaled-down version of our real masterpiece. A program I call Near Artificial Intelligence. Her name is Alice."

"Is that who found me when I searched for you and who you were talking to in the cab?" Drew asked.

Ben nodded. "She was monitoring local GPS receivers and surveillance cameras to verify we weren't being followed."

Drew raised an eyebrow. "Are you telling me your Alice hacks secure systems to gather information?"

Ben fidgeted. "Only when absolutely necessary. Alice is smart, Drew. You're going to love her." He whipped out a tablet and held it up to Drew's face. "Alice, look at this man. This is Drew Carter. You will respond to his commands and provide any information he requests."

"Yes, Ben," the tablet replied. "Should I have a record of his handprint and retina scan on file for classified access?"

"Yes," Ben replied and then lowered the tablet in front of Drew. "Put your hand on the tablet."

Drew obeyed.

"Your handprint has been captured, Drew," Alice said. "Please look into the camera, and don't blink."

Drew looked at Ben and smiled. He looked into the camera, and a gentle light turned on.

"Retina scan captured."

The more Drew learned about Ben and his last three years, the more impressed he was. The guy was a tireless machine of ideas. If the LASOK ever had a chance of working, Ben was the man to bring it alive. He learned that Ben had been able to keep the LASOK a secret from everyone else at Nex-Tech, working on it only at night. Although he had an apartment, he had a comfortable place to sleep in the LASOK lab for his many late-night work sessions.

Drew couldn't quite bring himself to tell Ben about his insight into the alien invader theory. It would be too painful and too embarrassing for both of them. For now, if it provided motivation to complete the LASOK, what could it hurt?

At four in the morning, Drew and Ben were ready to call it a night.

"Hey, this is awesome, Drew. Things are finally looking up. So the big question is . . ."

Drew knew what was coming.

"What's up with you and Sydney?"

Drew shook his head. "Nothing."

Ben just nodded. "Okay . . . that's probably good. But why?"

Drew shrugged. "She deserves better than me. My life is always in a state of chaos, and she deserves normal."

Ben smirked. "Boring people deserve normal. You and Sydney are any-thing but. So where is she?"

"I'm not sure," Drew said, trying to sound disinterested.

"Yeah, right! I don't believe that for a minute. You're telling me that with all the super spy stuff you know, you haven't looked her up and aren't tracking her right now?"

Who was he kidding? He couldn't even fool his geek friend who had never had a girlfriend in his life.

Ben continued. "She's got to be done with college. Is she back in Kansas? Surely you've seen her."

Drew huffed. "The University of Pennsylvania offered her a scholarship to get a graduate degree in microbiology, so she's not in Kansas. And no, I haven't seen her because my life is still crazy dangerous, which she doesn't need."

Ben waited, eyes wide in anticipation of a better excuse, which Drew had but wasn't going to say. It would mean confessing to his full-blown schizophrenia and then having to admit that the invaders Ben believed in were all just a figment of his subconscious.

"When's the last time you saw her?"

Ben's question triggered a multitude of painful memories. He replayed the events of the Chicago bombing and the precious time he'd spent with her in the hotel, saying good-bye and . . . making a promise, a promise he'd forgotten. He resolved to make good on it soon.

"It's just not in the cards, Ben. She's probably seeing someone by now anyway."

Ben just grunted and left it at that.

With Jake's permission, Drew took a few days to check in on Fortress East in York, Pennsylvania. The Fortress employees all knew that Drew was Jake's stepson, and at first there was the typical mild disdain from some who suspected nepotism, but Drew quickly dispensed with any such notion by showing respect to everyone he met and by setting the high scores for each of their range drills. By the end of his three days at Fortress East, he had won the respect of everyone there.

Drew especially hit it off with one particular East Division team leader named Gus when he discovered the man had a fascination and an amazing talent for understanding and wielding ancient weapons. Whether real or imaginary, Validus and his warriors had initiated a curiosity for such things in Drew that could not be satisfied merely by reading a book. Drew decided that if ever he had an opportunity to work with Gus in the future, he would tap into the man's knowledge and abilities to expand his own weaponry skill set.

During his time at Fortress East, Drew also found time to fulfill his promise to Sydney. He read through the Bible once more, but this time with a heart to discover Truth, if it was there. With each page he read, he came to realize something was different now, and he knew it probably had to do with the fact that he no longer believed in the alien theory. The words of the Bible seemed to penetrate and stir his soul like never before. However, there were still things he didn't understand, and if he ever had the chance, he would ask Sydney or Reverend Branson what they meant.

When Drew left Fortress East, he drove back to New York City and checked in on Ben the evening before he was scheduled to fly back to Rivercrest. Ben arranged to meet him at NexTech at eight.

"Ben, having worked in certain capacities for the government and now working for Jake, I find myself in need of some tech that I can no longer get my hands on."

Ben looked up from the LASOK and smiled. He set the soldering iron back in its holder, flipped off the switch, and crossed his arms as he leaned up against the lab bench.

"This sounds interesting. What kind of tech? Micro bugs and cameras, GPS trackers, document scanners, cell phone listeners and jammers?" Ben offered. "No sense reinventing the wheel, because that tech is all available off the shelf."

"Right. No, I was thinking a little more sophisticated than that."

"I'm listening," Ben said enthusiastically.

"I still have to wear sunglasses to keep my headaches away, so why not make them useful? How about glasses that give the full gamut of GPS capabilities, Internet access, facial recognition, infrared scanning, voice command interface, and anything else you can throw in?"

Drew could see Ben's mind already turning. "You don't ask for much, do you?" he said with a sly grin.

"Well, we do specialize in mobile applications, don't we? Can't think of anything more mobile than an awesome pair of sunglasses. Oh . . . and yeah, they've got to look cool. Nothing geeky."

Ben smirked. "Anything else, commander?"

"Yeah, actually. You know how we can get 360-degree images off the Internet because they outfitted a vehicle to drive roads and record it? I need the same thing, except in video and without a bulky vehicle. I need it around me."

Ben let out a low whistle. "What are my restrictions?"

"It's got to look natural to everyone around me."

Ben started pacing as he thought. "You can't count on Wi-Fi, and that much data would be impossible at current bandwidths. You'd have to store data until download. How much time do you need?"

Drew thought. "A minimum of two hours."

Ben stopped and looked at Drew.

"And," Drew continued, "it can't be detected by a bug detector or visual inspection."

"Wow . . . I have a few ideas, but this is going to take some time. I'll have to get my whole team on it in-between other projects." Then a thought hit him. "Maybe the CIA will be our next customer."

Drew raised an eyebrow. "Maybe."

"Just curious, why do you need this tech, Drew?"

Drew didn't like being forced into his position as a NOC. Not only was he unsupported, but he still had suspicions about Ross and his motives.

"I can't say much, Ben, but there are situations I face where no one is watching my back, and a device like this would be very useful to me."

Ben nodded. "Okay. I'd like you to come by tomorrow morning as a client and have my tech team do some brainstorming. I should be able to have a project request and a meeting set up with the CEO by then. His name is Nate Allen. Tell him you're here for Mr. Belvedere and that you want to work directly with the tech team to ensure that the specs are clearly outlined. I'll arrange the terms so that seventy percent will be paid up front and the rest on project completion. He should like that, and then we can give the project priority without any hassles."

"You got it. My plane doesn't leave until late afternoon," Drew said. "I've wanted to meet our CEO anyway . . . You know, see if I like him."

"Like has nothing to do with it, Drew. Allen is a tech-business guru. We pay him well, but he's worth it. Oh, and by the way, here my name is Chider Stevens."

The next day, Drew met with the CEO, who then passed him off to Ben for an office tour.

"Wow, Allen's good. I can see why we're doing so well."

"He's one of the best, and I'm sure we'll lose him soon. Talent like his doesn't stay in one place long," Ben said.

"He might if NexTech keeps growing. It's already quite a feather in his corporate hat," Drew added.

Ben gave Drew the full NexTech tour—finance, human resources, and sales, saving the IT and design department for last.

In the advertising and marketing offices, Drew met a smug, smooth-talking wisecracker he didn't like the moment they walked into the office. Drew noticed that Ben tried to avoid the guy, but he wouldn't have it.

"Who's your friend, Chide-man?" The guy had tight curly hair, a mouth large enough for the entire office to hear everything he said, and eyes that looked through Drew like he wasn't there.

Ben hesitated. "Drew, Glen. Glen, Drew."

Glen grabbed Drew's hand and held on to keep Ben from dragging him away. "Any friend of Chider's is a friend of ours," he said, his tone dripping with condescension. "Good to meet ya, Drew."

"Same." Drew loosened his grip to let go and move on.

"Yep, Chider and the geek team give us good stuff to market," Glen said, slapping Ben on the back like he was a dorky little brother. It was almost like replaying a scene from high school with Cameron O'Brian. Drew wanted to smack him. He couldn't believe that Ben had actually hired this creep.

"Hey," Glen said as he eyed Drew carefully, "you're not one of those tech monkeys too, are you?"

"He's a client, Glen," Ben snapped. "On a major project that Mr. Allen just approved."

That set Glen back on his heels. Drew could tell he didn't like being re-buked by Ben, and he was sure the guy would attempt to get back at him later.

"Good . . . good," Glen said with a forced smile. "Let us know if we can do anything to help out."

Drew nodded and turned to join Ben, happy to be moving on. When they were out of earshot, he turned to Ben. "Good grief! Why don't you fire that guy?"

"Are you kidding? Glen doesn't know it, but he's my perfect cover. No one would suspect that I own this place with him making snide comments every time I walk by." Ben laughed. "The other techs tell me I should complain. It's awesome!"

"Just make sure I'm here when you do fire him," Drew said. "I want to see his face."

Drew had already seen the IT department but not the people in it. He expected eight more Benjamin Bergs, bustling about in frenzied, driven activity, but that was not the case at all. The atmosphere was relaxed, and yet there was a sense of genius at every work station.

"I've scheduled us for a meeting with the senior design team right about now," Ben said, escorting Drew to a glass-walled conference room with ample room for all of the tech inside. He opened the thick glass door.

"Team, this is Drew Carter," Ben said as they entered what he had earlier heard Ben call the Blue Room, even though nothing in it was blue except for a bowl of blue M&M's sitting on a ten-foot-long, interactive glass-topped graphic table in the center of the room. When Drew had asked him why he called it the Blue Room, Ben replied, "It's a reminder for us to see beyond what normal people see. We all take the blue pill here." Also inside the room were four seventy-inch monitors, electronic whiteboards, comfortable chairs, a deluxe Keurig Brewer, and a well-stocked refrigerator.

"Drew is a friend and our next client," Ben continued.

Drew offered his hand to each member of Ben's tech design team as they were introduced.

"This is Crypt, that's Piper, he's Ridge, and this is Jester. These guys are the brains behind NexTech."

Drew couldn't help his smile. "Really? Don't you guys have real names?"

The one called Ridge shrugged. "Yeah, but they're boring . . . except for Piper. Her's is cool enough as is." Ridge was charming, friendly, blunt, and Indian.

Piper shot Drew a crooked smile, then pushed her glasses to the top of her nose. She was cute in a genius sort of way, plain brown hair in braids, round face, glasses, and just enough makeup to make it look like she tried. "Don't let Chider fool you," she said. "We're just his minions. All the cool ideas come from him."

"Hey," Crypt piped up. "I've had a couple of great ideas." Crypt was the unwilling poster child for the geeks—thick, black, uncombed hair, narrow chin, and eyebrows a little heavier than his slender face should have.

"Oh yeah, like the programmable whoopee cushion that gives different sounds based on the weight of the person sitting on it?" Jester cocked his head and smirked. "That was a real winner." Jester's slightly chubby form was atypical for what Drew would have expected from a brilliant Asian computer genius.

"Or the mobile app that rates girls you talk to by monitoring your heart rate," Ridge added. He looked at Drew. "It gave you a 'dateability' scale."

"Hey." Crypt pointed his finger at Ridge. "That one had potential, and you know it."

"Except that your heart rate was 160 beats a minute for every girl you met," Jester jabbed.

"Wasn't for Piper," Crypt rebutted.

"She doesn't count," Ridge countered.

"Hey!" Piper exclaimed and backhanded Ridge in the chest.

"All right, that's enough," Ben said. "It's amazing you guys—and gal—get anything done around here. Now pay attention. Drew needs some tech designed. Go ahead, Drew."

Drew told the team what he had told Ben the previous day about the glasses and a need for clandestine 360 video and audio capture. They asked a lot of questions, trying to get a sense for the purpose and performance specs. Then the five tech geniuses immediately began brainstorming, often talking in jargon way beyond Drew's technical vocabulary.

During the discourse, Drew noticed Piper looking at Ben a couple of times. It made him smile.

The session lasted well over two hours. Drew wondered if at the end of it they even remembered what he'd asked for.

Drew thanked each one and then followed Ben to his office. He sat down in the chair. "Wow, that was exhausting."

"Ha! You hardly did a thing except listen to us brainstorm and talk about your project," Ben said incredulously.

"Yeah, like I said, that was exhausting," Drew said with a wry smile. "By the way, Piper likes you."

Ben looked at Drew, expressionless. "Don't even try."

Drew held up his hands. "Don't blame me. I'm just stating the obvious."

"This project is big, Drew, if we do it right. What's our time frame?"

"Nice diversion," Drew said. "Well, considering I don't have anything now, it's whenever you can make it happen. What do you think?"

Ben took a deep breath, then swiped across his tablet and typed a few numbers. "Three to six months, if all goes well." He looked up at Drew for approval. "And it will definitely impede the LASOK for a while."

Deep down, Drew laid some of the blame for his mental condition *on* the LASOK. He wondered how his overly imaginative subconscious would react to a fully functioning LASOK that couldn't see what he saw.

"I'm okay with that. This is important."

Drew left NexTech and caught his plane back to Rivercrest later that afternoon.

DRESSED TO KILL

Over the course of the next few months, Ross's mission assignments for Drew steadily increased. Without access to the CIA database, it was difficult for Drew to understand the overall scope of what Ross was trying to determine, but it appeared to be connected to linking terrorist infiltration and activities to high-ranking government officials.

The extra missions also seemed to be oriented more and more toward the East Coast. Drew arranged with Jake to transfer to Fortress East to assist in their operations, which also allowed him frequent access to Ben and NexTech. It was a good move all around.

One of Drew's missions for Ross included a trip back to Puerto Rico to gain access to Andrés Zapata's database. With some help from Alice, Drew was able to place a miniature USB transmitter on his server that connected with a remote network router bypassing all the firewall and data security. Not only was Alice able to download Zapata's entire database, but they now had continual access to any updated information as it occurred.

Drew looked over the information before preparing it for the drop to Ross. Zapata had been busy and had grown his drug and weapons dealings. Drew noted a few customers whose goods delivered were simply annotated as "units." He wondered if this was a reference to the human traffic business that Zapata had alluded to when Drew was posing as a weapons manufacturing rep for Armstrong Industries. Thus far he counted ninety-two units delivered.

Ever and always present with Drew were Validus and his team. When threats weren't immediate, they often disappeared, but Drew knew they were near. Perhaps his subconscious needed a break from time to time, fabricating the images for him.

Four months after Drew had made his tech request of Ben, he was called back to NexTech.

"What's up, Megamind?" Drew said as he walked into Ben's office.

The jab didn't faze Ben in the least. "The glasses are proving to be a challenge," he said, "but I think we can have something for you in the next month or so. It's the 'cool' part that's stumping us. Nobody here seems to know what that is."

"Ha!" Drew burst out. Ben's humor had become increasingly witty as his confidence with NexTech grew.

Ben didn't crack a smile. He went to a cabinet in the corner of his office and opened the door. "But here's something I think you'll like." He took a black leather jacket off a hook and held it up by the shoulders.

"Nice jacket. Where'd you get it?"

"It's not mine, Metro-man. This is the video recorder you asked for . . . except it does a lot more than take video."

"Really? A leather jacket?" Drew was impressed. "If this works—"

"Here, try it on," Ben said, holding it open for him. "We call it Witness."

"You named a jacket?" Drew chortled. "Do you guys name everything you make?"

"Pretty much."

Drew carefully put his left arm into the jacket, then his right. When Ben set it on his shoulders, Drew felt the weight. "It's a little heavy but not bad. I suppose the electronics added the weight." He felt the material of the sleeve—it was real leather.

"Except for the batteries, the electronics added almost nothing. It's the Kevlar that you're feeling," Ben said.

Drew couldn't help noticing the proud smile Ben was trying to suppress. "Kevlar?"

"Well, knowing how hard you are on things, we decided to laminate our two-terabyte array of memory in thin wafers of Kevlar. And then I figured, what the heck, let's make the entire coat out of Kevlar cloth and thread, all except for the outer layer, which is real leather."

"This is incredible," Drew said, carefully moving his arms.

Ben laughed. "You don't have to be so gentle. Believe me, you're not going to break it."

"So the Kevlar is for protecting the electronics . . . not me."

"Don't get any ideas, Drew. It's not bulletproof," Ben said. "But it might stop a knife slice."

Drew rotated his arms. It would take some getting used to, but it wasn't bad. "So what's it do?"

Ben looked anxious to explain it. "The question is, What doesn't it do? The entire coat is laced with microSD cards for RAM storage and a host of other electronics, including two multicore processors—one for redundancy— six 170-degree wide-angle cameras with five megapixel high-definition CCD sensors. We can capture video up to 480 frames per second. The cameras are located here and here."

Ben pointed to subdued logos on Drew's shoulders, back, and chest. "The overlapping images are processed, then stitched together to form a seamless 360-degree image. Four microphones with auto–noise-cancelling for digital recording, built-in Wi-Fi, Bluetooth, and 6G wireless technology, accelerometer sensor, proximity sensor, barometer sensor, ambient light sensor, gyroscope sensor, magnetic sensor, gesture sensor, bug-and-scan detection sensors—"

"Whoa, Ben, how could you have possibly incorporated all that into a jacket?"

"Actually, it was easier than you think. We just took the newest, hottest smartphone, upgraded and expanded the features, and turned it into a jacket. In fact, we had a lot more space to work with. The visual interface for the jacket is going to be the glasses. That's why we aren't done with those. There's a lot of data to access, but by using the jacket's electronics, we were able to focus on just the visual technology and still keep the glasses lightweight. What's really going to make this thing sing is Alice."

"Your Alice?" Drew asked. "I thought she took a supercomputer to operate her AI."

"You're right," Ben said. "But we're working on a mobile version of her to make full use of the tech in the jacket, so until Alice and the glasses are done, you'll have limited functionality."

Drew laughed. "You mean it will only be able to do what I asked for it to do?"

Ben nodded. "Yeah, it takes 360 video and audio. However, with the two terabytes of memory we were able to pack into it, and depending on the frame rate, you can take up to five days of footage before having to download."

Drew slapped Ben on the shoulder. "Benjamin Berg, you are amazing!"

"As far as being invisible to bug detectors, it's not foolproof. Bug detectors are passive listening devices that check for all electromagnetic transmissions emanating from a source. Your jacket auto-silences all transmissions when not in use, kind of like airplane mode on your cell phone. I'm programming Alice to manage that and to make it a priority, but you'll still have to be careful."

"It's amazing," Drew said as he moved about. "It wears like a stiff new leather jacket. How did you make it so flexible?"

"We used nonmetallic, high-flex circuit technology in conjunction with electro-fiberoptic transmission for the high-bandwidth busses. Like I said, all the electronics are protected by thin wafers of Kevlar and Kevlar cloth."

Drew looked the coat over very closely. If Ben hadn't shown him, he would have never been able to tell that it was anything other than a normal leather jacket. "How do I activate it? What's the interface?"

Ben opened a drawer in his desk and lifted out a small plastic case. He opened it to show Drew. "Your standard nano earpiece, but the inductive loop is built into the jacket." He handed the miniature three-by-two millimeter unit to Drew. It was as small as anything the CIA had.

"How do I control the jacket?" Drew asked as he set the earpiece deep into his ear canal, unseen from any angle. He could feel it resting against his eardrum.

"Voice command, of course, but"—Ben held up his hand to stop Drew's protest before it came out of his mouth—"in case you don't want to be labeled schizophrenic by talking to yourself . . . *you* are the alternative interface."

Drew looked sideways at Ben. "Not following."

"With all of the sensors built into the jacket, it knows the positions of your arms and where the jacket is being touched. You can tell it to memorize any movement or touch you make and relate it to any command. Your pockets are lined with high-resolution sensors that you can also use to access Alice. Put one of your hands inside and press against your abdomen."

"Hello, Drew," Alice screamed into his ear.

"Ah!" Drew cringed. "Too loud!"

"Oh . . . I forgot about your sensitive hearing. I'm sure Alice has already adjusted."

"I'm sorry, Drew. Is this better?"

"Yes, much." Drew turned to Ben. "This doesn't sound like your Alice. It sounds like . . ." Drew didn't want to say her name.

Ben smiled. "Sydney?"

Drew scowled. "Are you trying to torment me?"

"No, just wanted to make sure you listened to her. I knew if she sounded like Sydney, you'd listen."

Drew shook his head. "I hear Sydney's voice in my head enough as it is. How about a Brit, or an Aussie, or a South African? And I thought you said Alice wasn't working."

"Mobile Alice isn't. She's accessing your jacket from the mainframe through Wi-Fi and Bluetooth. Once you're out of range, your jacket goes dumb. Why don't you tell her to change voices."

"Alice, change your voice to an English accent," Drew said a little too loudly.

"Okay, Drew. How's this? And by the way," Alice said in a charming English-accented voice, "I can hear you if you whisper."

"Remarkable. So real it's rather scary. How did she know it was me in the jacket?" Drew asked.

"The pocket sensors read your fingerprint. From now on no one else can access the jacket except you." Ben crossed his arms and looked on his work with pride.

"Ben, you've outdone yourself," Drew said. "How much did this little project cost us?"

Ben looked at him, then went back to his desk to close things up. "You don't want to know."

Drew just stared at him.

Ben sighed. "With three engineers and four programmers, custom fabrication, materials, and equipment . . . you're wearing about a two-hundred-thousand dollar jacket."

Drew just about fell over. "What? Ben . . . that's ridiculous!"

"Hey, you asked for it, and besides, the first one is always the most expensive.

When you're ready to commercialize it, I'll bet there are plenty of wealthy folks out there and maybe a few government agencies who would love to have a jacket like this. Don't worry, partner. We'll get a return on it."

Drew actually had no argument against that. Ben had become quite the savvy businessman. No wonder NexTech had mushroomed overnight.

"Okay," Drew said with nod. "Let's see how this thing works."

THE LASOK EXPERIMENT

D rew, take a look at this," Jake said, turning up the volume on the television in his office at Fortress Central. Drew was back in Rivercrest for a week to connect with Jake and visit his mother.

A major news network was broadcasting a press conference with the president of the United States. Anchorman Tom Vincent was getting a live feed from the conference, where reporter Sophia Bryant was on location.

"Hey, I know her," Drew said. "Looks like she made it to the big time."

The screen was split in two, showing the seasoned but agelessly handsome face of Tom Vincent on the left and the fresh, fiery face of Sophia Bryant on the right. Vincent was speaking.

"In an unprecedented move by President Harden, the security of Camp David is going to be turned over to UN troops. Sophia, what kind of a response are you seeing there?"

"Well, Tom, as you said, nothing like this has ever been done in the history of the United States. The feelings are extremely mixed. Many applauded the president for his move toward global unity, whereas others feel it is the final straw in handing over our sovereignty as a nation to the UN."

"Stay with us Sophia as we replay that announcement for the people who just tuned in."

The television screen filled with the image of President Harden, the American flag behind him on his right, but Drew immediately noticed that the presidential flag, normally behind the president's left, had been replaced by the UN flag.

"If we, the human race of this great planet Earth, are going to move beyond our borders of dispute, beyond our ethnic differences, we must change how we think of ourselves as nations. In 1831, French historian Alexis de Tocqueville came to study democracy in America and called our nation the Great

Experiment. If ever we can testify to the success of that great experiment, we can do so now, after two hundred and forty years of welcoming people of all color, faith, and ideologies. We are a nation of diverse ethnic differences . . . and we thrive. We are a nation of many peoples . . . and we thrive. Let the United States of America be the model for planet Earth as we absolve our differences and thrive as a human race."

President Harden paused and looked straight into the camera and into the eyes of millions of Americans.

"People of America, it starts with trust—trust in each other as human beings, trust in leaders of nations. I can think of no greater way to honor that commitment to trust than to offer the security of Camp David, a beacon of global unity, to the forces of the United Nations. On September second, I will be meeting with United Nations Secretary-General Felice Albano De Luca and Islamic Global Alliance Premier Aashif Hakeem Jabbar to commemorate this milestone in the unification of humanity."

The scene cut out and was replaced with the images of Vincent and Bryant again.

"Sophia, as we all know," Vincent began, "the Marine Presidential Guard has been charged with the security of Camp David for decades. Have you had any response from any military personnel there?"

"That's right, Tom. In fact, the Marines have been charged with the security of Camp David since it opened under President Roosevelt. As you might expect, we are getting no comment from any of the active-duty military personnel."

"Thank you, Sophia Bryant. Now we go to Kevin Watson, who's doing a follow-up report on the successful quarantine and treatment of over five hundred patients infected during the recent outbreak of Ebola in the Democratic Republic of the Congo. Kevin, tell us—"

"What an insult," Jake said, clicking off the TV. "I guarantee the Marines are not happy about turning Camp David over to UN troops."

Drew shook his head. "So much for national sovereignty. Another American travesty."

"You can say that again. How's Fortress East holding up? You guys have been pulling in some great government jobs out there," Jake said.

"Yeah, all is well. Moving Mick there was a great decision. He's doing a great job managing the team," Drew said.

"Good. How's he doing with your occasional absences?"

Drew winced. "I'm not fooling him, and we both know it. I think he knew the day I showed up at Fortress."

Jake smiled. "Mick's a smart guy. He knows the score."

"The problem is that my, ah, outside work is getting more frequent and"—Drew hesitated as he looked at Jake—"I get the sense that my handler is concerned."

"Is that really why you're here?" Jake asked.

Drew smiled and shook his head. "Never was any foolin' you, Jake." He looked out the window toward the range, then turned back to Jake and leaned forward. "Something's not right. I can't put my finger on it, but my last few missions have been all over the place—Puerto Rico, Congo, Washington, DC, Syria, Afghanistan, and even inside the UN. My last assignment to Pakistan was completely solo—no contacts, no support. I don't have the big picture, but I can tell that my handler is getting desperate for intel, and I seem to be the only one he's using to get it. Something's changed in the last few months, and it isn't good."

Jake thought for a moment. "I don't know what to tell you, Drew. But you have to know where the line is and pull back when you get close to it. A dead agent isn't any good to anyone." He thought for a moment. "Are you absolutely sure that you're not being manipulated or used for the wrong purpose?"

Drew sat back in his chair and rubbed his eyes. Jake had hit the nail on the head. Drew had been trying to figure out if Ross was good or bad from the day he met him.

"No. I'm not sure, and the truth is . . . that's a big part of my concern. I'm so isolated from the rest of the agency that I'm not sure who I'm really working for."

Jake looked straight into Drew's eyes just like he always did when he wanted Drew to really grab hold of his next few words. "If you find yourself in a place you can't fix, to heck with clearances—you call me and I'll be there. And Fortress will be right behind me."

Drew smiled. He realized that this assurance from Jake was exactly what he was looking for and needed. He stood and pushed his hand out toward Jake.

"Thanks, Jake. You've always been there for me, even when—" Drew choked up. "Even when my dad couldn't be."

Jake grabbed Drew's hand, pulled him in, and hugged him. "I never needed my own son . . . I've got you."

The rare moment of tenderness came and went quickly, but Drew had no idea how much he needed that.

On his way back to Fortress East, Drew detoured to New York to check in on Ben. He had received a message that appeared urgent and couldn't imagine what his genius buddy would consider urgent. His mind swept through the entire gamut of possibilities, from discovering a new widget to alien ships landing at NexTech.

He arrived at the office just a few minutes before the end of the business day. He was able to see Ridge, Jester, Crypt, and Piper and brag on their work creating Witness, his leather jacket turned smartphone.

"Hey, guys, show Drew the glasses," Ben said as he continued working at a station nearby.

Jester opened a case and lifted out a very impressive set of sunglasses.

"Excellent . . . and they even look cool," Drew said.

"Since we didn't trust ourselves to design 'cool,' we started with a pair of Oakleys and went from there," Crypt said.

"Your entire visual interface with Witness will be through these glasses. You can configure the display any way you like," Ridge added with pride.

Drew took the glasses and put them on. His vision immediately filled with icons, menus, and a variety of sensor displays. The shading automatically adjusted to the brightness of the room. "This is impressive. How do I clean this up and rearrange items?"

"Just look at what you want to move or change and tell Alice," Piper said, pushing her own glasses back up the bridge of her nose. "The glasses are linked to her through a Bluetooth connection."

Drew looked at the weather widget. "Alice, remove this widget." The widget immediately disappeared. He smiled and nodded. "Well done, team! Mr. Belvedere will be very pleased!"

They took a few minutes to explain all the features to Drew, and then Crypt, Ridge, and Jester grabbed a few things and started to leave.

"We also just finished our beta version of mobile Alice," Piper said with a grin. She looked at Ben, who was mesmerized by something on his screen. "Hey, Chider, you want me to stick around and help with the upgrade?"

Drew saw the hope in her eyes, but Ben was oblivious.

"Thanks, Piper, but I got it. You guys have a good night."

Piper flashed a sheepish smile at Drew, then left to catch up with the other three.

Drew wanted to smack Ben. "What are you doing? Are you seriously that clueless?"

Ben looked up from the screen. "What are you talking about?"

Drew pointed down the hallway, where Piper and the rest of his team had just turned the corner. "Her!"

Ben looked at Drew as if he were talking in some foreign language.

"We are quite the pair," Drew said, shaking his head. "I can't keep my girl, and you don't even know girls exist."

Ben turned back to the screen. "Alice, upload your mobile version into Witness."

Drew gave up and tried to focus on what really excited Ben. "So you finished mobile Alice. This is awesome. With the glasses and the upgrade, Witness will be fully functional and autonomous."

Ben turned from the computer screen and looked at Drew. "This isn't why I've called you here." His eyes started to gleam. He looked around Drew as if to make sure no one was left in the room, then stood up and motioned for Drew to follow him to his office. Inside, Ben shut the door and looked at Drew. "I did it, Drew!"

The excitement in his voice was unprecedented. Drew didn't dare jump to conclusions. There was no telling what Ben's quirky mind might be thinking of, but he could only hope.

"Did what, exactly?" Drew asked.

Ben could hardly contain himself. He began pacing back and forth, smiling from ear to ear. "With Alice's help, I finally solved Dr. Waseem's missing equation! I did it!"

"Wait . . . wait . . ." Drew grabbed Ben's arm so he could look him in the eye. "Are you telling me that you actually got the LASOK to work? Is that what you're saying, Ben?"

Ben grabbed Drew's arms. "Yes—the LASOK works! I've successfully accelerated light, and I can now precisely control the increase in speed. It works, Drew!"

Drew froze. He was excited *and* frightened. Did he dare hope that the invaders were real, not some fabrication of his subconscious? Or would he discover with absolute certainty that he truly was schizophrenic and would have to deal with this mental disorder for the rest of his life? He was almost too afraid to find out.

He turned his head and looked at the image called Validus, who stood in the corner of Ben's office. He stared back at Drew, his stoic expression impossible to read. Though Drew wanted desperately to be free of the schizophrenic prison his subconscious had created for him, he wanted Validus to be real . . . He *needed* Validus to be real. What if the LASOK overwhelmed the imagination of his subconscious with truth so that Validus disappeared forever? His heart ached as if he were about to say good-bye to a close friend—a friend who had risked his life for him time and time again.

"Drew, did you hear me? I did it! The LASOK works!"

Drew shook from his emotional stupor and smiled at Ben. "That is incredible! I knew you could do it!" He hugged Ben, then pushed him back while holding onto his arms. "You are the man, Benjamin Berg. You are the man! Have you seen anything?"

Ben shook his head. "I haven't used the optics yet, just measured the increased speed a few times." He looked a little nervous, and Drew realized that he was just as anxious about finding out the truth as he was. "I decided to wait for you to test the optics."

Drew nodded.

Ben took Drew into the LASOK lab after they were certain no one in the building would come looking for them. Ben fired up the LASOK, and Drew noticed that there was a lot less tweaking and a lot less time required getting it ready compared to the original LASOK Dr. Waseem had built.

When Ben was ready, he stood back with Drew, soaking up the technical masterpiece before them. A powerful argon laser reflecting off multiple mirrors, the orange glow of a plasma generator pulsing through a series of glass tubes, power supplies, test equipment, LCD displays, and a host of new equipment and interfaces that Drew couldn't even begin to guess at were all humming with life, ready to give rebirth to a new technology.

Ben took a deep breath. "I've installed two sets of external mirrors that will give the LASOK direct images from the outside. One set looks north down the street and the other looks south. I've arranged the images so that we can do a split-screen image, seeing both directions at once. And just to make sure we don't miss anything, this time I've installed a high-speed digital video recorder that is post lens acceleration so we can capture everything we see. The hard part is going to be finding the exact speed that was tuned in to the invaders. I've got it tuned to approximately the same speed as Dr. Waseem's LASOK when it exploded. This screen here is a display of what's being recorded." Ben looked at Drew. "No need to use the view finder and risk another plasma accident."

"Very thoughtful," Drew said. "Let's do this."

Ben opened the orifice that let the visual imagery into the LASOK. "Alice, begin video recording of LASOK imagery at three hundred frames per second."

"Recording," Alice responded.

"Can I see the raw imagery coming from the mirrors?" Drew asked. "That way I can tell you if there are actually any invaders, and you can tune the speed until you see them through the LASOK."

"Great idea," Ben said. "Here are the controls to align the mirrors. These two images are what is being directed into the LASOK."

Drew watched the images closely. Since it was the end of a business day, the streets were full of activity, and it wasn't long before Drew saw multiple dark and light invaders. His heart began racing as he called out each incident. Ben swept through the range of speeds, searching for the perfect setting.

After six unsuccessful attempts to lock in on any invader, Drew's heart began to sink.

"I don't understand," Ben said in frustration. He checked his equipment and verified that the system was indeed working.

"Last time we had to overload the system to reach the speed that allowed me to see them. Are you sure we're there?" Drew asked.

"Positive. I've been able to increase the speed of light another ten percent beyond what Dr. Waseem's LASOK could reach. And my adjustments are twice as precise. It should work!"

Drew's tenuous hope began to fade. They tried for another thirty minutes on another ten invaders and still got nothing. On the last attempt, Drew wasn't even hopeful anymore. He came to the inescapable conclusion that he truly was schizophrenic. He stepped away from the image mirrors.

"Whoa!" Ben said.

Drew looked at the mirrors. "Sorry, buddy, but there aren't even any invaders out there right now."

"Maybe not, but look at this," Ben said pointing to the people. Wherever there was a person, there was an aura around them, almost as if they were emitting light from their skin."

"What is that?" Drew asked.

"I'm not sure. It only occurs in a very narrow range of speeds. I missed it on all of the previous scans and just stumbled onto it now."

A woman with a dog walked through the field of view. The woman was glowing, but the dog was not.

"What in the world is going on?" Ben asked.

He carefully tuned the speed down until the glow disappeared, and then for one split second, the dog began to glow but the people did not. Ben tried to retune the speed, but the woman and her dog turned a corner and disappeared out of view.

Ben turned and looked at Drew, bewildered.

"Don't look at me . . . You're the genius," Drew said, still fighting the ache of truth about the invaders. Years of struggle just to find out it was all in his mind.

Ben scratched his head and tried to retune back to the speed where the people were glowing. It took him another five minutes before he found it. They stared at the images for a long time.

"What do you think it is?" Drew asked.

Ben shook his head. "Not sure. It could be just a visual anomaly, but . . ." He pursed his lips. "No . . . it's too consistent. It's the exact same speed every time. It's always there. And the dog . . ." Ben thought for a moment. "Alice, replay the sequence with the woman walking her dog."

They watched until they saw the people quit glowing.

"Advance at twenty-five percent normal speed," Ben commanded.

When the dog began to glow, Ben froze the image and recorded the speed at which light was being accelerated.

"Wow, that is just 4.3 meters per second slower than when the people were glowing. My adjustment isn't that fine. We're lucky to have even caught it . . . whatever *it* is."

"Yeah . . . lucky." Drew walked over to a chair and sat down, unimpressed with this new "anomaly."

Ben spun around in his chair, and the two of them just stared at each other for a minute. Drew noticed that Validus and two of his team had disappeared through the wall to leave him and Ben alone.

"I'm sorry, Drew. It should be working. I'll keep at it until we get it."

Drew forced a smile. "I don't think we're going to get it, Ben. But I guess we can look at the bright side. There should be some amazing spinoff technology from your research." He rallied himself for Ben's sake. "You've done great, Ben. Your work is truly amazing."

Ben forced a smile back at Drew, displaying the same disappointment he felt. "I'm not giving up, Drew. I'm sure there's a logical reason for it, and I will find it. There's a lot left to discover about this machine."

Just then Alice spoke into Drew's earpiece. "I've just detected two new messages from your contact."

Drew froze. "Alice, what contact are you talking about, and how do you know there is a new message?"

"I watched your last interaction online and ran an algorithm to determine the sequence. Would you like me to erase this smart prediction procedure?"

Drew looked at Ben. "Your Alice is scary smart."

"Kind of like having me in your head, isn't it?" Ben said with wry smile.

"No, Alice, don't delete. Display messages."

The first message read: *Priority 2. Package delivery to Washington, DC, Steam Cafe & Pizzeria, 1700 17th St NW, 10:30 p.m. Authenticate "rain." Authenticate "ice." Package to follow.*

Drew checked his watch. He had just over four hours to get from New York to Washington, DC.

"That's ridiculous," Drew said out loud. There was no way he could catch a flight in time.

"The second message is the location online of an encrypted file. Would you like me to download it?" Alice asked.

"Yes, Alice, and transfer it to a USB drive. Can you decrypt the file?"

"Perhaps. I can give you an estimated time of decryption once I receive the file."

"Make it so," Drew said.

"What's up?" Ben asked.

Drew looked at Ben. "Can I borrow your car?" He figured if he left immediately, he could drive the 220 miles and just make it in time.

"Sure. Where are you going?" Ben reached in his pocket and threw him the keys.

"Thanks. Washington, DC."

Drew caught the look in Ben's eye. It was the same look that he remembered seeing back at Rivercrest High School when he was an outcast for causing the death of the star quarterback, Joey Houk. A look of compassion and friendship.

"I should probably go with you," Ben said. "You know, to make sure my car stays in one piece."

Drew couldn't help his smile. It was only a priority two, a simple drop of some data. He could leave Ben in the car a few blocks away and then return. There would be no danger to Ben.

"Yeah, you probably should. My driving has been a little rough lately."

Ben nodded. "Alice, save all LASOK data recorded, and secure file with my authorization for access only."

"Complete," Alice replied.

Ben quickly shut down the LASOK. Ten minutes later, Drew and Ben were navigating toward Interstate 95 south. Alice helped Drew bypass the worst of the traffic, and before long, the lights of New York City were diminishing in the rearview mirror.

Drew looked over at Ben, thankful once more for a friend who was willing to bear his discouragement with him.

PLAUSIBLE DENIABILITY

Jayt and Brumak, you two provide protection for Carter as he travels."
The two angels left to catch up with Carter and Berg as they exited Nex-Tech. Tren, Persimus, Crenshaw, and Rake were still in the LASOK lab, waiting for Validus's next orders.

"The rest of you get to Carter's op location and evaluate the threat before he gets there. I don't want any surprises. I need to make a dash to Malak's headquarters and make sure he's ready if we need him."

"You expecting trouble?" Tren asked.

Validus hesitated. "Always, but after my last visit to see what Ross was doing, I think we may need those legions sooner than we think."

"Commander, why didn't it work?" Rake asked as he examined the LASOK. He seemed fascinated by the machine. "Isn't this machine how Carter was able to see into our realm in the first place?"

"It was never going to work," Validus said. "Not the way they wanted it to."

"Why not?" Persimus asked.

"That which is born of the flesh is flesh, and that which is born of the Spirit is spirit," Crenshaw said.

They all looked at him.

"Elohim would never allow a machine made with human hands to be able to peer across the fringe into our realm," Crenshaw said.

"He's right," Validus said. "It is not the way of Elohim."

Tren went over to the LASOK to examine something.

"But what about Carter?" Rake asked. "Why did it work for him the first time?"

Tren turned around. "Perhaps it never did."

Drew enjoyed Ben's company. They talked a lot about the LASOK and came up with a few more options they could try before giving up on seeing the invaders. They also became excited about how the technology could revolutionize many aspects of the industry.

Drew saw an Exit sign and checked his watch. They were making good time. He took the exit.

"Why the detour?" Ben asked.

Drew didn't reply. He knew it was foolish, especially with Ben there, but he couldn't help it. His detour was less than two miles off Interstate 295, so it was a minimal diversion.

He pulled the car over to the curb just across the street from a duplex in East Greenwich near Philadelphia. He scanned the windows of the home, hoping for a glimpse of the one woman who stirred his soul, who drove him crazy. The one woman he could never have.

"Oh . . . oh, I get it. I know whose place this is. Are we seriously doing this? Drew, I told you from the beginning what would happen, and you didn't listen. Here we are on some super-secret mission of yours, probably to save the United States of America, and you want to stop and stalk Sydney Carlyle."

"Be quiet, Ben," Drew said.

"Does she know you stalk her?"

"I'm not stalking."

Ben just crossed his arms and slowly shook his head. "We drove out of our way to sit outside her home at night and look through her windows. You're stalking. Why don't you just go and talk to her? What could it hurt?"

Drew shook his head. "I promised to stay out of her life. In my line of work, there's no future for us. Besides," Drew pointed to the house, "she has her own future now."

Ben turned to look at the house. They watched as Sydney came to the window to draw the shades. As she did, a man came up behind her and wrapped his arms around her. Seeing it hurt much more than Drew thought it would. Something broke inside him. He put the car in gear and drove away, back toward the interstate.

Ben was silent for a long time.

"I'm sorry, man. I know that has to hurt. Who is he?"

Drew merged onto I-295 and headed south to Washington, DC. "His name is Ethan Elsing."

"Ethan Elsing? What kind of name is that? He's got to be a loser with a name like that."

"Actually, he's a doctor, and he's a good man," Drew replied, then added, "the kind of man Sydney deserves."

Ben huffed. "She deserves you and you deserve her. I don't know why you guys have to make this so stupid and complicated. Are you intent on being miserable for the rest your life?"

"It *is* complicated, brainiac. She's a Christian and I'm not. She won't love a man who's not a Christian. I also happen to have a job I can't talk about. What kind of life is that for her? And there are other issues."

"There's more?" Ben asked.

Drew still didn't have the heart to tell Ben about his psychiatric evaluation and that he didn't believe in his alien theory anymore. The LASOK experiment sealed that truth.

"It doesn't matter. Sydney just got her master's and now has a great guy to make her happy. There's just not a future where we will ever be together."

"If you say so, boss."

When they arrived in DC, Drew found the café and drove past it a couple times to reconnoiter the area, then pulled over to the curb two blocks to the south. He put the vehicle in park and left it running. He looked over at Ben.

"This shouldn't take long. If for some reason I'm not back in thirty minutes, just turn around and go back to New York."

Ben looked a little surprised. "You like doing this?"

Drew wasn't sure how to answer that. It would help a lot if he could get a look at the file he was delivering so he could determine if he was really working for the right people. He looked at Ben, then stepped out of the vehicle.

"Alice, have you decrypted that file yet?"

"No, Drew. I estimate six hours and twenty-three minutes."

Drew walked the two blocks and entered the café. He scanned, not sure who he was supposed to be looking for. The café was mostly empty, and none of the people there looked like a contact. There was a couple at a table near the back of the seating area, a young man with a beanie near the front, and an older man at one of the booths along the windowed wall on the north side of the café. Drew chose an empty booth midway down the same wall and took the seat facing the entrance. He ordered a cup of coffee, then located the small USB in his pocket and slipped it between the folds of a napkin on the table.

At precisely 10:30, the café door opened and a man in his forties walked in wearing a jean jacket and a Red Sox baseball hat. After looking over the tables and booths, he sat down at a table near Drew.

He picked up the menu and then glanced toward Drew. "Feels like we've got some rain coming in."

"Yeah, and with the cold snap, I just hope it doesn't turn to ice on the roads," Drew replied, then picked up his menu and started perusing it. The authentication according to the message from Ross was complete.

The man slid into the booth seat opposite Drew. Drew scanned the restaurant and what he could see outside through the window. His eyes came to rest on the man across from him, and he studied his face. It was a face that didn't fit with a baseball hat. Seasoned, intelligent, political, confident but fearful.

Drew slid the napkin across the table. The man covered the napkin with his hand, scrunched it up, and stuffed it into his pocket. He replaced it with another napkin from his other pocket.

Drew wasn't expecting an exchange. That wasn't what the message said, and Ross never miscommunicated. Drew looked at the napkin, then at the man. Something didn't look right. Perhaps it was the apprehension he saw in the man's eyes.

Drew saw two dark invaders flash by outside and his subconscious Validus lunged after them.

"Do you know who I am?" the man asked.

Drew studied his face once more, then illumination hit him. "Senator Hanson from Massachusetts."

The café door opened and a woman hurried inside, dripping wet from the rain that had hit DC. She shuddered and shook the rain from her shoulders and arms. Then went to a booth behind Hanson and sat on the far bench.

Hanson looked down at the napkin and then back to Drew. "Tell Ross the infiltration is much worse than we thought. The Patriots are ready, but we need solid proof from him before we can move."

Drew tried to fit Hanson's message into the intelligence he had been gathering with Ross over the past year but didn't fully see the connection. Who were the Patriots?

He saw movement outside the window right next to their booth and two of his subconscious warriors exploded into action. Drew struggled—react? Ignore? He put his hand in his lap, close to his gun, just as a precaution, then reached for the napkin with his left.

Hanson started speaking again. "Tell him we are planning to—"

Drew heard it before he saw the consequences. Three distinct shots fired through a silencer at close range. Hanson's eyes bulged just before he slumped forward.

Drew reacted instantly. He drew his FN Five-Seven and dove to the floor just as another two rounds hit the back of his seat cushion. He squeezed off three rounds at the woman sitting in the booth behind them. She fell out of the booth, her silencer hitting the wooden floor with a thud.

Two seconds later, the café erupted into chaos and screams. More gunshots rang out as the couple at the back of the restaurant fired a volley of shots Drew's direction. He rolled, trying to find cover beneath the tables, but one of the shots found its mark. The bullet penetrated Witness and entered his left shoulder.

"Witness integrity compromised," Alice said.

Drew fought against the pain and returned fire, trying not to hit the old man who was hunkered down in his booth and hugging the wall. Drew looked for cover, but in an open café there was none to be had. Four more rounds blasted into the wood flooring around him, one of them nicking his thigh. He returned fire, but it was just a matter of time before one of the bullets would be fatal.

Drew was vaguely aware of his subconscious warriors in battle around him, fighting dozens of dark invaders. He ignored them and tried to focus.

He heard more gunshots ring out, but this time they came from behind him, near the front of the café. He knew he was done—bracketed by gunmen without cover. This was his last mission, and his last few seconds of life.

Remarkably, none of the shots he heard hit him, but instead the woman at the back of the café collapsed. Drew continued to focus on the man who was still unloading his gun in Drew's direction, but this time the bullets did not impact near Drew, but above him. He heard a thump just a few feet away. The break in the attack allowed him the split second he needed to zero in on the shooter and put two rounds into his chest.

The entire gunfight had lasted less than sixty seconds. Drew rolled, and his shoulder exploded in pain.

"Are you okay?" a familiar voice asked.

Drew looked up to see his friend from the Farm, Aaban Hadad, kneeling down to help him up.

"Hadad! What are you—"

Hadad shook his head. "We need to get out of here . . . now!" His dark brown eyes were fierce.

He helped Drew gain his feet. They started moving toward the door, but then Drew remembered the USB drive Senator Hanson was trying to give him.

"Wait," Drew said.

He went back to the table and grabbed the drive, wincing as he bent over to grab the drive out of the senator's pocket as well. He felt Hanson's neck and detected an extremely weak pulse. He didn't have a chance.

Drew heard sirens coming, and he couldn't afford to be taken in. He had no official cover. Ross had ensured that he and whoever Drew's operations were conducted for had plausible deniability. If Drew was brought in, Ross and the CIA would deny all connection with him.

Hadad grabbed Drew and hurried him out of the restaurant and down the street. They turned up an alley, then ran as fast as they could, dodging in-between buildings and streets.

Four invaders were near, swords drawn. Two were bleeding as well. Drew felt his own blood flowing down the front of his chest, and the pain was getting worse quickly. He had to stop. He leaned up against a brick wall in one of the alleys, the pain pulsing with each breath he took.

Hadad stopped and looked back at Drew. "We can't stop here. They've got others looking for you."

"Who . . . what's going on, Hadad? Why were you there? Did the CIA send you?"

Hadad came back to Drew. "The CIA is compromised, Carter. I'm a double agent. I've been Mossad all along. We knew they were targeting specific agents . . . agents who are key to exposing them."

"Who?" Drew asked as another wave of pain shot through him. This one made him nauseous. He wasn't sure how much farther he could go.

"The IGA," Hadad said.

A car turned up the alley and started coming toward them. Hadad pulled Drew to the ground, and both men leveled their guns.

"Ben is approaching," Alice said.

"Hold up," Drew said. "He's mine."

Hadad looked up and down the alley for other threats. "The IGA is planning something big, Carter. Our agents in the Middle East have just intercepted intel from the IGA that indicated September fifth as detonation day—not September eleventh like we'd expect. Whatever attack they have planned is supposed to happen at midnight. Whoever you're working with doesn't have much time. Here, I was instructed to give this to whoever was going to meet Hanson."

Hadad put another USB drive in Drew's hand. Drew stuffed it in his pocket just as Ben pulled up next to him.

Hadad reached to help Drew up. "If anybody can do something about this, Carter, it's you."

"Thanks for the help back there," Drew said.

Hadad nodded. "I'll be in touch. They'll be looking for you. Be careful who you trust."

Drew opened the car door and fell into the passenger seat. "Go, Ben. Get us out of here."

"What happened? Alice says your vitals are off. Are you okay?" Ben asked, navigating back to the street. He turned north.

Drew grimaced. "So much for your bulletproof jacket."

"Seriously? Where are you hit?" Ben said, swerving as he tried to look Drew over. "And I never said Witness was bulletproof!"

"Just get me—" Drew began, but he couldn't finish. He leaned his head back against the head rest, trying desperately to get on top of the pain.

"I'm taking you to a hospital," Ben said.

"No! No hospital. I'll be dead by morning," Drew said to make his point.

"Sheesh, Drew . . . What's going on? Don't tell me you're still CIA."

Drew's world began to fade. It took everything in him to fight blacking out.

INTERSECTION

I didn't know where to take him, Sydney. He says if he goes to a hospital they'll find him and kill him. Please help him."

Drew was pale and nearly delirious. Sydney grabbed one of Drew's arms and helped Ben get him through the door.

"Quick, get him in here. Who's 'they,' Ben?"

"They . . . them . . . you know."

"No, Ben. I don't know. We'll talk about this later."

Ben and Sydney half-carried Drew into the living room and laid him on the couch. He was bleeding badly.

Ben looked at Sydney. "What are we going to do? If we don't get help, he's going to die."

Sydney ran and got some clean towels to put on the bullet wound. Blood had soaked the upper half of his shirt. Sydney grabbed her phone and started dialing.

"What are you doing, Sydney?" Ben asked.

"I'm calling for an ambulance," Sydney said, her voice thick with worry.

Drew felt better just getting off his feet and being able to lie down. He reached up and grabbed Sydney's arm, shaking his head. "No ambulance, Syd. Call Jake," he wheezed.

Sydney stopped, her finger over the green phone icon. "Drew you need medical attention. You'll die here."

"I'll die there," he said and closed his eyes.

She erased the numbers and instead pressed one of her speed-dial numbers. "I need to talk to Dr. Elsing. It's an emergency. Tell him it's Sydney Carlyle."

"Sydney . . . no," Ben said, but he didn't stop her.

"Ethan, it's Sydney. I need you at my place right away. Please hurry, it's a matter of life and death. No, I can't explain . . . Yes . . . please hurry!" Sydney knelt down next to Drew and wiped his hair out of his eyes. "Ethan is my fiancé."

Drew opened his eyes and looked up at her. Her eyes mirrored the pain he was feeling. "Good for you, Syd." He attempted a smile, but it transformed into a grimace of extreme pain.

Sydney's eyes filled with tears. "What have you done, Drew?"

"I got in the way of a bullet," he quipped, but Sydney didn't laugh. "It'll be okay, Syd. It didn't hit any vitals or arteries or I would have bled out already. We need to get the bullet out; then I need stitches and antibiotics." He grimaced again. "And maybe some pain pills."

Sydney sent a text to Ethan relaying Drew's request, then pressed hard on the towel that was quickly soaking through with Drew's blood. She shook her head. "Can't you ever have a normal life? What is it with you, Drew?" She wiped her forearm across her forehead to keep the hair out of her eyes and to keep from wiping blood on her face. She told Ben to go get another towel. "When will you be done with this cloak-and-dagger stuff?" Her voice was laced with anger and worry.

Drew looked up at those beautiful blue eyes that had captured his heart years ago. "I don't have much of a choice, Syd, but I sure didn't want to drag you into this again."

He couldn't read her face enough to know if her expression was one of sympathy for a wounded soldier or pity for a crazy man. He was finding it harder to focus his eyes and his thoughts.

"Drew . . . what are we going to do with you?"

He mumbled something back, but he wasn't even sure what he said. After that there were fuzzy images of a man looking over him, pain, and voices.

"Is this the guy?" He heard a heavy voice say, but he couldn't hear the answer to the question.

The next time Drew had a thought that made sense, he could hear voices speaking across the room. He opened his eyes just enough to see Sydney and a man he presumed to be Ethan talking. He was a handsome guy with sand-colored hair and a face that belonged on *GQ*. Though more slender than Drew, he looked fit and in shape. They spoke in hushed tones, but Drew could hear every word.

"If he's working for the government, then why won't he go to the hospital? Didn't you say the FBI had charges against him once? Maybe it's the FBI that shot him."

Sydney crossed her arms. "I had to help him, Ethan. He's a good man in spite of what has happened to him."

Ethan ran his hands up and down Sydney's arms. "It's too dangerous, Sydney. Now that he's been treated, we need to call the police. Just by helping him, we could go to prison!"

"No!"

"He's right," Drew called out. His voice was gruff and slurred. He put one foot on the floor, hoping to find the energy and the will to sit up. "It's too dangerous. They'll be coming for me, and it won't take them long to figure out to look here."

Ethan and Sydney looked toward Drew. Ethan was angry. Sydney looked worried.

"Where's Ben?" Drew asked. He tried to sit up but didn't even get his good shoulder off the couch before shockwaves of pain flooded his chest.

Sydney rushed over to him. "Stay still, Drew. You're in no condition to move yet."

Ethan walked over and stood next to Sydney about the same time that Ben came in from another room. Drew examined the dressing the doctor had put on him. The blood was gone, and the bandage looked good. Ethan must have found and removed the bullet, and Drew imagined there were multiple stitches beneath the bandage. He also noted that his grazed leg had been attended to as well.

"How you feeling, buddy?" Ben asked. "I told you Witness wasn't bullet-proof."

Drew put out a hand for Ben to grab. With a grimace on his face, he slowly lifted himself to a sitting position. Sydney supported his neck and shoulder until he was upright and leaning against the back cushion of the couch. He closed his eyes and let the pain and dizziness fade from his mind for a few seconds.

"Dr. Elsing, thank you for treating me."

Ethan nodded, but his dour expression didn't change.

Drew looked at Sydney. "How long have I been out?"

"About three hours."

Too long. He had to move ... but to where? Drew's body felt like it weighed a thousand pounds. He couldn't imagine even having the strength to walk to a car, but they couldn't stay here a minute longer.

"We've got to go, Ben."

"Where to? The company may not be safe, and neither are our homes."

Drew nodded. "We need to get off the grid as much as possible. Did you call Jake?"

"No. You were sounding pretty paranoid, and I wasn't sure who I should contact."

"Good thinking, Ben."

"Wait ... just wait a minute," Ethan interjected. "Who are *they?*"

Sydney looked at Drew with narrowed eyes. She had asked the same question.

Drew looked up at Ethan. "Ethan, you have no reason to trust me, and every reason not to." He paused to catch his breath. "All I can tell you is that I'm one of the good guys, and the less you know, the safer you and Sydney will be."

Ethan didn't look convinced. His smirk was filled with skepticism.

Drew grimaced again, and he felt like he needed to lie down. But if he did, he might not get up for a very long time. He steeled himself against the temptation to give in to his fatigue and pain.

All four of them were quiet for a time. Drew was desperately trying to make his mind work and decide on some safe house they could hide out in so he could recover. He had a safe house in Minnesota, but it was too far. He needed something close and soon.

"I know of a place," Sydney said, "and I'll take you there."

"What? No!" Ethan stepped forward. "I won't allow it. You can't go with them, Sydney. Whether he's telling the truth—which I highly doubt—or he is a crazy man, it's too dangerous. It's absurd! No, I won't allow it!"

"He's right, Sydney," Drew added. "You can't come with us. It *is* too dangerous."

Her eyes narrowed. Drew had seen that look before, and it was a look that always preceded her getting her way. She glanced at Drew, then focused on Ethan.

"And you think I won't be in danger here, waiting for 'them,' whoever they are, to come and interrogate me about where Drew and Ben are?"

None of the three men said a word.

Sydney looked at Drew. "Drew, the people coming after you, are they government agents?"

Any information Drew offered would pull them in further, but just the fact that he was in her apartment put them beyond any safety net. "Probably, but they're not the kind you want to meet. They don't operate by the rules like we do. The constitution means nothing to them."

"Is he serious? Are you some kind of conspiracy nut? Sydney, how did you get mixed up with this guy?"

Sydney looked miffed. She pulled Ethan away from the couch. She was using a hushed voice, but it did little to stop Drew from hearing them.

"I know this looks a little crazy, but this is also the guy who saved my life—three times! The least I can do is help him now while he's bleeding with nowhere to go." Her voice steadily increased in volume until even Ben could hear them. "He can barely sit up, and I know him—he won't go to a hospital. He needs tending to."

"I'll take care of him," Ben shouted across the room.

Sydney came briskly back to the couch. "Oh, please! You can hardly take care of yourself, let alone someone with a bullet hole in him."

Ben smirked and then nodded in agreement.

Ethan grabbed Sydney's arm. "What are you doing, Sydney? This is ridiculous. This isn't like you. Where did this crazy behavior come from all of a sudden? I don't want you going with them!"

Sydney turned and looked up into Ethan's eyes. She took a deep breath, then transformed her stern look of determination into a gentle smile. Drew had also seen this look before.

She put a hand to Ethan's cheek. "I'll be okay, Ethan. I promise. In a few days when this is over, I'll come back to you, and we'll finish planning our wedding. Okay?"

Seeing Sydney being tender with Ethan hurt again. The hole in Drew's heart was more painful than the hole in his shoulder. He watched Sydney's magic work on Ethan as it had on him many times before.

Ethan's face softened and his shoulders relaxed. He shook his head as he took her hand and held it with both of his. "Don't do anything foolish. And I want to know where you're going so I can bring the police at a moment's notice. That's the deal."

"Don't tell him, Sydney. It will put everyone at risk, including Ethan."

"Shut up, Carter. I'm not handing my fiancé over to some crazy man with a death wish." Ethan brushed hair out of Sydney's face. "Tell me, Sydney."

Sydney leaned close to Ethan and whispered in his ear. Drew couldn't take it anymore. He wished Ben hadn't brought him here. His heart was bleeding out worse than his real wound.

"Ben, help me up and get me to the car. We need to leave now."

Ben struggled to get Drew off the couch, but Sydney helped and they were soon at the door of the apartment and ready to exit.

Drew turned. "Elsing, it would be smart to clean up the blood so that when they do come, there's no evidence I was here. And if you have any vacation days, you might want to take a couple and go visit friends in a different city."

Ethan scowled. "I will not burn my vacation time running from some imaginary conspiracy group made up in the mind of a madman. If anything happens to her, Carter, I'm coming after you."

Ben and Sydney looked at each other with wide eyes. Drew scrutinized Ethan. "I know, doc. I'll die before I let anything happen to Sydney. I'll bring her back to you, I promise."

Ben and Sydney helped Drew to the car, but he nearly collapsed twice. Once inside he leaned up against the door and tried to keep from passing out, but he only lasted a few minutes, and then the world went black.

∽o∽

Validus and his men gathered outside the cabin on Lake Willow, a secluded and remote resort area in eastern Ohio. Evidently Carlyle's father had taken her and her family here on a vacation once when she was a child.

Jayt looked like he was struggling with half a dozen deep wounds from the recent Washington, DC battle. It was the closest Validus had come to losing Carter, and Jayt nearly dissolved trying to get to their charge during the gunfight.

Validus looked at the faces of his war-torn team. He remembered the day he had to convince them of the significance of the Carter mission. Today there was no convincing necessary.

"Last night we just about lost him, and were it not for the valiant efforts by all of you, I'm afraid this mission would have failed. Our challenge has been that we never know when or how the Fallen will attack next."

Validus looked through the large picture window of the cabin to see Drew sleeping on the couch with Sydney sitting next to him.

"But that is not the case now. Drew Carter and Sydney Carlyle are together, and this is as urgent as our protection will ever get. We must prepare for an all-out assault by legions of the Fallen.

"The seven of us will provide the close-range protection for Carter and Carlyle. Crenshaw, I want you next to me 24/7. I want to know if any Fallen gets within five miles of Carter. Brumak, Jayt, Rake, and Persimus will be lookouts for each of the four quadrants. Tren, you are within ten feet of Carter at all times. There are no relief shifts until this is over. While these two are together, the gates of hell could unleash at any time. Rake, get to Malak and tell him I need two legions here immediately."

All the warriors seemed encouraged by Validus's words, even Brumak.

"Yes sir," Rake said, his wings morphing out.

Validus shook his head. "No wings. Not until you are two hundred miles from here. I guarantee the Fallen are watching us, so be careful. Deliver the message and get back. Brumak and Persimus will give you cover until you take flight. Any questions?"

Validus looked at each warrior. When his gaze fell on Jayt, he could see the warrior was struggling.

"Jayt, I need you at full strength. Get to the water and initiate the Curing now."

Jayt's eyes narrowed and his jaw clenched. He nodded.

"Let's move," Validus said.

Brumak, Persimus, and Rake took off in a southern direction along the shore of the lake. Jayt straightened and began walking toward the water.

Tren started to go with him, but Validus grabbed his arm. "He won't want you there."

The pain was going to be excruciating. Most warriors preferred a hand to grip or a face to focus on to fight against the pain, but that was not Jayt's way. Tren still looked concerned.

"You get to Carter, and I'll be near if Jayt needs me," Validus said.

Tren seemed satisfied with that. He returned to Carter and Carlyle as Validus followed Jayt at a distance. The stoic warrior walked straight into the water without hesitating. Validus cringed as his man screamed inwardly against the avalanche of pain.

Rake returned later that day with a promise from Malak to come through with the warriors.

But two days later there were still no legions.

Validus paced outside the cabin, anger mounting. What if the Fallen had attacked already?

"Rake, I thought Malak said those warriors would be here. Where are they?"

Rake shook his head. "I—"

Validus stopped. "I'm sorry. This isn't your fault. I'm just frustrated." He scanned the area, looking for some sign that help was on its way.

That was when Crenshaw jumped from the roof and joined Validus and Rake. His face said it all. His mesmerizing eyes were filled with angst.

Validus tensed. His anger now full. "How many?"

Crenshaw looked at Rake, then Validus. "Too many to count, sir. Many legions coming from the south."

∽o∽

The sun was nestling between the pine trees across the water, spreading the last of its warmth on the inhabitants of Lake Willow. There wasn't a single wrinkle in the glass-like reflection of the water, capturing a perfectly symmetrical image of the trees, setting sun, and deepening blue sky—double the beauty for the eyes of the beholders.

And yet in spite of being surrounded by the indescribable beauty of Lake Willow, and in spite of being in the presence of the one girl who had completely captured his heart, Drew was as miserable as he had ever been in his life. He was healing quickly, but today was the first time in two days that he felt strong enough to walk and move around again.

Sydney suggested a short walk along the shore of the lake. Drew wondered if perhaps her intent was for more than exercise, for neither he nor Sydney had said a word regarding their feelings toward each other since he had met Ethan. Even now they walked in silence.

Drew noticed that Validus and three of his warriors were surrounding them, but he tried to ignore the visions. Since the shooting, his subconscious had kicked into overdrive.

Here in the serene beauty of the lake, it seemed as though the invaders were trying to grant him and Sydney a little extra space, almost as if they were chaperones who didn't want to intrude but yet were obligated to be near. Drew dreamed of, but could hardly remember, the days when his mind and vision were free from such intrusions.

After they had walked for a couple hundred yards, Drew stopped and pointed to the brilliant orange, red, and blue colors dancing off the undersides of the noctilucent clouds ushering out the day.

Sydney stopped and put her hands in her back pockets. "It's beautiful," she said, but the tone of her voice didn't match the beauty of the sunset.

Drew needed to help her, and he knew it; he just had to rally himself for the right words. "Syd, I'm glad you found the right guy for you. I don't want you to second-guess yourself. Ethan seems solid, and he'll take care of you."

She turned away from him. "I couldn't keep waiting, Drew. I—" She turned back to face him, and the pain in her soul poured out through her eyes. "I just had to move on. Ethan loves the Lord, and your life is so crazy."

Drew nodded. "I know." He wanted to reach out and hold her, but things were different now. She and Ethan belonged to each other, and Drew was not about to add confusion. "You had to move on, and I'm glad you did. You deserve so much better than me and what I could offer. Ethan will be that for you."

Her eyes saddened, and she forced a weak smile. "You guys didn't meet under the best of circumstances, but I think you would like him."

Drew tried to smile.

"I love him, Drew."

He lowered his gaze to the sand they were standing in. "I know. I can tell."

They both turned and looked across the lake. After a minute of silence, Drew started them back toward the cabin.

"Now that we got that cleared up, congratulations on getting your master's. That is amazing. I'm proud of you, Syd. What's next?"

"Actually, I'm thinking of going for my doctorate. I really love microbiology."

Drew smiled. "I'm not surprised. I think it's a great idea."

She shrugged. "Thanks."

Drew knew that his time with her would be short. He took a few seconds to gather his courage. "I was wondering if I could ask you a couple of questions."

"Sure."

"I can't even begin to tell you what's happened in my life in the last couple of years."

She held up her hand. "I'm not sure I want to know, Drew."

"Don't worry, Syd; tomorrow I'll be gone for good."

She bit her lower lip.

Drew glanced at her, wondering if he should go on. Of all the people in the world, she was the closest to really knowing who he was and what he had experienced. Perhaps it was his wound, but whatever it was, he felt vulnerable and a need to share the whole truth with her.

"Not long after the bombing in Chicago, the individual I worked for somehow discovered that I was . . . well . . . seeing things."

Sydney glanced up at him. He tried to read her to determine if he dared go on.

"And?" she asked.

"He forced me to see a psychiatrist." Drew sighed and shook his head. "He was a sharp guy. He claimed that with all the tragedy in my life, I was dealing with a severe case of posttraumatic stress disorder, and it developed into"—Drew couldn't make himself say *schizophrenia,* so he didn't—"visions that my subconscious conjures up to help me cope."

He didn't know how to read Sydney's expression.

"Jake and my mom know, but not Ben." His head lowered. "My whole life is such a lie. Ben thinks I still believe in his alien theory, and the people I work for think I'm schizophrenic. I live a double life, and now the US government is trying to kill me." Drew leaned up against a tree and crossed his arms. "I'm such a mess I don't know what to believe anymore."

∽o∾

Validus could feel the darkness moving in, surrounding them . . . swallowing them. There was no way any of them would survive this, let alone Carter and Carlyle. Malak had let him down, and now humanity was going to pay the price.

"We need to get them back to the cabin," Tren said.

Validus shook his head. "The cabin won't provide any protection from this. We make our stand here."

He had positioned his men at different intervals out with orders to collapse inward as the Fallen came at them.

Crenshaw turned his head. "Commander, Malak's legions are coming from the west."

"Praise Elohim! Malak is late, but at least we have a fighting chance." He turned to Rake. "Find the commander and tell him our location. Tell him to enter from the north, watching his west flank. The lake should protect the east."

Rake morphed his wings.

"Be careful, Rake," Crenshaw said. "They are everywhere."

Rake nodded and bolted north, first on foot to gain speed, then exploding into flight, arcing around to the west.

∽o∾

Sydney touched Drew's arm. He wished she hadn't. It only made an already confusing life even more so.

She seemed to sense it and withdrew her hand. "Are you still seeing the visions?"

Drew lifted his head and scanned. Did he see visions! Validus was near and his face wore the look of war. Invaders were gathering everywhere. Drew closed his eyes to make them go away.

"Yes, I see them. Every time there's a crisis or something bad is about to happen. The doctor says my mind fabricates the images to help me cope."

"Tell me what you see," Sydney said.

Drew shook his head. "I don't want to. I'm tired of it. I'm tired of being . . .

crazy." He rubbed his eyes. Fatigue was starting to set in. "I'm sorry, Syd. I shouldn't have told you. It wasn't fair." He pushed off from the tree, but she grabbed his arm again.

"I'm glad you did. Sit down and look at me . . . only at me."

Drew knew he shouldn't. It would only draw her more into his life, and that was not what he wanted for her, but she was the only one who brought a sense of peace into his life. He tried to ignore the chaos developing moment by moment in his imaginary world. He sat down and faced Sydney.

She smiled, and his heart melted one more time. "You said you wanted to ask me a couple of questions. What are they?"

He looked into her eyes and saw such peace. He was so envious. "I used to think I had life all figured out and that you were the crazy one for your beliefs. Now I realize that I'm the crazy one, and all along you've lived with such peace, such confidence. I wish . . ." His gaze fell again. "I wish I had that, Syd. I need peace in spite of this crazy world I'm in."

She lifted his chin. Her eyes were glowing with hope. Though the day was darkening, the blue plasma flame began to dance across her hands and face. His subconscious was so convincing.

"In Philippians, it says that God's peace surpasses our understanding and that it will keep your heart and your mind through Jesus Christ. The peace you see in me is the peace I have because of my Lord and Savior Jesus Christ."

"I remember reading that."

"You remember?" Sydney's eyebrows lifted.

"You made me promise to read the Bible again and seek God." He drew in a deep breath and exhaled. "I did, and I realized that my view of your faith was all wrong. This Jesus was one of the most courageous men I've ever read about. Your faith isn't for the weak but for the strong." He filled his hand with sand and let it slowly sift between his fingers. "That's when I realized that you were the strong one all along, Syd, and I was the weak one."

He saw flashes of swords and bullets all around him. His heart began to race. It was evident that he and Sydney were surrounded by a war between the invaders like he had never seen before. There were thousands locked in battle everywhere he looked. What was happening? Why was his mind doing this to him now?

He reached for his gun. Whether this was fabricated or not, invader activity almost always meant something bad was going to happen. Or was this exactly what Dr. Whitton said it was—his subconscious refusing to let Sydney destroy its imaginary world? He was so weary of trying to figure it out.

Sydney put her hand on his arm and then he felt her gentle hand on his cheek, pushing his face back toward hers. "Look at me, Drew."

"But it's never been this bad before. Crazy or not, it always means something bad is about to happen."

"Whatever is happening is happening because you're close to discovering the truth. Keep your eyes on me."

Drew tried to look only at her eyes, but it was impossible.

‹∞o∞›

Validus ordered reinforcements to engage another wave of Fallen attempting to outflank them and get at Carter from the west. Malak's legions had arrived just in time, but there hadn't been enough time to properly position all the warriors. Validus was commanding the entire operation as Crenshaw fed him moment-by-moment movements and predictions. For a three-mile radius around Carter, the region was filled with the fury of the battle of the ages. Malak's two legions, over ten thousand warriors, were fighting desperately to keep the minions of Niturni at bay. Thus far they had been successful, but . . .

"Three more legions of Fallen coming from the east!" Crenshaw shouted over the mayhem of an all-out war.

Validus was out of options. They couldn't keep their protection of Carter and Carlyle up for much longer.

"Who commands them?" Validus took ten seconds to cut through a demon that had breached their line.

Crenshaw closed his eyes, concentrated, then pointed south . . . into the sky. "Niturni."

Validus looked and saw his distant dark-winged nemesis commanding the assault. He looked over at Carter and Carlyle. "Almighty God, give your servants the strength to prevail. Draw this man to your salvation!"

‹∞o∞›

Sydney slid closer to Drew and put her hands over his eyes.

"Close your eyes, Drew. It'll be all right. How much of the Bible did you read again?"

Drew let the scent of her perfume and the warmth of her hands and her voice soothe him. "I read it all. I don't understand it all, but this time I got a glimpse into why it's so important to you."

"Why's that?"

"Because it gives you more to live for than yourself and . . ."

"And what?"

"And because God loves you." He wanted to open his eyes, but Sydney wouldn't let him.

"God loves you too, Drew. He wants to give you His peace and a purpose greater than anything you've ever experienced. Is that what you want?"

Drew couldn't deny it. "I want what you have, Syd. Yes."

"Then just talk to Him. He's waiting for you. Tell Him that you know you have sin in your life and you need Him to forgive you. Tell Him that you believe Jesus died on the cross for your sins and you want Him to come into your life. You've read it; you know that Jesus changed the world. That kind of change doesn't happen unless it's real."

He reached for her hands and pulled them down. He opened his eyes and saw a world exploding around them. Thousands and thousands of light and dark invaders were engaged in an epic battle. The blue plasma was streaking out from Sydney in all directions, empowering Validus and his men, but their lines were collapsing. There were too many dark invaders. The whole scene was bizarre, his subconscious once again turning Sydney into a hero in the invader realm, just as Dr. Whitton had said.

He fixed his eyes on Sydney and forced himself to know that it was all in his mind.

"Just talk to Him," she said again as she placed her hands on each side of his face, shielding his eyes from the chaos around them.

"That's it? No ritual? No chanting? No ten steps to faith?"

She smiled and slowly shook her head. "No . . . that's it. Just ask Him."

Sydney closed her eyes, folded her hands, and bowed her head. They were now encompassed in a glowing orb of blue. Drew marveled at the beauty of such a soul. Ethan was the luckiest man on earth.

Drew bowed his head. "God, I've never talked to You, and I'm sorry for that. I guess I never believed You existed, and I'm sorry about that too. I've screwed up so many times I wouldn't know where to start, so I just want You to know that I'm sorry. Please forgive me. I've read Your Word and I believe it. I believe that Jesus is Your Son and that He died for me. I don't understand why, because I know I'm not worth it, but I believe it. I believe You. Please come into my life and give me the peace that Sydney has. Amen."

Drew and Sydney both opened their eyes and lifted their heads at the same time. Drew stopped breathing. The world of the invader realm was absolutely still. Light invaders and dark invaders with weapons ready were frozen, and all eyes were on him. He looked around, realizing that if the battle were to continue, Validus and his men would go down.

"What is it, Drew? What do you see?"

Drew turned his face upward and saw it. At first a pinpoint of blue, but then like lightning from heaven, a shaft of burning blue plasma exploded down upon Drew. He was bathing in the glory and holiness of God as his soul filled with the Holy Spirit. He lifted his hands toward heaven, and the Spirit of God exploded outward like a shockwave in every direction. And as it went, every demon it touched for hundreds of yards dissolved in a green vapor that descended into the bottomless pit.

"Sydney . . . it's glorious!"

He stood up, slowly rotating and feeling the power of God flow through him. It was as if he were being transformed from the inside out. There were no words to adequately describe it other than, as he remembered reading, he was becoming a new man.

Sydney watched, tears streaming down her face.

"Is it like this for everyone?" he asked. He looked down at her with eyes open wide and his face aglow.

"God works a miracle in anyone who is willing. Yes, you just seem to have a better view." She smiled wide.

A few seconds later, the shaft of blue dissolved away, but now the flames he had seen in Sydney licked across his arms. He touched them.

"I'm . . . like you!" he said.

Sydney nodded as she wiped away her tears. "Yes, you are. You are now a child of the King!"

Drew looked around and realized that Validus and his men had all lifted their arms toward heaven too. Though he couldn't hear them, they were singing and shouting victory to each other and to heaven.

Then as if the warrior came to understand something profound, Validus stopped and looked at Drew. He held out his hands for his thousands of warriors to be quiet. They were waiting for something, but whatever it was did not come. Their joy was replaced with concern and then apprehension.

"Are they gone?" Sydney asked.

Drew turned and looked at Sydney. Slowly the exhilaration he felt began to fade.

"No," he whispered. "They're still here, and something is wrong."

23

AMBUSH

W here is Gabriel?" Crenshaw asked. "Why don't we hear the trumpet?" The salvation of Carter had happened, and they had been saved by the power of Ruach Elohim, but something wasn't right. If Carter was indeed the last salvation, where was the trumpet calling all believers to heaven?

Validus's men gathered around him, swords still in hand, as an eerie calm in both realms caused them all to hold their breath.

"I don't know," Validus said. He was confused and unable to give his men an answer. This had been the moment they were waiting for . . . fighting for . . . dying for. Even the Fallen, those who were left, seemed confused.

Validus looked toward Niturni, then to Carter. Had they all made a mistake?

Then Validus caught movement on the ground out of the corner of his eye. More danger was coming, and he heard the whisper of Elohim to his spirit, *Protect the man.*

⌒o⌒

Drew first heard them in the trees. He scanned and saw movement in the gray of the night. He looked at Sydney, sorry once again for what he had brought into her life. He pulled his FN Five-Seven.

"We need to get back to the cabin right now! Run fast!" He grabbed her hand and pulled her down the beach.

"What's happening, Drew? Who is it?"

"Sydney!" Drew heard Ethan call out.

"Oh, crud," Drew said as he continued to pull Sydney toward the cabin as fast as her legs would carry her. He counted four commandos behind them and speculated another four would be ahead of them—fully armed and wearing night-vision equipment.

Ethan stood on the beach, looking up and down the shoreline for Sydney. When Drew and Sydney reached him, he was more than upset.

"Carter—"

Drew put Sydney's hand in Ethan's and shoved them toward the cabin. "Get in the house now!"

He hurried them toward the house, but just as they were entering the back gate, the bricks in the gatepost just above Ethan's shoulder exploded from multiple rounds of 9mm.

"Stay low and get to the house." Drew turned and spotted the shooter. He squeezed off two rounds, then ran to catch up to Sydney and Ethan.

He could see Validus and his men engaged with their enemies again, but he wasn't sure how to even think about them anymore. He hadn't had time to fully process any of this.

Inside the cabin, Drew locked the door and called for Ben, but his friend didn't answer. He pushed Ethan and Sydney to a corner in the kitchen behind a solid-wood island. Their eyes were wide with fear.

"Carter, what's—" Ethan whispered, but Drew held his finger to his lips.

He heard quiet footsteps coming down the hallway from the front door. The glass pane on the back door shattered, followed by the sound of the deadbolt turning.

"Stay here," he whispered.

Drew was struggling. He was still weak from the loss of blood, and the exertion he had already made was causing his shoulder to throb. He pushed the pain back and dug deep for the energy he was going to need.

He knew these men were American soldiers or agents just doing the job they were told to do. Unfortunately, it didn't appear they were here to take prisoners but to kill. Drew would do his best not to kill them, but he would protect Sydney at all cost.

He crawled to the corner of a stub wall that separated the kitchen from the back entrance and watched the reflection off the glass front of the microwave as two men approached. The man from the front door was nearly to the kitchen too.

The men entering from the back reached the opposite side of the stub wall, and Drew didn't wait. He shot six rounds through the wall at their legs, which dropped the two men immediately.

The house erupted in automatic gunfire as Drew dove into the living room to acquire the man coming from the front. He tumbled, came up on one knee, and unleashed two perfectly placed rounds into the agent's M16.

"Get on the ground," Drew ordered, but the agent dropped his damaged gun and drew a 9mm handgun. Drew attacked him before he could fully lift the weapon to get a shot. The next few seconds of fighting were desperate and happened just a few feet away from where Sydney and Ethan were hiding.

Drew disarmed the man and put him in a neck lock with a gun to his head just as three more agents entered the cabin. Drew felt like he was about to pass out at any moment. He wondered if he was even strong enough to hold his hostage for more than a few seconds.

"Put the gun down, Mr. Carter. There's nowhere for you to go."

Drew knew that they had infrared lasers pointed at him that he couldn't see, so he kept moving himself and his target at random intervals to foil any shots they might consider. The situation was bad—hopeless, in fact.

"Let these people go, and I'll give myself up," Drew said.

Another agent came down the stairs with a gun pointed at Ben's head, and two of the gunmen turned their weapons on Sydney and Ethan.

"You mean these people?" the leader said.

Ben looked terrified. Drew could hear the stark fear in Ethan's and Sydney's heavy breathing behind him. His mind raced through the calculations and options. Four agents inside, probably four more outside. If they were here to kill them all, he didn't have a choice but to take as many with him as possible.

"Who are you?" Drew asked.

"NSA. Now put down your weapon!"

Drew knew he was lying. The NSA didn't threaten hostages like they were doing with Ben.

Drew decided to make his move, but before he could, a dozen high-intensity light beams filled the ground just outside, and another dozen red-dot lasers landed on the agents inside the cabin.

"Put your weapons down! We have all of your agents in custody."

Drew recognized the voice. Jake had come to save them.

The Fortress team entered the home and held the fake NSA agents at gunpoint.

"I don't know who you think you are. You are interfering with a sanctioned NSA operation. I demand—"

"You're on the wrong end of the barrel to be demanding anything," Jake said without emotion. "If you're NSA, how come the serial numbers on your vehicles trace back to a UN account?"

The man just glared back at him.

"Zee, secure them. When you get to the facility, you know what to do. Lock it down."

"Yes sir."

Drew tried to help Sydney and Ethan to their feet but instead nearly collapsed to the floor. Sydney grabbed him and helped him stand. Drew held onto the kitchen island countertop and pulled away from her. "I'm okay. Just a little dizzy."

Drew found Ben and put him back together. A few minutes later, everyone exited the front of the cabin. Zee took eight Fortress soldiers and stripped the UN agents of their weapons and gear, then led them under escort into the woods. Drew, Sydney, Ethan, and Ben joined Jake, who was organizing containment and extraction.

"Taco, secure the perimeter. I figure we've got ten minutes before their op HQ responds. We extract in five." Jake turned to Drew. "You want to tell me what's going on?"

"Man, am I glad to see you. How did you know?"

"I got an inside tip that you might be in trouble," Jake said with a wry smile.

The man next to Drew pulled off his black mask. Reed grinned. "Carter, no matter where you go, trouble just follows you."

Drew had a range of mixed emotions about Reed. This was the man who had gotten him eliminated from the CIA, and now he had come to save him. Or had he?

"Reed. You saved our skin. Do you know what you've gotten into?" Drew could hear a chopper in whisper mode coming toward them.

"I have a feeling I'm about to find out."

Drew nodded toward Ethan and Sydney. Ethan's eyes were still wide with fear. "We have to bring them. There's no place safe until this is over."

Ethan realized the comment was about them. "What? No. No way. We've had enough G.I. Joe antics for a lifetime. Sydney, we're out of here."

"I'm sorry, Ethan, but we can't let you go. What you saw tonight is just the beginning. They know you're connected, and they won't stop unless we stop them. Your lives are in jeopardy. You have to come with us."

Ethan was about to protest, but Sydney grabbed his arm. "We'd better do what he says, Ethan. Drew knows what he's doing."

Ethan didn't look happy, but he nodded. The air around them began to swirl, and a few seconds later a black helicopter set down on the grass in front of the cabin.

"Wait!" Ethan yelled and ran back into the cabin. A few seconds later he emerged carrying a silver briefcase.

The seven of them loaded into the chopper. Once airborne, Jake radioed Taco to clear out of the area.

"Where are we going?" Drew shouted to Jake.

"Someplace secure and off the grid."

Drew gave him a thumbs-up. He hoped it wouldn't be too long. He needed to lie down soon.

By the time the chopper set down, Drew was done. Jake and Reed had to help him get into the main bunker, which was actually a hardened shelter covered in earth and shaped perfectly to match the surrounding terrain. Drew couldn't guess where they were, and he didn't even want to try.

Inside, the bunker was large and completely furnished with everything a crew of fifty would need to survive an apocalypse for twelve months. Though it was a survival hideout, Jake had taken extra measures to ensure it was comfortable and very livable. It was divided into multiple rooms. There was over ten thousand square feet of living space and another five thousand square feet of storage for equipment, weapons, and nonperishables.

They put Drew in one of the side rooms and laid him on one of the four beds. Sydney and Ethan followed. Sydney went straight to Drew and felt his forehead while Ethan went to a small table on the other side of the bed and set his silver briefcase on it.

"What's wrong with him, Ethan?" Sydney asked, her voice thick with worry.

"I'll be fine," Drew mumbled, barely coherent. "I jus' need ta res'."

Ethan grabbed Drew's wrist and checked his pulse. "He's right actually. He needs rest, but he also needs blood."

"We don't have blood here," Jake said.

"What do we do, Ethan?" Sydney asked.

"When I was cleaning up your apartment, I knew he had lost a lot of blood." Ethan opened the silver briefcase on the table and removed two pints of blood. "I typed him and brought this. It's why I came to the cabin."

Sydney looked dazed. "I didn't think you believed him."

"Believing him had nothing to do with it," Ethan said, trying to avoid looking like he cared about Drew. "I treat sick people no matter who they are."

"Oh," Sydney said, but it was clear she knew better.

Jake got a call on his radio, so he stepped out of the room. Ben took that as a cue for him to exit too.

Ethan began setting up the IV. "And I knew you cared about him," Ethan added, then turned away to prepare the needles.

Sydney didn't respond.

It took a few hours to administer the transfusion; then Drew slept the rest of the night. By morning, he felt like a new man.

There was a gentle knock on his door.

"Come in," he said.

Sydney peeked in. "Hey," she said with a smile. "Can I come in?"

"Please." Drew sat up in bed. His shoulder still hurt pretty badly, but it was bearable now that he had the strength to deal with it.

Sydney pushed the door open with her hip to reveal a tray holding a delicious breakfast—orange juice, scrambled eggs, sausage, and fruit. "I'm a little late, but I thought I'd return the favor."

Drew smiled. "Except I have a feeling you didn't call room service for this one."

"No, but that just means you'll have to deal with my runny eggs and burnt toast."

Drew laughed.

"Actually, it's all rehydrated, so it probably *isn't* that good," Sydney finished.

"It looks like a feast to me."

She set the tray in his lap, and there was a moment of awkward silence.

Sydney tucked her hands in her back pockets. "Well, I guess I should get going."

He didn't want her to go, but it wouldn't be right for her to stay, even for a few minutes. "I owe Ethan a lot," he said. "He's a good man, Syd."

She nodded. "Yeah. I know." She turned and went to the door.

"Thanks for the breakfast," Drew said.

Sydney spun around. "You're welcome. Glad you're feeling better." She turned back to the door.

"Sydney?"

She spun around again, her eyes searching him. "Yes?"

Oh, how he wished he could tell her how much he loved her. But instead he needed her help on something else that was just as important.

"Do you really think that what I'm seeing are angels and demons? I mean . . . really?"

With the turn of recent events, Drew needed his confidence back. He needed to know he was solid again. Asking Jesus Christ into his life seemed to change everything, and he began wondering if perhaps it might even change his perceived reality about himself.

Sydney looked down at the floor as she thought for a moment. "I don't think I can answer that for you, Drew. But I do know this—I believe God has called you to something great. His Word says to humble yourself in the sight of the Lord and He will lift you up. You've been down for quite a while. Maybe He's getting ready to lift you up."

She gave him a quick smile and then left, closing the door behind her. It wasn't the answer he was looking for, but strangely, it helped. Thinking that almighty God might have a specific plan for his life was both thrilling and frightening. It was like being handpicked for a secret mission for the CIA . . . only bigger.

He finished the breakfast, cleaned up, then went looking for Ethan. He found him in the kitchen, pouring himself a cup of coffee.

"I just wanted to say thanks, Ethan. I appreciate—"

"Don't, Carter." Ethan looked up at him with fierce eyes. He looked around to make sure no one else was near, especially Sydney. "You nearly got Sydney killed, just like I said would happen, and now we're hiding out in some godforsaken hole in the ground, and I don't even know if you and this gang of mercenaries are the good guys or criminals. You've got Sydney so messed up in this, she's not even thinking straight. So keep your gratitude to yourself."

Drew didn't know what to say. Ethan was right. Sydney had been put in jeopardy again, and there wasn't much to convince anyone that they were actually the good guys.

"Fair enough. Thanks anyway."

He left just as Sydney entered, and he grimaced as they passed. He found Ben at the table in the main room of the bunker, trying to ascertain the damage to the Witness jacket to effect repairs.

"Hey, how are you doing?" Drew asked.

"Much better now that a gun isn't being pointed at my head."

"I'm sorry about all that, Ben," Drew said. "Things have gotten out of control in a hurry."

"Elsing says Witness may have saved your life after all. The Kevlar kept the bullet from penetrating deep enough to do any serious damage."

"I thought so. A gunshot wound at that range should have really messed me up. I guess I owe you again." Drew put a hand on Ben's shoulder.

Then he reached into his pocket and laid the three USB drives on the table in front of Ben. One from Ross, one from the late Senator Hanson, and one from Hadad and the Mossad. Somewhere in those encrypted files was the answer to all of this.

"Ben, Alice told me she couldn't decrypt Ross's files. I need access to every file on all of these drives. Something big's happening, and I think that somewhere in these files is the answer."

Ben grabbed the drives. "I'll need to get back to NexTech to do it."

"I'll talk to Jake, and we'll come up with a plan," Drew said. "NexTech should still be under the radar of the government, since we are not officially affiliated with the company, so we should be able to get you back there."

Jake and Reed joined them at the table and sat down. Drew could hear Sydney and Ethan talking thirty feet away. He tried not to listen and instead focused on the three sitting at the table with him.

"I'm still waiting to hear what this is all about," Jake said.

"Honestly, I'm still trying to figure it out myself," Drew said. "A few days ago I was on a routine drop mission and things went sideways. For some reason, there appears to be a lot of people who want me dead, and I don't know why."

Reed stared blankly at Drew. "I thought you were out, Drew. No explanation was given to me. I guess they turned you into a NOC after all."

Drew scrutinized Reed. Of all people, he would be the one to know what had happened. "Reed, can I talk to you for a minute?"

"Sure," Reed said, looking surprised.

"Jake, Ben, we'll be right back."

They walked back to Drew's room, and Drew shut the door behind them, then crossed his arms. "Do you want to tell me what's really going on, Reed?"

Reed looked genuinely confused. "Carter, I haven't seen you for months, and then I come to save your butt. Now you act like I'm the bad guy. What's going on, partner?"

Had he read Reed wrong all along? Drew was starting to wonder if he could trust anyone. The words of Hadad began to work their paranoia on him.

"Why did you report to Ross so that he had me . . . reevaluated?"

Reed's face twisted into a look of concern. "What are you talking about? I haven't seen Ross since that day in Chicago when he asked me to watchdog you. And my last communication with him was when I cleared you three months after you left the Farm."

Drew looked for signs of deception in Reed's face and body language, but there were none. "You mean you didn't tell Ross that I was seeing things, that I needed to have a psych eval done?"

"Is that what happened?" Reed asked. "That's why they kicked you out?" He laughed, but it wasn't funny to Drew. "It makes perfect sense. Ross needed to get you out so he could use you as a NOC. He used a psych eval to do it." Reed seemed lost in thought for a moment. "So how did they justify it? What got reported?"

Drew stared at him, trying to decide whether to believe him or not. "PTSD," he said slowly.

Reed looked at Drew again. "Why would you think I had anything to do with it, Carter? Ross wouldn't need anyone to pull a hokey psych evaluation. After you disappeared I got transferred to Langley. I had no idea what went down or where you were until Jake contacted me."

Drew slowly came to the conclusion that Reed was telling the truth. "How did you know to help me and where to find me?"

"Actually, our pal from the Farm, Hadad, contacted me. Told me you were in trouble and that your stepfather might have the resources necessary to help you out."

Drew realized that the Mossad must have tracked him after the café incident.

Reed looked straight into Drew's eyes. "You've saved my life more times than I can count. I wasn't going to pass up a chance to return the favor."

Drew warmly offered Reed a hand and a hug. "I'm sorry for doubting you. It's really good to see you again."

They joined Jake and Ben back at the table, and by now Sydney and Ethan were with them too. Ethan stood back and watched. Drew figured he was trying to decide whether or not he was a real agent or a criminal.

"This mission, Drew, what was unique about it to trigger an assassination squad?" Jake asked.

"How about we watch and see if we can find out?" Ben asked.

Everyone looked at Ben, bewildered.

"You got a download from Witness?" Drew asked.

"A partial. Jake's got a decent system here . . . for a survival bunker."

"Let's do it," Drew said.

"What about revealing classified information?" Reed asked.

"It's just a video in a café—not much different from a security camera," Drew replied.

They gathered around the twenty-three-inch monitor as Ben initiated playback from the moment Drew entered the café. The video was crystal clear and so was the sound. When Senator Hanson sat down, Ethan stepped forward.

"Whoa . . . that's Senator Hanson from Massachusetts. You met with the senator?"

"*Tell Ross the infiltration is much worse than we thought,*" Hanson said. "*The Patriots are ready, but we need solid proof before we can move.*"

"Freeze," Jake said. "What does he mean by that, Drew?"

"I don't know yet. I think the answer is on those drives Ben is decrypting."

Jake wore a look of dread on his face. "That's why they came after you."

"I know . . . and watch what happens next," Drew said.

Ben resumed Play, and seconds later, Senator Hanson's eyes bulged and he dropped over dead. Ethan and Sydney both gasped. The gunfight that ensued was intense, and there were times when it was difficult to follow because of how fast Drew moved. Drew had Ben stop the video just before Hadad came to help him so as not to reveal his friend's identity.

Drew looked at his friends. "I'm sorry you've all been dragged into this. It's not what I wanted for any of you."

Sydney still looked horrified at having watched the murder of a US senator, and Ethan looked shocked. He turned and walked away, apparently numb from the fact that Drew really was who he said he was and not some insane criminal.

Drew felt as though he needed to give them all at least some measure of explanation. After all, their lives were now in danger.

"I can't give you details, and I must be careful about what I do tell you, but I think you all deserve to know why this is happening. When I was officially released from the CIA over a year ago, I was contacted by a high-ranking official to carry on nonofficial operations within the US. What you just saw was one of those missions. I was to deliver some encrypted files to Senator Hanson, and obviously someone didn't want that to happen."

Jake looked concerned. "Have you decided on your handler yet? Is he trustworthy?"

Drew took a moment to think. He shook his head. "I honestly don't know, Jake. I've asked myself the same question a hundred times. I've tried to piece together my ops over the last year, but I don't have the big picture. The information I've gathered could be used for good"—Drew hesitated—"or for evil intentions. Since he's my only contact, the only way to find out is to meet with him."

Reed was deep in thought. He knew exactly who Drew was talking about.

"We're all going to have to be extremely careful in the future," Reed said. "Whether we like it or not, we're all part of this now."

Drew and Jake agreed. They discussed their options and came to the conclusion that it would be safe for Ben to return to NexTech and Reed to the CIA, but everyone else needed to stay off-grid at the bunker until Drew could make contact with Ross and figure out what was going on.

"That can't happen," Ethan protested. "I have to get back to the hospital. My work is too important."

Jake looked at Drew.

"We can't force anyone to stay, but if you go back, your life could be in danger, Ethan," Drew said.

"I have patients whose lives are in danger if I don't get back there. I'm sorry, but I'm going. I think I'd go crazy in this place anyway."

"No, Ethan," Sydney pleaded. "It's not safe."

"I'm going, Sydney."

"We'll have to keep the location of this bunker secret from those who are leaving," Jake said, "so that if something happens, the safety of the rest of us will not be compromised."

Everybody agreed.

"I can have a chopper here in a few minutes," Jake said.

Sydney pulled Ethan to the far end of the bunker so that no one else could hear them—almost no one else. Drew tried not to watch and he tried not to listen, but it was impossible. To distract himself, he and Reed looked over Ben's shoulder as he worked on the computer system, uploading the encrypted files to Alice.

"You can't do this, Ethan. I don't want you to go," Sydney pleaded.

"Sydney, I don't want any part of this. Whatever he's involved in is contrary to everything that I am." Ethan's voice was easier to hear. "And I don't like what it's done to you. It's like I don't even know you anymore."

"I know it's a little bizarre—"

"A little?" Ethan interrupted. "No, this is beyond bizarre."

Sydney didn't respond. There was a moment of silence between the two of them that was filled with Ben's voice.

"Drew, the files from your café agent aren't even encrypted." Ben opened one that displayed a list of names.

"Make sure they're uploaded to Alice so I can access them through my glasses," Drew said.

"Done," Ben replied. "The others I'll have to work on when I get back to

NexTech." Drew nodded, but Ben could tell he was distracted. He glanced over at Sydney and Ethan ninety feet away, then back at Drew. "You can hear them?"

"Of course he can," Reed said. "He doesn't miss a thing."

Drew winced a smile, then looked at Sydney and Ethan.

"I'm breaking off our engagement," Ethan said.

"No, Ethan, please. Why would you do that? That's not what I want!"

Ethan took her hands and held them. "Sydney, you're an amazing girl, and I love you."

"And I love you!" Sydney exclaimed.

Ethan put a hand to her cheek. "I know you do, but you also love him."

She looked stricken. "But I choose you, Ethan."

Ethan shook his head. "You choose me with your head, Sydney, but your heart says something else." His voice lowered with sadness. "When you took care of Drew in your apartment, I saw something in you I've never seen before."

"He was shot and bleeding, Ethan. That's what you saw in me."

Ethan shook his head. "No, it was something deeper. Something I want my wife to have for me. I'm not going to live in his shadow, and I don't want you to live with regrets and what-ifs." He let go of her hands. "It's taken me a few days to sort this out, and as much as I hated it, I kept coming to the same conclusion."

"But Ethan—" Sydney began; Ethan stopped her with a shake of his head.

"Please don't, Sydney. Can you honestly look me in the eye and tell me you don't love him?"

She didn't say a word.

Ethan nodded, then pursed his lips. "Call me selfish, but I won't share my wife's love with anyone." He shrugged.

Sydney had no response. She wiped her eyes.

"I think I knew all along that something was holding you back," Ethan finally said. "I think you were trying not to love him, but sometimes, love just has its way with us."

Sydney released a nervous laugh through her tears. "You are too good for me, Ethan."

Just then Jake stepped in from outside. "Chopper arriving. Be ready to roll in five minutes."

Ethan smiled. "You just be careful around him, okay? Just because I won't be with you doesn't mean I don't care about you. He's a walking 911 wherever he goes."

Sydney nodded and smiled, then reached up and hugged him. "There's someone better than me out there looking for you," she said as she stepped back.

Ethan smiled sadly. "Take care of yourself, Sydney. I'll be praying for you." He turned and started walking toward Drew and Ben, leaving Sydney behind.

Drew looked at Reed and stuck out his hand. "I can't thank you enough, partner."

Reed took his hand and gave Drew a serious look. "I'll see if I can find out what's going on, but in the meantime, you be careful. This is deep."

Drew nodded.

"And if you need me, you let me know," Reed continued.

"You watch your back too, Reed. Whoever is behind this has a lot of power."

Reed joined Jake at the entrance to the bunker just as Ethan passed Drew. He stopped and turned to face Drew. Anger, pain, and regret were evident in his eyes.

"Take care of her, Carter, or the next time you need patching up, I'll put a few extra holes in you where they don't belong."

Drew nodded.

"You know you don't deserve her," Ethan said with a fierce look.

"Yeah, I know. Neither of us do."

Ethan snorted, then nodded. He grabbed the few things he had, then went outside with Jake and Reed.

Ben looked toward Sydney. "Not sure what that was all about, but that's my cue to leave too. Alice is functional, and I'll communicate with you through her."

Ben and Drew shook hands; then Ben joined Jake, Reed, and Ethan outside.

Drew watched as Sydney slowly walked toward him. He wasn't sure how to react or how she might react.

She sauntered up to him and gave him a froward grin. "I suppose you heard all of that?"

Drew didn't say anything. She just nodded in a matter-of-fact way.

They walked outside in time to see the chopper lifting up and away. Jake didn't hesitate. He returned to the bunker almost as if Drew and Sydney weren't even there.

The thumping of the chopper's blades slowly faded and was replaced by the chirps and songs of country birds. Suddenly Drew was aware of the beauty of God's creation, and he was in awe at the genius behind the design of life. Except for the four invisible warriors positioned fifty feet away in each direction, Drew could almost make himself believe he was once more a teenager on a camping trip with Jake in the gentle rolling hills of a Kansas landscape.

"Looks like you've messed my life up one more time, Drew Carter."

He lowered his gaze from the blue-and-green canvas of the earth to the beautiful masterpiece God had created and had called Sydney Carlyle. "I'm sorry, Sydney. I never wanted to—"

"Shut up, Drew," Sydney said softly. "Just shut up and walk with me."

She turned, put her hands in her hip pockets and started walking through a meadow sparsely populated with deciduous and evergreen trees. Drew took a couple of steps to catch up with her. A few steps later, she leaned into him, and he gently put an arm around her. Nothing else was said.

THE LAST AGENT

Drew's senses were peaked. He waited on one of the trails in the designated park in Philadelphia, the same one where Ross had first enlisted him as a NOC agent. Two days earlier he had made contact with Ross and left Sydney in Jake's care back at the bunker.

In the meantime, Ben had successfully decoded the files from Senator Hanson to find pages of e-mails and voice messages between other members of Congress and some of the White House cabinet regarding an event called Crossbow. Without the context to which the code name applied, it was difficult to discern intent. However, one of the messages mentioned the IGA, and Drew immediately thought about Hadad's warning. Was the IGA really trying to kill him? Had he been right all along in his suspicions about Jabbar and the terrorist connections to the IGA?

There were so many unanswered questions, but the one that needed an answer first was the one regarding Drew's sanity. He needed resolution before he could go any further.

Validus and his warriors stood nearby at the ready. Drew turned and faced Validus, eyeing the massive warrior, and their eyes locked.

"Are you real?" Drew asked.

Validus hesitated, then scanned the area while giving orders to his men. They spread out from their position to provide cover, leaving Drew and Validus alone. Seconds later, blue arcing flames momentarily encased the massive warrior's body as he translated into the world of men. As he did, broad, pearl-white wings morphed out from his back.

Drew just stared, amazed at the ominous and powerful winged warrior. He had never seen such a thing—warriors with wings. If these weren't visions of imagination, there was only one answer.

Validus lifted his chin slightly, then broke the silence. "I'm as real as you are."

Drew's eyes evaluated every minute detail of the warrior, looking for some reason not to believe him but hoping he wouldn't find one. "Then you are . . . angels?"

Validus nodded.

Drew's faith in God was real, but he needed his mind to be sound too. He shook his head. "How can I be sure? For a long time I believed you were a vision conjured up by my subconscious."

"This world is temporary, ours is eternal. Which one do you suppose is *more* real?" Validus replied.

Drew had never thought of that.

"Men do not find God in the fullness of their own confidence. Only the humble in heart find Messiah," Validus continued.

"But why me? Why is this happening?"

Validus stared blankly at Drew, then slowly answered. "There are things that the Lord God Almighty does not reveal until it is time, even to His angels."

Drew nodded. "What am I supposed to do then?"

"It's simple, Carter," Validus said, putting a closed fist on Drew's chest near his heart. "You obey the voice of God."

Drew could hear a man approaching behind him as Validus translated back into the spiritual realm. The slight pressure on his chest from Validus's fist disappeared with the warrior.

Drew turned and watched as the distant form of Ross approached through the trees. He still didn't trust Ross. He thought back to every mission he had accomplished for him and tried to determine if he had somehow undermined his oath to protect the United States. Was Ross running some rogue operation controlled by the IGA? Maybe Ross was done with him and this last op was a way to take out two targets at once. Hadad said the CIA had been comprised. Was Ross part of that?

He watched closely as Ross reached inside his pocket. Drew tensed, then heard the faintest click of a button.

"Transmissions in the immediate area are being jammed," Alice said calmly in Drew's earpiece.

Ross pointed to the park bench, but Drew waited until Ross initiated the move to sit down.

Ross looked straight ahead. "You've been part of an operation code-named Torrent. For the last five years I've been recruiting, training, and assigning NOCs to this operation . . . without the director's approval."

Drew's eyes narrowed. "Why?"

"Because I believe that the Islamic Global Alliance has penetrated our government with agents, but I don't know how deep they've reached. After what's happened in the last two months, it looks worse than I thought. And now I think they are on to me." Ross looked at Drew and hesitated. "I had you removed from the CIA and your files redacted because I needed the very best agents on this op. Every one of my other Torrent agents—*every* one—has been eliminated. You're the last one, Carter, and from what I heard, they just about got you when they assassinated Senator Hanson. They're coming after me now too."

Drew eyed Ross. He wanted desperately to trust him.

He gave Ross the USB drive that Senator Hanson had given him. "Senator Hanson told me to give this to you. Perhaps this will tell you how deep the corruption is."

Ross took the USB. He looked more than concerned. He looked sad.

"What is Operation Torrent?" Drew asked.

"When Aashif Hakeem Jabbar formed the Islamic Global Alliance eight years ago, our intelligence agencies aggressively tried to link the IGA to militant terrorist groups, but no connection could be made. When Jabbar began to gain the trust and respect of governments throughout the world, we started getting pressure to stop investigating him and his organization. You discovered that when you started looking into the IGA on your own. Your investigation raised flags, and they shut you down. But when you wouldn't let it die, I knew I had to get you to the outside and into Operation Torrent. The problem was that I couldn't release you without drawing attention, unless there was a legitimate reason for dismissal. You were too good to go missing unnoticed. Agent Reed gave me exactly what I needed when he told me that you confided in him about seeing things."

Drew was confused and angry. He had nearly confessed to Reed but never actually told him. And Reed had said he had nothing to do with telling Ross. Someone was lying. How could he trust either one of them now?

Drew was about to get up and walk away, but something happened that made Drew's skin crawl with shivers and goosebumps. Validus and one of his warriors were positioned slightly behind Ross and out of his view. Validus whispered something to the warrior standing next to him, and seconds later, the warrior translated into the world of men and took on the perfectly replicated form of Agent Reed.

Drew's eyes widened, and he squelched the gasp forming in his throat. Three seconds later, the form of Agent Reed translated back into the invisible warrior impersonating him.

Ross's voice continued, but Drew could hardly concentrate under a flood of wild thoughts. Angels could appear as anyone? Had they instigated his dismissal from the CIA? And to what end? Then Drew remembered Validus's words. *"Only the humble in heart find Messiah."* Validus had done it to break him.

"I had Dr. Whitton draw out the process to validate the dismissal," Ross said, "and evidently no one suspected a thing or you would have been killed a long time ago."

Validus stared at Drew, and Drew came to a conclusion. The warrior Validus was indeed an angel of God, and for some unknown purpose, Drew was supposed to live. Perhaps it was for this very reason—to help Ross discover the truth about the IGA and America's involvement with them.

Ross continued. "After the last two elections, all investigation on the IGA was completely shut down, and I began suspecting a cover-up. But I wasn't the only one. Senator Hanson from Massachusetts and I served together as officers in the Navy. He's a man I knew I could trust. He contacted me about his concerns, not only about Congress, but about some of the people who were being appointed to some very strategic and powerful offices."

Ross stopped and wiped his hand across his face. It was the only time Drew had seen even the slightest hint of anxiety in him.

"I've never seen Hanson scared before. He told me there were a handful of other congressmen and congresswomen who were just as concerned. Five years ago we secretly launched Operation Torrent. It was my job to recruit and investigate connections between the IGA and worldwide terrorist attacks. But even that wouldn't be enough. I had to prove that key US political and military figures friendly to the IGA knew that Jabbar was orchestrating the terrorist attacks and supporting him, thereby making them accomplices."

Ross looked squarely at Drew. "The deeper I dug, the further Jabbar's influence went. When my investigation led me to the White House, things got ugly quick. My NOC agents began disappearing. It was only a matter of time before they would discover Torrent, me, and the Patriots—the members of Congress still loyal to the Constitution. Hanson told me he would feed me the evidence to implicate members of the cabinet and some of the directors who have been appointed." He looked at the USB drive, then tucked it into his pocket. "I guess he gave his life getting this to me."

Ross looked away, then back at Drew. "Jabbar is taking over the world, Carter. Only God knows how many other governments he's secretly overthrown. He's already in control of high offices in our government. I don't even trust our intelligence directors. All of his global unification rhetoric has duped even the well-intentioned US citizens and officials. They don't understand the freedom they'll give up if they submit to his influence and power."

Ross paused to let Drew absorb his words.

"I'm sorry about Hanson," Drew said. "He confirmed what you just said, that the infiltration is much worse than originally thought. He said that the Patriots are ready but that they need solid proof from you before they could move." He hesitated as he remembered Hanson's last words. "He said they were planning something, but he didn't finish the message. Whoever else is a member of the Patriots, they're in danger too." Drew felt like he should have been able to protect the senator.

"Hanson was a good man. America needed him," Ross said. "What concerns me the most is the rhetoric associated with Jabbar. He is being heralded as the Mahdi, the Twelfth Imam, by many Islamic leaders."

Drew shook his head. He wasn't following.

"The Shiite Muslims believe that the Islamic messiah is the Twelfth Imam, a man who will bring justice and peace to the earth through a global fight against an evil enemy. Martyrdom is their ticket to heaven. Death is not a deterrent. These are extremely dangerous people."

Drew had to ask the question that frightened him most. "What about President Harden, sir? Do you think he is part of this?"

Ross's face turned gray. He licked his lips, apparently choosing his next words carefully. "I don't know. So far I don't have any direct evidence of such. On the other hand, he's appointed dozens of pro-IGA officials to his staff and cabinet. Unless we act now, I'm afraid Jabbar will soon control the United States. I only hope we haven't waited too long and that we have enough evidence to convince the people before it's too late.

"We know that Jabbar has used terrorism in multiple ways to garner support for the IGA, at times planning an attack and then exposing the jihadists at the last moment, thereby fooling governments into believing they are the true heroes of peace they claim to be. My last agent believed that the IGA was planning something big in the US, something so big it would incapacitate us, but he didn't discover what it was before he was taken out."

Drew shook his head. "Why take over the government only to incapacitate it? It makes no sense."

"Jihadist Muslims view Israel as the little Satan and the United States as the great Satan. They envision a world free of both Israel and the US. Once they've crippled the US, Israel will be next. Right now the United States is the only thing standing in their way to world domination."

Ross handed Drew a folded piece of paper. "Agent Foster died getting this to me. It's a list of 163 IGA members who have come across the border in the last six months, both legally and illegally—many of them probably through Zapata's human-traffic route with his arms dealers. The problem is, if they are planning something, we don't know what it is. We know it's big, and with Iran's nuclear program running unchecked by the UN, we suspect it must be a small tactical nuclear bomb, perhaps near the capital. September eleventh isn't far away."

Drew shook his head again. "I still don't buy it, Ross. Why would our own leaders be a part of their own demise? Even if they don't believe in the Constitution or our American ideals anymore, they wouldn't die for Jabbar's cause."

"It's because they actually believe Jabbar's message of world peace and unification. All Jabbar needs is to cripple the US government long enough to take out Israel. A nuclear bomb in Washington, DC would do just that. It would take us years to recover."

"If that's true, then just tell the president the truth," Drew protested.

"He'd never believe me without proof, Carter. And once I raise the flag,

I'm a dead man. The US goes down without a fight. You don't understand how loved and feared Jabbar is—worldwide!"

Drew didn't want to believe Ross. Everything inside him rejected the notion that high-ranking officials in the government would erode the people's constitutional freedoms for the sake of Jabbar's Muslim world vision.

As Drew considered Ross's words and as his analytical mind kicked into overdrive, the pieces of an ominous plan fell into place. All the intel he had been studying the last few days, along with what he had seen on dozens of missions, connected and synchronized all at once. The existence of such an evil plot choked him. For a moment he became a statue in a world of chaos, watching the foundations of freedom and justice crumble beneath him. He unfolded the list of names of IGA members, and as he read them, Jabbar's sinister plot was confirmed.

"Jabbar isn't trying to cripple the United States, Mr. Ross." Drew lifted his head and looked straight into Ross's eyes. "He's going to destroy it—all of it!"

Ross looked at Drew, eyes narrowed. "That's not possible."

Drew continued. "If all you have said is true, then Jabbar has atrophied our security and intelligence to the point that the IGA will be able to pull off the perfect terrorist attack and destroy all of America."

"What are you talking about, Carter? It would take a hundred nuclear bombs to pull that off. There's no way they could do it."

"This is worse than a nuclear attack, sir, and Jabbar doesn't need to fire a shot or set off a single explosive."

Ross's eyes widened.

"When I met Hanson, an agent from the Mossad helped me escape, and he gave me this." Drew handed Ross another USB drive. "He also told me that they had discovered that 'detonation day' was September fifth, not September eleventh. That drive contains a list of 112 jihad terrorists that the Mossad has linked to the IGA. All of them have been associated with a training camp in northern Pakistan along the Afghanistan border. It's the same camp you had me recon two months ago. They're all suicide bombers, and nearly all the names on his list match the list you just gave me."

"Perhaps, but even a hundred suicide bombers couldn't accomplish what you're talking about."

"They could if the bombs they were carrying were inside them. When I

reconned the camp, I discovered that it wasn't just a training camp for terrorists—it was an incubator site for bioterrorism. I dispatched a micro drone that
recorded a conversation between two trainees mentioning Ebola." Drew looked
at Ross. "They're going to hit major US cities with Ebola."

Ross seemed dazed as he considered Drew's analysis.

Drew shook his head. "I was slow to understand it because I just couldn't
fathom the magnitude of what they were plotting."

"How will they spread the disease? Once an outbreak occurs, the CDC
will immediately quarantine," Ross said.

"They'll have to do it quick so that by the time a quarantine is put in place,
it will be too late. The fastest way to spread the disease will be at restaurants. If
we could find these terrorists"—Drew held up the paper—"we will discover
that most of them are employed at fast-food restaurants near transportation
hubs—interstate junctions, bus and train stations, airports—to ensure quick
and uncontainable spreading. They will probably also target restaurants in
political, financial, and business districts. They could easily contaminate the
food they prepare with saliva and sweat." Drew's analysis was sobering and
dreadful, but he was convinced it was true. He considered the consequences.
"Within two weeks, millions of Americans will be infected. Within a month,
the Ebola epidemic will be unstoppable. The rest of the world will quarantine
the North American continent. In less than two months, Jabbar and the IGA
will have wiped America from the face of the planet, paving the way for global
domination."

Ross looked stunned. "How can you be sure?"

"Because the Mossad successfully tracked three of the terrorists to the US,
where they have all been hired as cooks in fast-food restaurants. One in Los
Angeles, one in Portland, and one in Memphis. At first I thought that was an
odd coincidence, but now it makes perfect sense. It's in the files," Drew said,
pointing to the USB in Ross's hand.

"God help us!" Ross said. "Evidently the Mossad trusts you more than
they trust the CIA."

"What do we do, sir?"

Ross seemed lost, and it worried Drew. If there was anyone in all of the US
government who could see through to a solution, Ross was the man, but instead he sat in silence. Drew began analyzing, strategizing, calculating. He had

never had to take his abilities to such a global scale before. Continually interjected into his thoughts, however, was one irreducible truth: America was on the brink of annihilation.

"We need to know how they plan to infect the terrorists all at the same time. The virus can't survive without a living host for more than a couple of days," Ross said.

Drew thought for a moment—it clicked. "There's only one way they could do it. They would have to use a number of 'trigger' host carriers to infect everyone at the same time." Drew snapped his fingers. "That's it! September fifth . . . midnight . . . detonation day. Three days from now on detonation day, over one hundred IGA suicide bioterrorists will infect themselves with an active Ebola virus from trigger carriers. Six days later on September eleventh, when they are all contagious, they will begin spreading the disease in our largest cities."

"It makes sense. Does any of your intel specify infection locations?" Ross asked.

"I'm afraid not."

"Then we're too late already," Ross said. "Our only hope is to convince the president that this terrorist threat is real. I'll arrange an emergency meeting with the cabinet tonight. You're flying back to DC with me now, Carter."

Drew's eyes opened wide. "I don't think I can—"

"Too bad. You're coming with me. You know the details, and you're my last man. We don't have to convince them that IGA and Jabbar are bad, only that the viral terrorist attack is real and imminent."

"What about exposing Jabbar and the corruption in our government?" Drew asked.

"First we have to make sure there's a country left to govern. We'll launch the witch hunt later . . . and it *will* be a witch hunt."

"It sounds like this time there are actually witches to hunt," Drew replied.

 భంం

Validus and Persimus watched Carter and Ross stand up and walk down the sidewalk. The rest of Validus's team joined them. Each mighty angel stood solemn and silent.

"What does it all mean?" Crenshaw asked. "What have we missed?"

Validus struggled to offer an answer. The Carter mission had exploded to global proportions in just a few days, and Validus felt like he had stumbled into a minefield uninformed and unprepared. Clearly he had misinterpreted the message from Tinsalik Barob about Carter being the last salvation. What could he offer his men now? Did Malak know what was happening, what was in store for America?

"It means Carter is just as important as Michael said he was."

Validus and his team turned to see General Brandt and an entourage of escorting angels approaching. They all snapped to attention.

"And it now makes perfect sense why you were assigned this mission, Commander Validus," Brandt continued.

"General Brandt. I wasn't told you were coming. What are your orders?"

Brandt closed the last few steps and took a moment to evaluate each of Validus's team. He slowly nodded, then gazed back at Validus. "Your orders are to keep doing what you have been doing—protect Carter. The team you've assembled is exactly what is needed. I'm here to brief Malak and get him up to speed on the situation. We knew that Apollyon was close to implementing an initiative that would take out America. Until now, the momentum seemed unstoppable. That is, until Carter."

The corner of Brandt's mouth turned up ever so slightly. "Looks like General Danick was right all along. This is all about the survival of Israel, and Carter is the key." He scanned the circle of valiant angels who had seen more intense action in the last few months than any other angel warrior on the planet. His face hardened. "I don't need to remind you all of what's at stake here or what the cost may be. I am initiating over a hundred missions to counter Apollyon's efforts, but yours will be the most important. Failure is not an option!"

"Yes sir," Validus snapped.

"Keep Malak up to date on all developments so he can respond quickly with support. And beware—Apollyon is near."

The words sent chills up and down Validus's spine. His men glanced his direction. General Brandt nodded; then he and his accompanying angels turned to depart eastward toward Colorado and Malak's headquarters for North America.

25

AMERICAN ANNIHILATION

The director for National Intelligence, James Ward, drove Ross and Drew in a black SUV north to Catoctin Mountain Park in Frederick County, Maryland. During the ninety-minute drive to Camp David, Ross and Drew pre-briefed Ward on the details of the terrorist threat. Per Ross's instruction, Drew omitted any references linking the current administration to previous terrorist plots and the IGA.

The director was cold and harsh, but Drew expected as much. His reputation was on the line if Ross and Drew were right. Drew also knew that Ross suspected Ward's motivation and perhaps even his loyalties, though he didn't say so outright.

"The timing for this couldn't be worse," Ward said as they pulled up to the entrance of the famed presidential retreat. "The president has just finished talks with UN Secretary-General De Luca and IGA Premier Jabbar. Security will be tighter than usual, especially since the change of the guard from the Marines to the UN is tomorrow morning."

"Doesn't the timing of this terrorist plot seem a little coincidental to you, Jim?" Ross asked.

Drew knew Ross was probing and observing responses, but Ward remained silent, which in itself could be telling.

Three Marines with a bomb-sniffing dog halted their vehicle. Ward rolled down the window to greet one of the Marine sergeants and present IDs for all three of them. A UN officer appeared behind the Marine, almost as if to supervise his performance.

"We're expecting you, sir," the Marine said firmly. He was the epitome of professionalism and military pride. Drew had a flashback to the statues of flesh and blood at his father's funeral more than a decade ago. A lot had changed since that day.

"The timing of your visit is inconvenient," the UN officer said in a thick European accent. He stepped up beside the sergeant. "We prefer you delay your appointment until the UN and IGA delegations have left the premises."

Drew watched as Ward looked from the UN officer to the Marine. There was the slightest look of consternation on the Marine's face.

"This is the director of National Intelligence, sir," the Marine said.

The UN officer looked unimpressed. "As I said, we prefer you delay your appointment until the delegations have left the premises."

Ward looked like he was going to launch himself through the window at the UN officer. "Sergeant, finish your inspection and let us through!" he ordered.

The Marine stepped in front of the UN officer and snapped a salute. "Yes sir. Please open your trunk, sir."

The Marines cautiously and carefully inspected every inch of the car, using mirrors to look beneath the chassis. Two UN troops followed behind the Marines, double-checking the inspection. After a few minutes of thorough searching, the sergeant appeared at the window again, handing the IDs back.

"I apologize for the extra measures. We are—"

"Carry on, sergeant," Ward barked.

"Yes sir!" the sergeant said and snapped another salute.

Once on base, Alice informed Drew that all wireless communications were being monitored. Drew tapped on his jacket to confirm silent mode.

There were multiple facilities and two main lodges on the Camp David premises. Ward drove them to Laurel Lodge, where the president would be meeting with De Luca and Jabbar. Aspen Lodge, just a quarter mile away, was the residence of the president and his family while they were at Camp David. According to the news report, the First Lady and their two children would be staying at the lodge for a week's vacation after the global conference as a symbol of their trust during the changing of the guard from the Marines to the UN forces.

As they approached Laurel Lodge, two Secret Service agents were waiting for them. They were directed to park and remain inside their vehicle until the delegations had left.

"It should only be ten to fifteen minutes, sir," one of the agents told Ward.

Drew noticed that Validus and his contingent of warriors had surrounded their car with swords drawn and the look of battle on their faces. He had never seen Validus so anxious. Then Drew saw something so glorious and so frightening that shivers skittered up and down his spine. All around him, warriors just like Validus began to appear, and many of them came down through the trees on pearl-white wings. Something warmed inside Drew's chest, but it was short-lived.

Ward whispered Jabbar's name, almost as a cuss word.

"There they are, Carter," Ross said quietly. "Premier Jabbar and Secretary-General De Luca."

Drew saw them, but he also saw so much more. Shivers flowed again, but this time shivers of great fear, for walking among the men of global power was an army of dark invaders—or demons, or whatever they were. Their swords were drawn too. Was this to be a battlefield of the unseen?

And leading the legions of darkness was one who was as unholy as Drew had ever seen or imagined. Eyes of pure black, stature none other could compare to, and authority like that of a god.

Drew pondered in his heart at what he saw. Was this the cause of Validus's apprehension, of his entire army's apprehension? The dark master turned his fierce gaze left, then right, then to Drew and stopped.

Drew felt the hairs on the back of his neck stand straight. When Validus had told him they were all coming for him, was this being the cause of it all? Drew wanted to hide, to disappear from the gaze of this dark being, but it was not to be. The dark lord lifted his hand and pointed at Drew, and every dark invader eye turned to look at him. Drew feared greatly, and he began to think that there was nothing that could save him from such a powerful vessel of darkness.

And then the whisper came. A whisper from inside, where the true words of God were hidden and no dark invader could steal them away.

"He who is in you is greater than he who is in the world." It was a whisper that brought peace from one so holy and so powerful that the loathsome gaze of one thousand demons could not shake it. Drew wondered if perhaps this was the great enemy of God the Bible spoke of. He didn't know for sure who this demon of great power was, but he did know who had saved his soul.

"I trust in you, God," Drew whispered.

"What's that?" Ross said.

"Nothing. I was just hoping the president doesn't delay the briefing too long," Drew said.

He watched closely as the angels and demons kept their distance from each other. Evidently the battle was not yet to be. When the delegations drove off, the horde of demons went with them . . . at least most of them.

"Let's go," Ward said as one of the Secret Service agents approached. They exited the car.

"I'll escort you to the president, sir," the agent said.

Just before entering the lodge, an agent scanned each of them for weapons and bugs. Drew was relieved when his jacket passed without a blip. Ward, Ross, and Drew were then taken to the Laurel Lodge conference room, where the meeting between the three global leaders had just occurred. Drew noticed that Validus and his team were staying close-by. He tapped out a sequence in his pocket.

"Three-sixty recording active," Alice said coolly. Drew envied her calm detachment.

He scanned. Clear, except for Validus and two of his warriors, who were on the opposite side of the table from him.

Ward sat in one of the chairs next to the head of the table where the president would sit, and Ross sat across from him. Drew sat beside Ross.

As the minutes ticked by, Drew became anxious. Ward paged through the files that Ross had given him. Drew noticed that the director was getting edgy too. At one point he closed the files and looked across the table at Ross.

"You'd better be right about this, Ross. I hope your boy got his facts straight." He gave Drew a stern look, then glared back at Ross. "If you're wrong, this isn't something you'll recover from."

"If we're right, it could mean the end of America," Ross countered.

Ward's glare eased. "Convince the president, and things will move fast." Drew could tell he was feeling the full weight of his responsibility. Under his watch, the nation was on the verge of enduring the worst terrorist attack ever orchestrated on the planet. The potential casualties would make American deaths in World War II look like a drop in the bucket.

Minutes later, the door opened and a sharp-looking man entered. Drew recognized him as Michael Dougherty, the president's senior advisor.

"The president needed a few minutes to recover from the conference. He will be with you shortly." Dougherty glanced at Drew. "Is this the agent who will be briefing us on the terrorist threat?"

"Yes," Ross said. "This is Agent Carter."

Dougherty stuck out his hand, and Drew grabbed it. "Michael Dougherty. I hope this isn't as serious as Mr. Ward indicated. The president is ready to call an emergency cabinet meeting depending on your brief. Keep it short and to the point. The full briefing will come later."

Drew nodded. Dougherty left the room.

Ten minutes later, President Harden entered with Dougherty. Ward, Ross, and Drew stood up.

"Mr. President," Ward said.

"Jim, Trent," the President said as he greeted the director and Ross. It was the first time that Drew had ever heard Ross's first name. Harden reached out his hand to Drew. "I assume you're Agent Carter."

"Yes sir," Drew said, shaking his hand. He had extremely mixed feelings about the encounter. He didn't like Harden or his liberal policies, but he was honored and nervous to have the ear of the most powerful man in the world. However, now that Drew knew this man was handing their nation's sovereignty over to the IGA and the UN on a silver platter, his dislike for him was even greater. Drew tried to respect the office and separate the man from it, but being in the same room made that almost impossible.

Just give him the facts, Drew thought. *Surely he still wants what's best for our country.*

Dougherty turned and talked to the Secret Service man outside the door. "Make sure we're not disturbed for any reason."

The agent nodded and Dougherty shut the door. President Harden sat down at the head of the conference table and leaned back in his chair. Dougherty sat next to Ward. The president looked tired. Drew could only imagine the energy such a conference would take. The last thing he wanted to do now was to get a briefing on terrorism.

Harden rubbed his eyes. "Based on your message, I wanted Michael to hear this too. What's going on, Jim? What's so important that couldn't wait until tomorrow?"

"We have a serious national emergency—a clear and present danger to the security and very survival of the United States."

President Harden dropped his hands to the arms of the chair. He looked skeptical, but when Ward didn't retreat from his dramatic words, the president leaned forward. "Come on, Jim—survival?" His face sobered to stone. "You'd better not tell me that those blasted jihadists actually got a nuke onto our soil!"

"No sir," Ward said. "I'm afraid it's worse than that. Agent Carter?"

Drew took a breath, formulating the right words. "Sir, I've been running covert operations in the United States, investigating a plot by Muslim extremists to incapacitate our nation."

"Which terrorist group are we talking about?" the president asked.

"It's not a single group, sir. It's a joint effort," Drew replied.

"Joint effort?" The president squinted at Drew. "Surely one group is spearheading the attack."

Drew looked at Ross. Ross nodded.

"Yes sir, our operation has discovered direct ties to the Islamic Global Alliance."

"Preposterous!" Harden said, anger flushing his face. "I don't know where you got your information, agent, but there is no way Premier Jabbar is behind any terrorist attack, either here or worldwide." The president tapped his index finger on the table in front of him. "I just spent the last four hours with him discussing our unified effort to bring about global peace, and specifically peace to the Arab-Israeli conflict." President Harden glared at Ward. "Who authorized this operation?"

"I initiated the op, sir," Ross piped in. "Without the director's approval."

"What in Jack's name is going on, Ward?"

Ward leaned forward, about to speak, but Dougherty interjected. "If I may, sir. As outlandish as it may sound, we should hear what the threat is and evaluate the evidence before jumping to any conclusions."

"He's right, Mr. President," Ward added. "This is one scenario we never imagined and aren't prepared for."

President Harden glared at Ward, then at Dougherty. He leaned back in his chair and crossed his arms. "Of course. Proceed, Agent Carter."

"Over the past six months, various jihadist groups—Hamas, ISIS, Al-Qaeda, the Muslim Brotherhood, Al-Shabaab, and others—have been successfully penetrating our borders and placing suicide terrorists in at least one hundred of our most populated cities. We have evidence that these terrorists have taken up employment at various restaurants, most of them in fast-food chains where thousands of people are served daily."

President Harden glanced toward Ward, Ross, and Dougherty. Drew continued.

"Two days from now, over one hundred suicide terrorists will infect themselves with the Ebola virus. Six days later on September eleventh, when they are all contagious, they will begin spreading the virus to tens of thousands of people. Within two weeks, millions of Americans will be infected. Within a month, the Ebola epidemic will be unstoppable. This terrorist attack will make the concerted attacks of 9/11 seem insignificant by comparison."

The silence in the room was deafening.

"Mr. President, the United States of America won't survive. The terrorists are suicide bioterrorists who, in the name of Islam, consider it their duty to Allah to destroy us."

The president looked to Ross for some assurance that what he'd heard was true.

"The threat is real, sir," Ross said.

"God help us!" President Harden said.

Drew glanced at Ross and noticed he was studying Ward and Dougherty.

"Ebola needs a living host to survive, doesn't it?" Ward asked. "How will they do it?"

"We believe they've kept an active Ebola virus alive using hostages as incubators for months," Drew said. "They plan on using 'trigger' carriers and a number of infection locations throughout the US to spread the virus to the suicide bioterrorists."

President Harden ran his fingers through his hair. Horror filled his eyes. "How reliable is this information, Carter? Are you sure?"

Drew hesitated. His response would dictate how seriously the president would take the threat. "Nothing is one hundred percent, sir, but we've confirmed a suicide terrorist training camp in Pakistan with Ebola, and we've confirmed 112 terrorists that have landed in the US who were trained there. The Mossad has also given us warning. It's happening, sir, and we don't have much time to respond."

Harden nodded. "Have we identified and located the suicide bioterrorists or the trigger hosts?"

"No sir. And we don't know the infection locations. We're working on that."

"How do you know the IGA is behind this?" Harden asked.

Drew looked at Ross. This was his question.

"With the intel I've gathered over the last three years and with recent intel we just received from the Mossad, we have direct links of eight recent terrorist attacks that tie Jabbar and the IGA with Hamas, ISIS, Al-Qaeda, the Muslim Brotherhood, and Al-Shabaab. Jabbar used the attacks to gain political power and influence, often thwarting the terrorist plots at the last minute to look like the hero."

Harden's face turned from fear to anger. He looked at Ward and then at Dougherty.

"Get a hold of my chief of staff, and have him call an emergency cabinet meeting. Now!"

"Yes sir," Dougherty said. He jumped up and hurried out of the room.

Harden turned to Ward. "Blast it, Ward, how did you let it get this far? The IGA . . . really?"

Ward was difficult to read. Anger, embarrassment, frustration? He fidgeted with the folder in front of him. "It's a good thing Ross ran his own operation or we would be walking ignorantly into oblivion. Ross, I want you to take lead on this. You will have any and every resource you need. I want you to pre-brief Alex Webb, director of Homeland Security, prior to the cabinet meeting."

Ross continued. "You should also know, Mr. President, that the IGA is getting help from someone deep inside our government. I had three other agents on this operation, and they were all assassinated. Agent Carter is the only one left. Although unconfirmed, I believe Senator Hanson's murder was also a result of the mole."

Harden turned an icy glare toward Ward. The director's cheeks flushed slightly.

"I'm reading extreme stress in the face of the subject thirty degrees to your right," Alice said, but Drew was already getting cues from Validus and his men. The warriors had their hands on the handles of their swords and were eyeing Ward closely.

Ward opened his mouth to answer, but Dougherty reentered the room carrying a briefcase.

"Marine One is on its way to pick you up, sir. The cabinet members are being called and will convene as soon as we get you back to the White House. I've sent an agent to Aspen Lodge to let the First Lady and your children know you will be leaving immediately." Dougherty walked back to his seat and set the briefcase on the table. "Mr. Ross, who else knows our situation? Is there anybody else who might have pertinent information we should call to the meeting?"

Ross shook his head. "Agent Carter put it all together this afternoon. This is our first briefing. We are the only four."

"Good," Dougherty said as he unlatched the briefcase and lifted the lid.

Drew saw the expression of Validus and his men change from concern to all-out alarm. Validus drew his sword, but six dark invaders collapsed on him and his men, materializing through the roof at once.

For one fraction of a second, Drew questioned his decision to believe if what he was seeing was real or still some figment of his subconscious. What if he reacted and made a fool of himself in front of the president and the director? His chance to stop the terrorist attacks would be over before it started.

But that slight mental hesitation proved to be deadly, for in that fraction of a moment, the terrorist attack on America began, and Drew was too late to stop it.

∽○∾

Despite realizing how serious of a threat Dougherty was to Carter, there was little Validus could do to stop whatever was about to happen. The Fallen were on him in full force, and these were some of Apollyon's best.

How had they missed this? Validus chided himself for relying on Malak's men for information on the IGA's infiltration into the United States government. Obviously Dougherty was a sleeper agent and had been for a long time. Then it dawned on Validus that the mistake had probably happened on his watch as North American continental commander—a mistake that could prove to be unrecoverable.

Validus's sword flew to meet the onslaught of vicious attacks that came at him. With extreme skill and overpowering force, the Fallen pushed Validus back and out of the conference room. Just outside the lodge, every one of his men was fully engaged with an assault team of Fallen. They were all fighting for their lives. Where were the reinforcements that Malak said would be standing by?

Validus's team paired up to cover one another's backs.

"We need to get back into that conference room. First team to break loose covers Carter!" Validus shouted above the fray.

The seven warriors eliminated multiple waves of Fallen, and yet with each second that passed, Validus knew that Carter's chance of survival diminished exponentially. He began taking risks he had never taken before in an attempt to get to his charge. Something akin to panic welled up inside him as his fight became desperate. Time dragged on with no break in the fight.

Validus eventually maneuvered toward Rake and positioned himself to take on his fight long enough to allow the swift angel to break free.

"Get to Carter, now!" Validus ordered.

THE FATE OF
THE NATION

Dougherty lifted a Glock 17 with suppressor out of the briefcase. Drew's first glimpse of the deadly black weapon caused an explosion of synaptic responses, but he was too late to act on any of them. He had no weapons, there was a broad, five-foot oak table between them, and there was nothing behind which to take cover. He set his hands on the table to give himself leverage as Alice voiced a warning in his ear.

"Warning! Weapon twelve o'clock."

The muzzle was pointed directly at Drew's chest. "Careful, Agent Carter. No sudden moves." Dougherty spoke as casually as if he were holding a cell phone. "Besides, these bullets aren't for you, not yet."

Drew watched Dougherty's finger flatten against the trigger. He calculated his response vector, but at the last second, the muzzle turned ten degrees, and one hollow-point 9mm round ripped through Ross's abdomen.

"No!" Drew screamed as he tried to shield Ross with his body, but it was too late. Ross slumped in Drew's arms as he fell out of the chair. Blood soaked Drew's hands as he gently laid Ross on the floor. One bullet to the abdomen was no accident. Dougherty wasn't trying to kill Ross, he was trying to torture him. Whatever was coming, he wanted Ross to hear it before he died.

Drew turned and glared at Dougherty, calculating the odds of his attack.

"What are you doing!" Ward exclaimed. "Have you lost your mind?"

"Shut up, Ward," Dougherty said with a calm voice. "You were the one who gave the kill orders for the other three agents. In your incompetence you didn't know there was a fourth, and now I have to clean up your mess."

The president hadn't moved. Horror laced his face.

"Don't look so shocked, Harden," Dougherty said. "This is what it looks like up close and personal. You pretend to run the world from your ivory tower, untouched by the grisly consequences of your orders. You're both pathetically weak."

President Harden finally broke from his stupor. "You idiot!" he exclaimed. "Ross is the key to stopping this terrorist attack!"

Harden started to stand up, but Dougherty shoved him back in his chair. "Sit down, Harden."

Ward jumped to his feet. "You *are* mad, Dougherty!"

Dougherty aimed the Glock at Ward. "Not mad, Ward, just committed."

Ward's eyes widened. He held up his hands. "Calm down, Michael, we'll handle this."

Dougherty sneered. "Shut up and sit down."

Ward slowly sat, his eyes glued to the Glock. This was Drew's chance, while Dougherty was distracted.

"Don't be stupid, Carter," Dougherty said as he turned the pistol to the president's head. "The president will be dead before you reach the table."

"Had to expose them," Ross whispered.

Drew looked down at the man who had trusted him, who had seen potential that no other had.

Ross winced. "You're not here by accident."

Drew touched a preset sequence on the left arm of his jacket.

"Sit down, Agent Carter. Now!"

Ross nodded, and Drew returned to his chair just as a rogue Secret Service agent entered the room. Odds were diminishing fast.

"What amazes me is how easy it was to get both of you to betray your own country," Dougherty said.

Drew glared at Director Ward, then at President Harden.

"What are you talking about?" the president said carefully. "You're the one betraying us!"

"Oh really? What about the five terrorist attacks that you approved in New York, Texas, California, Washington, and Illinois on American citizens?" Dougherty pulled out a two-way radio and clicked the transmit button. "Clear."

"Dougherty, you treasonous pig! Those attacks were based on your recommendation. You said the people needed a push toward global unification," President Harden said.

"And it worked, didn't it?" Dougherty smiled. "Premier Jabbar and the

IGA condemned the attacks and worked with the US intelligence offices to provide invaluable information and resources to thwart the next three attacks. President Harden and Premier Jabbar are heroes, the American people are safe, and global unification begins. Except that we are not really concerned about global unification. We are more interested in global domination. Allah is God and will rule the world through his people!"

"Code Viper! Code Viper!" President Harden shouted to the Secret Service agents outside the door.

Dougherty walked behind Harden and gruffly shoved the muzzle of the gun up against his temple. "Save your breath, Harden. All agents not loyal to the IGA have been killed, and tomorrow morning when the UN takes over and your pathetic Marines are gone, we will have complete control. Oh yes, and in case you're wondering, the agents guarding your lovely wife, son, and daughter are mine too. If you don't do exactly as I say, I will have them killed right now."

Drew added that variable as he calculated strategies. The odds were turning grim fast.

The radio clicked on. "In position."

"Roger. Send him in," Dougherty radioed back.

The door opened and a man dressed like a Secret Service agent stepped in carrying another briefcase. He walked to the table and set the case down.

"Our bleeding friend Ross over there has unfortunately forced my hand, but we have a contingency."

The man snapped open the locks and handed Dougherty a transmitter, then lifted out a syringe. Dougherty pointed the gun back at Ward. "Him first," Dougherty ordered. "Show them the syringe."

Inside the syringe was a light green liquid that seemed to be in a constant state of motion.

"Each syringe contains millions of nanobots engineered to find clogged arteries and clear them, compliments of a Swiss technology firm. Unfortunately they found it difficult to control the little devils. But where they found frustration, we found opportunity. These nanobots are kept in a suppressed state by a signal from this transmitter." Dougherty entered a code, and the greenish liquid immediately became still. "I must enter a secure code every thirty minutes for each of you or the signal linked to your nanobots stops. When the signal stops, they are no longer suppressed, and they do exactly what they're supposed to do and more. It turns out that the nanobots can't tell the difference between a clogged artery and a healthy one. They just don't know when to stop. The poor test monkeys bled to death internally in a matter of minutes. They tell me it was rather gruesome to watch."

"Your arm," the man ordered.

"What are you doing? Just tell us what you want," the president said.

"You can't give me what I want, Harden. That's why I have to take it."

Ward looked like he was about to retaliate, but Dougherty shot a round into the headrest beside Ward's left ear.

"Don't worry, Ward. As long as you do what I say—and stay within fifty or so feet of me at all times—the nanobots are harmless."

Slowly Ward put out his arm. The Secret Service agent grabbed it, located his vein, then inserted the needle of the syringe. Ward winced as the fluid slowly disappeared into his bloodstream.

Dougherty smiled. "Now Harden."

The man prepared to repeat the procedure on the president.

"Why, Dougherty? Why are you doing this?" President Harden asked.

"I need to make sure that no matter what happens in the next few days, you will do exactly as I say. With my little nanobots, your puppet strings just got stronger." Dougherty smiled as he gloated over Harden and Ward. "America is the great Satan, and it is time for you to die. This is a glorious time. With America gone, we will wipe the people of Israel from the face of the earth. Our messiah has come—the Twelfth Imam has returned, and now is our time to rule the world! But before peace comes, we must purge the world of infidels."

The greenish liquid in the syringe emptied into the vein of President Harden.

"I trusted you, Dougherty. I chose you to be my senior advisor!"

Dougherty laughed. "Ha! You didn't choose me. We chose you. You're nothing but a puppet whose strings are being pulled to perform a much greater purpose."

"You'll never get away with this," Ward said.

"Oh yes, I will, and you're going to help me."

Dougherty motioned to Drew with the Glock. The Secret Service agent reached for another syringe. Drew knew that Dougherty had no reason to keep him alive. He'd already shot Ross. President Harden and Director Ward were necessary to control so that the terrorist attack could be carried out without interruption, but Drew was only a threat and very expendable. He was surprised he hadn't already been shot. Then he realized he was going to be used as a guinea pig to show Harden and Ward what would happen to them if they didn't follow Dougherty's instructions to the letter.

The man stood next to Drew. "Take off your coat."

Drew stood up and took off his coat. He stuck out his arm as if feigning a "do your worst" attitude. As the man set the needle against his right arm, Drew saw that the nanobots had not been suppressed—the liquid was in a constant state of motion.

Drew grabbed the man's wrist with his left hand while simultaneously sliding his right hand into a position that allowed him to rotate the man's hand and snap the bones in his wrist. Before the syringe hit the floor, Drew caught it, then spun the screaming man in front of him just as the first of three rounds from Dougherty's gun reached them. The bullets penetrated Drew's human shield, and in the split second following, Drew threw the syringe directly at Dougherty before he could react.

The needle plunged completely into his throat. Dougherty dropped the gun and the nanobot transmitter to reach for the imbedded syringe as Drew cast the body of his shield aside and lunged at the rogue senior advisor. The impact pushed the plunger of the syringe halfway down, dispensing less than half of the active nanobots into Dougherty's neck, but it was enough. Dougherty's eyes bulged with terror as he became a victim of his own ghastly plan.

Drew rolled to the gun and came up on target just as the door opened and two more of Dougherty's men entered. Four perfectly aimed shots put them down. He didn't have time to waste. If there were more outside the room, there would be no chance of saving Ross, Ward, the president, or the United States.

He dove through the door into a somersault, knowing that anyone alive outside the room would belong to Dougherty. As he came up on his knee, he had already positioned three men and unleashed one round into the chest of each of the first two men. By the time he acquired and targeted the third, one bullet had been fired and another was imminent. Drew began to twist, but there was not enough time or distance to avoid the bullets.

In the split second that remained, Validus's red-headed warrior dove from above and deflected the first round with his brilliant silver sword. It was the fastest Drew had ever seen a warrior move.

Drew continued his twisting motion while simultaneously squeezing off two rounds at the shooter. The bullet grazed his head just above his left ear as his rounds found their mark.

He quickly recovered and made a search of the surrounding area to verify there were no more of Dougherty's men. Besides the rogue agents, six Secret Service men lay dead at various places in the lodge.

Drew returned to the conference room to discover two panic-stricken men sitting motionless in their chairs, their eyes glued to the gruesome sight of Dougherty's body lying in a pool of blood on the floor.

"What do we do?" Harden said. "We don't know the code—we're going to end up like him!"

Ward pulled out his cell phone.

"No!" Drew ordered. "Any communication outside this room will tip off the terrorists, and you obviously don't know who you can trust." Drew looked at the two men. "Stay calm, Mr. President. We'll sort this out."

Validus and his men were still immersed in a ferocious fight with the enemy. This battle was just beginning.

Drew grabbed the nanobot transmitter, noticing that he had twenty-eight minutes before the next code had to be entered. He found an extra magazine for his gun in Dougherty's briefcase, then went to Ross and knelt beside him. He looked like he was barely hanging on.

Drew found himself in the worst of predicaments. Any attention to what had just happened would tip off the terrorists and they would disperse into the populace. The outbreak of Ebola would still happen, just at a slower rate, and they would have no way of stopping them. Their only hope was to keep this entire tragedy undisclosed so they could find, capture, and possibly kill those responsible. But then how could he get help for Ross?

"How are you doing, sir?" Drew asked. "We'll get you medical attention."

Ross shook his head, then wheezed. "Get to the Marines, you can trust them. Secure Camp David, protect the president, find and take out the terrorists." He grabbed Drew's arm. "It's up to you, Carter."

Drew looked at the transmitter timer—twenty-seven minutes.

"We've got to get someone in here who can disarm these things," Ward said.

"There's no time, sir." Drew grabbed his coat and put it on. "Alice, analyze transmissions emanating from this device."

"Complete," Alice responded. "It is an encrypted frequency modulated signal."

"Can you duplicate the signal?" Drew asked.

"Who are you talking to?" President Harden asked.

"My coat," Drew replied.

"Yes, but it will take me approximately thirty minutes to decipher the encryption," Alice replied.

"Do it," Drew said, then turned to Harden and Ward. "Dougherty had to have help to get this far, and since the UN and the IGA appear to be in this together, I'm betting those UN troops out there aren't exactly trustworthy."

Harden cursed. "What do you suggest?"

"I need to contact the OIC of the Marine Guard and tell him to disarm and secure the UN troops. We need to keep this under wraps if we're going to have any hope of eliminating the terrorists."

"My wife and children," President Harden said.

"I'll take their guards out first, then get to the Marines."

"And us?" Ward asked.

"Hope I don't die and that I get back here in twenty-five minutes. What's the distress word for the Marine Guard, sir?"

"Shadowman," Harden said.

Drew bolted from the conference room and then exited Laurel Lodge. He sprinted down the road toward Aspen Lodge, less than half a mile away, where the president's wife and children were.

"Alice, scan infrared," Drew commanded as he donned his glasses, now tint-free. Though his night vision was very clear, the infrared would illumine people much quicker. Validus and his six warriors were with him, scouting before and behind. He kept a close eye on their cues as he went.

When he arrived at Aspen Lodge, he circled the cabin and noticed two bodies lying in the woods—Secret Service agents who had been eliminated.

Drew watched Validus, who let him know where the two rogue agents were. Within three minutes, Drew had taken out the agents and assured the First Lady and her children that everything would be all right.

"Stay here until the Marines come," he told them.

Drew checked the timer—twenty-one minutes. He ran through the woods straight toward the double fence that surrounded the camp. He needed to get the Marine officer in charge, the OIC, alone to explain the situation. That was going to be tough with the UN forces shadowing the Marines' every move.

He looked for a perimeter guard and moved that direction. A UN soldier was walking slightly behind and to the Marine's side. There could be no radio calls. Drew positioned himself in the trees so they would pass within ten feet of his location. Since they were protecting Camp David from intruders from the outside, surprising them on the inside was a much easier task.

First the Marine guard passed, then the UN soldier. Drew attacked from behind, quickly disarming and knocking the UN soldier out cold. The Marine immediately spun and brought his weapon to bear on Drew.

"Arms in the air! Arms in the air!" the Marine commanded. He reached for the transmit button on his radio.

Drew raised his hands. "Corporal, if you do that, the president will die. Shadowman. Shadowman."

The corporal froze.

"Listen to me, Corporal, my name is Drew Carter. I'm a special agent with the CIA. President Harden and Intelligence Director Ward were attacked in Laurel Lodge. These UN troops are part of the plot. I need to speak to your OIC immediately—without UN troops hearing what I have to say."

Drew stayed still with his hands in the air. The young Marine's eyes were wide and searching. He was indecisive. This was not procedure, and Drew had just taken out a UN soldier.

"I know this stinks, Corporal, but right now the life of the president of the United States and the very fate of the nation will depend on what you do in the next thirty seconds."

Drew could see sweat forming on the brow of the Marine. His finger hovered over the transmit key.

"Fifteen minutes remaining," Alice said.

"Get on the ground now!" the Marine ordered.

Drew shook his head. "I'm going to slowly open my coat and show you the gun that I could have used to kill both of you." He slowly dropped his hands to his coat and the Marine became nervous. His finger tightened on the trigger.

"Keep your hands where I can see them," the Marine ordered, but instead Drew slowly opened his coat to reveal the silencer tucked in his belt.

"Corporal, if you make that radio call, the president dies. I need to speak to your OIC now."

The Marine pressed the transmit button. "Sentry Three, this is Rover Two. I need to speak to Barracuda."

"Come again, Rover Two?"

"Get me Barracuda ASAP."

There was a long pause. "Roger, Rover Two."

The Marine was still struggling.

"If any UN troops find out what's happening, the president will die," Drew said. "You have to help me get the OIC by himself so I can talk to him. We have less than fifteen minutes."

The Marine looked at the unconscious UN soldier, then back at Drew. He slowly dropped his weapon. "At least one UN officer will be with him if I call him out. What do we do?"

Drew breathed a sigh of relief. "Make the call and help me get him into the woods." He motioned to the unconscious UN soldier. When the OIC called back on the radio, the corporal requested he come to their location. They then gagged the UN soldier and tied him to a tree while they waited for the OIC to arrive.

Five minutes later, a Humvee pulled up on the road near them.

"Ten minutes remaining," Alice said.

A US Marine captain and a UN captain exited the vehicle and approached them. The Marine had his gun on Drew, who was on his knees.

"Corporal, what are you doing?" the captain shouted. "Why wasn't this reported to Sentry?"

"Is this how you run security, Captain?" the UN captain said with disdain in his voice. He lifted his radio to his mouth.

The corporal lifted his rifle from Drew to the UN captain, and Drew brought his 9mm to bear on him as well.

"Put your radio down," Drew ordered.

The Marine captain drew his weapon and pointed it at Drew. "What's going on, Corporal?" he asked.

"You've got to listen to him, sir," the corporal said, his voice unsure.

"Captain, I'm Special Agent Carter with the CIA. Shadowman," Drew said bluntly.

The captain lowered his weapon. "Explain yourself, Agent Carter. Why is your weapon on my UN counterpart?"

"The president and Director Ward have been attacked by IGA agents, and these UN troops are part of the plot to take him out and initiate a terrorist attack against the US. Captain, I need you to disarm him and remove his radio. If any transmissions are made, the president will die."

"This is absurd," the UN captain said in a thick accent.

"How do I know the distress code hasn't been compromised?" the Marine captain asked. He glared at the UN officer. There was no love lost between them.

"Secure this man, and I'll take you to the president myself," Drew replied.

"Seven minutes remaining," Alice said.

"Captain, I don't have time to explain why, but I have seven minutes to get back to the president or he dies. We have to go now!"

The captain turned to the UN officer and removed his radio and gun. "Corporal, guard this man. If he runs, shoot him."

"Yes sir," the corporal replied.

Drew and the captain jumped in the Humvee and headed toward Laurel Lodge. Drew learned that the captain's name was Bates. He gave him a two-minute brief on what had happened to the president.

"Alice, have you decoded the transmission signal yet?" Drew asked.

"Not yet. Two minutes remaining," she said calmly.

Drew and Captain Bates quickly made their way to the conference room, where President Harden and Director Ward sat staring at the transmitter. The timer was now down to the last sixty seconds. *Fifty-three, fifty-two, fifty-one.*

Drew first went to Ross and knelt beside him. He checked for a pulse, but there was none. Drew hung his head. Anger boiled up inside him. Why was he trying so hard to save these two corrupt men when they disregarded the lives of greater men like Ross?

"Do something, Carter!" Ward yelled.

Drew stood up, walked to the table, and looked at the timer. *Forty-one, forty* . . . "Alice, what is the status of your transmission analysis?"

"Analysis complete. There is a twenty-three percent probability that the transmission will not be an exact duplicate," Alice said.

Thirty-four, thirty-three . . .

President Harden looked at Carter. He was surprisingly calm. "Are my wife and children safe?"

Carter nodded. At least he had some shred of humanity left in him. Drew would have to count on that if there was any hope of saving America.

Fourteen, thirteen, twelve . . .

"Alice, transmit duplicated transmission."

Five, four, three . . .

Ward closed his eyes and grimaced.

Two, one . . . Dougherty's transmitter emitted a high-pitched five-second tone that caused everyone in the room to jump, but neither President Harden nor Director Ward seemed affected by the nanobots. After three minutes, it was obvious that Alice had been successful and was keeping the men alive.

"Thank God it worked," Harden said. "But we can't live like this forever."

Drew wanted to ask the president if he was actually thanking God or if it was just an expression of relief. He saw such things so differently now. He picked up Dougherty's transmitter and read the nameplate. "Alice, I want you to access the Biobot Technologies database and see if there is a way of permanently disabling the nanobots. Override all security and firewalls."

"Yes, Drew."

"We'll get it figured out, sir. For now we need to focus on securing Camp David," Drew said.

"What do you want me to do, sir?" the Marine captain asked.

Ward, Drew, and Captain Bates developed a plan for disarming and securing the UN troops while maintaining radio silence. Forty-five minutes later, Captain Bates left the lodge to retake Camp David.

"Captain Bates," Drew called after him. "Once you've contained the situation, I need any transmission jammers turned off."

"Yes sir," snapped the captain, then turned to leave.

"Drew, I've successfully accessed the Biobot Technologies database. There is a transmission code to permanently disable the nanobots. Would you like me to initiate transmission of the code?"

"Yes, Alice."

He looked at President Harden and Director Ward. There was no change.

"The nanobots have been disabled," Alice replied.

"Mr. President, Director Ward, the nanobots have been permanently disabled. We'll need to get a doctor to figure out how to extract them from your bloodstream."

Both men took a deep breath.

"Well done, Agent Carter," President Harden said. He shook his head. "It looks like I've made a deal with the devil."

Drew remembered the dark master walking beside Jabbar and De Luca. Goose bumps covered his body until they ached. He slowly turned and looked at Validus and his band of mighty warriors. The angels stood like statues, watching, waiting, protecting. Harden had indeed made a deal with the devil. Drew alone was privy to the ancient war between God's holy servants and Satan's vile demons. The stark realization frightened him, and then the whisper of God came as he looked upon the mighty servants of the Most High God.

I am with you.

The flame of the Holy Spirit swelled within him, restoring his mind, his body, and his soul with the confidence and strength of a servant of God. Validus offered the subtlest of nods, but it was all Drew needed. They were not some invisible alien-invasion force. They were not some figment of his subconscious. They were warriors from heaven, and they were here for him. Was it for this time—to save the United States of America from annihilation? What else could it be?

"What are you looking at, Carter?" President Harden asked.

Drew turned back. "The hope of our future. You have indeed made a deal with the devil, Mr. President, but God Almighty, Creator of heaven and earth, has not abandoned us yet."

President Harden rubbed his eyes. "If only that were true."

"That He hasn't abandoned us?" Drew asked.

"No . . . that there was such a God." Harden frowned and looked at Ward. "What do we do now?"

The director took a deep breath. "I don't know who I can trust, even in my own intelligence offices. Not after today. Not after discovering what Jabbar was really after."

"You've put many pro-IGA people in power," Drew added.

Ward nodded. "The military's our best bet, but we've even been grooming their leadership. Right now, as far as we know, the terrorists are moving forward with their plot. If we let it out that we know, they will scatter and disappear and we may still have an epidemic to deal with. All it takes is one more mole, and we're done—CIA, FBI, NSA, Homeland Security, military."

"And I have reason to believe there are a lot more than just one," Drew added. "The IGA has penetrated deep."

President Harden folded his hands and looked at Drew. "Then it's up to you, Agent Carter. I don't care what it takes. The resources of the United States government are at your disposal. You must stop them!"

Drew suddenly felt the weight of the world on his shoulders. Millions would live or die by his actions. "With all due respect, sir, the resources of the United States government are severely tainted, and as Director Ward said, we can't afford a single leak. If you really want me to handle this, I'll be using my own tech team and assault force. People I can trust."

President Harden looked at Ward.

"Fortress Security is owned by Carter's stepfather," Ward said. "We've contracted them numerous times in the past two years. All ex-military—they know their stuff."

The president hesitated, then nodded. "Very well. What's your plan?"

"We have just over forty-eight hours. The trigger hosts are already inside our borders. Our only hope now lies in discovering the infection locations," Drew said.

"But Ross said you didn't know who the trigger hosts are or where the infection locations are," Ward replied.

"Yes, but we do know who many of the terrorists are. If we can find them, we may be able to locate the infection points," Drew replied. "Then we'll have to take them out on the ground, one by one."

"But even then, how will we know if we get the trigger carriers?" the president asked.

"I think there may be a way," Drew replied.

"Two days isn't much time, Carter," Ward said.

Drew nodded. "If we haven't eliminated the threat in forty-eight hours, we'll need to initiate the CDC's bioterrorism emergency procedures as well as shut down all air traffic, close the borders—including all shipping ports—shut down all restaurants, and broadcast emergency instructions to all citizens, explaining the threat."

"Agreed," Ward said.

"I will also need complete access to the CIA, Homeland Security, and FBI computer systems and databases—all of them so my tech team can tie into the information we need. Please get me all access codes immediately."

"That would be the biggest breach in security in history," Ward said. "Mr. President?"

"Whatever it takes, Jim. Give it to him. We have no other option."

Ward wrote three access codes and corresponding passwords on a piece of paper along with a phone number. "There are three levels of security for this kind of access. Once you're past the third level, you will have access to any system you need. The last number is my direct line. Call it and you can reach me anywhere."

Drew held the paper up and tapped for Alice to record the numbers. He gave the paper back to Ward and nodded.

Captain Bates entered the conference room. "Mr. President, we have secured Camp David. All UN forces have been contained and are being held in the field house for now. No communication was made that we are aware of."

"Well done, Captain," President Harden said.

"It's going to be difficult keeping this under wraps," Ward said, looking at Drew.

"We just have to keep this quiet for forty-eight hours," Drew replied. "Alice, break radio silence. Tell Ben to assemble the team immediately."

He inwardly cringed as he considered that the fate of America was in the hands of five computer geeks with video-game nicknames. He didn't even know their real names.

"Alice, call Jake," Drew commanded. "Director Ward, I need aerial access to Camp David. A chopper will be coming for me shortly."

"Done," Ward said.

"Oh yes, and I need an open account for expenses."

Ward looked to the president.

"Wire fifty million to his account, Jim," the president said, then looked at Drew. "Give Director Ward your account info, and if you need more, let him know." He looked at Director Ward. "If by some miracle we can put down this attack, how are we going to fix this?"

Drew felt his anger rising. Here was a man who had just handed the nation over to terrorists and he was worried about *fixing* it? "*Fix* this, sir?" He clenched his teeth. "I don't see how this can be 'fixed.' The American people deserve the truth—all of it."

Harden looked fiercely at Drew. "The people are too ignorant to be able to handle the truth, Carter. You do your job, and let me worry about governing the people."

Drew quelled his rising anger and tried to focus on the challenge of saving three hundred million people. "Yes sir," he replied slowly.

Ward went to the far end of the conference room to arrange airspace and money on his secure cell phone.

President Harden stood up and looked Drew in the eye. He put a hand on his shoulder. "Pull this off, son, and you'll be a hero." His gaze turned ice cold. "Don't fail me."

"I understand, Mr. President," Drew said. And he did.

"What's going on, Drew?" Jake's voice sounded in the earpiece.

"Jake, I need a chopper to pick me up immediately."

"Okay. Where?"

"Camp David. I'll be at the field house in ten minutes."

There was only silence on Jake's end.

"Jake?"

"Are you messing with me, Drew?" Jake asked.

"I wish I were. You have airspace clearance. Get here fast, Jake, and bring Sydney and Mick."

Ward returned. "It's all arranged."

"Good."

The president, Director Ward, Captain Bates, and Drew went to the front entrance of Laurel Lodge. There were no less than eight Marines inside with weapons drawn and ready.

Drew turned to Captain Bates. "Well done, Captain. You and your men have served this nation well tonight."

Bates saluted Drew. "My honor, sir."

Drew looked at Ward. "Director, I also need Agent Thomas Reed flown into LaGuardia Airport in an hour."

Ward nodded. "Keep me informed, Agent Carter. I want to know what's going on."

Drew's anger seethed again as he thought of Ross and the other nameless agents who had died at this man's hand. He glared at the director. "Unless I need something, I'll let you know when it's done."

Drew got into the Marines' Humvee and closed the door. Out of the corner of his eye, he saw Ward lean toward the president.

"You ready, sir?" the Marine sergeant asked.

The director whispered something to the president.

"Almost, sergeant," Drew said.

The president's lips moved in response, but his words were lost behind the reinforced glass and the sound of the diesel engine.

"I'm ready, Sarge."

During the ten-minute ride to the Camp David field house, Drew put on his sunglasses again and tapped out a command to Alice inside his pocket. *Replay video, sixty seconds, three o'clock camera.*

He found the time frame just as Ward began to speak and zoomed in on his lips. *Interpret,* he commanded Alice. In her soft English accent, she spoke the words of Director Ward.

"We're going to have trouble with him."

Then of President Harden. "We'll deal with him when it's over. I *will* fix this."

⌒o⌒

Validus and his team escorted Carter to the field house, keeping close and alert. Validus clenched his teeth as he thought of the near-fatal mistake that had just been made. His team had narrowly escaped dissolution themselves. Four of his men had been wounded but not seriously. With Apollyon this close, everyone should have seen this coming—Brandt, Malak, and especially himself. He vowed such a thing would never happen again.

The entire team sensed his frustration and anger. No one said a word, and not a single sword was sheathed the rest of the evening.

When they arrived at the field house, Validus watched Carter pace, knowing his mind was screaming through the strategies and scenarios necessary to pull off the impossible mission before him.

At one point he stopped and looked up at Validus. His eyes filled with deep concern. He almost looked afraid. "Is this possible?" he whispered.

Validus had found it necessary to rally thousands of warriors to significant battles in centuries past, but now he was at a loss as to how to encourage this one solitary man with the weight of the world on his shoulders. He could not deny the pangs of sympathy in his heart for Carter, but what could he say? The future was not set.

Persimus came to stand next to Validus. "All he needs is the confidence of a commander, Validus," he said quietly.

Validus looked Carter straight in the eye, filling his gaze with a fiery resolve, then nodded. One by one, Validus's valiant warriors came to stand beside him, swords drawn and jaws set firm.

Validus saw Carter's fear dissolve away as the blue flames of Ruach Elohim spilled from his soul.

THE TEAM

Drew ran to the chopper and jumped into the cabin. Sydney reached for him as he took the seat next to her. She grabbed his hand and held on as if he might disappear at any moment. Drew wrapped an arm around her.

"Thank the Lord you're okay," she said as the door closed and the blades spun up.

He hugged her tighter and turned his lips to her ear. "Whatever happens, Sydney, I want you to know that I love you. I always have."

Drew felt her hand on his neck and cheek. She didn't reply, but he didn't expect her to. It was much too soon. He just didn't know what the next forty-eight hours might hold and didn't want to miss the chance to tell her.

As the chopper lifted, he released Sydney and reached for the seat belt. He looked at Jake. "LaGuardia, as fast as this thing can fly. Once there, we need to become invisible."

Jake nodded. "I'll arrange it." He clicked on his headset and relayed the destination to the pilot, then looked back at Drew.

Drew marveled at how much he could tell Jake with just a look. It was just a natural part of their relationship, and it developed the first time they camped together. It was a connection that allowed no secrets, even when there was one. The details would come later, but with a glance, Jake knew the gravity of the situation. With one hand, Drew subtly signaled the number five. It was Jake's method within Fortress to silently relay the threat level of a situation. From a thumbs-up, meaning "all clear," to a three, meaning "many will die." Jake stared at Drew's hand—Mick saw it too.

While en route, Drew had Alice send a coded message; then he called Ben. "Ben, get your team ready for a briefing, and if you have any processor or mainframe upgrades you were planning, now's the time, and cost is no factor. You just need to have it ready in two hours."

"I just got a data upload from your mobile Alice. Is what I'm seeing real, Drew?" Ben asked.

"I'm afraid so, partner."

"We'll be ready," Ben replied.

An hour and a half later, they picked up Reed at LaGuardia Airport, then flew to the top level of a vacant parking garage. A utility van was waiting for them. One more clandestine vehicle change and they were inside NexTech thirty minutes later in downtown New York City.

Just over two hours after leaving Camp David, Drew, Sydney, Jake, Mick, Reed, Ben, Piper, Crypt, Ridge, and Jester were gathered in the NexTech Blue Room. Also present were Validus and three other angels. Drew noticed that other angelic forces were positioned on the roof and throughout the building. In the midst of impending doom, their presence was comforting, especially now that he knew who they were and Whom they represented.

"How we doing?" Drew asked Ben.

"Upgrades complete and Alice is running at peak performance. And we have an additional fifty million in our account," Ben said with a smile.

"Good. When she connects with the government systems, can you hide our location? I want to keep our base of operation off their radar."

"I can for a while," Ben said, "but the longer we're connected, the greater the chance of them finding us. I'll give Alice some additional encrypting and masking routines. She might be able to hide for a couple of days."

"That should be all we need," Drew said as he slapped Ben's shoulder.

"Ah . . . Chider, we've got someone lurking around our south entrance near the service door," Ridge called from one of the work stations. "Looks fishy to me."

Drew looked at the monitor. "I've got this. Unlock the door once I get there."

A few minutes later Drew returned with a middle-aged woman wrapped in drab clothes, but there was nothing drab about her eyes or personality. When they entered the Blue Room, Drew noticed Ben and his crew had gathered together. Jake, Mick, and Reed were talking, and Sydney was standing at the table by herself, eyes ever on him. The woman with Drew took off her coat, went to Sydney, and introduced herself.

Drew wasn't sure how to even begin to explain what he had commissioned them to do—save the United States of America. He heard conversations from the three groups as if he were standing next to them.

Crypt: "So why are we here in the middle of the night, and why is your friend acting like he's all in charge of everything?"

Piper: "And what's with the dudes with the guns? They scare me. Is this some sort of government takeover?"

Woman: "Pleased to meet you. I'm Sarah."

Jake: "I'm sorry, Mick, you know how tight a cover has to be. I'm not even sure what agency he's with."

Reed: "I had no idea he was still involved until an old contact from the Farm told me he needed help and that I should talk to you guys."

Ridge: "I seriously don't think Mr. Allen is going to like this middle-of-the-night thing happening. What's going on, Chider?"

Mick: "I knew there was something more to him. I just don't like not knowing, Jake."

Ben: "Don't worry about Mr. Allen. I can take care of him."

Drew scanned the room, but this time not for "invaders." He looked at each of the people he had called to this epic moment in time and realized that he had lived a life of deception with every single one of them and that each one believed a different story. How could he keep the lies straight, let alone get them all to work together as a team?

Then a gentle message penetrated his thoughts. *Just be honest with them.* It was Sydney's soothing voice.

The woman had gone to get a cup of coffee, and Sydney was looking at him again. Drew was warmed by her strength and smile. She seemed to know his thoughts. He nodded, then stepped to the head of the table.

"Everybody, please gather around," he began. Within a few seconds, all eyes were on him. "You all have a lot of questions, questions that deserve answers. The problem is that I can't answer all of them because time is short and people's lives are on the line. I have deceived each of you in one way or another, but I need you to trust me even though I haven't earned it." He stopped and looked at each face. "So let me at least set a few things straight and hopefully start to gain your trust. I have been working for the CIA for the last three and a half years and as a nonofficial cover agent for the past year. I recently discovered an Islamic terrorist threat that has the potential to wipe out the entire United States. The president has commissioned us to eliminate that threat."

Jester snorted, then fell silent as he realized Drew wasn't kidding and no one else was laughing.

Drew continued. "At Camp David, terrorists succeeded in killing many agents and nearly took out the president and the director of National Intelligence because of the intel I had gathered and presented on the Islamic Global Alliance. With the corruption that has leeched into our government and with the infiltration of Islamic extremists into some of the highest offices, the president has had no choice but to hand over this mission to us." Drew held out his hands, gesturing to everyone in the room. He let his words settle for a few seconds.

"I can't make this sound any less dramatic than it is—standing in this room is America's only hope for survival. Allow me to give each of you a brief introduction to the rest of the team." Drew motioned toward Jake. "Jake Blanchard is the president of Fortress Security, a company with decades of military combat experience. The US government has contracted Fortress Security to handle some extremely delicate and dangerous missions in the last few years. Mick Trotter is Jake's East Coast division commander in York, Pennsylvania.

"Agent Thomas Reed is a current CIA asset. I've asked him to be part of this team because he's the only one in service I fully trust.

"Now for the tech team." Drew looked at Ben. His friend nodded his approval of what Drew was about to reveal. "Ben, aka Chider, and his tech team, Crypt, Ridge, Piper, and Jester, are the genius behind NexTech, a technology company that is second to none in state-of-the-art technology advancements. What none of you know"—Drew hesitated, but there would be no way to hide it over the course of the next two days—"is that Ben is not only the genius behind the company . . . he *is* the company. With money that we acquired in previous years, Ben secretly launched NexTech by hiring all personnel, including upper management, casting the vision, setting priorities, and orchestrating projects to put NexTech at the frontline of the industry. In short, Ben and I own NexTech."

Everyone turned to look at Ben with shock on their faces, including Sydney. Piper's eyes lit up, then diminished to disbelief. Ben flashed a brief smile.

Crypt threw his hands in the air. "Okay, the charade is up." He pointed his finger at Drew. "*You* are crazy, I don't know *who* these goons with the guns are, we still don't know who the bag lady is supposed to be, and you"—Crypt pointed at Ben—"Chider, you're just as nuts as he is. I'm out of here. I need to get some sleep before work tomorrow." He turned to leave.

"Alice, have you finished uploading the video from Witness?" Drew asked.

Crypt stopped at the door.

"Yes, Drew," Alice responded.

"Play 360 video beginning at 8:15 this evening."

The four seventy-inch screens, one on each wall, sprang to life with images captured by Drew's jacket at Camp David. The occupants of the Blue Room became Drew as each monitor gave its seamless view of events that occurred just hours earlier. Dougherty held the gun to President Harden's head. Director Ward sat in his chair with a look of horror on his face. On another screen, Ross was on the ground, wincing in pain as blood pooled on the floor beneath him. The only face not visible was Drew's. Perfectly clear audio filled the room.

"Save your breath, Harden," Dougherty was saying. *"They're dead. And the agents guarding your lovely wife, son, and daughter are mine. If you don't do exactly as I say, I will have them killed right now."*

Drew let the events in the Laurel Lodge conference room play out for five minutes. "Alice, stop video."

The monitors went blank. The truth and severity of the moment hung in the air as Drew's team continued to stare at the black screens. Crypt silently returned to stand beside Ben.

Drew motioned toward the woman. "This is Senator Sarah Boyd from Oklahoma. She and five other members of Congress are part of a secret coalition called the Patriots. They enlisted Director Ross, the man who died tonight, to investigate the IGA's association with terrorist activities in the US, as well as high-level officials in the government, who are working with the IGA, to manipulate policies that would destroy our freedoms and national sovereignty."

Crypt swallowed hard. "Beg your forgiveness, ma'am."

"Not necessary," Senator Boyd said. "I've been called a lot worse than a bag lady."

Drew looked at Sydney, and she shook her head. She clearly felt out of place, but little did she know how important her role would be.

"This is Sydney Carlyle."

Sydney lifted a timid hand and waved, clearly embarrassed.

"Sydney has a master's degree in microbiology. You will soon understand the necessity for her expertise."

Sydney's hand slowly fell. She looked at Drew, confused.

"In approximately"—Drew looked at his watch. It was just after 1:00 a.m.—"forty-seven hours, over one hundred suicide bioterrorists will inject themselves with the live Ebola virus in order to infect the largest cities in the US. All of them work at restaurants where they can directly infect the greatest number of people possible before they are discovered. Sydney, what will be the consequences if this terrorist attack is successful?"

Sydney looked stunned, along with everyone else in the room. "Well . . . as you know, the Ebola virus is one of the deadliest viruses known to man even though it only has a reproductive ratio of two, which is considerably less than, say, measles, which has a ratio of seventeen, or malaria, which is one hundred." Sydney paused to gather her thoughts.

"What's that ratio mean?" Piper asked.

"The reproductive ratio is the average number of secondary cases caused by an infectious individual in a totally susceptible population," Sydney explained. "In spite of its low reproductive ratio, what makes Ebola so deadly is its fatality rate. In undeveloped countries where medical treatment is limited, it can be as high as ninety percent. In the US, it would be significantly lower at first, say sixty percent, but . . ." Sydney shook her head. "On a scale like Drew is talking, the epidemic would quickly overwhelm the medical system, and the fatality rate would rise to near that of a third-world country. It would become a vicious cycle, causing an epidemic that within two to three weeks would be unstoppable even with a reproductive ratio of only two." Sydney seemed stunned by her own analysis.

Drew finished for her. "The US would quickly be quarantined from the rest of the world. In two months, the epidemic becomes a pandemic—millions would die." Drew looked at Sydney and saw the pain in her eyes. "In less than six months, the United States of America would cease to exist as a viable nation. We are talking about a biological apocalypse."

Once again the gravity of what they were facing sobered every soul there. Seconds passed as they all considered the weighty burden on their shoulders.

"And you expect our little band of merry men to fix this?" Ridge said.

Jake crossed his arms. "The odds *are* low, Drew, considering the scope of the threat and the time frame. The risk of failure is—well . . ." Jake didn't finish. He didn't need to. "Something of this magnitude needs the full resources and attention of our intelligence agencies, our medical personnel, and our military. Isn't there some way of utilizing them? I know there are still many good people in those organizations."

"I agree, Jake, but all it takes is one mole inside any of those organizations and we fail. Yes, they might not be able to hit us as hard or as fast, but millions of people will still die."

"He's right," Senator Boyd interjected. "The Patriots have been concerned for years in regard to the number of known and unknown radical Islamic ideologists infiltrating every system of government. There is no way to ensure confidentiality outside of what you are doing right here."

"So this whole War on Terrorism campaign was just a bunch of bologna?" Ridge asked.

"No," Drew said. "We still have hundreds of thousands of patriotic, solid people doing their jobs, including Muslims who are not aligned with the extremists. Unfortunately our security has been compromised, and we don't know who we can trust. The bottom line, people, is that we don't have a choice, and in this room are some of the most brilliant and skilled individuals in the world. Besides this, we have help that you cannot see."

Drew glanced at Sydney. "For those of you who believe in God, I ask you to pray. For those of you who don't, I ask you to reconsider, because what lies before us is going to take a miracle to accomplish. As our forefathers did before bearing the weighty task of forging a nation, I think it would be wise to pray to our Creator and ask that He grant us wisdom, strength, and protection through this mission."

Drew glanced around the room filled with geeks and soldiers, men and women, believers and nonbelievers, angels and humans. It was a strange assembly that had come together to save the nation.

Everyone bowed their heads.

"Dear God, I . . . I'm not very good with prayers."

Drew felt awkward. He opened his eyes and glanced toward Sydney. She was looking at him. Her eyes brimmed with tears as she mouthed the words,

"God loves you . . . and so do I." Then she bowed her head, and Drew saw God's Spirit well up from within her and reach out to everyone in the room. What a mighty warrior she was. He felt God's Spirit rise up within him too, and he closed his eyes once more to continue his prayer.

"Lord, we are mere men and women, inadequate for the mission before us. We desperately need Your divine help. Forgive us, Lord, for the people of this nation have forgotten You. We have trampled underfoot the Son of God and treated the sacrifice of His blood as something unholy. We have grieved Your Spirit and cursed Your name. We have preyed upon the innocent and embraced perversion and called it good. In faith our forefathers placed the foundation of this great nation on Your Truth, on the rock of Jesus Christ, and now we have gone astray. Forgive us, almighty God, and restore us. Grant us, dear God, the strength to endure the coming battle, the wisdom to discover the plots of the Enemy, and the protection to accomplish Your will. Let us be once more the wings of a great eagle to deliver Israel from the mouth of the dragon. We humbly set our future and our fate in Your hands. In the name of our Lord and Savior, Jesus Christ, amen."

Drew kept his eyes shut as the presence of God lingered. What had just happened? Words from the Bible had flowed from him as if his voice were not his own. He opened his eyes and slowly lifted his head. Every eye was on him, and all, including Sydney, looked stunned. His cheeks flushed in embarrassment. He felt silly and ashamed, and now he had to try to lead this odd band against a global network of terrorists.

Behind his team, he saw Validus and his men glowing in power. It gave Drew the strength to begin. He took a deep breath.

"We're facing bioterrorism on a grand scale, and we have less than forty-seven hours to find and eliminate the threat."

The other ten team members seemed to awaken from their stupor.

"How do the terrorists plan on infecting themselves?" Sydney asked. "As deadly as Ebola is, without a living host, it dies rather quickly."

"We suspect they will be using trigger hosts infected with the virus who have already entered the country," Drew said. "We're not sure how they plan on transferring the virus to the rest of the suicide bioterrorists. What would be the most effective way?"

"The most efficient method would be by injecting contaminated blood directly into the bloodstream. The virus would never be out of contact with a living host, and it would spread quickly throughout the body of the receiving host." Sydney shuddered. "Death would be almost certain, but it also means they would be highly contagious in a relatively short time."

Drew turned to Jake. "We're going to have to mobilize every resource Fortress has. Money is no object, but again, confidentiality is paramount. Every one of those terrorists is one phone call away from being warned. We must keep the element of surprise, and we can't trust anyone outside of Fortress and NexTech. Ben, with the codes I gave you, you should have complete access to the intelligence agencies' database and mainframes. We need to keep our intentions hidden from prying eyes on their end."

Ben thought for a moment. "I think we can swing that. We'll use their databases for data acquisition only and keep the computations and analysis of the data on our end. We can also run some dummy searches to hide what we're looking for." He hesitated. "Do you really think the IGA has access to their systems too?"

Drew nodded his head. "I know so. You'll have to be careful."

Ben and his crew all nodded.

"Drew, how do you propose we find the infection locations?" Jake asked.

"From the intel I've received from Mr. Ross, the Mossad, and Senator Hanson, I have confirmed IDs of thirty-eight of the bioterrorists. If we can locate them, we could track them, and they would lead us to the locations."

"We wouldn't have enough time to respond," Mick said. "We would need at least a four-hour head start before the first terrorist arrives to make sure we got there in time."

"And that's with prepositioning our men in strategic geographic locations," Jake added.

"Triangulation!" Piper exclaimed.

Ben nodded. "Yes!"

"Explain," Drew said.

"You said these terrorists are already in their respective cities." Piper swiped the interactive glass table and pulled up a map of the US. "If we can locate as many as possible and track them . . ." She tapped three cities in the Midwest. "Terrorists from each region should be converging to the same point." She drew lines from the three cities to a fourth city as a point of convergence.

"Theoretically, we just need to track two of them and find their travel intersection point. With each successful terrorist we track, the resolution of our prediction narrows."

"That's good," Drew said. "Based on the intel, we're fairly certain that there are four infection locations. We'll call them zero points. We can only hope that of the terrorists we find and trace, we will have at least two for each zero point. I'm guessing that timing for them is going to be important, which we can use to our advantage. They are going to want to infect all suicide terrorists as close to the same time as possible, so not only will their paths converge, but so should their times of arrival at the zero points."

"Now, how do we find them and trace them?" Ridge asked as he swiped a digital clock onto the table, then initiated a countdown to midnight on September 5. "Considering we have only forty-six hours and twenty-six minutes."

"How about what the CIA and FBI already do—facial recognition? That's one of Alice's prime routines, and I guarantee she's better at it than anything the government has," Crypt said. "We tap into the government databases, access security cameras everywhere, and let her go to work."

"That would work," Ben said.

Jake shook his head. "We need multiple methods. We can't afford to rely on just one. Besides, once they start moving toward their zero points, there's no guarantee we will get another facial ID along the way."

"Agreed." Drew shot Reed a glance.

"RFIDs," Reed said.

"Exactly." Drew nodded. "Radio Frequency Identification tags. The CIA uses tags that are basically the size of a speck of dust. We locate and physically plant RFIDs on as many terrorists as we can find before they move."

"But how do you plant them if they're that small?" Crypt asked.

"The tags can stick to clothes or hair for a long time, but the surest way is bonding it to the skin. The CIA developed a method for that," Reed said.

"I'm sure they did," Jester said.

Reed ignored the comment. "Twenty tags are suspended in a thin film of permanent adhesive, like superglue except that this glue completely evaporates, leaving no residue when not between two substrates. They come on small dots the size of a hole punch. Peel one side and stick it to the back of your hand. Peel the other side and you have five minutes to brush the permanent adhesive on the tags against a target's skin. The bond can last from three days to two weeks."

"RFID radios are everywhere—airports, railways, turnpikes, bus stations, schools, museums, and even traffic lights," Drew said as he looked at Ben.

"Alice, are you connected to the government network and databases?" Ben said.

"Yes, Ben."

"Mask all searches. How many RFID radios can you access throughout the continental US?"

There was a three-second pause. "Approximately 246,000."

Jake and Reed looked satisfied, but Ben and his crew wore sour expressions.

"Big Brother is here," Piper said soberly. "What we're doing is scary in many ways."

"Man, this is everything we're against," Crypt blurted.

"He's right, Chider," Jester added. "We've spent years fighting this kind of government invasion of privacy. I hate it."

"I'm pretty sure those terrorists couldn't give a monkey's tail about your privacy rights," Mick said.

"Right now we don't have the luxury of being impeded by ideological thinking," Drew said. "You're going to have to worry about that later. Reed, we need ten thousand RFIDs so Alice can program their codes and track them. See if we can get them straight from the manufacturer and bypass the CIA."

"It won't be likely. The manufacturer for the tags is in Texas. We'll probably have to utilize the CIA's inventory," Reed said.

"Check them before you bring them here," Drew said. "I think we can assume that most of the terrorists won't fly for fear of being identified. That means they'll probably be moving to their zero points in the final twelve to twenty-four hours. Jake, we'll need your men to place the tags on the ID'd terrorists within the next twenty-four hours."

"All personnel at all three divisions have been placed on alert," Jake said. "We have choppers and charter jets on standby. Get us the tags, the locations, and photos, and we'll take care of the rest."

"Maybe this is a dumb question," Mick began, "but if we can get close enough to place tags on them, why not just follow them?"

"All it takes is for one terrorist to make a tail and the whole operation could go down," Drew said. "And if we take any of them out, they might miss a scheduled check-in and raise suspicion. We would never find the four trigger hosts, and the epidemic would still happen, although at a much slower pace. But you do bring up a good point. Tell your men to stay visual with the terrorists until we can confirm we are tracking them. If any of the terrorists have vehicles, plant a GPS tracker. If we aren't able to track with RFID or GPS, we stay with them all the way to the zero points. Make sure your men understand the need for absolute invisibility."

Mick nodded. "You got it."

"What about satellite imagery?" Crypt asked. "The new Spectator Sat4 was launched last month. With 15-cm resolution, you can count zits on a face."

"Alice, do you have access to Spectator Sat4 imagery?" Drew asked.

"DigitalGlobe is requiring an access fee," Alice replied almost instantly. "The National Geospatial-Intelligence Agency has an account. Confirm authorization to access."

"Alice, call Director Ward," Drew said. "Make it untraceable."

A few minutes later, Ward relayed the account access codes.

"Alice, complete authorization," Drew said.

Four seconds later Alice responded. "Access granted."

Drew handed Ben the USB drive containing the names of the terrorists. Ben plugged it into a port on the edge of the table. "Alice, access this drive and correlate the names to database information on file for each individual. Display records on the monitors."

The monitors began filling with photos and information on the terrorists. Where there was no information, only a name appeared.

Ben continued directing Alice. "Using the photos, use surveillance cameras and satellite imagery to identify and locate each person. This is going to take some time," he said to the team. "The amount of data she is processing is immense."

"And it's the middle of the night when few people are working," Piper added. "Probably won't find much until morning. We're going to lose precious hours unless . . ."

Ben looked at her and smiled. "Unless we access historical imagery, but it would really slow the search."

"Nighttime is the time to do it, though," Piper shot back.

Ben nodded. "Alice, optimize search to include historical imagery when appropriate."

"Please specify," Alice requested.

"Limit your search to restaurants. If the restaurants are closed, attempt to access historical imagery. Display photo, name, and date stamp on the table showing locations."

A few seconds later, a photo of the first terrorist appeared on the graphic table, pinpointing his location at a fast-food restaurant in downtown Los Angeles—Hassan Atef.

"There we go," Drew said. "Let's hope Alice is fast enough to get us IDs in time for us to predict the zero points." He looked at his team. They all seemed hopeful—all except Sydney. "Is there anything else we're missing? Any concerns?" he asked, looking at her.

Sydney was staring at the second terrorist that Alice had just ID'd and was now showing on the table. "You won't really know," she said quietly.

Everyone turned their gaze to her. She looked up, panning the faces.

"You won't really know if you get the trigger hosts. I mean, if you don't know who they are or what they look like, you won't really know until weeks later if the country is safe. When an outbreak occurs, every measure is taken to contain the spread. If just one of these terrorists leaves the zero points infected, or if a trigger host himself escapes and they aren't trying to contain but rather trying to spread the virus, it could still escalate into an epidemic."

The room sobered again.

"We need a foolproof method of knowing," Jake agreed.

Sydney shook her head. "There isn't one, or the CDC would be using it."

Drew looked at Ben. They were both thinking the same thing.

"Perhaps there is a way," Drew said.

B en looked at Drew as they led their team to his office. "Once we do this, it's over, you know." There was a look of defeat in his eyes.

Drew put an arm across Ben's shoulders. "I know, but it's okay. When we have some time, I've got a few things to tell you. After all, I think you may have discovered a whole new market for this thing." He lowered his voice. "Besides finding aliens. Have you been able to do some additional testing to verify the results since I was here?"

"Yes. It's pretty remarkable," Ben replied.

Drew ushered the entire team into Ben's office.

"Now I get why you have the big office," Crypt said.

Ben placed his hand on the scanner in his desk, and the section of the wall leading to the LASOK lab opened.

"Get out!" Ridge exclaimed.

Piper looked at the LASOK lab, then back at Ben, eyes sparkling with admiration. Ben caught the look, and Drew saw his genius friend flush, then attempt to ignore it.

"Chider, you dawg!" Jester exclaimed. "You really do own this place!"

By the time everyone had entered the lab, Crypt was already drooling all over the equipment. He looked up at Ben, confused by the array of seemingly unrelated equipment all configured into some mysterious puzzle. "What is it?"

As everyone gathered around the LASOK, Ben stepped forward. "This is the light accelerator by stimulated optical kinetics, or LASOK. It's a device I've re-created from Dr. Waseem's research at Drayle University . . . with a few enhancements."

Crypt's eyes opened wide, then his eyebrows furrowed. "Are you seriously trying to accelerate light? Come on, Chider. Now I'm back to thinking you're crazy again."

Ben shook his head. "Not trying, Crypt—doing. The LASOK already works."

Only Ben's tech team seemed to fully grasp the significance of what Ben was saying. Jake, Mick, Reed, and Senator Boyd looked anxious to be on with the mission.

"Why are we here, Drew? What does this have to do with the terrorist attack?" Jake asked.

"Ben has discovered an interesting anomaly that occurs when you accelerate light. Not the particular anomaly we were originally hoping for, but it could be extremely useful for what we are facing right now. Tell them, Ben . . . in English."

"There's a very narrow range of velocities above the normal speed of light that produces what can only be described as bizarre visual effects. We didn't see them at first because we couldn't tune the velocities with enough precision. When I did discover them, I thought at first they were just some strange phenomena that occurred in the visual spectrum unique to light acceleration—something like the aurora borealis."

Ridge wrinkled his nose and squinted.

"He said English," Ben responded. "Anyway, what I discovered is that each incremental change in velocity highlighted different life forms."

"What?" Piper exclaimed. "In what way?"

Ben seemed hesitant to answer. "They glow."

"They glow?" Jester repeated.

Ben nodded. "Seriously, they glow as if emanating their own light. And every life form seems to have its own velocity associated with it. Humans, dogs, cats, mice, insects—every single species has its own associated velocity. It's as if life has been categorized and can be identified by the velocity of the visual spectrum. It took me a while to develop a velocity tuner fine enough to differentiate between similar species, but I can tell you the species of ant by the velocity at which the LASOK glows."

"It sounds a little like the spectral analysis that can be used to identify gases and compounds," Jester said.

Ben nodded. "I suppose in a way it is spectral analysis of living organisms."

Sydney's face lit up. "You can tune in to the Ebola virus velocity so we can see it!" Drew couldn't remember the last time he had seen her so excited.

"But the virus is inside the body," Mick said. "Can this thing see through other substances?"

"No, it can't," Ben said.

"That doesn't matter," Sydney replied. "Within just a few days of becoming infected, there will be up to one hundred trillion virions inside and outside the body. It lives in all bodily fluid—saliva, tear ducts, urine, sweat. A trigger host's body would be teeming with virions."

"He would light up like a glow stick," Ben said.

Crypt turned away from the electron microscope he'd been inspecting. "As awesome as this machine sounds, it's a little too large to haul to four different locations at the same time while we ask the trigger hosts to stand still so we can conduct a spectral analysis on him."

Ben held up his finger. "Early on we had an accident that ended up being fortuitous for a couple of reasons. As a result, I recently discovered that a lens could be kinetically stimulated and set by a burst of plasma. When a relatively small electrical current is applied transverse to the crystalline structure of the glass, it becomes its own miniature LASOK. It's set at a fixed velocity, but it allows a user to see as if they were looking through this machine."

"That's what happened to me?" Drew asked.

Ben smiled. "As near as I can tell, that's what happened."

Drew was astounded once again by the absolute genius of his friend. If those arrogant kids from high school could see him now! *Geeks really do rule,* he thought.

"What does this mean?" Mick asked.

Ben went to a cabinet and returned with a bulky set of glasses. He clicked a switch on the side and handed them to Mick. "It means I should be able to make Ebola-tuned glasses that will help you spot the host triggers."

Mick slid the glasses over his eyes. "Wow! Like infrared but clearer."

"This set is tuned to humans, but I've yet to find a life form that the LASOK can't tune to," Ben said.

"But I didn't think that viruses were actually alive," Senator Boyd protested. "Will this still work?"

Ben hesitated.

"It's true," Sydney said. "Viruses were first considered poisons, then life forms, then biological chemicals. Today most biologists consider them somewhere in between."

"I've never tried a virus. We won't know until we try," Ben said. "Which means to do this, I will need a sample of the Ebola virus in order to tune the lens to it."

"Do we have the time?" Jake asked.

"Tuning the lens is relatively easy and fast. Then we'd have to build the glasses." Ben thought for a few seconds. "If you can get me the virus, I can have the glasses tuned and built within six hours."

Drew looked at Sydney. "Where do we get Ebola?"

She shook her head. "You don't. Only biosafety labs with a level 4 rating are allowed to work with dangerous and exotic agents like Ebola. There are only fifteen labs in the country with that rating. There is no way they would let you walk out with a vial of Ebola."

"Would an order from the president of the United States make it happen?"

Sydney raised an eyebrow and shrugged.

"Where's the nearest lab?" Ben asked.

"The nearest lab that may have the active virus is the NIH, the National Institutes of Health Clinical Center in Bethesda, Maryland. I've been following their research on the development of a vaccine for Ebola. But there's also a level 4 lab at Fort Detrick, Maryland, at the US Army Medical Research Institute of Infectious Diseases. I think there's a new one in Boston too."

"Bethesda sounds like our best shot. I'll talk to Director Ward and see what he can do." Drew looked at Sydney and hated what he had to ask her to do. He grimaced.

"You get me approval, and I'll take care of it. Ben and I will work on it together," Sydney said. "They may insist on delivering it themselves and on sending one of their laboratory scientists with the sample to ensure containment. I would."

"Yeah, that's not happening," Drew said. "NexTech has got to stay undisclosed as our base of operation."

He looked at Jake. This was the moment in the mission that a clear line of leadership needed to be established. He could tell Jake felt it too.

"Drew, this is your operation. Tell us what you need, and we'll make it happen," Jake said with a nod.

Drew was humbled by Jake's trust in his leadership. He nodded his thanks.

"Timing is going to be critical. Jake, you and Sydney need to take the chopper to Bethesda and get that virus. I want her surrounded by six fully armed soldiers while she's in custody of the virus. This should give the NIH at least some level of assurance. If they insist on sending an escort, then he stays at NexTech with no communication until this is over. Once you get the virus transported back to NexTech, prepare your men at Fortress East for tagging our targets. Based on the population distribution, you'd better prep three teams for assault in case our East Division has to cover three zero points."

"Depending on timing and the number of men we have to send out to tag targets, those three teams could be lean—twenty to twenty-five soldiers each," Jake said.

"That'll have to do." Drew turned to Jake's second-in-command. "Mick, you need to get on a charter back to Fortress Central and manage operations there. We'll use Teterboro Airport, not LaGuardia. Geographically you're going to have the greatest challenge. You'll need to cover any target tagging and zero-point assaults west of Chicago to east of Phoenix."

"You got it," Mick replied.

"West Division will take from Phoenix west. Can Sanchez handle this?" Drew asked Jake.

"We're not fully equipped there yet, but the men are solid. I'm confident in Sanchez, but I recommend having Fortress Central tag all targets west of Chicago and have Sanchez focus on getting his assault teams ready," Jake replied.

"That makes sense. That way we can deliver the RFIDs to just two locations." Drew turned to Reed. "Once you get the RFIDs back to NexTech and programmed, deliver them to Fortress East then Central. Then I want you back at CIA headquarters in Langley. I want eyes and ears there and direct access to resources if we need them. I'll remain at NexTech to coordinate efforts and work out details with Ben and his team until the LASOK glasses are built, then I'll join Jake at Fortress East and command one of the assault teams. Sydney, I need you to be the courier of the glasses to Fortress Central and West. You also need to be prepared to brief our assault teams on potential Ebola contamination. I'm going to have Ward get the CDC to run emergency deployment exercises so they'll be ready to deploy for real as soon as the terrorists are taken out."

Sydney nodded.

Drew scanned the faces of his team. "Any tech you need, try to get it here or from trusted, private, and local sources. Keep in contact with NexTech as Ben and his team hone in on terrorist movement and zero-point identification. Ben, when the terrorists begin to move, get us your predictions of the locations for the four zero points immediately. Even if they're not accurate, it will get our assault teams moving in the right direction. You can fine-tune the locations as we move. Reed, we can't deploy men to tag targets until we get those RFIDs. Here's Director Ward's secure line. Work directly with him and no one else. Just keep NexTech a secret."

"I'm on it," Reed replied. "But can we trust him?"

"No, not really, but I do believe he wants us to eliminate this threat. Just keep your contact with him minimal." Drew turned to Sydney. "Hopefully the timing will work out so that you can deliver the glasses and RFID tags to our Fortress Divisions at the same time because travel time west is going to be a big factor. Ben, shut down NexTech for the rest of the employees until this is over. If you need more than your tech team, do what you think is necessary. Make sure Alice bounces all data and voice communication outside of NexTech so that our location can't be traced." He looked at the faces of his antiterrorist team. "Any questions?"

The silence said it all.

"Then it's time for us to move, team. God be with us."

As they exited the LASOK lab, Senator Boyd pulled Drew aside. She looked worried. Sydney looked over her shoulder at Drew as she walked on with Jake, Mick, and Reed.

"Jake, wait for me at the dock door. I'm riding with you to the chopper," Drew called.

"Will do," Jake called back.

Drew turned to Senator Boyd. "What is it, Senator? Is there a flaw in our plan?"

"Not that I can see." The senator crossed her arms. "If we get through this, you know that every one of these people is going to be in serious danger. Harden and Ward won't allow loose ends to jeopardize their power."

Drew knew that he would be a target but hadn't considered that everyone else would be just as threatened. "That video is proof enough. It will be our protection."

Senator Boyd shook her head. "Not good enough, Drew. You've broken just about every privacy law we have to get that, and it won't hold up legally. Because of that, the Patriots can't use it. I don't think you know how far the corruption goes. Harden will manipulate, lie, coerce, bribe, and even kill to stay in power, and he still has all of the resources of the United States government at his disposal. The judicial system has been compromised too."

"I don't care if it's legal or not. All I need to do is convince the American people of the truth. I don't really see any other option. We can either be illegal or dead." Drew looked at his dispersing team. "And I won't allow anything to happen to them."

The senator nodded. "I know, and I'll make sure the Patriots are prepared to run this to the finish line. Somehow the government needs to be purged, and perhaps this will be the catalyst."

Drew began strategizing on a whole new level. He looked at Ben, who was in deep conversation with the rest of his techs. "I think I can help you with that, Senator. Ben!"

Ben came to stand beside Drew and Senator Boyd.

"When you can spare some processing time, I want you to run a search on all government, private, and military personnel scheduled to travel out of the country from September fifth to September eleventh. Isolate all that are unique."

"What's this for?" Ben asked.

"If you knew there was going to be an epidemic and the borders would be shut down in a matter of days, would you stick around and wait to die?"

"Ah . . . like rats leaving a sinking ship," Ben said.

"It would be a great starting point," the senator said. "Those would be the worst of them, the ones looking to destroy us."

"If we make it out of this, I want those rats to hang," Drew said. "Thank you for being here, Senator. You be careful too."

She looked Drew in the eyes. "We'll be praying for you."

Drew found Ben and his team back in the Blue Room, where they began analyzing Alice's data and prepping to program the RFIDs when they arrived.

"Ben, I've got to take care of a couple of things. I'll be back in an hour," Drew said, then went to catch up with Sydney.

Mick and Reed were already in a taxi on their way to Teterboro Airport twelve miles north to catch charter jets to Fortress Central in Rivercrest and CIA headquarters in Langley.

Drew, Sydney, and Jake made their way back to the van and then to the chopper. This was where he would have to say good-bye to Sydney. As they exited the van, the pilot began spooling up the blades. Jake looked at Drew and Sydney, then ran to the chopper.

Drew grabbed Sydney's hand. "Here I am, dragging you into danger once again. Are you tired of me yet?" He looked into her beautiful blue eyes, grateful that at last there was nothing to keep them apart anymore . . . except perhaps a bioterrorist apocalypse.

"Disaster does follow you," she said. "Or is it that you follow disaster? I've never been quite able to tell." Then she grabbed Drew's other hand with her free hand. "But no . . . I'm not tired of you and never will be. I always knew that God had a great purpose for you. I just never dreamed it would be this big." She took a big breath and glanced toward the chopper. She looked anxious. "I'll bring the glasses and the RFIDs to you as soon as they're complete."

"You be careful, Syd. I mean it. I don't want to lose—"

Drew's words stopped when Sydney lifted herself up on her tiptoes and kissed his cheek. She wrapped her arms around his neck.

"I don't want to lose you either," she whispered into his ear.

Drew held her for a moment; then they parted. He grabbed her hands once more. "While you're waiting for the virus, I need you to do something for me."

"Of course."

He watched as two of Validus's warriors morphed wide pearl wings and moved toward the chopper. He looked at Validus and caught the glint in the mighty warrior's eyes. "We need you to pray. Without breeching the security of the mission, we need you to enlist every believer in the nation to pray. Pray that God will look favorably once more on our country. The soldiers in both realms are going to need it."

Sydney's eyes lit. "Are they with us, Drew?"

He watched as the majestic beings took flight. "They are, Sydney, and it is a sight to behold."

"Reverend Ray will be my first phone call."

Drew smiled. "Perfect. I can't wait to see him again and tell him."

"I want to be with you when you do," Sydney said with a smile that disarmed Drew once again.

He followed her to the chopper and helped her in. He gave Jake a thumbs-up. "See you at Fortress East," he said, then closed the door. He ran back to the van and waited until the chopper was in the air.

Though Drew couldn't hear it, he could certainly feel it—the bioterrorism bomb was ticking.

A WAR FOR SURVIVAL

Drew stood on the street corner, waiting, his hands in his pockets and his glasses displaying Alice's progress. Five blinking red dots were now overlaid on a map of the United States. It was almost 3:00 a.m. Drew wondered if he was waiting in vain.

After a few minutes, a Lincoln MKX Crossover pulled up to the curb. Drew opened the passenger door and sat down.

"It's been a long time. I thought perhaps you'd forgotten about me." The woman sitting behind the wheel turned and looked at Drew. Her dark brown eyes searched his face.

"I'm just glad you remembered and took my phone call seriously," Drew replied.

"You could have picked a better time. I don't normally let strangers in my car at three o'clock in the morning. These streets can be dangerous this time of night."

"Miss Bryant, I need your help," Drew said.

"It's Sophia, mystery man," she interrupted. "And if I'm going to take you seriously any further, I need to know who you are."

Drew gazed into her eyes with the same warmth he had when she had accosted him at the Chicago bombing. He saw the effect in her eyes as her news-anchor professionalism softened.

"My name is Drew Carter. I'm an operative for the CIA, the kind that the US government disavows if I'm ever captured or discovered. What I'm about to tell you is bigger than anything you've ever heard or any story you've ever run."

Her gaze hardened. "Why should I believe you?"

He reached into his pocket and pulled out a two-terabyte solid-state USB drive. He held it up. "Because of this. Last night I thwarted an assassination attempt on the president of the United States, and right now I have less than forty-five hours to stop the largest terrorist attack ever plotted against our country. If this isn't handled properly, what I'm about to give you will either sign my death warrant or will be instrumental in restoring the freedoms we once believed in and are about to lose."

Bryant smiled and Drew knew he had lost her. It was too much, but he didn't have time to break it to her in pieces that she could digest slowly. He held the drive out for her to take anyway. She was his only hope.

She reached for it, one eyebrow raised. "Well, you certainly are dramatic." She flipped the drive in her hand as if it were an interesting but unimportant obscure item she had just lifted from the street to inspect. "People like you don't exist," she said, looking once more into his eyes. "I suppose you're going to tell me that many have died to get this information."

Drew's eyes narrowed. "Sophia, it's going to take you some time to get through that drive, but don't delay—time is short. When you're done . . ." He hesitated. He was asking her to sacrifice just as much as anyone else who had been caught up in this web of global corruption. "You're going to have to make a choice. I just hope you have the courage to make the right one, because by handing that information to you, I just broke the law, and if you choose to report any of it, you will be breaking the law too. Unfortunately, you and I have been put in positions where we must choose the higher ground and pay the consequences to save others."

Drew held her gaze for a few seconds, then reached for the door handle. He stepped out of the car, then leaned down and looked in at Bryant. She was still holding the drive, gazing at it.

"I chose you because you're smart and the people trust you. Thanks for meeting me." He stood and closed the door, then turned and walked away.

"Alice, how many terrorists have been identified?" Drew asked as he headed back toward NexTech.

"Seven terrorists have been identified and located. Would you like them displayed?"

"Yes."

Drew's glasses filled with a map of the USA showing seven blinking red dots with names attached to them.

"Call Reed." After a few seconds, Reed answered. "Reed, Alice has already ID'd seven terrorists. What's your ETA back to NexTech so we can get our men moving with the RFIDs?" Drew asked.

"Ward has the tags waiting for me, so I can have them to NexTech in two hours."

"We'll have a chopper waiting for you at the airport. I think the National Institutes of Health may prove difficult to work with in getting that virus, so we won't wait for Sydney and Jake."

"Roger that," Reed said. "We should be able to get the tags on their way to Fortress within the hour. Your men should be able to deploy to the first few targets in three to four hours."

At 5:13 a.m., Reed arrived at NexTech with the RFID tags. Ben and his team had the tags programmed and coded for Alice to track thirty minutes later.

After dropping Reed back off at Teterboro Airport to catch a charter back to Langley, Drew took the chopper straight to Fortress East in York, Pennsylvania. As soon as he arrived, he briefed his men and began deploying them to the identified terrorist targets.

Over the course of the next twelve hours, Jake's men had tagged nineteen of the terrorists without being discovered. And of the thirty-eight previously identified terrorists, Alice had successfully located and was now tracking twenty-seven of the targets using facial recognition and the planted RFIDs. Just after 6:00 p.m. on the evening of September 4, the targets began to move. Ben's team was able to predict four infection locations, or zero points, just as Drew had determined from the intel—New York, Louisiana, Colorado, and California. Each zero point looked geographically placed so that terrorists from all parts of the country could access one of the four without having to travel more than seven hundred miles.

What concerned Drew was that each of the zero points had been pinpointed to rural farms, which was completely unexpected. He began to wonder if there was a flaw in their strategy. As it was, they proceeded as planned. Fortress West would take California, Fortress Central would take Colorado and Louisiana, and Fortress East would take New York.

Under extreme protest and after a personal phone call from President Harden, the National Institutes of Health allowed Sydney to procure a sample of the Ebola virus. The stipulation was just as she suspected—an accompanying scientist who was level 4 certified and a containment chamber that looked like the outer casing of a nuclear bomb. Jake and six fully armed guards accompanied Sydney and the scientist. The acquisition, transportation, and delivery of the virus to NexTech were completed under extreme secrecy.

By the morning of September 5, detonation day, Sydney and Ben successfully isolated the speed of light that categorized the Ebola virus. By the time Ben and his team finished constructing the Ebola-tuned glasses, they were only two hours behind schedule.

Thirty minutes later, Sydney was on a Cessna Citation X to hand deliver a set of glasses each to Fortress Central and West divisions. When she arrived at Fortress West in California at 2 p.m., Jake set up a videoconference with Fortress East and Fortress Central so that Sydney could brief all members of the assault teams on the use of the glasses and how to protect themselves from exposure and infection.

Drew addressed them first. "Men, you have to assume that every terrorist is already infected with Ebola, which makes them deadly both to you and to thousands of others. Our goal is to capture, but if they attack, take them out before they get close to you. If they run—" Drew stopped. The thought of shooting someone in the back as they were fleeing was almost incomprehensible. "They are running to kill thousands and thousands of US citizens. You must shoot to kill. None can escape. Sydney?"

Sydney filled the screen. Drew was proud of her—so intelligent, so gutsy.

"The Ebola virus is one of the most deadly viruses we have discovered. It is not airborne but is passed through all types of bodily fluid. Therefore keep all your skin covered at all times, especially your hands and face. If you come in contact with a terrorist or any sweat, blood, or urine, you must consider yourself contaminated for the safety of the rest of your men. Put on the red armband so they know your status. You will be quarantined as 'high risk' by the CDC when they arrive. Everyone else will also be quarantined simply for the safety of the populace until they can guarantee you have not been infected."

Jake jumped in. "We don't expect armed resistance, as it would be highly unlikely that they would have risked acquiring weapons once inside our borders. However, we will still handle this as we would any other terrorist armed threat. Are there any questions?"

There were no questions from the ninety-six soldiers that made up the four assault teams.

"Okay, men. Load up," Jake ordered.

The videoconference terminated, but Drew immediately got a call from Sydney.

"It's all working just as you planned," Sydney said, trying to encourage him.

"Yeah . . . too well."

"What do you mean?"

"No mission this complicated ever goes this smooth," Drew said, then realized that he didn't need to add to her worry. "But perhaps God is working things out for our benefit. There's a lot at stake here."

"Well, you have thousands praying for you." Sydney's voice was strong, but Drew could hear the worry between her words. "You be careful, you hear?"

Drew smiled. "I promise. Then I'm going to ask you out on a proper date when you get back here."

"And I'll say yes."

"I've gotta go, Syd. I'll be in touch when this is over and get you on a flight back here tomorrow."

"Okay, Drew. God be with you."

Ten minutes later, Drew, Jake, and their assault team were loaded up into three choppers and flying northeast toward their zero point. Out the windows of the chopper, Drew could see an armada of angels, and he imagined the same held true for each of the teams now deploying to each of the other three zero points. There were thousands upon thousands of angelic warriors in the sky around them, but Drew had to stay focused on the world of men for the next few hours so he could effectively lead this team.

Drew tried once again to grasp the logic of the terrorists meeting in rural farmhouses when their goal was to infect large, densely populated cities. The infection could have easily been accomplished in an apartment in downtown New York. As it was, the unfortunate owners of this rural upstate New York farm were probably dead. The nearest neighboring farm was over a mile and a half away.

At 11:45 p.m., Drew made a call to the county sheriff's office, explaining the operation and directing them to set up a five-mile radius quarantine. Drew followed with a command to Alice.

"Alice, relay coordinates of all four zero points and mission brief to Director Ward, the CDC, the FBI, the CIA, the NSA, and Homeland Security."

By 11:50, Drew and Jake had positioned six-man teams on each quadrant of the farmhouse at a distance of two hundred and fifty yards. The call sign to be used was Posse. Drew, as the commander of the entire assault team, was Posse Boss.

A north-south road separated the cleared farmhouse land from thick forest to the east. Drew and his men, Posse East, had positioned themselves just across this road, seventy-five feet east of the farmhouse. From there, Drew could manage the whole operation. Fifty feet to the southwest of the farmhouse was a large steel Quonset building that gave ample cover for Posse South to approach from that direction. Jake and his men, Posse West, were positioned in a small grove of trees. There were also two smaller outbuildings to the west. Posse North had the least amount of cover and was the most vulnerable. Fortunately this was the back of the house with the least amount of activity by the terrorists.

Drew wore the virus-tuned glasses because they would interfere with Jake's infrared goggles. For Drew this wasn't an issue, since he could already see at night, but he wondered how the other four teams were dealing with it. It was a problem they hadn't thought through.

Drew could see a dozen vehicles positioned around the southern and eastern areas of the house, and he could faintly hear chanting and prayers being said in Arabic. He gave the order to close in. "Clear each outbuilding as you go."

Slowly, carefully each team maneuvered and cleared buildings until they were all within fifty to seventy-five feet of the farmhouse.

"Posse South, get positioned behind the autos," Drew radioed. One click from each was their acknowledgment.

Three minutes later—"Posse South set. Posse West set. Posse North set."

Drew set a bullhorn to his lips, but before he could speak, Jake's voice filled his ear.

"Posse Boss, this is Posse West, we have a problem," Jake said. "Two of the targets are carrying automatic weapons."

Drew's heart beat harder. This was a complete game changer. He took a moment to analyze.

"Be prepared to take them out at the first sign of hostile fire," Drew called. "Roger."

"If this turns hot, watch the crossfire," Drew radioed to everyone, then lifted the bullhorn again. "Attention!" His amplified voice blasted across the road. "You are surrounded!"

But that was the last word Drew voiced.

Automatic gunfire filled the night air. He heard bullets zing above his head. There was a pause as Jake's team took the two men out. Would that be it? But Drew's answer came quickly.

Windows broke, and the farmhouse erupted in automatic gunfire from all directions. Drew's men returned fire. The farmhouse and surrounding land filled with hundreds of flashes and the unceasing sound of automatic weapons. Somehow these terrorists had equipped themselves with an arsenal of weaponry and ammunition.

At various times, two or three terrorists would attempt to climb out of a window and make a run for it, but Drew's team was able to contain them each time. The gunfight was ferocious, but in spite of the surprising number of weapons the terrorists had, the Fortress soldiers were better equipped for a nighttime fight and far better trained. Over the course of twenty minutes, the gunfire began to subside.

Drew called for surrender once more, but it only seemed to intensify the return fire. When the return fire stopped, Drew knew the worst was still to come—clearing a farmhouse with dozens of small rooms and narrow hallways. And although he had not yet been able to see any indication of Ebola through his glasses, he knew that the house was rich with the deadly virus. He heard sirens in the distance.

"Status," Drew radioed.

"Posse South, clear."

"Posse West, one injured." Drew couldn't tell if it was Jake's voice or not.

"Posse North, clear."

"Move in," Drew commanded.

He motioned for two of his East team to stay back and cover any attempts by a terrorist to make a break for the trees. It was the only possible route that had enough cover for such an attempt. The rest of Drew's East team crossed the road. Drew positioned himself further south so he could see the entrance of the home better. As the assault team closed in from all four quadrants, he began to hear shouting from the house in a thick Arabic accent.

"Don't shoot . . . surrender . . . don't shoot! We're coming out!"

"Hold," Drew ordered over the radio. "Keep your distance."

The six men to the south were the closest to the entrance of the house. They had left their cover behind the vehicles to approach the now-silent farmhouse. Drew counted eleven bodies on the porch and on the ground just in front of the porch. He knew there were more west and north, but he didn't yet have an exact count. Of the bodies he could see, all seemed to be virally clear, but perhaps he was still too far away for the LASOK glasses to work.

They waited as one by one the terrorists came to the porch in a huddled group. Drew still couldn't quite see the door.

"On the ground!" he shouted. "Lay on the ground!" he repeated in Arabic.

The group of terrorists began stepping off the porch, but none of them went to the ground. He shouted again, but still no response. Posse South was now just forty to fifty feet away.

Then Drew saw it. At the back of the group was one man glowing in green, phosphorescent light.

"Trigger host at the rear! Keep your distance," Drew radioed but it was an order that would not help them.

All at once the men in front of the trigger host fell to the ground and the terrorist filled with trillions of Ebola virions began running toward Drew's closest men. Drew saw the dead man's switch in his hand, and the realization of what was about to happen struck fear into his heart. There was nothing he could do except attempt to minimize the death and the contamination that was about to happen.

Before the terrorist had run ten feet, Drew took aim and shot as the terrorist shouted, "Praise be to Allah! Death to the great Satan!"

The instant Drew's bullets hit the trigger host, the detonator for the vest bomb he was wearing went off. The bomb's explosion assaulted all of Drew's peaked senses. Although the men closest were on the outer edge of the forty-five-foot lethal blast radius, there was just as deadly an outcome waiting for them. Drew watched in horror as green phosphorescent, Ebola-laden tissue and fluid sprayed upward and outward, reaching much farther than the lethal radius of the concussion.

"Back away! All units back away!" Drew shouted as he motioned for the three men with him to quickly retreat. Fragments were raining down from above.

Drew heard more gunfire to the north of the house. The bomb was a diversion so the other terrorists could attempt a break for it. He looked down the eastern side of the house just in time to see two more terrorists climbing out of windows there. He motioned, and his men turned and opened fire.

"This is a diversion. Keep eyes on all exits from the house," Drew radioed. He looked back at the blast area, horrified by the sight of it. A sixty-foot radius around the suicide bomber glowed with thousands of fragments of Ebola-laden fluid and tissue.

He heard more gunfire to the north and west this time.

"All units hold your positions. The entire area is contaminated with Ebola. Posse South, what's your status?" They would have taken the worst of the blast. Drew checked his own clothing and the three other men with him as he waited for an answer. He could see no trace of the virus on any of them. They were the farthest out and partially shielded by two vehicles in front of them.

"Two men down," came the strained reply.

Drew motioned for his men to keep their eyes on the house. He then backed away from the house and circled around to the south. He carefully approached from that direction until he could see miniscule glowing fragments splayed on the ground and all over the vehicles. His Posse South team was just on the other side of the vehicles, fifteen feet into the contaminated area. He could see two men on the ground, both alive but hurt badly. The other four were still recovering from the shock.

"Posse West, what's your status?" Drew asked Jake.

There was no reply. Drew's heart sank. *Please no,* he prayed.

Gunfire erupted off to Drew's left, west of the house near the Quonset. Then came gunfire inside the Quonset.

"Don't move. Keep eyes on the house," Drew ordered, then turned toward the Quonset. "Posse West, state your status," he radioed as he ran.

"Targets acquired along the north wall in the Quonset," Jake's voice returned.

Drew ran to the north side of the Quonset just in time to see a side door open.

"Stop!" he yelled in Arabic, but the two terrorists turned to fire.

Drew took them both out, then covered them to make sure they were dead or incapacitated. As he approached, he kicked their rifles away from their hands and immediately noticed that they were Heckler & Koch G36 assault rifles. "What the heck?" he said quietly.

One of the terrorists' right arm was exposed. A pinpoint of glowing light was evident just where a needle would enter the vein. He sidestepped the bodies.

"Two targets down, north entrance of the Quonset," Drew radioed.

"Copy. Quonset clear," Jake's voice returned. "Posse Boss, you'd better take a look in here."

Drew entered the Quonset and quickly made his way to Jake. He had to get back to his injured men and the mess at the farmhouse. Jake and two of his men were standing beside opened crates. There was a small patch of glowing green on the back shoulder of one of the men.

"You're contaminated, soldier. Stay clear."

The soldier stepped back three steps, then put his red armband on. Drew quickly inspected Jake and the other soldier.

"We saw these earlier but missed the markings," Jake said as he kicked over one of the crate lids. They were marked UN.

"They're brand-new G36s," Drew said.

"Now we know why the zero points were all rural. They must have had a secondary attack plan after infection or in case of capture," Jake said.

Drew shook his head. "We've got men down and a viral mess out there."

When they exited the Quonset, Jake repositioned his two men back on the west side of the house, advising the contaminated soldier to keep his distance from the others. Jake and Drew went to within a safe distance of Posse South. All six of them were contaminated. Two of the men were watching the house while the other two were administering first aid to the two injured soldiers.

"All units, there is a sixty- to seventy-foot radius out from blast point that is contaminated with the virus. Keep clear and keep eyes on all possible exits from the house. We may still have terrorists."

"Posse North, copy."

"Posse East, copy."

"Posse West, copy."

"What's their condition, Pete?" Jake called out from thirty feet away.

"One fair, one serious. Bleeding restricted but we need medical treatment," the detachment leader replied.

"Roger that," Jake said.

Drew dialed Director Ward.

"Drew, we still need to clear that house before any medical or CDC personnel get on site," Jake said.

"Agreed. The front entrance is massively contaminated. We'll go in the west entrance and clear from there. We'll have to be careful. I'm sure the house is severely contaminated too."

"We can clear it, sir," one of the Posse South men said. "We're already contaminated. It won't matter now."

Drew looked at Jake. He nodded.

"Take two men with you, and keep contact with all surfaces minimal," Drew ordered.

"Yes sir."

Director Ward's voice came in over the headset. "What's your status, Carter?"

"Director, we have an Ebola disaster here. We need a full CDC containment facility and medical treatment personnel immediately."

"They're already en route to all four locations, just like you asked. The FBI is en route as well to help manage security," the director replied.

"Be advised that local law enforcement are at each location, as well as news teams from the Associated Press and World Media News," Drew added.

Silence, then, "That was a foolish move, Carter."

"Carter out," Drew said, ending the call.

He got status reports from the other assault teams in San Francisco, Denver, and Shreveport. Each of the other teams reported successful missions with only three soldiers injured—one in critical condition. The other teams also faced heavy return gunfire, but none of them endured a suicide bomber with the viral disaster Drew and Jake's team faced. A total of one hundred and twelve terrorists had been identified, of which seventy-six were killed, twenty-three were captured, and thirteen were still at large.

"Posse Boss, this is Posse South. The house is clear."

"Roger, Posse South. Exit the west entrance and return."

"Copy."

Drew and Jake finished securing and positioning their men as they waited for the FBI and the CDC to arrive. Twenty minutes later, Drew received a call from Ben.

"I think you'd better get back here ASAP," Ben said.

"What is it?"

"Can't say for sure. It's something you need to see."

Ben's voice sounded strained, and it made Drew anxious. He took a moment to inspect every square inch of his body, including the soles of his boots.

"Jake, every man here needs to be quarantined until the CDC declares them clear. Keep Posse South isolated, and inform CDC. Ben will have gotten the additional LASOK glasses to the CDC to equip their mobile containment facilities to help verify containment. I need you to see this through. I can't stay."

Jake removed his night-vision goggles and looked at Drew. "You sure that's wise, Drew?"

"No, but I don't have a choice. Doesn't sound like we're out of this yet. I'll keep this set of glasses with me to do an hourly inspection. If I am infected, it'll show long before I'm contagious."

Jake nodded.

"Your men were outstanding tonight," Drew said. "America owes them a great debt of gratitude."

Jake nodded. "Be careful, Drew."

Drew began making his way back to one of the choppers. He would continue to inspect himself thoroughly for any contamination, but as an added measure, he would have to strip naked and burn his clothes. Once on board, he would get further updates from the other three assault teams, brief Ward on the details of the mission, and give Sydney a call to let her know that all had gone well.

America had been saved, at least from the worst of the attacks, but he knew more potential devastation was coming. Would the country survive it? Would he and his team survive it?

∽◦∾

"Commander, Brumak is hurt badly, and Crenshaw's not doing well either," Rake reported, pointing with his sword to the west side of the farmhouse. He was bleeding badly from two of his own wounds.

Validus looked at Carter, who was already twenty yards out, making his way back to the choppers nearly a mile north of their location.

"Persimus, find Jayt and join up with me to cover Carter. Tren, you and Rake recover the rest of the team and make sure the Fallen's assault here is fully contained. Stay with Brumak and Crenshaw until they can move to a better location and fully heal. This isn't over yet."

"Yes sir," Tren and Rake responded, then left. Validus hurried to catch up with Carter as Persimus moved swiftly to find Jayt.

Validus and Carter walked side by side, each scanning their own realms for threats.

"We're not out of this yet, are we?" Carter asked, taking a second to look toward him.

Validus shook his head, then stopped and held up his hand. Carter complied as Persimus and Jayt joined them, both with swords ready.

"What is it, Validus? I don't see anything," Persimus said.

"I don't know, but something's not right."

Then, in the murky dark sky above, five winged demons came at them at once. Validus was confused because he didn't see any physical threat to Carter and an aerial assault against experienced warriors, even at night, was suicide. What were the Fallen attempting? Their assaults were always coordinated with a terrorist or criminal threat from one of their human pawns, but the area seemed clear for miles.

Then Validus witnessed something unprecedented in Fallen history. Just as he, Jayt, and Persimus positioned themselves and pushed off the ground to execute their fatal cuts, the demons demorphed their wings while simultaneously translating into the physical world of men. The angels' swords passed through them as if they weren't there.

This was indeed a suicide mission, for according to the Noahidic Accord, their fate of dissolution to the Abyss was sealed. But for the few seconds of existence that remained, there was never a more dire threat to Carter than right now. In earthly form, these demons could take immediate and effective deadly action against him.

The instant Validus realized what was happening, he began translating, and so did Persimus and Jayt, but he feared it would be too late. Carter could never survive such an assault.

$$\sim\!\!\circ\!\!\sim$$

Drew was half a mile from his team when it happened. In spite of all that he had seen, this was something new and horrid.

Three demons translated into physical form before his eyes, each one brandishing a dark and grisly sword meant for him. He brought his AR-15 to bear on the closest one, but one lightning-fast slice from the demon's blade crumpled the front barrel and tore the weapon from his hands.

The force of the blow gave Drew his first indication of the frightening power these dark warriors wielded. All five senses immediately kicked into overdrive, but the most dramatic one was the smell of evil. It was indescribable . . . some strange mix of decaying flesh and sulfur.

Drew dove to his right, toward the blue arcing flames of a translating Validus, while drawing his FN. He rolled and came up on one knee, targeting a demon, and put three rounds into it. Before the demon hit the ground, his body dissolved and disappeared into the earth, but two more demons translated to take his place.

Drew turned just in time to see another blade coming down on him from behind. He rolled and kicked at his assailant's feet as the blade tore into the dirt beside him. The demon pounced on Drew before he could get another shot off, and a massive, powerful hand ripped the FN from Drew's grip.

It felt to Drew that each passing second would be his last. The sound, smell, weight, and sight of a demon this close was nearly paralyzing. How could anyone survive such a thing?

The demon dropped his sword in exchange for a knife, but Drew beat him to the first blow. His knife sank deep into the demon's side, and the curses that spewed from its lips revolted Drew in the darkest of ways. The weight of the demon quickly dissipated as his flesh dissolved to a green vapor and sank downward through Drew.

He had momentarily escaped death, but more demons were coming. He rolled to his hands and knees, trying to regain his feet, but out of the corner of his eye, he caught the sight of another dark blade slicing toward him. This time, there would be nothing he could do to stop it. His last sensation would be the sound of clashing swords as Validus and his warriors finished translating into earthly warriors.

∽o∾

Validus didn't wait to finish translating to initiate his first cut. Carter had miraculously survived two demon attacks already. His quick and skilled actions had bought Validus and his men a few precious seconds to complete their translations, but now a third demon was executing a fatal slice that would surely end the man.

The demon's blade was already inches from Carter. Validus had no choice but to slice upward through Carter, attempting to precisely time the translation of his blade to intersect the demon's. A fraction of a second too late, and the demon's blade would finish him. A fraction of a second too soon, and Validus's own blade would kill Carter.

The collision of these two powerful blades sent sparks flying in all directions, and Validus hardly dared look to see if Carter had survived. The demon cursed, and Validus finished him with two quick counter slices.

Before the demon fully dissolved, he grabbed its dark sword and maintained the translated weapon. He turned to see Carter on his feet, knife in hand, waiting for the next attack. This was a man worthy to protect!

Carter glanced at Validus as more demons came, translating from spirit to physical form all around them. Without a word, the man seemed to know his thoughts. Validus threw his golden sword to Carter, and together, they began to fight the strangest battle of blades the world had ever seen.

∽o∽

Drew reached for the gleaming sword and snatched it from the air just as a demon came at him. The golden handle of the sword felt good in his hand, like it belonged there . . . like it had always belonged there.

Never in his wildest dreams—or nightmares—had Drew thought that working with Gus at Fortress East might determine his survival. He had learned everything Gus could teach him in the art of swords, but he felt wholly inadequate to stand beside such legendary warriors and fight against the forces of evil in such a way. Although this sword was the epitome of perfection in weapon design, he needed both hands to wield it effectively. It was meant for a larger bearer like Validus.

Drew sliced the brilliant blade to meet the demon that came at him. He wondered if there was any chance of surviving such a battle. But what he lacked in skill, the sword itself seemed to provide, knowing just where to move. And with each cut and slice, Drew's hyper senses and heightened mental acuity and motor skills learned and adapted to this bizarre arena.

He was also keenly aware that Validus and his two fellow warriors were taking great risks to protect him. Why should such valiant angels risk their very lives for *him*? *They* were the holy ones. *They* were the perfect ones. And yet even now, they seemed willing to sacrifice it all to keep him alive.

Their four blades flew in a flurry of synchronous combat. It seemed to Drew that the attacking demons were nearly suicidal in their attack once translated to physical form. Once when a blade was nearly to him, the demon and his sword dissolved away before he could finish his cut. It was a strange thing, almost as if the demons had less than sixty seconds of existence in the physical world.

The battle seemed to last for hours, but Drew knew it had only been a matter of minutes. It was the effect of adrenalin and his hyper mental activity.

Just when it seemed the fight was over, another wave of demons surged for a final attack, and that was when Drew faltered. Three demons came at him at once, the first two simply to block his blade and the third to execute a deathblow.

It was a final, desperate attempt, and it worked.

∽०∾

Validus lunged toward the third demon that was executing a slice toward Carter. The demon didn't even seem to care that his blade would take out at least one of his cohorts as well.

In a tangled mesh of bodies and steel, one dark blade from an unseen fourth demon found its way to Carter. Validus turned and yelled, but Jayt was already reacting. His sword was bound by the blade of an assaulting demon, so he left it and became Carter's shield. The sword pierced him through as the last of the demons dissolved away.

"No!" Validus screamed.

Carter reached for Jayt as he fell to the ground, his wound now open and empty where a dark blade had just been.

Validus knelt across from Carter as Persimus stood guard against any final assaults. "Hang on, Jayt," Validus said, but he had seen too many wounds to believe there was any hope.

Jayt held up his hand, and Validus took it. He coughed and his lips turned red with blood. "Didn't think much of you or your mission." Jayt fought to utter each word as he shot a quick glance toward Carter.

Validus lowered his head. Losing a warrior was never easy. Guilt seemed inescapable, especially as a commander.

Jayt squeezed Validus's hand to get his attention. "But you . . . and this mission . . . were worth . . . dying for, Commander."

Validus squeezed Jayt's hand as he drew his final breath and dissolved away to Mount Simcha.

"I'm so sorry," Validus heard Carter say. "I don't . . . I'm not . . ."

Validus looked up at the reddened eyes of the man. Carter knew the score. He knew that Jayt and many others had given their lives for him. If Validus felt the burden as a commander, he could only imagine what this man was feeling.

"Don't question your resolve or your mission, Carter. Elohim has called you. Make the sacrifice of this warrior and all of those before count for something."

He saw the man's soul fill with a quiet confidence that only a soldier could muster. Carter nodded.

They had fought together and survived. Such combat forged brothers of the most unlikely of men . . . and of angels.

COVER-UP

Drew arrived at NexTech two hours later to meet up with Ben. Before Ben would let him past the roof stairway entrance, he took five minutes to inspect Drew with another set of Ebola-tuned LASOK glasses. When they finally made it to the Blue Room, Drew congratulated the tech team, then downed an entire bottle of water as he sat next to Ben at the table.

"What have you got, brainiac?"

Ben looked at his team. "Guys, you know the procedure when we finish a project. Go take care of it."

When the room was clear, Ben asked Alice to pull up some data.

"It may be nothing, but Alice continued to monitor the government databases and servers before they cut our access just a few minutes ago. Running a threat analysis algorithm we were subcontracted to develop for a defense contractor, she found a host of anomalies and potential threats our agencies seem to be completely ignorant of."

Drew looked over Alice's assessment. "That is amazing, Ben. When the dust settles, we'll get this to the CIA so they can use it."

"Yeah," Ben said absentmindedly. "And then she found this too."

Ben had Alice display the details of one specific assessment linking classified communiqués and directives that had been initiated in the last twenty-four hours. None of them, in and of themselves, specifically indicated an operation, but Alice's threat analysis algorithm had connected enough dots to trigger an alert.

"There is a thirty-two percent chance of action against the designated target," Alice offered.

"Alice, who is the designated target?" Drew asked.

"You are, Drew."

"Even though the probable threat ratio is low, it's specific," Ben said. "I think you'd better be careful, Drew. Besides the IGA, who did you make angry?"

Drew looked at his friend. He hadn't told Ben just how corrupt the director and the president seemed to be. Senator Boyd's warning certainly seemed justified.

"Thanks, Ben. Maybe you're right. Some precautions might be warranted." He looked over Alice's report again. Just how far would the president and Director Ward go? Ben was right, he'd better be careful.

At 5:00 a.m. Drew and Ben sent the tech team home. "I think they deserve the next couple of days off," Drew said.

Ben agreed. "By the way, I got that list of names that you asked for before Ward shut us out of their network."

"Perfect." Drew grabbed the USB out of Ben's hand. "Go get some sleep, Ben. I'll meet you back here at ten."

Drew could hardly stand upright any longer. The last forty-eight hours had been grueling.

When he got back to his hotel room and finally laid down, he couldn't even remember shutting his eyes. When Alice woke him up at 9:30, it felt as though he had just blinked, and the sun was streaking through a slit in the curtain.

He struggled out of the pillow-topped bed. After slowly swinging his feet to the floor, he reached for the remote. He clicked on the television to discover three major networks running minute-by-minute stories on the thwarted bioterrorist attacks in California, Colorado, Louisiana, and New York. Drew cycled through the channels until he found Sophia Bryant with World Media News reporting that a press release by the president was scheduled for 2:00 p.m. A short news conference would follow. She would cover the conference live for WMN.

Before Drew jumped into the shower, he put on the LASOK glasses and inspected himself once more. Still clear. He was anxious for the Fortress men who had been contaminated, especially those with open wounds and damaged protective clothing.

"Lord Jesus, please protect those men who risked their lives to save many.

Amen." The prayer was short, but he loved what it felt like to turn a situation that he couldn't control over to a God who could.

Drew hurried through his shower and stepped onto the floor mat just as Alice informed him of an incoming call. He wrapped a towel around himself.

"Answer the call, Alice," Drew said.

"It's Sydney Carlyle," Alice replied. "Would you like video?"

"Of course not!" Drew said, perturbed. "Wait . . . Alice, did you just make a joke?"

"Joke about what?" Sydney's voice came through on speakerphone as Drew scrambled for his clothes.

"Nothing. I was talking to Alice. You can't see me, can you?" Drew asked.

Sydney laughed. "No, why? Should I be able to? Are you all right?"

"I'm good . . . I'm good," Drew said as he stumbled trying to get his right foot into his jeans and nearly fell on his face.

"Are you sure? 'Cause you sound a little flustered."

"I'm good. What do you need, Syd?"

"I'm just getting ready to head to the airport, and I thought I'd see how you were doing." Her voice softened. "I can't wait to see you again."

Drew finished throwing on his shirt, then sat down on the bed. "I'm looking forward to seeing you too," he replied. "How about you and me take a vacation when you get here?"

She sighed. "That would be really nice. You set it up, and I'll be there. Just make sure there's a beach involved."

"You got, it," Drew said. "Alice sent you the flight information, didn't she?"

"Yeah, I've got it."

"It's a Citation X, so your flight won't be too long."

"I'll see you in a few hours?" Sydney replied.

"Can't wait, Sydney." He wanted to say more, but that would have to do for now.

Drew made it back to NexTech by 10:05. Ben was already busy working on a dozen tasks at once.

"Did you sleep?" Drew asked as the coffee machine purred to life.

"We collected a lot of data, so I thought I'd better make a second backup. Alice is nearly done," Ben said, his fingers feverishly working the keys on one of the computers.

Drew shook his head. "You're going to burn out, Ben. Alice, display the live broadcast of World Media News." He tapped Ben's shoulder. "Take a look at this."

"We have confirmed reports that the CDC has established mobile containment facilities at four locations throughout the US." Tom Vincent was at the top of his game, working his correspondent magic—assimilating news bits, interviewing eyewitnesses, and managing the heartbeat of the World Media News command center. "We also have information indicating that these four facilities, all located next to major metropolitan cities, were part of a concerted bioterrorist plot. As of yet, no terrorist organization has claimed responsibility for the attempted attack. Sophia Bryant is live at the White House as we await the presidential statement and news conference. Sophia, what have you learned there?"

"Well, Tom, the White House is remaining silent until the conference. But sources have told me that this is indeed a major bioterrorist attack on the United States with the intent of infecting millions of Americans with a deadly virus on the anniversary of 9/11. We also have reports that this terrorist attack could be linked to the unconfirmed reports of an assassination attempt on President Harden just two days earlier at Camp David. Everyone here is anticipating information released by the White House on both incidents."

She's smooth, Drew thought. He knew she was using some of the information he had leaked to her, but she was also playing it safe so as not to cause the news network any embarrassment should the information turn out not to be accurate or true at all.

"Tom, whether speculation or fact, the term *Ebola* has been used numerous times. Whatever happened on those remote farms, the people have a right to know and a right to be concerned. Let's hope the president will give us some answers and some assurance that the threat has been completely eliminated."

"Thanks, Sophia Bryant." The scene cut back to Tom Vincent. "Here is some video our team captured at one of the locations just after the Special Forces team was taken into quarantine."

"Alice, stop broadcast," Drew said.

Ben looked up at Drew from his chair. In spite of the success of the mission, there was no joy in his eyes. Ben was always serious, but Drew could tell there was something deeply wrong.

"I watched the rest of the video Alice took while you were with the president." Ben slowly shook his head. "You agreed to work with two men who are that corrupt? You trusted them?"

Drew set down his coffee cup. "I didn't have a choice, Ben. Millions of people were going to die."

Ben's gaze went to the far wall and some distant thought he was having. Without looking at Drew, he asked the question Drew knew he was thinking. "These are powerful people, Drew. In that super strategic mind of yours, is there any scenario where we survive this?" He turned his eyes back to Drew.

Drew shrugged. "Hey, we saved the United States of America, didn't we? That's got to be worth something." He flashed a sheepish grin, but Ben didn't respond. "Ben, I'm sorry. Maybe God put you and me on this earth for this very purpose—to save millions of lives. No one may ever know, but—"

"God?" Ben asked. "You really have bought into this religious stuff. It's not just for Sydney, is it?"

"No, it's not. We have been invaded, Ben, but not by aliens. When you're ready to hear it, I'll explain it all." Drew's phone signaled a received text. He glanced at it. "But right now we need to check on the LASOK. That machine could be our ticket out of this mess."

Ben nodded.

When they got to the machine, Drew noticed that a box of LASOK glasses were ready. "These Ebola-tuned?"

"Yep. We need to get them to the CDC ASAP."

"Good. This is going to revolutionize disease control," Drew said.

"You have a phone call," Alice's calm voice said in Drew's earpiece. "The number is unlisted. Do you want to take it?"

"Yes, Alice." Drew heard the line connect. "Hello?"

"Drew, this is Director Ward. How are you doing?"

Drew looked at Ben and raised an eyebrow. "I'm well, Director Ward. What can I do for you?"

"I just wanted to congratulate you again on a successful mission. Once the president is finished with his press conference today, he will be personally calling you to congratulate you on behalf of the nation. You and your team did well, Agent Carter, with the exception of that little media stunt you pulled."

"This call is being traced," Alice said. "Do you want me to terminate the connection?"

Drew hesitated then tapped "no" on his sleeve. He wanted to know what Ward had in mind.

"Thank you, sir. It was an honor for all of us to serve our country. Tell me something, Director, how much will you tell the American people?"

There was a couple of seconds of silence. Drew heard a faint whisper in the background. "Another sixty seconds."

"Well, Carter, you need to understand that the people often don't know what's best for the people. That's why men like President Harden become leaders—to make decisions and take action that is in the best interest for the masses. The less they know, the better off they are. Your little media stunt at the terrorist sites is going to take some time to fix."

Drew could feel his anger rising up again. "Your definition and my definition of 'fix' are vastly different, Director."

Drew's sensitive ears could hear the words "Got him!" in the background. Drew knew he should hang up, but he figured he had at least fifteen minutes before he had to disappear. It felt as if Ward was about to show his hand, so he waited one more minute.

"I imagine you're right, Carter. It's men like me who have the guts to clean up messes that others make. That's how I fix problems."

"And who cleans up your messes, Director? And the president's? The mess of political corruption that authorizes terrorist attacks on our own people?"

There was a moment of silence again. Drew faintly heard some chatter in the background but couldn't make it out. Then his heart nearly stopped as he picked up one final phrase—"Impact in thirty seconds."

"Good-bye, Carter. You and your team have served its purpose. Now for the good of the country, it's time you all disappear." Director Ward's voice was filled with smug contempt, and they were the last words Drew heard.

"Run, Ben!" Drew shouted just before the connection was lost.

His last thought before the concussion hit was of Sydney. Would she be targeted too?

The AIM-9 missile struck the left engine of the Cessna Citation X at nearly the same time that two top-secret hypersonic scramjet missiles impacted NexTech, traveling at Mach 5.2, faster than radar could track or the naked eye could see. The kinetic energy transfer combined with the moderately sized warheads completely obliterated the entire building in just seconds. The blast shattered windows for four city blocks, killing dozens of innocent passersby.

Within minutes, the entire city of New York was in a state of emergency, with police, ambulance, and firefighters rushing to the scene. News agencies around the world were declaring that America was under another 9/11-scale terrorist attack, attempting this time to wipe out the president and a major US city, and strike fear into the hearts of the common citizens through bioterrorism.

In the CDC quarantine quarters near San Francisco, Denver, Shreveport, and New York City, hundreds of FBI agents converged on the disarmed Fortress soldiers. Jake was the first to see the muzzles of the MP5s.

THE FACE OF CONSPIRACY

What's going on, Reed?" Jake asked as he eyed the two dozen FBI Special
Weapons and Tactics Team agents, all carrying MP5s.

When the CDC had arrived at the zero point, Jake's men had been disarmed and stripped for quarantine. Now the FBI had shown up in force. There was nothing they could do. No one had said a word to them since the assaults on the terrorist locations nearly twelve hours ago. Jake figured they would all be dead by now if they were to be executed, so he advised his men to cooperate.

Agent Reed was the first person Jake recognized, and he began to wonder if the corruption Drew had alluded to had reached this man too. He tried to read the agent's face as he looked through the visor of his HAZMAT mask.

"We're here to protect you," Reed said. "Carter figured some heavy stuff was going to go down when this was through and knew that you would be vulnerable until you and your men made it out of quarantine. We took the risk and trusted our former assistant director at the FBI."

Jake relaxed. "What about Drew and the rest of the team?"

Reed hesitated, which made Jake anxious, then shook his head. "I'm not sure. I just received word that NexTech was bombed. I don't know, Jake. Drew and Ben were trying to get more LASOK glasses to the CDC. I haven't heard from them."

Jake's eyes filled with fiery wrath. "Somebody has to take them down!"

At 2:01 p.m., President Harden entered the White House press-briefing room to flashing cameras and journalists anxious for updates and an opportunity to ask questions. All forty-nine assigned seats were filled, and another fifty reporters and cameramen stood in the aisles along the sides of the room and at the back. The air was thick with solemn and heavy hearts.

President Harden took a moment to gather himself at the lectern, then gazed across the room with presidential resolve. "Fellow Americans, the United States has been fighting a war on terror for nearly two decades. It began on that fateful morning on September 11, 2001, when terrorists hijacked four airplanes in a coordinated attack against our nation's economic, political, and military institutions. Since that day, we have been successful in taking the fight to the terrorists, to their camps, and to their host countries. We have hunted down those responsible and brought them to justice. But today that war has returned to our soil. And though precious lives have been lost, we have prevailed, and we will continue to prevail."

Harden paused. "Two days ago at Camp David, a terrorist attack on my life was thwarted by our Secret Service agents and the Marine Presidential Guard. Last night, this same terrorist group attempted a bioterrorist attack against four US cities. Once again our Special Forces, in conjunction with the FBI, thwarted the attack, and it has been contained. This morning, however, terrorists were successful in blowing up a New York tech company in an effort to strike fear into the heart of Americans. We were able to evacuate most of the people from the building before the bombs went off, but in every one of these cowardly attacks, courageous Americans lost their lives, Americans to whom we owe a great debt of gratitude."

Harden looked straight into the camera and hesitated. The dramatic pause was powerful. "Let the world know that we will not be conquered. We will rise, and we will overcome! We will not stop until our nation is free from the threat of terrorism!"

The moment lingered and then the president took a deep breath.

"I'll take a few questions."

The room exploded in shouting and hand raising.

"Yes, Susan." The president pointed to a journalist in the front row.

"Mr. President, has any terrorist group claimed responsibility for all three attacks?"

"Not yet, but our intelligence agencies are zeroing in on those groups responsible, and we will soon be taking both military and clandestine action to bring them to justice." The president moved on. "Yes, Bob."

"Was the assassination attempt on your life the reason the security of

Camp David was not transferred to the UN as planned, and are the IGA and Premier Jabbar involved in any way?"

"As for your first question, yes, I decided the timing of the transfer should not be clouded by such terrorist activity, and we are revisiting if and when that transfer of security should happen in the future. Regarding your second question, I would prefer not to answer that until we have completed a full investigation into the attempted terrorist attacks. Next question . . . Kent."

"What type of virus were the terrorists planning to release on our cities, and how do you know the virus has been contained?"

President Harden thought for a moment. "The virus was Ebola, the same strain from the outbreak in the Democratic Republic of the Congo six months ago, but it has been contained. The CDC is in possession of new technology that allows quicker and easier isolation of the virus. We believe the terrorists chose to attack NexTech Corporation in New York City because they were involved in developing this new technology." President Harden scanned the room. "I have time for one more question. Sophia Bryant."

There was an unusual pause. Bryant looked around the room, then back at the president. She stood up. "Mr. President, can you tell us why you authorized five previous terrorist attacks on US cities and justified it in the name of global unity?"

The room fell deathly silent as the president glared at Miss Bryant.

"I don't have any idea what you're talking about, Miss Bryant, and please show a little respect for the office of the president of the United States."

Harden turned, but Bryant shouted back. "Then why do I have video showing you and Director Ward confessing to orchestrating those attacks?"

Harden froze, then turned an icy glare at Bryant. White House aides started moving toward her.

"Tell us the truth, Mr. President. Operation Torrent revealed that you and Premier Jabbar of the IGA coordinated with our own intelligence agencies to plan those attacks in addition to ordering the murder of the agents who discovered the truth."

Harden sneered, then quickly exited.

"Which of these recent attacks have been orchestrated by your administration?" Bryant shouted after him.

The pressroom erupted in mayhem as Bryant moved with the rest of the news crews to escape the grip of Harden's men, but she was detained.

Moments after the dramatic close to the press conference, America watched as World Media News began playing the video of President Harden and Director Ward's conversation with Dougherty on all of its media channels. At its conclusion, Tom Vincent mesmerized millions of viewers with a promise of details regarding Sophia's dramatic announcement to the world of President Harden's corruption.

"WMN and, in particular, Sophia Bryant has taken great risk to bring you this story. Sophia is, in fact, right now being detained by White House officials," Vincent said with an edge of anger in his voice. "In anticipation of such a response, we prerecorded an interview with our own Sophia Bryant in order to help you, the American people, understand both the scope and the legitimacy of this alarming information. Here it is."

The image of Sophia Bryant filled the screen, eyes filled with concern, eyes that Americans had come to trust regardless of race or political affiliation.

"America, what I'm about to share with you will change the course of our nation forever. Agent Drew Carter, the man who both saved the president from an assassination attempt and also saved America from bioterrorist annihilation, met with me two nights ago." She held up the drive Drew had given her. "He gave me information that exposes the corruption of President Harden and his administration." Sophia's face sobered even further. "I can only report the truth. What the people of this great nation do with that truth shall be determined in the days, weeks, years, and centuries to come. The response of this present generation of Americans will determine whether this is to be our worst hour or our finest hour."

Sophia went on to explain how Drew had met with her and how Operation Torrent had discovered irrefutable ties of terrorist activities to the IGA and Premier Jabbar. Over the course of the next few hours, all major news networks throughout the world were replaying the video, and the entire nation was turned on its head.

The outcry from the American people quickly reached a frenzy, with immediate demands of impeachment of President Harden. There were riots in two of the cities that had been hit the hardest by the previous terrorist attacks. Islamic nations that had earlier seemed pacified by Premier Jabbar's rhetoric and political maneuvering seemed to turn vicious, with cries of "Death to America."

By evening, the United States of America's political, economic, and military systems were being shaken at their very foundations, and Sophia Bryant and WMN were at the epicenter. The White House had no choice but to release Bryant for fear of riots in the streets of Washington. President Harden attempted to implement marshal law, but he quickly retracted the order when he learned that both Congress and the Pentagon fiercely opposed him on the basis that it could initiate the complete collapse of the government. Placing the people under military rule when they already felt betrayed would not stop anarchy but ignite it.

Both the House of Representatives and the Senate, led by the Patriots, called emergency sessions to launch formal chamber investigations into the actions of the president and the director of National Intelligence. As more was revealed, the momentum of the collapse of Harden's regime became inevitable.

High-ranking officials in numerous agencies began to come forward. Many were subpoenaed to testify before Congress. The list of those who had planned to flee the country surfaced in the hands of Senator Sarah Boyd and was presented to the congressional investigating committees. Evidence tying the IGA to terrorist activities was publicized, which shook the political powers throughout the world.

And through it all, the question that kept being asked was, Who is Agent Carter, the man who single-handedly saved the president from assassination and the United States of America from annihilation? The world turned to Sophia Bryant for an answer, but she could not offer one.

"The corruption in Harden's administration runs deep, and impeachment is an eventuality," Tom Vincent said as news banners scrolled across the bottom of the WMN screen, updating the public on dozens of breaking stories regarding the Harden scandal.

"This goes beyond impeachment, Tom. We are talking criminal charges and possible time in prison for the man holding the highest office of the United States," Sophia Bryant said. "We may never know how deep the corruption went. If this administration was willing to commit murder, who's to say what else has been done."

Tom shook his head. "Is it possible, Sophia, that President Harden took action to eliminate Agent Carter as part of the cover-up? Could the man who saved the president's life and pulled America back from the brink of annihilation have been killed by the very man he saved?"

Bryant's eyes captured the sadness and the anger at the heart of Americans from coast to coast. "It's chilling to imagine, especially coming from a man whose rhetoric these past years has been filled with talk of world peace and unification," Sophia replied. "We've also just learned that Senator Boyd from Oklahoma was privy to Agent Carter's task force planning to take out the bioterrorists. She testifies before the Senate and House over the next two days, and I think that we are going to learn a lot about those final hours."

"And what about NexTech Corporation, the company that was supposedly destroyed by terrorist bombs?" Vincent added. "Senator Boyd has stated that NexTech was actually the base of operations for Agent Carter and his team. That seems much more than coincidental. If this was a cover-up, I can only imagine the public outcry against such further blatant disregard for life and liberty coming from the highest office of the United States. It is simply unthinkable!"

THE TRUTH SHALL
SET YOU FREE

Do you want to explain to me how we ended up on an island somewhere in the Caribbean Sea?" Crypt exclaimed. "There's no tech worth looking at in this place."

"I like it," Piper said. "If the US government wants to give us a vacation on the beach, I'm all for it."

"You would be," Ridge said. "Crypt is as white as a ghost and gets sunburned from a 40-watt bulb, and Jester thinks the only thing a beach is good for is the silicon we get from it to make integrated chips."

"Yeah . . . and what about you, Ridge?" Jester asked.

Ridge smiled wide and crossed his arms behind his head as he stretched out on the towel beside Jester. "I already have the perfect tan, so what do I need a beach for? Admit it, you're all just trying to look like me."

Sydney rolled over next to Drew and whispered in his ear. "You know, when I asked for a vacation with a beach, I really didn't picture them being here with us."

Drew opened his eyes and turned his head toward Sydney. He raised himself up on one elbow and looked over her to see Ben typing away on a laptop next to his four geeky and out-of-place friends. The Caye Island Resort Hotel in Belize was just behind them.

"Do you think we should have left them at NexTech?" he asked with a sly smile.

"No, but we could have dropped them off on a different island." Sydney lifted one eyebrow as she glanced toward the odd crew.

"Hey, a guy can only plan so far. Next time there's a national emergency and we have to run from the president, Homeland Security, the CIA, the FBI, the NSA, and every other alphabet agency there is, I'll plan that in."

"Deal," Sydney said. "Actually, they're not so bad. It's a little like having built-in entertainment." She looked back at Drew with narrowed eyes. "How did you know they would try to take us out?"

"Alice told me," Drew replied.

"Really?"

"Indirectly. She helped me interpret a silent conversation between President Harden and Director Ward by reading their lips," Drew said. "Knowing what they had done to other agents, I figured their way of 'fixing' things would be drastic. Ben and I arranged to transfer the LASOK and all our critical equipment and data via a moving company to a warehouse in another part of the city, then had Alice bounce our calls through NexTech to make it look like I was at that location when I was talking to Ward. Reed helped arrange things to protect Jake and his men. Your protection was the most elaborate and expensive. I chartered two jets. One with you on a flight plan to New York, piloted remotely. The other to Belize. The owner of the charter company was a friend of Mick's, otherwise I would have never been able to pull it off." He leaned close to Sydney. "I couldn't take any chances . . . not with you."

Sydney touched his cheek. "So what's your plan now, mystery man?"

He leaned into her a little closer. He could feel the warmth of her breath on his lips; then he smiled and leaned back on his towel and closed his eyes. "You're lookin' at it. I've done my job. It's time for the rest of America to do theirs."

Sydney was silent for a long time. He opened one eye to see if she was still there. She was glaring at him.

"What?" he exclaimed. "You want me to do more? Seriously? What more can I do, Syd?"

"You just dropped a bombshell that is rocking our entire nation's political system and then disappeared. America needs you now more than ever, Drew Carter. You have to see this through to the end."

He frowned.

"Congress needs your testimony, and the people need your hope." Her voice softened with each syllable until Drew was putty in her hands.

"You know I don't do well speaking in front of people. It's not my thing," Drew petitioned.

Sydney leaned close to him and his heart skipped a beat. "Well, you weren't my thing either." She smiled, and then her voice almost became a whisper. "But you are now. People can change, Special Agent Carter. And maybe God is asking you to change one more time."

"Just so you know, I don't like you anymore. You don't play fair."

Sydney smiled. She knew she had won. She jumped up and looked down at Drew, then yelled, "Last one to the water buys food tonight!"

She took off running, and Drew just watched her. She always surprised him. How could a person be that amazing? And how could he be this blessed?

Piper pulled a resistant Ben up off his towel and away from his laptop. Jester and Ridge joined in the race too. When Crypt saw he was the only one left, he made a halfhearted attempt to join in as well. Within a few minutes, all seven of them were laughing as they attempted to body surf the four-foot waves rolling in over the reef and onto the white sands.

For a few hours, Drew forgot about the burden he was obligated to bear.

One week after the infamous presidential press conference, Drew and his crew were on a flight back to New York City.

"It's going to take a lot of time and money to rebuild NexTech," Ben said, showing Drew the estimates and his plan for their new facility. "But I think we can make some significant improvements."

"What about the LASOK?" Drew asked. "Planning that in?"

"Of course. Once our new facility is ready, we'll pull the components out of the warehouse we're renting and rebuild."

"Sounds like a plan, partner. I have to say, I am impressed with how fast you got the machine disassembled and transported out of there."

"Actually, you gave me plenty of time to arrange it all. Once the building was clear, I changed all the security codes so no one could get back in. I still can't believe Harden would actually bomb our facility—right in downtown New York! I hope it's safe to go back."

Drew nodded. "Me too. Guess we'll find out soon enough."

Ben went back to his seat, and Sydney came to sit by Drew. She reached for his hand and leaned her head on his shoulder. "Thanks for saving me again," she said.

Drew squeezed her hand. "You've got it wrong, Syd. You're the one who saved me."

When they reached New York City, they were not prepared for the state of political, economic, and military chaos that surrounded them. And the impact of the last week's events reached much further. People all over the world were angry with the United States for the "conspiracy" America had conjured against the IGA, Premier Jabbar, and the UN. It seemed the only allies America had left in the world were Israel and a couple of NATO countries.

Within the borders of the US, there was unrest and mayhem like the nation had never seen before. From the White House to Congress, from the Pentagon to the local police force, from Wall Street to the corner coffee shops, emotional turmoil was everywhere. And the range of emotions and attitudes was as varied as the people displaying them—anger, fear, gratitude, sadness, joy, disgust. The one emotion not present, however, was apathy. The country had catapulted into a period of reevaluation and sober reflection. In awe, Drew and his team watched the transformation, both good and bad, as a result of what they had done.

"Yeah, I'm pretty sure we're in big trouble," Jester said, watching the news in the airport.

"You'd better contact Senator Boyd," Sydney said to Drew as they caught a taxi to a hotel.

Throughout their escape from Harden's execution attempt, Validus and his warriors had never left Drew's side. Even now Validus was sitting in the front seat of the taxi, which was reassuring, as the cabbie kept looking at Drew in the rearview mirror. Drew watched his hands closely. Perhaps it wasn't safe to come back yet after all.

"I owe the first phone call to Miss Bryant," Drew said. "Then they can do with me what they want." He looked at Sydney. "You sure this is a good idea?"

Sydney grabbed his hand. "Look at the state the country is in. You're the only one who can give them answers right now. It's the right thing to do."

"Maybe, but I've broken so many laws they could crucify me if they had a mind to."

The cabbie looked over his shoulder and Drew tensed, ready to make a move. He hadn't seen a gun, but maybe this guy was that good. He glanced at

Validus to see if the angel was preparing for action, but he wasn't paying attention to the driver at all.

"You're the guy!" The cabbie's face lit up. "You're the guy they're all talking
about! The guy with the video! The agent who saved America."

Drew looked at Sydney, concern in his eyes; then he dialed Sophia Bryant's
number. After a short conversation, Drew called Senator Boyd and told her his
plan. She tried to persuade him to come directly to Washington.

"I'll be there tomorrow afternoon," he told her.

By the next morning, Drew was at the WMN studio prepping for an interview.
When he first saw Miss Bryant, she looked relieved and nearly gave him a hug.

"You had us worried, Agent Carter," she said with a shake of her head. "I'm
sure glad to see you."

"It's good to see you too, Miss Bry—" Drew caught the disappointed look
in her eye. "Sophia. Are we ready to do this?"

She grabbed his elbow. "Let's go. This is what you can expect." She explained the interview procedure as she led him to their chairs in the studio.

When the cameras went live, Drew wondered if he was going to sound as
much like an idiot as he felt.

Sophia opened with a heartfelt call to every American watching. "America
has been turned upside down by a tidal wave of terrorism and corruption." The
camera slowly zoomed in to show her perfect olive complexion and penetrating, trustworthy brown eyes. "Many Americans have been left feeling like the
very foundation of our great country has been damaged. For a country that has
been pulled back from the brink of calamity, we are left to ask, how do we
move forward? This morning we are privileged to talk to the man who may
have some answers."

Bryant turned to look at Drew as the camera zoomed out to frame them
both.

"First, let's settle the question that's on everyone's mind right now. Are you
the Drew Carter who single-handedly saved the president from assassination
and the United States of America from terrorist attacks that would have resulted in biological annihilation?"

Drew instantly regretted agreeing to this interview. He looked at Bryant, angry that she would pull this right off the bat. He had thought he could trust her. He took a moment to form his careful reply.

"Sophia, I'm just an average guy from Kansas who wanted to play college football, find a wife, get a good job, and raise a family. There's nothing special about me except for the opportunities I've been given to serve my country. Yes, my name is Drew Carter, and I worked for the CIA, but there was nothing 'single-handed' in any of these missions. Hundreds of people sacrificed, some with their lives, and they are the ones who deserve our praise and thanks." Drew thought of Mr. Ross and was saddened. "There are thousands of men and women who serve our country every day whose names we will never know. They are the true heroes, defending our country with their lives to protect the freedom we still enjoy. Given the same opportunity, all of them would have done exactly the same thing."

Bryant's eyes glowed with satisfaction. "You're right, Agent Carter, but I think what America needs right now is a person to whom they can offer their thanks. So on behalf of grateful Americans everywhere, we thank you and all of the nameless men and women who have risked so much to save so many."

Drew pursed his lips and lowered his head in humility. There was no adequate reply to such a statement. Bryant let the moment stand for a few seconds, then began the story.

"I first met you in Chicago at the suicide bombing of the bistro on Seventh Street. Was that attack the beginning of your investigation into the IGA?"

Drew shared his story as Bryant strategically navigated them through the details of a saga that would expose the most corrupt administration the country had ever seen. But it also exposed President Harden's ignorance of the plots of Premier Jabbar and Secretary-General De Luca.

After two hours of gripping interview, Drew was finally done and ready to wash his hands of this life.

"Thanks, Agent Carter. America needed that," Bryant said with a gleam in her eye once the cameras were off.

"Why did you start out with that question?" Drew asked, still a little perturbed. "I thought we agreed—no undue hero-making."

She didn't hesitate. "You know spy stuff, and I know media. With the answer to that single question, you captured the heart of every American, and they believed everything else you said after that."

Drew huffed and laughed. "I guess that's why you are where you are. Looks like I picked the right one."

Bryant offered a sheepish smile, then looked at Drew with different eyes. "Is there somebody special?"

He smiled. "Yes, there is."

She nodded and shrugged. Drew wasn't sure how to interpret that. "Well, she's a lucky one. Tell her I said to take good care of you."

Drew shook his head. "Actually, I may have been given an opportunity to save the country, but she's the one who saved me."

Sophia tilted her head and gazed at him with her dark brown eyes. "Then tell her thank you . . . from all of us." She straightened her shoulders. "I'm told you have an escort downstairs waiting for you."

"I imagine so," Drew said. "Thanks for believing me and for having the courage to see this through. The country owes you a great debt of gratitude too."

She smiled, then looked at the camera team. "We're not done, boys. I want the next few minutes on camera."

Bryant and her camera crew walked with Drew to the door, where a host of armed FBI agents were waiting for him. Though they were there to protect him, they were also there to arrest him. He had broken many laws by leaking classified information to the press, and he would have to face the consequences.

Bryant filmed it all as they respectfully handcuffed Drew and placed him in a black SUV.

The next few months were filled with congressional testimonies, hearings, and trials. When it was all over, Harden, Ward, and more than thirty additional high-ranking officials were in prison.

Vice President Newman was cleared from all allegations and was sworn in as the new president. His first official act was to pardon Drew Carter of all charges against him, and he did so publicly.

It was a moment the nation cheered. It was a moment that cauterized the people of America to return to the place they had come from, a place most eloquently spoken of by Abraham Lincoln: "We here highly resolve that these dead shall not have died in vain—that this nation, under God, shall have a new birth of freedom—and that government of the people, by the people, for the people, shall not perish from the earth."

LIGHT OF THE LAST

Validus and his warriors stood outside Emmanuel Church in Chicago, which Carter and Carlyle had just entered. Validus was pleased with his men. They had each given their all over the last three and a half years, some with their lives. They had lost Sason in the suicide bombing in Chicago and Jayt in the assault against the terrorists in New York, but Crenshaw, Rake, Brumak, Tren, and Persimus survived, ready even now to carry on with their mission. But what was their mission?

"You've done well, warriors, and now is a time of respite. We have protected Carter, and he is now a child of the King. The United States has survived and is a stronger ally with Israel than ever before." Validus slowly nodded. "Yes, our mission is complete for now. Take a few days and recover. You all deserve it and need it."

"Are you sure, Commander? What about you?" Crenshaw asked.

"My time will be later. Teriel is here at Reverend Branson's church if anything should happen. But why would the Fallen attack now?"

No one could think of any reason. And so one by one, they left for a time of rest and recovery. Tren and Persimus were the last to leave.

"Go," Validus said. He could see the hesitation still lingering in their eyes.

They looked at the homeless and the unwanted making their way toward the church for a meal. A place for the least, a place for food, drink, clothing, and comfort, just as Jesus had commanded.

Tren and Persimus turned and left.

∾○∾

When Drew and Sydney entered the church, Reverend Ray was surrounded by a team of young people all working to prepare the evening's meal. Ray looked up and smiled as big as Drew had ever seen. He hurried to greet them, hugging them both with exuberance. He stood back with one arm on Drew's shoulder and one arm on Sydney's for just a moment. His smile was uncontainable.

"How good to see you!"

"It's so good to see you too, Reverend Ray," Drew said.

"I can see just by looking at the two of you that there is much more than just friendship between you, although I could always see that."

Sydney blushed as she leaned into Drew, and he wrapped an arm around her. "Yes, but now, it is with the blessing of God. I'm a believer in Jesus Christ, Reverend. And we came here to thank you for all you've done for us."

Drew didn't think Reverend Ray's smile could get any bigger, but it did. He reached for Drew and hugged him again, then Sydney. "Praise God! Our prayers were answered," he said with eyes sparkling as he looked down at Sydney.

Sydney nodded, her eyes welling up with tears.

They spent a few more minutes catching up as the homeless entered and sat down, waiting for the meal.

"What can we do, Reverend?" Drew asked.

Drew and Sydney dove into the labor of meeting the needs of hundreds of Chicago's castaways. Reverend Ray's tireless ministry was at the heart of God, and Drew could feel it. He looked at Sydney talking and loving the people. His heart warmed for so many reasons.

But then something inside Drew shivered. He stood up and turned around just in time to see the thing that always preceded tragedy.

∽∘∾

Validus found Teriel standing next to the wall at the front of the church, his ever-watchful gaze looking over the people who came to Emmanuel. He didn't look very happy. Validus offered an arm of greeting, and the mighty angel took it.

"How have you been, Teriel?" Validus asked.

"Well, but"—he looked at Drew—"your charge always brings danger." Then he looked at Validus. "And so do you."

Validus understood his concern. "I think the Fallen are through with him. There's very little more he can do."

Teriel slowly shook his head. "Commander Validus, what Drew Carter can do has just begun."

A blackened, grisly sword pierced Teriel from behind, bursting through the wall. Shock and horror hit Validus like a tidal wave as he reached for Teriel, whose face was twisted in pain. Teriel fell forward and Validus tried to catch him, but he dissolved away before his body hit the floor.

"No!" Validus shouted as Niturni materialized through the wall.

Validus ducked and rolled away, just narrowly escaping the next crosscut that Niturni executed. Validus came up with sword drawn and vengeance boiling in his heart. He stood ready to take on an entire legion. He looked for more Fallen to collapse on him, but they did not come.

Niturni began to laugh. "Don't worry, Validus. I am the only one. I finally realized how to defeat you. Your divining angel always allowed you to be just ahead of my forces, so I decided that I would not use an army to destroy you. I would do it myself."

Niturni's smile transformed to a loathsome scowl of hatred as he lunged toward Validus with both his long sword and his short sword drawn. Validus met his attack while simultaneously drawing his short sword just in time to thwart a slice to his abdomen.

In the minutes that followed, the inside of the church became the arena for an epic duel between ancient friends turned enemies. They jumped from tables to walls, swords flashing faster than bullets could fly. The homeless people filling the tables were oblivious to the raging battle as both angel and demon passed through them in their brutal duel.

Validus tapped into all his battle experience just to keep Niturni's blades from piercing him. He fought against his feeling of inferiority because he was the last God had created and Niturni was of the One Hundred. Would he ever be free from that?

Niturni fought with the ferocity of a dragon, relentless in his deviant skill. Out of the corner of his eye, Validus saw Carter watching in angst. Only now did Validus realize that Teriel was right. God was not through with Drew Carter.

However the forces of the Fallen and the angels had misinterpreted Tinsa-lik Barob's message, one thing was clear: Elohim had more in store for Carter than even saving the United States of America.

The genius mind of Niturni must have figured it out as well, for this duel was for more than to satisfy a vendetta.

Niturni seemed flawless in his attack, and his strength was unmatchable. Validus was retreating, and he knew from the experience of a thousand battles that such a thing was a prelude to defeat.

The first wound came as the tip of Niturni's short blade sliced across Vali-dus's chest, opening a three-inch gash that flowed with blood. The two war-riors stared at each other. It was the first time that either of them had ever drawn blood on the other, and in spite of six millennia of enmity between them, Validus's spilled blood seemed to cut them both much deeper than expected.

Niturni swished his sword from side to side in defiance of the silent pain they both felt. "You are so predictable and pathetic," he taunted. "You didn't really think I could ever have stooped so low as to call you friend, did you?"

"I admired you once, Niturni. I thought you an angel of courage. But Apollyon has turned you into nothing but one of his cowardly pawns of evil."

Niturni yelled and attacked with renewed vigor, and Validus did his best to counter against his fury, but he could feel the end drawing close.

Carter could see it too. Just months earlier, the man would have drawn a weapon forged by the hands of men, but now . . . now he drew a weapon forged by the hands of God.

Carter knelt and prayed just as another powerful slice came at Validus. The warrior recovered, just barely thwarting the crosscut from Niturni that would have severed his neck. But he was not done. The flames of Ruach Elo-him began to fill the place, and Niturni felt it.

"No!" he screamed, along with blasphemies against the Almighty.

The power of God strengthened Validus, and he slowly turned the duel against his enemy. From one wall to the other, their battle continued with such violent intensity that neither realm had ever witnessed such a thing. Slowly Validus advanced until Niturni's eyes filled with alarm.

Validus continued his advance until at last, with one mighty cut, he slammed his gleaming sword against Niturni's long blade, and it flew from his wearied hand. A table of unsuspecting homeless separated them. Niturni swung his hand up through the table, translating a tray of food and hot soup, but Validus was unfazed by the trickery of his nemesis. He swung his short sword across the elements and translated them back to nothingness while simultaneously preparing his final cut that would end Niturni's life in the Middle Realm.

Validus could see stark fear in Niturni's eyes, and for just one brief moment, his gaze softened to the ancient kindness Validus had seen long ago while standing next to the Crystal Sea.

"Friend," Niturni pleaded.

Validus had never felt the pain of sin so powerfully as he did in that moment, gazing into the eyes of his ancient friend whom he must now kill. He had told Persimus never to hesitate, and yet he did. With all his might, he tried to strike Niturni down, but his arms would not obey. He yelled, but still he could not strike. He shook his head and stepped back. Why couldn't he finish him?

His sword lowered just as a homeless man came to sit at the table between them, and then Validus's nightmare became reality. The blackened eyes of the unforgiven demon returned to Niturni's gaze, and he lunged at Validus with his short sword, but it never reached him.

The homeless man translated and stood to take Niturni's blade into his own chest, the very blade that would have pierced Validus through. Niturni's eyes bulged as Persimus simultaneously plunged his own short blade into his chest.

Validus screamed his horror to the world as he reached for Persimus. "No, Persimus—no!"

Niturni dissolved away, and as he did, so did his blade. Validus caught his friend and laid him on the floor, tears filling his eyes.

"No, Persimus . . . why?"

Persimus grabbed Validus's arm, struggling to speak his final words. "Because. . . . he was going to kill my friend."

Validus shook his head, tears spilling from his eyes. "You came back. You shouldn't have come back."

Persimus attempted a weak smile. "I realized that my respite has always been at your side. You are . . . my great friend."

"Stay with me, Persimus. I'm not so strong."

Drew Carter knelt beside Validus, and together their tears mingled in mourning for the fall of a great angel of God.

"I'm so sorry," Carter whispered.

Persimus shook his head and looked into Validus's eyes. "You are the last . . . just like Carter. Finish this, my valiant friend."

Persimus slowly closed his eyes and slipped away to the majestic essence of his beautiful soul, then lifted to heaven. Carter stayed beside Validus, his shoulders shaking with each heave of grief.

⌒o⌒

Sydney knelt down beside Drew between the tables of homeless people and slipped her arm over his shoulder.

"Drew, what is it?" she whispered.

He lifted his head, unconcerned about the strange stares from the people watching him weep over empty ground. Unconcerned with a drunk man mumbling about how some guy just disappeared beside him.

"I don't know why, but I think perhaps God is not done with me, and the price of my understanding is great indeed."

Drew saw the sorrow etched permanently on the face of his protector, Validus, and it caused him no small measure of reflection. He prayed with all his heart that God would not let such great sacrifice be in vain.

"Call me, God, and I will listen. Send me, Lord, and I will go," he prayed.

He didn't understand why or how God would use him, but he did understand the severity of praying such a prayer. Many had fought and died on his behalf, but the sacrifice that motivated Drew beyond all others was that of the Son of God. It was time to fully serve the One who bled and died for him.

The next morning, Drew and Sydney attended Reverend Ray's church and worshiped with the people of Emmanuel. When Ray stood up to deliver his sermon, he opened his Bible and read one verse, Isaiah 6:8.

"I heard the voice of the Lord, saying: 'Whom shall I send, and who will go for Us?' Then I said, 'Here am I! Send me.'"

Reverend Ray looked up from his Bible and gazed across the congregation.

"Today I am compelled to set my prepared sermon aside and ask you"—Ray looked straight at Drew—"is He calling you? Drew, will you come and share what God has placed on your heart today?"

Drew grabbed Sydney's hand, and she squeezed back. Fear filled his heart. This was not something he had expected or was prepared for.

Sydney leaned into him. "Just tell them the story of how God saved you. God will give you the words."

Ray waited while Drew tried to find the courage to stand. Slowly his shaking legs lifted him, and he walked forward. He would have rather faced five terrorists at once than stand up and speak before so many. Ray welcomed him to the pulpit and stood beside him for support.

Drew looked out and saw the warm smiles of many believers, but he could also see into the hearts of many who were not filled with the Holy Spirit. He ached for their confusion and loneliness, and in that he found the courage to speak.

"When I was twelve years old, my father died while serving our country. The pain of my father's loss was etched in my heart forever."

Drew spoke for thirty minutes, mesmerizing the people of Emmanuel Church with the story of how God showed compassion for a hurting soul and saved him.

When it was over, Reverend Ray put an arm around Drew and asked if any felt the call of God on their lives just as Drew had—some to a renewed walk with the Creator, some to salvation, some to deliverance from evil. And as the choir sang, the chairs of Emmanuel Church emptied to the front until no more could come. Drew watched in humbled amazement as the Spirit of God filled the congregation and drew the hearts of all to Him.

Drew and Sydney spent the next two weeks in Rivercrest with Jake and his mother. One Monday afternoon, Reverend Ray asked Drew to come back to Chicago to meet someone. When he arrived, Ray introduced him to Dr. Worthington, the pastor of New Life Church, the largest evangelical church in Chicago, the church Sydney had invited him to years earlier. It had doubled in size since then because of the powerful biblical preaching of Pastor Worthington. It was Sydney who had connected the two churches, and ever since, New Life Church had been a supporter of Reverend Ray's inner city ministry both financially and in labor support.

"I would love for you to give your testimony at our church," Pastor Worthington said.

Drew's first thought was of how many people he would have to stand in front of. But God would not let him ask the question.

"I'm not a preacher or a teacher, sir, but I would be honored to share how God saved me."

Pastor Worthington and Reverend Ray smiled. Then Pastor Worthington looked at Drew as a mentor would.

"What you have done for our nation, Drew, took great courage. You may have thought that you were working to save our country, but in reality you were fulfilling prophecy and saving two nations. The United States of America exists for two reasons—to spread the gospel of Jesus Christ to the world and to protect Israel. When we quit fulfilling that purpose, it will be our end. Israel must continue to be at the heart of our purpose as a nation. The USA has been and will continue to be a key instrument in fulfilling the prophecies of the End of Days. You, Drew Carter, are part of that as well. And I think perhaps more so than anyone realizes."

That week, Drew spoke at New Life Church, and the response from the people who heard him was the same. Hundreds of people came to accept Christ, and Drew was crushed by how God had chosen to use him.

Other pastors began calling him, and Drew hesitantly said yes to everyone. Over the next few weeks, Sydney and Drew traveled throughout the country, giving testimony of what God had done in their lives.

On occasion, Jake and Kathryn came to hear Drew speak. Drew could tell God was drawing them, but he didn't push. This was a whole new experience for them, so he let them ask questions, and he and Sydney gently gave them answers. Drew also began to study the Bible with zeal, and it came alive, just as Sydney promised it would.

One Sunday morning after Drew had spoken at a small church in Dallas, Texas, a middle-aged gentleman came to shake his hand.

"Thank you for all you've done, and for being willing to be used of God."

Drew noticed the man wore an army chaplain pin. "And thank you, sir, for ministering to our troops."

The man's smile warmed his heart. "I'm retired and don't normally attend here, but when I heard you were speaking, I had to come see you. I remember a man by the name of Ryan Carter when I was serving as a chaplain in Afghanistan."

Drew's smile faded, and his world fell numb around him. A man from his dad's past. What grieved him beyond words was that he had never heard his dad talk about God or Jesus Christ as Savior. He couldn't dwell on it too long or it would break his heart. Now it looked as if he might have to face it head on.

"You have his resemblance. Are you related?" the man asked.

Drew struggled. He didn't want this to happen . . . not now. "Ryan Carter was my dad."

The man's smile faded too.

"He passed when I was twelve," Drew said.

"I'm . . . so sorry. I never knew." The man was obviously embarrassed. "I was moved around a lot, so my time with him was brief."

"How did you know my dad?"

"Ryan began attending my Bible studies when he could fit it in between missions. I had the joy of leading him to the Lord."

Drew's eyes immediately filled with tears. How could it be? Was it really possible? He tried to talk, but he had a hard time forming the words. "How?" he managed.

The man looked somewhat bewildered. "Didn't you know?"

Drew just shook his head as tears spilled down his cheeks. Sydney joined him.

"Watching you today, I was reminded of him." The man reached for Drew's hand again and held it with both of his. Now his eyes welled up with tears. "Your father had questions that let me know he was really searching for God. I think the missions in Iraq and Afghanistan really affected him. When I started sharing God's love with him, he was anxious to receive it. The day I knelt with him and heard him pray to accept Christ as Lord was a marvelous day. He said he couldn't wait to tell his family."

Drew had read the last letter from his dad so many times he had memorized it. Even now he could hear the words of his dad in his ear as he thought of the last part of the letter.

"Kathryn, I have some very exciting news to share with you, but it is something

I feel I need to share in person. I love you so very much and can't wait to see you again soon. Please tell Drew that I miss him and that . . ."

Was this the news that he wanted to share with Drew and his mother? News untold until now?

Drew sat with the man for the next hour, soaking up every detail he could from the chaplain who had led his dad to the Lord. That which Drew had dreaded since he had come to Christ was instead a blessing beyond belief. Drew arranged for the chaplain to meet with his mother and Jake a few days later. In great tears of joy, this same chaplain led Kathryn and Jake to Jesus Christ, just as he had done for Ryan Carter over twelve years earlier.

Four months later, Pastor Worthington, Reverend Ray, and six other pastors from around the country hosted an event calling all of America to spiritual renewal. Drew would be their voice as television stations throughout the nation broadcasted the event.

Ohio Stadium in Columbus, Ohio, began to fill two hours before the event. After a time of powerful worship, Drew looked up and saw the air above the people filled with thousands of angels singing praises to God along with His saints. And then Pastor Worthington took the stage.

"Sydney, help me . . . I can't do this," Drew said as he looked around the stadium filled with people.

Sydney lifted his hand to her lips and kissed his fingers. "It's not for you to do. It's for God to do." She smiled and gazed into his eyes. "Just be you, Drew, and God will take care of the rest. 'Take no thought how or what you shall speak: for it shall be given you in that same hour what you shall speak.'"

Her words and loving eyes soothed him. He covered her hand with his and squeezed. The butterflies in his stomach subsided until he heard Dr. Worthington begin an introduction.

"We have the privilege of hearing a man upon whom God has poured out His anointing. This is a man who has been in the trenches of spiritual warfare. A man who has been in the trenches of physical warfare. A man who helped save the United States of America from the tyranny of terrorism and political corruption. Please join me in welcoming to the stage Drew Carter, the guardian of our freedom!"

The stadium immediately erupted in thunderous applause, and as Drew stood up to approach the stage, so did over 100,000 people. Drew froze—terrified, humbled, and overwhelmed.

Sydney grabbed his hand again and whispered in his ear. "God is with you. He has been from the very beginning."

Drew looked down at her with reddened eyes. She was the one who should be speaking to these people, for her faith had been his guiding light all along.

He squeezed her hand and began the long journey to the podium. On stage, Pastor Worthington greeted him with a vigorous handshake and an encouraging smile. The roaring applause and cheers were almost too much for him to take as the continual waves of sound assaulted his ears.

Worthington leaned close so Drew would be able to hear him. "They just want to hear your heart, Drew. God will give you the words to speak."

Drew swallowed hard and tried to smile back. Mr. Worthington ushered him to the podium, then left the stage. Drew placed his hands on the podium and hung on. He lifted his eyes to see a sea of humanity that refused to cease its applause. His tongue and mouth became dry, his hands shook, and his mind was blank. He lifted his eyes farther and prayed.

"Dear God, please give me the strength, and give me Your words to speak."

Drew tried to talk, but the people would not stop. After two more attempts, the applause slowly began to diminish until the stadium fell to complete and utter respectful silence.

And as Drew opened his mouth to speak, the Holy Spirit filled him and gave him utterance.

∽○∽

Validus stood next to Michael, enthralled with the power of Ruach Elohim to change the heart of one and to also change the hearts of tens of thousands. He ached for Persimus to be with him, for he knew how thrilled his friend would have been to see this day.

"I don't understand, Archangel. Tinsalik Barob said that Carter was the last salvation before the End of Days, before Gideon's trumpet would sound."

Michael's gaze swept across the stadium—one hundred thousand souls here and millions more listening on television.

"The Fallen never heard the whole message. Carter is not the last salvation," the archangel said with a rare wisp of a smile. "He is the last witness!"

It took a moment for Validus to assimilate that one simple truth and compare it with all that he had experienced with the man. *Of course,* he thought. *How could I have missed it! A great witness of the gospel would be a thousand times more devastating to the enemies of God. The last salvation would happen through the last witness . . . Drew Carter!*

Validus looked at Michael. The first angel always knew more, always saw further.

Michael turned and looked at Validus, his smile fading to his usual stoneserious face. "But although he is the last witness, he is not alone. There is another."

Validus's mind ran wild with speculation. *Another . . . another like Carter? One of the lineage?*

"Another, Archangel?"

Michael's gaze tore right through him. "You don't think Apollyon is just going to give up do you? Yes, there is another."

Illumination hit Validus with near physical force. John the Revelator was given the prophecy of two witnesses. He smiled as he thought of General Danick and the Lineage Legion. How precious now was the knowledge that they were protecting prophecy all along. Nothing had been sacrificed in vain.

Michael turned back to look at the man. Carter's arms were raised toward heaven, and the blue flames of God were bursting through him, piercing the souls of tens of thousands. Validus thought of the billions of souls in the Middle Realm yet to hear the truth of the Holy One. Earth needed more than just two, it need an army of witnesses!

"You've done well, Validus, but Carter is more of a target for the Fallen than ever before. Elohim has great work for him to do, and you must be by his side, ready and vigilant. The days are short, and this man will play a vital role in it all. We dare not slumber."

As Carter offered up a powerful prayer of praise to Elohim, the arcing flames of Ruach Elohim pierced men, women, and angels alike. Validus felt His power resonating in his soul. "I am ready."

∽o∾

And this gospel of the kingdom will be preached in all the world as a **witness** to all the nations, and then the end will come.

—MATTHEW 24:14

READERS GUIDE

CHAPTER 1

In My Distress

Drew Carter finds himself in a very distressing situation with all odds against him. As an unbeliever, he has no one to turn to for help when there seems to be no solution to the problems he faces. A Christian has access to strength and hope through the Lord.

> In my distress I cried to the LORD, and He heard me. (Psalm 120:1)

> Trust in the LORD with all your heart, and lean not on your own understanding; in all your ways acknowledge Him, and He shall direct your paths. (Proverbs 3:5–6)

CHAPTER 2

Life for a Life

Drew attempts to bargain his life for Sydney's, Ben's, and Jake's freedom, but in the end he is only partially successful. Only a perfect, guiltless mediator could successfully accomplish such a thing, and that is exactly what Jesus Christ did for humanity through His sacrifice on the cross. In exchange for our freedom, Jesus paid the brutal price by His death. How precious is the blood of Christ!

> And if you call on the Father, who without partiality judges according to each one's work, conduct yourselves throughout the time of your stay here in fear; knowing that you were not redeemed with corruptible things, like silver or gold, from your aimless conduct received by tradition from your fathers, but with the precious blood of Christ, as of a lamb without blemish and without spot. He indeed was fore-ordained before the foundation of the world, but was manifest in these

last times for you who through Him believe in God, who raised Him from the dead and gave Him glory, so that your faith and hope are in God. (1 Peter 1:17–21)

CHAPTER 3

Lose Sight, Lose Fight

As a fighter pilot, I once learned a valuable lesson while dog-fighting with a fellow pilot who was more experienced than I. During the engagement, I lost sight of his jet, and he was able to quickly maneuver into position and launch a simulated missile to kill me. During the debrief he told me that if you ever lose sight of the enemy, you will lose the fight. It is very easy to lose sight of who we are fighting in this world. Sydney tries to open Drew's eyes to the real battle that is raging around him by offering Ephesians 6:12.

> For we do not wrestle against flesh and blood, but against principalities, against powers, against the rulers of the darkness of this age, against spiritual hosts of wickedness in the heavenly places. (Ephesians 6:12)

We must keep our eyes upon Christ as the author and finisher of our faith, but it is also very wise to take Peter's warning to heart and never lose sight of who the real enemy is.

> Be sober, be vigilant; because your adversary the devil walks about like a roaring lion, seeking whom he may devour. (1 Peter 5:8)

CHAPTER 4

A Haunting Past

When Kathryn discovers a forgotten letter from her mother, a frightful past is revealed. Her mother tries to encourage Kathryn to be free from their past, but there is only One who can truly give us a new beginning: Jesus Christ.

> Therefore, if anyone is in Christ, he is a new creation; old things have passed away; behold, all things have become new. (2 Corinthians 5:17)

Then He who sat on the throne said, "Behold, I make all things new."
And He said to me, "Write, for these words are true and faithful."
(Revelation 21:5)

Lineages

The tracing of lineages throughout the Bible, especially that of the Messiah, is deemed of utmost importance. This theme seems to continue on into the book of Revelation, when 144,000 people are sealed, 12,000 each from the twelve tribes of Israel. In *Light of the Last,* the lineage theme is used in a speculative way in regard to our hero, Drew Carter.

And I heard the number of those who were sealed. One hundred and forty-four thousand of all the tribes of the children of Israel were sealed. (Revelation 7:4)

CHAPTER 5

No Greater Joy

Every good parent desires their children to make wise choices and to walk in truth and integrity. Even people who don't love God but are moral and upright hope for this in their children. The angst and then great relief we see in Kathryn is evident when she sees that Drew is a young man of integrity who is committed to doing that which is right.

I have no greater joy than to hear that my children walk in truth.
(3 John 1:4)

CHAPTER 6

The Personalities of Angels

It is easy to homogenize God's holy angels into flat, personality-less beings, but that just doesn't fit the creative genius of God Almighty. One could argue that angels are potentially more dynamic and varied in personality than even their human charges. At a minimum, Scripture indicates that angels are perfect, holy, fierce, and joyful (see Isaiah 37:36; Job 38:7; Matthew 25:31). This chapter's speculative glimpse into some of the different personalities angels may have is an attempt to offer a more realistic view of God's mighty warriors.

Desperately Wicked

The Holocaust was the systematic persecution and murder of approximately six million Jews by the Nazi regime between 1933 and 1945. This was two-thirds of the Jews living in Europe during World War II. The Holocaust is a dramatic reminder that no matter how "advanced" mankind becomes, its propensity to do evil is always great.

> The heart is deceitful above all things, and desperately wicked; who can know it? (Jeremiah 17:9)

Only by accepting Jesus Christ and receiving the Holy Spirit can a person be renewed and changed into a vessel of righteousness.

> For we ourselves were also once foolish, disobedient, deceived, serving various lusts and pleasures, living in malice and envy, hateful and hating one another. But when the kindness and the love of God our Savior toward man appeared, not by works of righteousness which we have done, but according to His mercy He saved us, through the washing of regeneration and renewing of the Holy Spirit, whom He poured out on us abundantly through Jesus Christ our Savior, that having been justified by His grace we should become heirs according to the hope of eternal life. (Titus 3:3–7)

CHAPTER 7

Recruitment

Validus recruits angels with varying skills and abilities with the intention of being well prepared for the battles to come. When a person accepts Jesus Christ as Lord and Savior, not only is he saved from an eternity in hell, but he is recruited into an army that is called to battle evil on every front. It is important to understand this vital aspect of following Christ, for it is a weighty responsibility God has placed on us. The souls of millions hang in the balance.

> You therefore must endure hardship as a good soldier of Jesus Christ. No one engaged in warfare entangles himself with the affairs of this life, that he may please him who enlisted him as a soldier. (2 Timothy 2:3–4)

When God enlists us into this spiritual war, he bestows on us different gifts to fight well. According to 1 Corinthians 12, these gifts are the word of wisdom, the word of knowledge, faith, healing, miracles, prophecy, discerning of spirits, and the interpretation of tongues. It is also extremely important and rather ironic that our greatest weapon in this epic spiritual war is love.

> And now abide faith, hope, love, these three; but the greatest of these is love. (1 Corinthians 13:13; see also 1 Corinthians 13:1–12)

CHAPTER 8

The Sin of Unbelief

Validus is frustrated because of Drew's unbelief. The natural conclusion is that if Drew could see a sign of the truth, he would believe. But the heart of a prideful person will always find some excuse not to believe. Jesus had harsh words for the scribes and Pharisees when they asked for a sign.

> Then some of the scribes and Pharisees answered, saying, "Teacher, we want to see a sign from You." But He answered and said to them, "An evil and adulterous generation seeks after a sign, and no sign will be given to it except the sign of the prophet Jonah." (Matthew 12:38–39)

The sin of unbelief is always rooted in pride.

> Beware, brethren, lest there be in any of you an evil heart of unbelief in departing from the living God; but exhort one another daily, while it is

called "Today," lest any of you be hardened through the deceitfulness
of sin. (Hebrews 3:12–13)

Chapter 9

Terrorism and the Tactics of Satan Versus the Love of God

There are more than coincidental similarities between terrorism and the tactics
of our spiritual enemy, Satan. The goal of both terrorists and Satan is to strike
fear into the hearts of people. Both attack when you least expect them. Both are
invisible before they strike. Both have goals to destroy and kill. And finally,
both intend to destroy freedom and put people into bondage. The mastermind
behind earthly terrorists is clearly the archenemy of God, Lucifer. Contrast his
tactics with the tactics of God.

> For God has not given us a spirit of fear, but of power and of love and of
> a sound mind. (2 Timothy 1:7)

> And you will seek Me and find Me, when you search for Me with all
> your heart. (Jeremiah 29:13)

> Therefore if the Son makes you free, you shall be free indeed. (John 8:36)

> Rejoice that we serve a good God who offers life, liberty, and love!

Chapter 10

When God Draws a Soul

Drew feels the tug on his heart as he encounters the holy Word of God for the
first time. The Bible is clear that only those that God draws can come to Jesus.

> No one can come to Me unless the Father who sent Me draws him; and
> I will raise him up at the last day. (John 6:44)

But the Bible is also clear that God desires that none should perish.

> The Lord is not slack concerning His promise, as some count slackness, but is longsuffering toward us, not willing that any should perish but that all should come to repentance. (2 Peter 3:9)

Since both of these scriptures are true, the natural conclusion is that God draws all people to him at some point in their life. Whether they choose to follow Christ and receive the gift of salvation is up to them.

CHAPTER 11

Mighty Weapons

Drew finally gets a chance to ask Sydney directly about her apparent superpowers over the dark invaders and is still amazed at her influence over them. What he doesn't understand, and unfortunately many Christians don't understand, is that a believer in Jesus, filled with the Holy Spirit, is a powerful vessel through which God can work to disrupt and even destroy the works of the Enemy.

> For the weapons of our warfare are not carnal but mighty in God for pulling down strongholds, casting down arguments and every high thing that exalts itself against the knowledge of God, bringing every thought into captivity to the obedience of Christ, and being ready to punish all disobedience when your obedience is fulfilled. (2 Corinthians 10:4–6)

The Burden of Command

When Sason dissolves because of his severe injuries, Validus experiences the painful and overwhelming burden of command. Few possess the ability to lead men and women into harm's way and bear the burden when loss occurs. As long as sin continues to taint the universe and work its evil, God will raise up men and women who are able to make the tough calls without becoming callous and uncaring. Jesus was just such a man, for He prepared His disciples for lives of tremendous trial and persecution. He did not flinch from the pain that was in store for those He loved, because He knew their sacrifice would not go unrewarded or be made in vain.

> Blessed are you when they revile and persecute you, and say all kinds of evil against you falsely for My sake. Rejoice and be exceedingly glad, for great is your reward in heaven, for so they persecuted the prophets who were before you. (Matthew 5:11–12)

CHAPTER 12

The Ultimate Search

Sydney makes Drew promise to read the Bible once more but this time with the intention of discovering truth and of knowing God. When a person earnestly seeks God, the Lord promises that person will find him. Acts 17:27 says that He is not far from each one of us.

> And you will seek Me and find Me, when you search for Me with all your heart. (Jeremiah 29:13)

> But without faith it is impossible to please Him, for he who comes to God must believe that He is, and that He is a rewarder of those who diligently seek Him. (Hebrews 11:6)

CHAPTER 13

Betrayal

Drew felt betrayed by his friend and partner Reed when he discovers that Mr. Ross knows Drew is seeing beings no one else sees. Betrayal hurts worst when it is done by someone close to you. Jesus felt the sting of betrayal too when Judas, one of His disciples, gave Him over to the chief priests to be crucified.

> From that time he sought opportunity to betray Him. (see Matthew 26:14–16)

Jesus understands every hurt we feel and every temptation we have endured. He is a Savior whom we can turn to even when we feel betrayed.

> We do not have a High Priest who cannot sympathize. (Hebrews 4:15)

CHAPTER 14

Great Men Sacrifice Greatly

Dr. Whitton makes a statement when Drew opens up about his admiration for his father. Dr. Whitton says, "Great men sacrifice greatly." Perhaps an add-on to this would be "The greater the man, the greater the sacrifice." When there is evil in the world, there are continual opportunities to sacrifice on behalf of others. Great men and great women sacrifice time, money, freedom, prosperity, comfort, and health for others all the time. Good parents sacrifice for their children. Ultimately, the greatest sacrifice of all was made by the greatest man of all, Jesus Christ. He sacrificed His life so that we could be saved.

> For the grace of God that brings salvation has appeared to all men, teaching us that, denying ungodliness and worldly lusts, we should live soberly, righteously, and godly in the present age, looking for the blessed hope and glorious appearing of our great God and Savior Jesus Christ, who gave Himself for us, that He might redeem us from every lawless deed and purify for Himself His own special people, zealous for good works. (Titus 2:11–14)

CHAPTERS 15–16

Brought Low to Look Up

Although Drew doesn't seem like a man full of pride, it is his pride that is keeping him from discovering God—pride in his intellect, pride in his abilities, and pride in his thinking that Christians are weak-minded. Imagine what God might think about a person who considers that His children are foolish and weak-minded. Validus and his team take action to bring Drew to a point in his life where there is very little left to be prideful about. Unfortunately it is often when we are at our lowest that we can finally look up and see our Savior for who He really is. A prideful man can't repent, so the first step toward salvation is to humble oneself.

> And whoever exalts himself will be humbled, and he who humbles himself will be exalted. (Matthew 23:12)

Humble yourselves in the sight of the Lord, and He will lift you up.
(James 4:10)

CHAPTERS 17–19

Friendship

When Drew and Ben are finally reunited, Drew is overjoyed with being able to reconnect with his friend. Friendship is a gift from God. The Bible tells us in Proverbs 18:24 that there is a friend who sticks closer than a brother. God fulfills our need for friendship through the lives of others, but perhaps one of the most remarkable offers God makes to us is His friendship.

No longer do I call you servants, for a servant does not know what his master is doing; but I have called you friends, for all things that I heard from My Father I have made known to you. (John 15:15)

CHAPTER 20

The Great Experiment

President Harden borrows a concept from French historian Alexis de Tocqueville when he calls America "the Great Experiment." His improper application of the concept to justify dissolving the sovereignty of the nation is a trick of the devious. Perhaps the most significant aspect of the Great American Experiment was the implementation of biblical thought and principles into a government that was to grant equality and freedom to all people. In a ten-year study conducted by the University of Houston, researchers examined fifteen thousand documents by our founding fathers and discovered that 34 percent of their quotations were from the Bible, the highest by far of any source. Never before on planet Earth has such a government with its foundation placed squarely on God's Word been formed. As politicians, judges, lawyers, and educators drift further from biblical thought and closer to secular humanism, the Great American Experiment may end with dire consequences warned of by our forefathers.

If the foundations are destroyed, what can the righteous do?
(Psalm 11:3)

Chapter 21

Failed Experiment

Validus and his men discuss why the LASOK didn't work for Drew and Ben. This is an appropriate place to be reminded that no matter how advanced man becomes and no matter how successful the Enemy seems to be, God is sovereign and is in control. There is a barrier that separates the spiritual world from the temporal world that is not to be transcended without the express permission of the Creator. Crenshaw testifies to this fact by quoting Jesus in John.

> That which is born of the flesh is flesh, and that which is born of the Spirit is spirit. (John 3:6)

Chapter 22

The Threat of Salvation

Validus and his mighty warriors prepare for an onslaught from the Fallen as Sydney and Drew come together to discuss God. To our Enemy, Satan, salvation is a serious threat because he doesn't know what this new creation with the power of the Holy Spirit will be capable of. Will the new believer receive the Spirit of God only to stifle His promptings and retreat to a life of mediocrity? Or will he rise up to be a powerful vessel through which the gates of hell cannot prevail? If the angels in heaven rejoice over one sinner coming to repentance, can you imagine the angst among the demons when the same occurs?

> Likewise, I say to you, there is joy in the presence of the angels of God over one sinner who repents. (Luke 15:10)

The Simplest Hardest Thing to Do

When Sydney explains how simple it is to ask Jesus into his life, Drew is amazed. John 3:16 is the clearest explanation of what it takes to be saved.

> For God so loved the world that He gave His only begotten Son, that whoever believes in Him should not perish but have everlasting life. (John 3:16)

But simple doesn't mean easy. Jesus makes it very clear that following Him would not be easy. Accepting Christ as Savior is not a ticket to easy street but rather a promise of victory, joy, renewal, and persecution.

> Remember the word that I said to you, "A servant is not greater than his master." If they persecuted Me, they will also persecute you. If they kept My word, they will keep yours also. (John 15:20)

The Miracle of Salvation

Drew is saved because he repents of his sin and puts his faith in Jesus Christ. The depiction of salvation from a spiritual perspective is purely speculative, but we do know that such an event is a miracle of God, for only by the power of God can a soul be saved from hell. Paul testifies to this in Romans.

> For I am not ashamed of the gospel of Christ, for it is the power of God to salvation for everyone who believes, for the Jew first and also for the Greek. (Romans 1:16)

CHAPTER 23

The Last Salvation

There is much conjecture and opinion about the sequence and timing of the End Times events. Although Validus and his angels thought that Drew's salvation might trigger those events, the Bible makes it clear that no one, not even the angels, knows when Christ will return again. Our duty as believers is not to be so concerned with the "when" but with the "how." Jesus charges us as to "how" we should behave until that day comes, and it has everything to do with being obedient, faithful servants of God, sharing the gospel with a lost and dying world until the very end.

> But of that day and hour no one knows, not even the angels of heaven, but My Father only. (Matthew 24:36)

> Who then is a faithful and wise servant, whom his master made ruler over his household, to give them food in due season? Blessed is that

servant whom his master, when he comes, will find so doing. (Matthew 24:45–46)

CHAPTER 24

Secret Missions

Mr. Ross has had Drew on secret missions for many months now, and it appears that what Mr. Ross is asking of Drew could mean he might even lose his life. Believers in Jesus Christ have had a veil removed from their minds so that they can see the reality of the spiritual war being waged around them. We are, in essence, secret agents on mission for God. The lost do not see what we see and do not understand what we understand. Our struggle is fierce and our cause desperate, for millions of souls are at stake. Sometimes God may even call us to a mission that may require our very lives. Whatever God calls us to, He promises to go before us and equip us.

> And He Himself gave some to be apostles, some prophets, some evangelists, and some pastors and teachers, for the equipping of the saints for the work of ministry, for the edifying of the body of Christ, till we all come to the unity of the faith and of the knowledge of the Son of God, to a perfect man, to the measure of the stature of the fullness of Christ. (Ephesians 4:11–13)

CHAPTER 25

Dark Lord

Drew sees Satan for the first time in his life, and the encounter momentarily incites great fear in him. The most powerful created being in the universe would certainly have that effect on anyone. But then Drew hears the whisper of God, and his peace and confidence is restored. We need to remember that our Enemy is already defeated and Jesus made a spectacle of it on the cross. Furthermore, the Holy Spirit lives within us, and thus we are protected by His presence.

> God has not given us a spirit of fear, but of power and of love and of a sound mind. (2 Timothy 1:7)

You are of God, little children, and have overcome them, because He
who is in you is greater than he who is in the world. (1 John 4:4)

CHAPTER 26

Six Things the Lord Hates

Drew discovers that although Senior Advisor Dougherty is guilty of playing a
key role in a major terrorist plot, President Harden and Director Ward are also
guilty of egregious acts that have cost many Americans their freedom and their
very lives. God calls such men "workers of iniquity." There is a specific list of
actions that God spells out as things He hates.

These six things the LORD hates, yes, seven are an abomination to Him:
a proud look, a lying tongue, hands that shed innocent blood, a heart
that devises wicked plans, feet that are swift in running to evil, a false
witness who speaks lies, and one who sows discord among brethren.
(Proverbs 6:16–19)

Drew is disgusted by Harden and Ward, and rightly so, for they have committed all seven of the things God hates.

CHAPTER 27

Prayers That Move the Hand of God

Drew offers up a prayer to God on behalf of his team and on behalf of the nation. It is quite apparent that during the prayer the Holy Spirit leads him to
speak words of genuine repentance and petition. There are some outstanding
examples of effective prayers throughout the Bible, prayers that move the hand
of God. We ought to pay attention to such things because Jesus Himself told
how to pray and how not to pray. Vain, repetitious prayers are worthless. Effective prayers are initiated in absolute humility, asking first for forgiveness and
offering heartfelt praise to God. The Lord tells us to ask Him for help in our
time of need, but He also tells us that many ask with the wrong heart and
wrong intentions. The noblest prayers of all are those offered up on behalf of

other people or even an entire nation. Below are examples of prayers that move the hand of God.

> And when you pray, do not use vain repetitions as the heathen do. For they think that they will be heard for their many words. Therefore do not be like them. For your Father knows the things you have need of before you ask Him. In this manner, therefore, pray: Our Father in heaven, hallowed be Your name. . . . (Matthew 6:7–13)

> And I prayed to the LORD my God, and made confession, and said, "O Lord, great and awesome God, who keeps His covenant and mercy with those who love Him, and with those who keep His commandments, we have sinned and committed iniquity, we have done wickedly and rebelled, even by departing from Your precepts and Your judgments. . . ." (Daniel 9:4–19)

> And the tax collector, standing afar off, would not so much as raise his eyes to heaven, but beat his breast, saying, "God, be merciful to me a sinner!" (Luke 18:13)

> And Mary said: "My soul magnifies the Lord, and my spirit has rejoiced in God my Savior. . . ." (Luke 1:46–55)

CHAPTER 28

A Deadly Virus

Drew and Ben reveal the LASOK to their team with the hope of being able to use it to identify the deadly Ebola virus. Here's a tidbit of sheer speculation about viruses. It is interesting to note that unlike bacteria, there are no "good" viruses. All viruses are designed to invade a living host, replicate itself, and destroy its host. That doesn't sound like part of God's "good" creation. For decades, scientists and biologists have been trying to determine if viruses are living organisms. At first they believed them to be a type of poison, then a living organism like bacteria, but now they agree that viruses are not true living organisms because they lack the ability to reproduce without the aid of a living host and don't use the typical cell-division approach to replication. They are a complicated "assembly" of molecules that include proteins, nucleic acids, lipids, and carbohydrates. It is almost as if they have been engineered to destroy life whenever possible. The creation of life can only be accomplished by God Almighty. Is it possible that the Enemy has attempted to imitate the creation of life but for the sole purpose of destroying it? Has he somehow been able to devise a molecular system that can only function when it invades or "possesses" a living host and change its very nature? Again, this is the sheer speculation of this author.

> The thief does not come except to steal, and to kill, and to destroy.
> I have come that they may have life, and that they may have it more
> abundantly. (John 10:10)

CHAPTER 29

The Physical Manifestation of Demons

Validus and his warriors experience a new and desperate tactic by the Fallen— demons translating to physical form in an attempt to kill Drew. Although there are many biblical examples of angels translating to physical form to communicate with and interact with people, there are no such examples of demons doing so. In fact, when Satan wanted to try and defeat Jesus before He went to the cross, this fallen angel did not translate but instead possessed Judas to accomplish his purpose. There is no biblical basis to argue that demons have translation ability. I have taken literary freedom to write a scene about something the Bible is silent on and therefore should not be confused with the definitive truths of God's Word on such matters.

CHAPTERS 30–32

Sin Is Always Judged

Drew enlists the help of Sophia Bryant from World Media News to reveal the evil schemes of President Harden and his corrupt administration. Although it appears that sin is not always judged, we know according to the Bible that at some point in time, all sin will be judged. For believers, our sin was judged on the cross when Jesus offered His life as propitiation. If we continue to sin, there are still earthly consequences, for we are not being obedient to our loving Father. For nonbelievers, all sin will eventually be judged accordingly. This is clear in the book of Jude.

> Now Enoch, the seventh from Adam, prophesied about these men also, saying, "Behold, the Lord comes with ten thousands of His saints, to execute judgment on all, to convict all who are ungodly among them of all their ungodly deeds which they have committed in an ungodly way, and of all the harsh things which ungodly sinners have spoken against Him." (Jude 14–15)

CHAPTER 33

The Great Commission Is Personal

It is revealed that Drew is not the last salvation but rather the last witness. We have all been charged to go out into the world and make disciples of all the nations. At some point in time, there will be just one more soul to win for Jesus. Perhaps you are the one that heaven is waiting for to be a witness. Go and be bold in sharing the truth of God's love with those around you.

> And Jesus came and spoke to them, saying, "All authority has been given to Me in heaven and on earth. Go therefore and make disciples of all the nations, baptizing them in the name of the Father and of the Son and of the Holy Spirit, teaching them to observe all things that I have commanded you; and lo, I am with you always, even to the end of the age." Amen. (Matthew 28:18–20)

DON'T MISS THE ACTION
THAT BEGAN
THE WARS OF THE REALM!

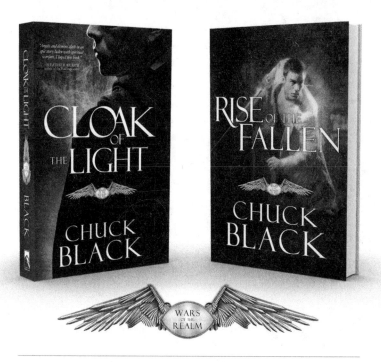

Follow Drew and Validus on an epic adventure of mystery, plot and intrigue as they try to defeat the spiritual forces that seek to destroy the United States.

The Kingdom Series

A riveting Medieval parallel to the Bible

Weaving together moral principles with high adventure and fierce imagination, Chuck Black's six books in the Kingdom Series profile heroic characters with values that readers will want to emulate. Each book also contains a study guide.

Find these and other captivating titles at
WaterBrookMultnomah.com

The Knights of Arrethtrae Series

Brimming with adventure and intrigue, The Knights of Arrethtrae books are a series of Medieval adventures with powerful parables that entertain without compromising Biblical truth. Includes maps, illustrations, and discussion questions.

Find these and other captivating titles at
WaterBrookMultnomah.com